HOLIDAYS WITH THE WONGS

THE COMPLETE SERIES

JACKIE LAU

A Match Made for Thanksgiving Copyright © 2019 Jackie Lau.

A Second Chance Road Trip for Christmas Copyright © 2019 Jackie Lau.

A Fake Girlfriend for Chinese New Year Copyright © 2020 Jackie Lau.

A Big Surprise for Valentine's Day Copyright © 2020 Jackie Lau.

ISBN: 978-1-989610-19-0

Editor: Latoya C. Smith, LCS Literary Services

Cover Design: Flirtation Designs

CONTENTS

A MATCH MADE FOR THANKSGIVING

BOOK 1

MEET NICK & LILY...

Advertising executive Nick Wong enjoys living in Toronto. He loves late nights partying and taking women back to his penthouse. And so it is with great reluctance that he returns to his boring hometown of Mosquito Bay for Thanksgiving.

This year, however, is even worse than usual. His interfering parents and grandparents, frustrated with the lack of weddings in the family, have invited blind dates for him and his three siblings. Nick's brother Greg has been set up with Lily Tseng, who just so happens to be Nick's latest one-night stand, the one he can't get out of his mind.

Although Nick has never been interested in settling down, Lily has him reconsidering. Perhaps he's good for more than a single night of sex, dumplings, and bubble tea after all. But first, he has to get through this painful weekend with his family and convince her that she should be with him, not Greg...

"WHEN WILL you be home for Thanksgiving?" Nick's mother asked. "We're doing dinner on Saturday this year, remember?"

As he held the phone to his ear, Nick Wong looked out at the spectacular view of Toronto from his penthouse. This was his home now. He did not want to go to Mosquito Bay. He'd left the small town on Lake Huron as soon as he'd finished high school and hadn't looked back.

Seriously, it was called *Mosquito Bay*. Why would anyone want to go there?

"Nick?" his mother prompted.

He sighed. "I'll be there by four on Saturday."

"Don't be late. Not like last time."

"I'll do my best."

To be honest, he was sort of looking forward to seeing his family, but he was dreading it at the same time. His family was a bit...much, that was all.

Nick liked to do his own thing. Be his own man. Be in charge.

But in Mosquito Bay, his control seemed to slip away. There were his parents, his white mother and Asian father, who had been high school sweethearts and were confused as to why, at the age of thirty-two, Nick had yet to settle down and have four kids, like they had. Then his father's parents, Ah Ma and Ah Yeh, who were pushing ninety but still surprisingly good at interfering in his life. Well, that was mostly Ah Ma. Ah Yeh, Nick's grandfather, was more interested in ordering things on Amazon—he thought online shopping was the pinnacle of human achievement. He would also make his famous noodles for Thanksgiving.

Nick was already salivating at the thought of those noodles.

"Do you want me to bring the usual char siu?" he asked.

"Yes, please," Mom said.

"Will do. See you next weekend."

"Nick, are you getting off the phone already? I haven't had a chance to ask you any questions."

"You asked when I'd be coming back for Thanksgiving."

"You know what I mean! How's life in Toronto? Your job?"

They talked for fifteen minutes, and then Nick said, "Sorry, I have to go."

"Hmph. Sure, get drunk and pick up women, then nurse your hangover with dumplings and bubble tea."

"Thanks for your insightful description of my life."

"See you next weekend, Nicky. Love you."

"Love you, too," he said before ending the call.

Alright, time to get his Friday night started. It was six thirty—still very early, but he needed to get out. He'd have a drink or two at Lychee before he met up with Trystan.

Work hard, party hard. Enjoy all the delicious food and women the city had to offer. Why would he live in Mosquito Bay when he could live in Toronto?

Lily Tseng was boring. It was just a fact.

She'd always known it. It shouldn't have been a shock when her ex broke up with her because she was dull and bland.

Yet when he'd said those words, it *was* a shock.

They'd been together for a year. Surely he hadn't been bored the whole time?

Anyway, she'd turned thirty last month, and it was time to make a change. Next weekend, she'd attempt skydiving and bungee jumping.

Ha! No. She never even dreamed of doing such things.

But tonight, maybe she'd have her first one-night stand.

In the past few weeks, she'd spent a lot of time scoping out possible venues to meet men. She had no interest in going to a club. Not her scene, and she wouldn't venture *that* far out of her comfort zone. Instead, she'd focused on stylish downtown bars and had settled on Lychee. It was a restaurant owned by some up-and-coming Chinese-Canadian chef who'd won a cooking show last year, and it was located on Elizabeth Street, near the former location of Lichee Garden, a well-known Chinese restaurant in decades past—hence the name.

In addition to the main dining area, Lychee had a bar and lounge with eight-dollar cocktails before eight. Lily had peeked in a couple times, and it looked like it had a decent crowd of young, attractive men in suits.

She really did like men in suits.

But maybe all this preparing for her one-night stand defeated the purpose. She was planning it the way she planned everything else in her life. Wasn't part of her goal to be more spontaneous?

Lily sighed and stirred her drink with the straw. She wasn't very good at this.

She was sitting at the bar in Lychee now, waiting for her friends Tara Kim and Sam Rubenstein to show up, but she didn't expect them for another half hour.

That was Lily. Always early.

It was a lovely space, she had to admit. Wood, chrome, and exposed brick that somehow went together just right. High ceilings.

And her drink was delicious. It had black tea-infused vodka, mango juice, lime, and…some other things. She'd forgotten what, but she didn't care. She was just trying her best not to drink it too quickly.

She crossed her legs and smoothed out her red dress. A special dress that she'd bought for this occasion, with Tara's help. It showed more cleavage than she'd normally be comfortable with, but Tara had convinced her it looked smashing, and Lily had to agree.

Now she needed a guy.

What if she didn't find anyone suitable tonight?

Oh, come on, Lily, it's not even seven o'clock. You have lots of time.

She was eager to cross "one-night stand" off her list, though. She loved crossing things off lists. Though perhaps she shouldn't have a list for learning how to be more fun and less boring.

But even if she found a suitable guy—attractive, no creepy vibes, those were the main criteria—how would she approach him? What would she say?

I, Lily Tseng, sensible accountant, am trying to have my first one-night stand. Will you sleep with me, please and thank you?

Dear God. She was hopeless.

She had a sip of her cocktail and looked around. At the other end of the bar, there was a group of men who were a few decades older than her. Next to them were a couple of men closer to her age, but they gave off douchebag vibes.

Nobody made her want to take a second look.

And she was just looking for a potential guy! She hadn't even tried to talk to anyone yet.

"Why is it so difficult to have a one-night stand?" she muttered.

Maybe she should cancel Operation Get Laid Tonight.

"What did you say?"

She startled at the unfamiliar male voice, and a little orange liquid sloshed over the edge of her glass.

"Sorry. Let me get that."

A large hand wiped the spill away with a paper napkin. She looked from the hand to a wrist with an expensive watch, up an arm sheathed in a gray suit jacket and...

Oh.

Her mouth fell open, but she promptly snapped it shut so she didn't look stupid.

Although it was hard not to stare.

The man had nearly black hair with a hint of a wave that made him look roguish, if that was a word anyone used anymore. He had dark brown eyes, a teasing smile, and he caused a pleasant hum in her body, even more so than the delicious cocktail. He looked ever so slightly like Henry Golding.

And he was standing right next to her and—

"Did you ask why it was so difficult to have a one-night stand?" he inquired politely.

—and he'd heard her say that.

Right.

Normally, she was a fairly put-together person who always thought before she spoke, and yet she'd muttered that under her breath when *he* was right next to her.

Though she was trying to act less like herself tonight.

But she wished he hadn't heard. Her cheeks heated in embarrassment, and they heated even more as his gaze slid from her face down to her chest, down to her silver stilettos, the ones she hardly ever wore because they were so high and not at all sensible.

And then, she did something even more shocking.

"Are you offering?" she asked.

She didn't say it with a sassy flick of her hair, nor did she reach out and trail her finger down his arm, but she said those words all the same.

Oh, God. She covered her mouth.

He chuckled and it reverberated in her chest.

"One-night stands are my specialty," he said, "but let's get to know each other first. Can I buy you another drink?"

Was this happening?

This was really happening.

It was probably best that she stop after one drink.

"Um, I'll just have some juice," she said. "Mango, if that's possible." The mango juice in her cocktail had been excellent.

"Maybe some food? The char siu sliders are quite good."

"Sure."

The stranger got the attention of a bartender and placed their order, and a few minutes later, Lily had a glass of mango juice, garnished with a cherry. It probably cost six dollars, and there wasn't even any alcohol.

She pushed aside that annoying voice in her head and sipped her juice.

"What's your name?" she asked.

A one-night stand with a man whose name she didn't know sounded extra naughty, but she couldn't do it. She needed to call him *something*.

"Nick."

"I'm Lily."

He sat down on the barstool next to her, then shrugged out of his suit jacket. He rolled up his sleeves, and the sprinkling of dark hair on his forearms was so damn erotic, for some reason.

Lily squeezed her legs together. She wasn't used to being this physically affected by a man.

Yes, he was perfect for Operation Get Laid Tonight.

She couldn't help feeling a little surprised that he seemed interested in her. Not that she was unattractive—she thought she looked quite good in this outfit, in fact—but he really was *that* sexy. Surely he could have almost any woman he wanted. Why, there was a group of three women on the other side of the bar who were looking in his direction.

"I've never done this before!" she blurted out.

"Done what?"

"Tried to pick someone up at a bar. Had a one-night stand."

He chuckled again, all cool, not flustered like she was.

"You're doing fine," he said, then had a sip of his Old Fashioned.

His drink had a single large ice cube, and she was stupidly amused by it. The ice cube was just so...big. They must have used a special mold to make it.

"What do you do for work, Lily?"

Ooh, she quite liked the way he said her name.

"I'm an accountant at a large engineering firm. And you?"

"Oh, I work in advertising," he said vaguely.

She suspected he had an important position. Management or something.

She didn't ask for details, though. It was only one night; she didn't need to know much about him.

A server set a plate with three char siu sliders in front of them, and Lily suddenly realized she was quite hungry. She picked up the first one. Egg bun, from the looks of it, with barbecued pork, cilantro, pineapple, and some kind of sauce. She attempted to take a dainty bite. It wasn't the sort of food that lent itself to dainty bites, but she tried her best.

"Good?" Nick asked.

She held up a finger. She wasn't quite finished chewing.

"Yes," she said at last. "Very good. You were right."

He picked one up, and she watched his Adam's apple as he swallowed, wondering why she'd never been so captivated by a man's throat before.

Maybe it was just Nick's throat. Hmm. She wanted to kiss it right...there.

"You want the last one?" He motioned to the plate.

"Mm. Yes, please."

"Will you be this polite later?" he asked, leaning closer.

A sizzle of energy traveled down to her toes.

Oh, she liked this. She couldn't remember the last time a man had talked to her this way.

She grinned. "May I touch your thigh, please?"

His eyes seemed to darken, and he held her gaze as he laced his fingers in hers and brought their hands to his muscular thigh.

She ate the last slider with her other hand, then chased it down with some mango juice.

"You can touch me wherever you want," he said. "I promise I'll like it all." He paused. "You said you'd never had a one-night stand. Why do you want to have one now?"

"I'm trying new things. Stepping out of my comfort zone. I have a list."

∾

Nick tried not to laugh.

"Of course you have a list," he murmured.

"Why do you say that?" Lily asked. "You only just met me."

True, but he felt like he'd known her for more than twenty minutes, even though that was all it had been. When he'd seen her sitting alone in that incredible red dress, he'd been struck by the way she carried herself with such poise. Everything about her appearance was perfect, not a hair out of place.

He desperately wanted to mess it up.

Then she'd made that comment about a one-night stand, and he'd instantly gotten hard.

When she spoke, she was honest, straightforward, not quite as poised as her appearance would suggest—he wondered if she was like this with everyone. And she got an adorable flush when she was embarrassed.

"You just seem like a list person," he said. "I can't explain it."

"Well, lists are amazing. There's nothing like the satisfaction of crossing something off your to-do list."

"Nothing? Nothing at all?" He stroked the back of her hand with his thumb.

Her pretty red lips parted.

"Why did you pick tonight for your one-night stand? Has it been a while for you?"

"Six months, which actually isn't that long to me, but I was…"

"Horny?" he supplied.

"Yeah. That."

"Say the word."

"No! Not here. Plus I've always hated that word. It makes me think of monsters."

"Monsters?"

"Yeah. Monsters with lots of horns."

He bit back a laugh.

Lily squirmed in her seat, and he hoped that was because she was *horny*, but more likely, she was embarrassed again.

"Okay," he said. "I won't repeat it. You felt…like fucking." He danced his fingertips over her thigh, and she shifted closer to him, her hip pressing against his. "Will you say that word?"

"I only swear around certain people."

"Certain people?"

"My friends. I don't swear with strangers. Or colleagues. Or family."

"You said you want to try new things."

"I do."

"So swear in front of someone you just met. Me."

"That was a fucking good char siu slider."

He laughed. "Now say it in another way. You haven't had sex in a while, and you feel like fucking tonight."

"Alright." She cleared her throat. "Nick, I would like you to fuck me. Please."

Oh, she was killing him.

He wouldn't meet Trystan tonight. When he and Lily left Lychee, he'd take her straight home, and he couldn't help but anticipate her look of delight when she saw his place. The view, the bed. He looked forward to introducing her to *fucking* someone she hardly knew, and tomorrow he could...

He pushed that thought aside. It was a one-night stand, and he was glad that had been clear at the outset. Sometimes he saw a woman more than once—it wasn't *always* a one-night stand with him—but nothing that could be described as more than a fling. Much to the frustration of his parents, he liked his bachelor lifestyle here in the city.

So, no, he wouldn't be introducing Lily to a whole bunch of new experiences.

He shrugged off his curious twinge of disappointment and rested his hand on her thigh, pushing up her knee-length skirt just a little so he could touch her skin.

"Thank you for propositioning me," he said. "I accept. But you are free to change your mind at any time, okay?"

She nodded and had a sip of her mango juice.

He was getting jealous of that red straw.

He leaned forward and pressed a kiss to the top of her neck. She was as sensitive as he'd imagined. Then he worked his way along her jaw, planting a kiss to her chin before claiming her mouth.

She tasted sweet, of mango and pineapple, and he pulled her closer so he could taste her more fully.

"Nick," she said. Quietly, but he still heard it above the background noise in the bar.

"Lily?" another female voice said.

She jumped away from him and looked at the two women behind them, one East Asian and the other white.

"Please continue," the Asian woman said, smirking. "Don't mind us."

"It's not what it looks like!" Lily said.

He put his hand on her shoulder. "Lily, I think it's exactly what it looks like."

"Right. Well." She gestured to the two women. "These are my friends, Tara and Sam, and this is Nick. We, um, just met."

Sam—the white woman—held up her hand for a high five, but Lily didn't slap it.

"I didn't think you were serious about meeting a guy at a bar," Tara said. "I should have known you always do whatever you set your mind to, but I thought you'd need some encouragement."

Lily stood up. "You two will be okay without me, won't you?"

"We can hang out with your friends for a while," Nick said. "I don't mind."

He'd prefer to bring her home right now, but it was only seven thirty. The night was still young. He almost never took a woman home before midnight, but it would be nice to have extra time with Lily.

"No, no," she said. "We'll go."

"As you wish." He paid their bill, then stood up and tucked her hand in the crook of his elbow.

Sam was staring at them, her mouth hanging open.

"Don't worry, we'll find someone else for you." Tara tugged her along. "Lily, remember to text me, okay?" she said over her shoulder.

Lily nodded.

And then Nick was alone with Lily, and they had a whole night ahead of them.

2

"WHAT THE FUCK," Lily said under her breath as she took in the view from Nick's living room. "What the fuck."

He definitely had an important job if he could afford a place like this. It was a penthouse on the fifty-third floor of a new building downtown, only a short walk from Lychee, thank God, and everything was sleek black and metal. And the view!

When she'd imagined having a one-night stand, she hadn't imagined being with a guy who looked as hot as Nick and who seemed to be a hotshot CEO or something like that. She couldn't help feeling a little inadequate, like she didn't belong in his world, but she'd try to ignore those thoughts and enjoy the night.

This would be quite the memory.

"There you go," Nick said, coming up behind her. "Swearing again."

"It's a view that encourages obscenities," she said.

"Mm. You want anything? Water?"

"No, I'm good."

He was standing behind her, infuriatingly close. Infuriating because she could feel the heat radiating off him, but he wasn't actually touching her, and he hadn't kissed her since they'd been interrupted at the bar.

But tonight, she was a sexy, confident woman, and she could make the first move.

She leaned back against him, and he folded his arms around her. He'd only turned on a light near the door; it was still mostly dark here, aside from the lights of the city. Just the two of them, and this night that felt like a dream.

He'd probably done this with lots of women. *One-night stands are my specialty.* She tried to push that out of her mind. She didn't care what he did on any night but tonight, and tonight, he was with her. They would use protection. It would all be fine. She'd texted Tara his address and phone number, just in case.

He kissed the crook of her neck.

"You're beautiful," he breathed, leaning down to rest his chin on her shoulder.

"I'm nervous," she said, which wasn't the way she usually responded to a compliment.

"We don't have to do it."

It. *Sex.* Something she'd only ever done within a relationship, but she wanted this night with him.

He really was a very nice man. In her mind, she gave herself a high five for making such a good choice. She felt safe, safer than she'd thought she would feel with someone she hardly knew.

"I want to," she said. "I very much want to."

"Say it again. Like you did at the bar."

"Nick, I would like you to fuck me."

"You forgot the 'please'."

"Please."

"It would be my pleasure." He pulled her closer and rubbed himself against her.

She gasped. He was—

"Feel how hard it makes me when you talk like that."

Stupidly, it made her think of the ice cube in his Old Fashioned, the ice cube that was a bit bigger than any ice cube she'd ever seen before.

"Don't worry," he murmured. "I'll take good care of you."

She continued to stare out the window as he pressed himself against her and ran his hand under the hem of her dress and up her thigh.

"Okay?" he asked, the tips of his fingers inside the waistband of her panties, the lacy black ones she'd bought for tonight.

"Yes." She pressed herself back against his cock.

His fingers dipped inside her underwear, running over her slit and casually stroking her.

"It's a very nice view, isn't it?" he said. "That's part of the reason I got this place. Good location. Lovely view."

"Gunh." She was unable to form proper words.

With his other hand, he undid the zipper at the side of her dress and slid one thin strap down her shoulder. He slipped his hand inside her strapless bra and gently kneaded her breast as he planted kisses up and down her neck.

She was drowning in sensations.

He pushed a finger inside her. An intimacy she'd never allowed a man she'd only met an hour before, but the fact that she hardly knew him made her blood pump quicker.

Lily needed to kiss him. Properly this time, now that it was just the two of them.

She turned in his arms, and he kept his hand inside her panties as she set her lips to his. His mouth was soft and warm and overwhelming, especially with everything else he was doing to her.

She could lose herself in this kiss.

When he deepened the kiss, his tongue touching hers, she unbuttoned his shirt in a hurry and moved her fingers over his chest. Exploring. Making a memory she'd never forget.

He hissed out a breath.

When she undid his belt and pants and slid her hand inside his underwear, he did it again.

She wasn't nervous anymore. No, just eager.

Lily wrapped her hand around his cock. Ooh, yes, that was nice. She slid her hand up and down, ran her thumb over the bead of precum at the tip.

"Nick, I—"

She squeaked in surprise as he lifted her onto the couch. He pulled off her panties and raised her skirt, baring her to him, and then he set his mouth on her.

His very talented mouth.

She'd always loved oral sex, and it was the one way she could reliably orgasm, but he put all of her previous boyfriends to shame. And the curtains were wide open in front of them! The whole city could watch her being pleasured!

Except it was dark in here, and they were on the fifty-third floor.

But it gave her a thrill to be able to see the city before her as a man had his head between her legs.

He slipped one finger inside as he licked her, and she bucked against him.

"More," she panted.

He gave her more, adding a second finger and sucking on her clit.

And then she was coming for him, this man she hardly knew, and it felt like she was letting go of all the times she'd played it safe, all the times she'd been the good daughter rather than having fun.

She was free.

She said his name quietly, but she shook and soared like never before.

He lifted his head and smiled lazily at her, then picked her up and carried her to another room. He set her down on a bed and flicked on the lights, giving her a better look at him.

When he slid off his shirt, exposing all of his chest and arms, it was a magnificent sight. Once again, she congratulated herself on making such a good choice for a one-night stand, though it was still hard to believe this was actually happening.

Next, he pushed down his pants and boxer briefs. His cock jutted out, and he pumped it a few times.

Dear God. She breathed rapidly as she stared at him.

Nick climbed onto the bed and crawled toward her. Predatory, but like a very friendly predator, and she chuckled at that thought.

"What?" he asked.

"Nothing," she said.

He pulled her dress over her head. "You are stunning, Lily." He said it solemnly, but she caught a hint of a smile before he leaned down and kissed her as he pressed his hand between her legs once more.

He kissed her leisurely for a while, the expanse of his skin against hers, and then his kisses became sloppier, more desperate. She squirmed beneath him.

"God, I want you," he murmured. "You ready?"

"Yes. Do you have a condom, or should I get my purse?"

He picked up a condom from the night table and quickly rolled it on. "I think I'd like you in this position."

The next thing she knew, she was on all fours, her ass in the air.

"Is that okay?" he whispered.

She nodded.

She'd take him any way he wanted, if only he'd ease the ache inside her.

He knelt behind her and pressed the tip of his cock to her entrance. Slowly, he eased himself inside, and she gasped. Soon, he was all the way in, and he was big, yes, but she could take him, no problem.

"Okay?" he asked.

"You feel amazing," she said.

He started to move, in and out, and nothing mattered but her pleasure.

He leaned down and kissed the side of her neck, fondled her breasts with one hand, and it was all she could do just to keep breathing. She couldn't even hold herself up on her hands and knees anymore; she slid down so she was lying on her stomach.

And still he fucked her and kissed her neck.

"You're incredible," he whispered. His breath tickled her, made her break out in goose bumps. She pushed back against him, wriggled her ass. "Yes, that's good. Take it, Lily."

He pulled out of her, much to her dismay, but only so he could roll her onto her back, and then he was inside her again. He held her gaze as he licked his finger, then brought his hand down and touched her clit.

The pleasure was so sharp that she nearly flung herself off the bed. Pressure built up inside her, and everything in her contracted then expanded for a long, glorious moment.

Nick growled and picked up his pace, finishing inside her as she came down from her high.

One-night stands were *awesome*.

Nick pulled on his boxer briefs and climbed back into bed with Lily.

"Hey, you." She giggled and pulled him against her, and he was happy to oblige.

"Hey," he said. There was an unfamiliar sensation in his chest as he wrapped his arms around her.

They lay in silence for a minute, and he idly stroked her hair. It was silky and long, well below her shoulders, and smelled faintly of something floral. He wasn't sure what, but he liked it.

"So what happens now?" she asked.

"What do you mean?"

"In a one-night stand. I thought you were the expert."

"Well, we might do it again or go to sleep." He glanced at his alarm clock. "It's only nine o'clock, so we're about four hours ahead of schedule. If you want, I can get a taxi, and you can go home or join your friends."

She jerked up to a sitting position. "You want me to leave?"

Her disappointed expression was so guileless.

He bit back a smile. "No, I just thought you might prefer to, so you didn't have to spend the night, but I'd be more than happy to have you stay."

Yes, he very much wanted to do that again. Once hadn't been enough.

"Could we get some food first?" she asked. "Maybe bubble tea, too. I'm craving it."

He laughed. "I know just the place."

They got dressed and headed outside. It was early October, cool enough for a light jacket but still pleasant. He led her to a nearby bubble tea shop on Dundas, where she got an oolong milk tea with tapioca pearls, and he got a taro milk tea.

This was what he loved about Toronto. He could walk outside his condo and have so many different kinds of food and drink within ten minutes. There were endless choices. Whereas in Mosquito Bay, there were only a handful of restaurants and one bar.

No, this was the life.

He and Lily moseyed onward. She looked so radiant right now, and *he* was the reason for that. He had a strange impulse to hold her hand, but he quashed it.

It was unusual for him to be out with a woman like this, wandering about with a drink in hand. They'd already had sex, and they would do it again, but there was no rush. He'd simply enjoy being with her.

"Here." He led her down a side street, to a cramped dumpling shop called XLB. "Don't worry, they're fast. Six soup dumplings for three bucks. What do you think?"

Her eyes widened. "Six for *three* bucks? In that case, I'll have twelve."

Fifteen minutes later, they were sitting on a bench in the park behind the art gallery, eating their juicy soup dumplings from take-out containers, their bubble tea nearly finished.

"These are delicious," Lily said before putting another one in her mouth. "I've never heard of this place before. I'll have to go back."

"The best cheap xiaolongbao you can get," he said. "Not the very best I've had, but very good for the price."

She smiled at him, her face lit by the nearby streetlight.

"So," she said, "any plans for Thanksgiving next weekend?"

He felt momentarily disoriented, but she was just making pleasant conversation.

"I'm going to my hometown to see my family," he said. "Where there are no dumplings or bubble tea, and I'll be itching to escape as fast as possible."

"Same here." She chuckled. "Where is your...never mind."

Yes, there was no sense in talking details, not when they were just together for a night.

This was different from a regular one-night stand, though. It felt almost like a dream.

God, he was losing it.

His phone chirped. "Sorry, I should get that. Could be work."

"No worries. Go ahead."

It wasn't work. No, it was a message from Greg, asking who was bringing the char siu home for Thanksgiving.

"Anything important?" she asked.

"Nah, just my older brother." Whom he wouldn't give another thought to tonight.

After she disposed of the containers, he pulled her onto his lap. He wound her hair around his hands and kissed her until she was breathing quickly and her face was flushed.

He loved how she responded to him.

She rubbed herself against his erection, only the thin fabric of her panties covering her.

He groaned and stood up. "That's it. Time to take you back to bed."

And that was exactly what he did.

When he was lying in bed afterward, listening to Lily's rhythmic breathing as she slept, he realized he'd almost perfectly followed his mother's description of his life: he'd picked up a woman and had dumplings and bubble tea. Not to nurse his hangover—he hadn't drunk much today—but it was a horrifying realization nonetheless.

Still, he couldn't regret tonight. It was the best night he'd had in a long, long time.

～

Lily walked out into the sunshine with a big smile on her face.

It was ten o'clock in the morning, and she was wearing the same dress as the night before. Although she'd cleaned up her make-up and run a brush through her hair, she looked a touch bedraggled.

Walk of shame?

Ha!

She was on cloud nine.

After dumplings and bubble tea, they'd had sex twice more at Nick's place before going to sleep. He'd suggested she sleep naked, but she'd insisted on borrowing a shirt. A plain white T-shirt that smelled deliciously like him.

This morning, she'd woken up to find him lounging in bed next to her, working on his laptop, but he'd set it aside the instant she sat up, then made love to her again.

Made love?

What was she talking about? It had been sex, plain and simple. Damn good sex.

Really, she needed to have one-night stands more often. She suspected they wouldn't all be this amazing—she'd just gotten lucky her first time—but still.

She pictured going to another bar and meeting a man who looked suspiciously like Nick. It was hard to think of anyone else right now. When she'd stepped out the door, she'd nearly asked if she could see him again, but then she'd snapped her mouth shut.

That was part of the magic: it was only one night. One perfect night.

There was a hollow feeling in her heart, but she pushed it aside and held her head high. She'd had sex four—four!—times in twelve hours. Nick was gorgeous and talented, but also kind and attentive, and he'd made her eggs and toast and coffee for breakfast *while wearing only his underwear*. Like some kind of fantasy man, except he was utterly real, and he'd wanted her.

A great night, sure, but this was for the best. She couldn't imagine he'd want anything long-term with her anyway. If one-night stands were his thing, he probably got bored easily.

Her phone rang, interrupting her thoughts. There was only one person who would call—not text—at ten in the morning on the weekend.

"Lily!" her mother shouted. "I have a surprise for you!"

Dear God. A surprise from her mother. This could be anything. Hopefully just some kind of face cream. "What is it?"

"Next weekend, don't come here for Saturday dinner, okay?"

"Why not?"

Ma was giggling. Actually giggling. "You have a date!"

Oh, no.

No, no, no, no.

It must be because Lily had recently turned thirty.

She hadn't been allowed to date in high school. When she'd

3

NICK PULLED up to the old brick house where he'd spent his childhood and released a breath as he put the car in park.

Suitcase in hand—his mother always insisted he stay overnight—he walked up the driveway and opened the front door, which was never locked. As he took off his shoes, his brother ambled over.

"Hey, man," Zach said, slapping him on the back. "Good to see you."

Zach was the third sibling, the only one who'd stayed in Mosquito Bay. He worked as a science teacher at the local high school they'd all attended back in the day.

"How was the drive?" Zach asked.

"Oh, not bad. Bit slow coming out of Toronto, but I can't complain."

"Who's that?" yelled their mother from the kitchen.

"Nick's here!" Zach shouted back.

The next thing he knew, there was a stampede to the front hall, Mom and Dad in the front, and Ah Ma and Ah Yeh hobbling behind them.

"Nicky!" His mother threw her arms around him. His father was next and gave him a more restrained hug.

"Ah, Nicky!" Ah Ma said. "You stop bossing people around in the city long enough to visit us. How nice of you. We have a big surprise."

"A big surprise?" Nick said as she patted his back. She didn't come up to his shoulder. "What is it?"

"It's a *surprise.*" Mom turned to her mother-in-law. "You weren't supposed to say anything."

"Okay," Ah Ma said, "there is *not* a surprise. I have been forbidden from talking about it. Now I will go back to the kitchen."

"No!" everyone shouted.

She laughed. "Don't worry, I'm just teasing!"

In Nick's experience, most people thought their grandmothers were amazing cooks. People assumed he ate delicious Chinese food made by Ah Ma all the time.

No.

Ah Ma was, frankly, a pretty terrible cook. When they'd had a restaurant in town, Ah Yeh had done most of the cooking.

Now that the initial excitement of his arrival had passed, Nick brought the char siu to the kitchen, then followed Zach, Ah Ma, and Ah Yeh into the living room, where Greg was sitting on the couch. He raised his hand in greeting. "Hey."

That was Greg, a man of few words. Never one to get caught up in the excitement of anything because, well, he didn't find many things exciting. He enjoyed model trains and CBC radio—Greg was an old man in some ways—but even then, his enjoyment was more restrained.

Like Nick, Greg lived in Toronto. Sometimes they drove down together, but Greg had wanted to stay in Mosquito Bay for two nights this Thanksgiving, and there was no way Nick was staying more than one.

"Is Amber here yet?" Nick asked.

"No," Zach said, "but you know Amber."

Yes, their little sister was always late.

It was only four o'clock, though, and they probably wouldn't eat until six. There was still plenty of time. Amber lived about an hour away in Stratford, where she worked in marketing at the theater festival.

Nick made himself comfortable on the couch. He could check if his parents needed any help in the kitchen, but based on past experience, they'd either shoo him out immediately or fail to notice his presence because they were making out. Personally, Nick couldn't imagine being with the same person for so long and still wanting to make out like that.

"What's that?" he asked, nodding at a green furry thing on the coffee table.

Ah Yeh leaned forward and picked it up. He put it on his hand.

It was a green puppet, a velociraptor from the looks of it.

"You got that on Amazon?" Nick asked, though it didn't need to be said. His grandfather *loved* buying things from Amazon.

"Of course. You can find everything on Amazon."

"Yes, but why do you need a green dinosaur puppet?"

"For your children, of course."

Nick coughed. "What?"

"My great-grandchildren. I think I will be getting some soon, if today's surprise—"

"Aiyah!" Ah Ma said. "They forbid us from talking about it, weren't you listening?"

Well, this was truly bizarre.

Nick could also make out a very small sweater sitting on one of the end tables. What the hell? Sure, his parents and grandparents had occasionally talked about him and his siblings getting married and having kids of their own, but actually buying things for these hypothetical children seemed a bit much.

"So, what's new in Mosquito Bay?" he asked.

"The diner changed hands," Zach said, "and Mrs. Meyer—remember her? She finally retired."

Zach caught him up on all the news about town, Ah Ma adding her opinions here and there. Ah Yeh fell asleep in his chair. Greg grunted occasionally.

Nick was about to ask Zach how his job was going when the doorbell rang.

"I'll get it," Greg said.

He got up and went to the door, returning to the living room a few minutes later with a woman who definitely wasn't their sister, but she wasn't a stranger, either.

Diana Lam.

The Lams were family friends of the Wongs. Diana was twenty-seven now, if Nick remembered correctly, a year older than Amber. He hadn't seen her in several years.

Strange. Sure, the Lams were friends, but Thanksgiving was always just family. And if Diana was here, where were her parents? It wasn't surprising that her brother, Sebastian, wasn't present, though. Last Nick heard, Sebastian was doing his residency on the other side of the country.

But the rest of her family?

"Hey, Diana," Zach said. "Wasn't expecting to see you today. What's up?"

"I'm your date!"

"My date?"

"Ah, the first surprise is here," Ah Ma said.

Zach turned to their grandmother. "I don't understand."

Ah Ma was grinning evilly, which always heralded bad things.

"You see," she said, "we have a problem. All four of you are grown-up. Thirty-four, thirty-two, thirty, and twenty-six. Yet no one is married. Not even engaged. When your parents were twenty-six, they were already married and had Greg. Rosemary says maybe romance is not for everyone, but out of the four of you, I would think at least three would be interested, yes?"

Nick scrubbed a hand over his face. "So you set us all up for Thanksgiving? That's the surprise?"

"Yes! The woman we found for you is—"

"Don't ruin it!" Mom came into the living room. "You'll meet her when she arrives."

"I don't want to get married, Mom," Nick said, "but Greg does, and he's the oldest. You could have set him up without involving the rest of us."

"Go big or go home!" Ah Ma said gleefully. "That's the expression, right?"

"Besides," Nick continued, "I'm perfectly capable of meeting my own women."

He recalled the woman he'd had in his bed last weekend. He'd thought of Lily many times in the past week. Once, he'd even spaced out for a whole five minutes at work, remembering how it felt to have her legs wrapped around him.

He pushed that thought out of his mind.

"Then why don't you bring these women home with you?" Mom asked.

"He does bring them home," Zach piped up, "but he doesn't think of this place as home."

Mom looked scandalized.

Ah Ma looked confused.

Ah Yeh was snoring in the corner, the velociraptor puppet on his hand.

"What does he mean, Nicky?" Ah Ma tugged his sleeve. "I don't understand."

"He's not serious about any of the women he meets in Toronto," Greg said. "That's why he's never brought them to Mosquito Bay. He just brings them to his bed."

"And why haven't you brought women here, Greg?" Ah Ma asked.

"Greg isn't very good at meeting women," Nick said. "He's too busy grunting in the corner."

"Am not," Greg said…with a grunt.

His brother did have a sense of humor. Sort of.

"So this matchmaking business is good for him," Nick continued, "but not for the rest of us."

"But my life is in Toronto," Greg said, "not Mosquito Bay. I don't need to meet a woman who lives in Mosquito Bay."

"Ah, but your date lives in Toronto!" Ah Ma said. "Very pretty girl. Daughter of your mother's friend."

"You convinced her to come all the way to Mosquito Bay for dinner?"

"She is visiting her family for the weekend. Not so bad a drive from there."

"Hmm," Greg said uncertainly.

"Why did you set me up with the girl who ran an electric train through my hair when I was a kid?" Zach asked.

"I did not do that," Diana said.

"You did so."

"Ah, you are arguing." Ah Ma nodded sagely. "Good, good. This is always, what do you call it? A *prelude* to kissing."

Just then, Amber stormed into the living room, followed by Darren, her boyfriend.

Well, *ex*-boyfriend.

"Darren claims you invited him as my date!" Amber said to Mom. "He's lying, isn't he?"

"No," Mom said, "he isn't."

"They arranged Thanksgiving dates for all of us," Zach said. "Guess you got stuck with one you've already dated."

Amber crossed her arms over her chest. "There is no way I'm having pumpkin pie with that turd of a human being."

"Excuse me?" Darren said.

"I always liked you together," Ah Ma said. "Why did you break up?"

"I am not having this conversation." Amber turned away.

This was going to be interesting.

Nick wondered who they would set him up with, though he couldn't say he was looking forward to his date's arrival. Amber had gotten her ex and Zach had gotten a family friend, so it seemed likely that Nick would get a woman he already knew, too.

He headed to the kitchen, where his father was working on the potatoes.

"You knew about this whole matchmaking plan?" Nick asked.

"Sure," Dad said. "Not that I expected anything to come of it, but I thought it would be entertaining, at the very least."

"And you wonder why I don't come back here more often!"

"That's not fair." Dad set down his knife. "We've never attempted matchmaking on this scale before."

"You've attempted it on smaller scales?"

"Only with Zach, since he lives here."

This was great. Just great. Nick couldn't wait until he could return to Toronto tomorrow, knock back a couple drinks, maybe pick up a woman at a bar. Eat a few Korean tacos, or some other food that didn't exist in Mosquito Bay.

He couldn't help picturing someone who looked like Lily. Why did he keep thinking of her?

The doorbell rang.

"I'll get it," Nick shouted, heading to the front hall.

He opened the door to reveal a young woman, who was smiling hesitantly and carrying a large Tupperware of what looked like Nanaimo bars.

Nick loved Nanaimo bars, but he didn't care, not now. Because this woman, who was wearing jeans and a light pink sweater, was very familiar.

He blinked, trying to clear his mind. He must be imagining this.

But when he opened his eyes, she was still standing there.

Lily.

4

OH, no.

This couldn't be happening.

How was this happening?

Lily was never supposed to see Nick again. It was supposed to be a one-night stand. He was meant to be a pleasant—*very* pleasant—memory, not someone she would ever encounter in real life.

He was wearing a polo shirt and jeans today. She'd always been partial to men in suits, but he pulled off the casual look well, too. And the naked look.

Get it together, Lily!

She should not be recalling when he lifted her onto the couch, spread her legs, and went down on her, without even closing the curtains, and—

Okay, seriously, Lily. Not important right now.

Her face flamed.

She was supposed to be set up with a man named Greg and meet his family. She'd even made Nanaimo bars for this whole-some occasion. And now she'd discovered that she'd already slept with someone in Greg's family. Likely Nick was his brother.

Her only one-night stand! What were the odds?

She couldn't help wishing she'd been set up with Nick instead, but then she felt stupid and naïve. To him, she was probably just another woman he'd spent an enjoyable night with. Whereas he was the man who'd given her the hottest experience of her life.

There was no way she could actually go out with Greg. Not that she'd had high hopes for this matchmaking event—she'd done it to satisfy her mother—but now it was an impossibility. It would be too weird.

She'd just try to get through dinner and hope Nick wouldn't say anything. She didn't want his family judging her.

Well, she didn't mean she wanted him to say *literally* nothing, like he was doing now. He was simply staring at her. Shocked, like she was.

But she'd prefer if he didn't let on that they knew each other.

"Lily," he whispered, "are you my date?"

She shook her head. "Your brother's, I think. Don't say anything, okay?"

He nodded just as another man walked over to the door. The man looked quite a bit like Nick. Maybe an inch or two taller. Good-looking, nice build.

He didn't affect her nearly as much as Nick did, however.

Plus, he was frowning.

Mind you, Nick was frowning now, too, but during the night they'd spent together, he'd smiled at her a lot, aside from the times when he was looking at her intensely, like he wanted to rip her dress off. And when he *was* ripping her dress off.

Stop it, brain!

"Lily, is that what you said your name was?" Nick said.

"Yes. I'm supposed to be Greg's date."

"Hi," said the other man. "I'm Greg."

"Well, um, nice to meet you!"

She couldn't think of anything else to say, not with Nick standing there. It was hard to think clearly in his presence.

"My mom says you're an engineer?" she managed at last.

"Yes," Greg said.

Hmm. He wasn't the greatest conversationalist. No mention of what kind of engineer he was, or anything else.

"I wonder when your date will get here," Greg said to Nick.

"I'm told your parents invited dates for all of you?" Lily said.

"Yep, all four of us," Nick confirmed. "Though I suspect my sister's date will be heading off any minute."

Just then, there was some yelling from another room.

"I never want to see you again!" shouted a woman.

"How did things get so bad so fast?" Lily asked.

"They already know each other," Nick said. "In fact, they used to date, and apparently it did not end well."

He left and came back with his hand grasped around a smaller man's upper arm.

"I don't care that my parents invited you," Nick said. "My sister never wants to see you again, so you're not staying for dinner."

"But..."

Greg opened the door and Nick shoved the man out. He slapped his hands together afterward.

Lily had to admit, the whole thing turned her on a little.

"Ah, who is here?" said a female voice.

Suddenly, there was a whole crowd of people in the front hall, just as Lily was in the process of taking off her shoes.

"You are Lily!" said the elderly woman, presumably Nick's grandmother. "Yes, your mother is right, you are very pretty."

"Uh, thank you."

"Welcome to our home. I'll take those for you." A middle-aged white woman held out her hands, and Lily passed her the Nanaimo bars. "I'm Rosemary, Greg's mother."

"Uh, hi. Nice to meet you."

"This is my husband, Stuart." She gestured toward an Asian

man with long, graying hair. He bore a slight resemblance to Nick.

"You can call me Ah Ma," said the elderly lady. "You will be part of the family soon, so you might as well."

"Let's not get too far ahead of ourselves," Rosemary said. "This is just a setup since Greg here isn't very good at meeting women. Like our other sons."

A moment later, the doorbell rang, and Nick opened the door to reveal a petite white woman with wavy blond hair. She wore jeans and an off-the-shoulder floral top.

"You must be Nick!" She grinned, then gave him a hug. "I'm Janice."

Janice had a rather squeaky voice.

Or maybe she didn't, and Lily was just jealous because Janice was touching Nick and she wasn't.

She tried to push those feelings aside. She had no claim on him, and if Nick was genuinely interested in this woman, what was Lily going to do? He was welcome to be interested in any woman he liked. He'd done nothing wrong.

Then he looked at Lily. Was it her imagination, or was that a lustful look in his eyes?

Nah, must be her imagination.

She took a deep breath. This was going to be a long dinner.

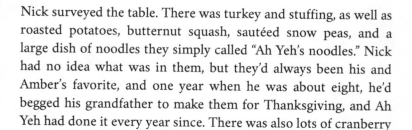

Nick surveyed the table. There was turkey and stuffing, as well as roasted potatoes, butternut squash, sautéed snow peas, and a large dish of noodles they simply called "Ah Yeh's noodles." Nick had no idea what was in them, but they'd always been his and Amber's favorite, and one year when he was about eight, he'd begged his grandfather to make them for Thanksgiving, and Ah Yeh had done it every year since. There was also lots of cranberry sauce and gravy and warm rolls, plus the char siu he'd brought from Toronto.

It might not be strictly traditional, but in Nick's family, this was tradition, like Pictionary at Chinese New Year.

And this year, they might actually eat most of the enormous quantity of food, since there were three more people than usual.

Lily was sitting next to Greg. He said something to her quietly, and she laughed.

Nick tightened his hand on his fork. Dammit.

Why did his brother get set up with Lily? Why couldn't Nick have been set up with Lily instead? His brother was all wrong for her, that much was obvious. Lily needed someone to add a little excitement to her day-to-day life. To introduce her to one-night stands and having soup dumplings as a late-night snack.

She and Greg together? It would be dull.

Not that he thought Lily was dull by herself, oh no, but...

Nick gave his head a shake. He was acting like he knew Lily well after they'd spent a grand total of one night together; in truth, he hardly knew her at all.

Except he felt like he did.

He turned his attention back to the woman sitting beside him. Janice was a pig farmer. He had not expected the pint-sized blonde to be a pig farmer, of all things, but she'd taken over the family farm—about twenty minutes from Mosquito Bay—from her father.

Which meant she was totally wrong for Nick.

Despite having grown up in this small town on the shores of Lake Huron, he was very much a city guy, and Janice was committed to her pig farm. She also grew soybeans and corn and was telling him unnecessary details about the crops. Details he was sure someone else would be delighted to listen to.

But he wasn't that guy.

She also seemed to think his family would be particularly

interested in soybeans, perhaps because they were Asian? It was a little weird.

"What's that?" she asked, pointing at the char siu.

"Barbecued pork. I brought it from Toronto. Here." He picked up a piece with his fork and placed it on her plate. "What do you think?"

She put it in her mouth and cocked her head to one side. "Not bad."

Not bad? It was the best char siu in Toronto. He'd tried dozens of places over the years he'd lived in the city. This one was the best.

Though the char siu in the slider at Lychee had been pretty good, too. Or maybe that was just the company.

He shot a look across the table. Lily was already looking at him, and her gaze suffused him with warmth.

Jesus, he was losing it.

He'd already slept with her, for God's sake. He shouldn't be this affected by her.

Nick enjoyed a variety of women, had never felt the need to commit to just one. He was young and rich and good-looking, and he enjoyed flirting with new women in bars, dancing with them in clubs. He was always honest about what he was looking for and never led anyone on.

But now, what he wanted more than anything was to sit next to Lily at Thanksgiving dinner. Then he could put his hand on her leg, like he'd done at Lychee, and admire her from up close. Whisper in her ear and hear her laugh just for him.

His parents had done a piss-poor job of matchmaking. Lily made no sense for Greg, and Janice made no sense for Nick. His parents had also done a bad job with Zach and Diana, who seemed to grate on each other's nerves.

Amber, lucky her, was seated next to an empty chair, where Darren should have been, but Amber had gotten so angry at the sight of him that Nick had thrown the bastard out. Why did Mom and Dad think setting her up with an ex was the way to go?

Yes, once this dinner was over, he would make his feelings clear to his parents.

There would be no more matchmaking. End of story.

"So, Lily," Ah Ma said. "What do you do for Thanksgiving in your family? You have turkey?"

Lily shook her head. "One year when I was in elementary school, I begged my parents to have a normal Thanksgiving dinner, like all the other kids. So they bought a turkey, and I'm not sure what went wrong." She chuckled. "But there was lots of yelling, and by nine o'clock that night, the turkey still wasn't done, so we ordered Kentucky Fried Chicken. And that's what we have for Thanksgiving every year now. KFC and an apple pie my mom buys at the grocery store."

"Where did you grow up?" Nick asked.

"Ingleford."

Ah. It was a small town south of London, Ontario if he remembered correctly; Mosquito Bay was to the northwest.

He wanted to ask her more questions. He wanted to know more about her than what kind of bubble tea she liked and how she ate her soup dumplings.

But she was Greg's date.

God, he could barely stand it.

"What about you?" he asked Janice. "You do the whole turkey thing?"

"Yeah. All my extended family. There's twenty-six of us. Or is it twenty-seven now? I keep forgetting."

Nobody said anything for a few minutes, all busy eating their turkey and stuffing and veggies and noodles. Amber, as usual, had loaded up almost entirely on noodles and stuffing. Zach had mostly meat. Greg's plate was perfectly balanced, as always.

Conversation was not flowing naturally.

This, Nick supposed, was what happened when your parents unexpectedly invited dates for all their children. It probably didn't help that he was thinking about how he wanted to rip off his brother's date's pink sweater and feed her Nanaimo bars.

He hadn't eaten a Nanaimo bar in a long time, and he was craving one now.

Did Greg actually like Lily...like that? Or was he just being nice?

Nick and his older brother had never fought over a woman before, perhaps because Greg only occasionally showed interest in anyone and rarely bothered with anything as pedestrian as socializing.

Though he seemed to be doing a good enough job with Lily now.

"Nick, how are things in Toronto?" Ah Ma asked. "You do good business? You trick lots of people into buying things?"

"Thank you for that wonderful description of my job."

"What do you do?" Janice asked. "My parents didn't tell me, just said you were some fancy Toronto businessman."

"I work in advertising."

"Like *Mad Men*?"

"Sure," he said. "Just like *Mad Men*."

"You like living in the city?" She made a face.

"Yeah, I love it."

"Don't you find it noisy?"

"I live on the fifty-third floor. It's not too noisy up there."

"Fifty-third floor?" Janice sputtered. "I'm afraid of heights. What happens if there's a fire? Or a wind storm? What possible advantage could there be to living in downtown Toronto? There's so much traffic. And crime."

"There really isn't. Though the traffic is bad, I'll give you that."

"Hmph."

Nick couldn't stand it anymore. He finished his noodles in a hurry and didn't help himself to seconds—even though he *always* had seconds of Ah Yeh's noodles—and headed to the kitchen.

He needed a break.

5

LILY EXCUSED herself to go to the washroom, and on the way back, she went looking for Nick. He wasn't hard to find.

He was in the kitchen, eating her Nanaimo bars.

Nanaimo bars were her favorite dessert to make. The bottom was a mix of graham cracker crumbs, coconut, cocoa powder, nuts, butter, egg, and sugar. Next came the creamy filling: butter, cream, sugar, and custard powder. Lastly, the top layer of chocolate.

They were delicious and extremely unhealthy.

But it was Thanksgiving, and she was being forced to sit through a dinner with a family she didn't know. Perfectly nice people, but she felt like she was intruding.

Worse, she had to sit across the table from Nick and his date.

Not that Nick seemed interested in Janice, and it was clear they had nothing in common, but it was hard to watch all the same.

She just...dammit.

Maybe Lily sucked at one-night stands after all and couldn't help getting attached to a man she'd slept with. She was trying to be less boring, but she couldn't truly change the kind of person she was.

Nick turned as she approached. "Do you like him?"

"What?"

"Greg. Do you like him?"

They were whispering, so nobody could hear from the dining room, but something crackled between them. Like a fire on a cold winter's day. There was an unexpected edge to Nick's words.

"He's nice," Lily said, not giving Nick what he wanted.

"Nice," Nick repeated faintly. "He's a little stern and grumpy. Is that the kind of guy you usually go for?"

She shrugged. Greg was perfectly fine, and maybe if she hadn't met Nick first, she would have been interested enough to see him again.

Or perhaps not.

The thing was, she and Greg had no chemistry. Sometimes that developed with time, but it was impossible not to compare him to Nick.

There had been lots of chemistry from the start.

Now he was looking at her with an expression she couldn't decipher. It wasn't an expression she'd seen on him last weekend, when he'd been charming and kind, and then very *purposeful* when he'd started to touch and undress her.

She couldn't help releasing a little squeak at the memory.

Nick plucked a Nanaimo bar out of the container and lifted it to his mouth. She couldn't help staring as he ate.

"These are amazing," he said. "I have no idea what's in Nanaimo bars, but they've always been my favorite."

"Mine, too."

"Yours are especially good."

"I know."

His lips twitched.

"What if I tried to feed one to you?" He took a tiny step toward her.

She breathed in sharply. "You're jealous."

"Very jealous."

"Are you jealous of every woman your brother shows a slight interest in?"

"It's never happened before. I'm not the jealous type. But I still really want you, Lily."

She hadn't expected this.

"How do you want me?" she asked.

"Preferably over the counter."

They were both quiet for a moment, and she could hear laughter and the clink of cutlery from the dining room. She wished they were completely alone.

She squeezed her thighs together.

"It was only supposed to be one night," she said. "I thought you were great at one-night stands. You told me they were your specialty."

"So I did."

"And?"

"You've thrown me off my game."

"Me?"

"Yeah, you."

He reached out and touched her arm; it felt like he was branding her. Then he pulled back and picked up another Nanaimo bar. She'd cut them into small pieces so they could be eaten in a couple bites. He removed the top layer of chocolate and held it to her lips.

"You're not supposed to eat Nanaimo bars like that," she protested. "You're supposed to eat the layers all together. It's the perfect combination." She gestured to his hand. "This is *wrong*."

"There's still a bit of filling, whatever it is—"

"Butter, cream, tons of powdered sugar, and custard powder."

"Don't ruin the magic for me. I don't need to know what's in it."

"I'm not ruining the magic. I know exactly what's in Nanaimo bars, and I still love them." Though knowing the ingredients and quantities made her very conscious of the fact that they weren't healthy.

He held the square of chocolate, with a little of the creamy filling clinging to it, closer to her lips, and she took a bite and chewed slowly. After she finished the chocolate, he held up the rest of the Nanaimo bar, and she licked the filling off the base. Nice and slow.

This wasn't like her.

This wasn't like her at all.

But when his eyes flared with desire, she couldn't deny that it was fun to tease him.

"Okay," Nick said hoarsely. "You've answered the question of what you'd do if I fed you a Nanaimo bar. Now tell me, what would you do if I kissed you? Do you want me to?"

His family was so close, just in the other room. One of those men was her blind date, but it wasn't like he was her boyfriend.

She felt deliciously naughty. She wasn't used to feeling this way, but with Nick...

"I'd like that very much," she said. "I'd like that very fucking much."

He chuckled. "Just like you enjoyed those 'fucking good' char siu sliders last weekend."

"Oh, much more than that."

He stepped closer and rested his hand on her shoulder, and she was overwhelmed by his nearness. His handsome features were mere inches away.

Why wasn't he kissing her yet? Hadn't she already sexily eaten a Nanaimo bar for him?

She needed his lips on hers.

She wasn't used to needing anything this badly. She usually felt restrained, in control, but with Nick, it was different.

Finally, he kissed her, and it was even better than a Nanaimo bar.

His hands stayed firmly on her shoulders. He didn't explore her body, didn't move anything except his lips against hers, but that was enough. It made her feel like she was all that mattered.

He pulled back. "We should head to the dining room. They might wonder where we are."

By the time she'd found her voice, he'd already left, and she leaned against the counter for a moment in a daze.

There was pumpkin pie, apple pie, cherry cheesecake, and Nanaimo bars on the table, plus vanilla ice cream and whipped cream as accompaniments.

Nick enjoyed dessert, but today, he didn't much care.

Sure, he helped himself to a slice of pumpkin pie with a generous dollop of whipped cream, as well as another Nanaimo bar, but all he really cared about was Lily.

Lily, who certainly wasn't going to think about Greg again after that kiss.

She kept catching Nick's gaze, then quickly looking away, as though embarrassed. But when it was just the two of them, she wasn't shy.

They were good together, dammit.

"So, anyway," Janice was saying, "the manure was…"

This wasn't his preferred topic of conversation, especially while eating, and it drove home the point—once again—that they were all wrong for each other.

He could only think of Lily, who was sitting there sweetly across the table from him, focused on her plate of dessert. He wanted—*needed*—to be alone with her again, to feel her shudder at his touch.

"Alright." Zach put his fork down with a clink. "Mom and Dad, why on earth did you set me up with Diana, and Amber with her ex-boyfriend? Why do you feel the need to interfere in our dating lives?"

"We already told you!" Ah Ma said. "Four grandchildren, all single. Clearly you need help."

"No," Zach said, "we don't."

"And Diana is your best friend's little sister."

"Sebastian isn't my best friend. I rarely see him anymore."

"But he was your best friend when you were children, yes?"

"What does that have to do with anything?"

"We did our research." Ah Ma stuffed a bite of cheesecake in her mouth. "Well, mainly Rosemary, because she is the one who reads all the romance novels, but I read a few, too. And this best friend's little sister? We see it in a few books. It always results in a happy ending. So we think, maybe it will work for you!"

Mom turned to Amber. "Sometimes second chance romances turn out well, too, so we figured we'd invite Darren."

"What about Greg and me?" Nick asked. "How did you pick our dates?"

"You and Janice are opposites," Ah Ma said. "Opposites attract, no? And Lily...well, from all I've heard, she sounds like a wonderful woman"—she looked at Lily, who blushed—"and I thought she'd be best with Greg. Though there was that runaway bride..."

"Runaway bride?"

"A new woman in town," Mom said. "Left a guy at the altar. She was supposed to get married again last week, and I thought for sure she'd leave this guy, too, and then maybe she could fall into the arms of one of my sons. But she went through with the wedding. You know Mrs. Meyer? She lost thirty dollars in a bet!"

"Mom," Zach said, "why would you want to set one of us up

with a woman who'd left two men at the altar? Seems like a bad bet."

"Aiyah!" Ah Ma said. "Clearly you don't understand these things."

"Clearly not," Greg muttered.

Nick didn't know why his elders were treating their dating lives like they were in a novel, but he didn't bother voicing any complaints. This ridiculous plan of his family's had brought Lily back into his life, and she didn't want Greg the way she wanted Nick.

And Nick was going to...

Well, he didn't know precisely where to go from here. One-night stands were his area of expertise, as he'd told Lily. He didn't know how to do other things, whatever those entailed.

Her tongue darted out of her mouth to lick some whipped cream off her lip, and he nearly growled in frustration. Frustration that he couldn't touch her right now.

All he knew was that he needed more of her.

To no one's surprise, Janice and Diana left soon after dinner was over. Nick attempted to help with dishes, but his parents wouldn't let him. They never let him help when he came back to Mosquito Bay for the holidays.

"I'm going to get some fresh air," he said, hoping Lily would understand what he was after.

Indeed, she came out the front door a couple minutes later, and he led her around the side of the house. She had her arms wrapped around herself—it was cooler than it had been earlier.

"Allow me," he murmured. He hauled her against him and replaced her arms with his, holding her close.

She felt amazing; she felt *right*.

Geez, he was having some weird thoughts tonight.

She slid her arms around his neck, tilted her head up, and pressed her mouth to his, just once. "I feel so naughty."

"Mm." He couldn't speak; he was too busy burying his face in the crook of her neck. There was one particular spot that he'd found last weekend, right—

"Ohh."

Yes, right there.

He hoisted her up, his hands under her denim-clad ass. He'd loved her in the red dress, but he also loved her like this, in jeans and a sweater, her back against the brick wall of his childhood home. He set his lips to hers.

"Nick," she said, "what are we—"

"Nick!" someone else shouted. "What are you doing?"

It was Ah Ma.

6

SUDDENLY UNSUPPORTED BY Nick's hands, Lily fell to the grass, unable to get her legs underneath her in time. He'd dropped her the moment he'd seen his grandmother standing before them.

Dear God, they'd been caught.

When she was younger, Lily's sister, Marla, had been caught sneaking out of the house multiple times, sneaking a boy into her bedroom, smoking pot, and many other things.

Lily, on the other hand, had only been discovered while eating Oreos in the middle of the night at the age of eight. That was all.

Oh, she'd also taken an extra box of Pocky from the pantry.

Once.

She'd certainly never been caught in the middle of a make-out session by the man's grandmother. This was a totally new experience, one she wished she weren't having.

She took Nick's extended hand, and he pulled her up to standing.

"I'm so sorry," he said. "You okay?"

"Aiyah!" Ah Ma said, grasping Nick's wrist. "I hear stories about how you are—what do you call it? Playboy? Manwhore? Am I saying this correctly?"

Nick made a strangled sound in his throat. "I think you—"

"What happened?" Rosemary and Stuart rushed around the side of the house, followed by Zach and Greg.

"It's not what it looks like!" Lily said.

Which was stupid.

But it was the first thing that came to mind, because that's what Marla had always said when she got caught, though the phrase had never helped Marla get out of anything.

It was also exactly what Lily had said when Tara and Sam found her kissing Nick.

This past week had certainly been something.

"No lying! You were making out." Ah Ma pointed at Nick, then Lily. "Against the wall! I saw it!"

"Your vision isn't that great," Stuart said, placing a hand on his mother's shoulder.

"I know what I saw! Kissing! Nick kissed Greg's date! Playboy! Man—"

"Okay, okay," Nick said, lifting his hands. "Ah Ma is correct."

"Stealing your brother's woman? I raised you better than this."

"What are you talking about?" Rosemary interjected. "*I* raised him."

Zach was smirking, and Greg looked…well, Lily couldn't read him at all. He always wore the same expression.

Nick curled his arm around her waist in a protective gesture. "Lily and I met last weekend, actually, in Toronto. We went on a date."

"A date!" Zach laughed. "You don't date."

Nick shot him a glare. "I had no idea she was coming to our family Thanksgiving, because that was sprung on us without warning."

"Why didn't you say anything earlier?" Rosemary asked.

"It seemed awkward."

"And I told him not to," Lily added.

"You like Nick better than Greg?" Rosemary asked.

"I'm sorry," she said to Greg. "I was going to tell you, if we ever got a chance to have a private conversation. I didn't mean for you to find out like this."

Greg nodded. "No worries."

"Are you sure?"

"It's fine."

"Where did you meet Lily last weekend?" Ah Ma asked Nick.

"At a bar," Nick replied.

"Is it only physical? Or love at first sight? Maybe we did good matchmaking after all, we just set Lily up with the wrong man!"

"I'd call that bad matchmaking," Stuart said, and Ah Ma gave him a look.

"What's going on out here?" Ah Yeh stumbled around to the side of the house, and Stuart steadied him.

"You missed all the excitement!" Ah Ma said. "Nick was making out with Lily! Why are you always napping? You miss all the good stuff."

Ah Yeh waved this off. "I know this already. I saw them in the kitchen earlier. Feeding each other Nanaimo bars."

"And you didn't tell me?" Ah Ma screeched. "We have such boring lives, and you keep the exciting things to yourself? Wah, you are a bad husband!"

"That's enough," Nick said. "Lily and I are going for a walk now, okay? The rest of you are going back inside, and don't you dare even think about following us. I can't believe that has to be said, but it does."

Ooh. Lily rather liked this commanding voice of his.

As well as the thought of being alone with him once more.

Nick led Lily to a small park overlooking the beach, Lake Huron a dark shape just beyond. It reminded her of last week, when she'd seen Lake Ontario from his penthouse.

One week. It had only been one week since she'd met him.

It felt like so much longer.

They sat on a bench. It was a touch cooler by the lake, but when Nick put his arm around Lily, it felt like there was a fire burning inside her.

"Why is the town called Mosquito Bay?" she asked, not feeling like talking about what had just transpired. They were probably due for an important conversation, and she wanted to delay that a little longer.

"No idea. They've tried to change the town name a few times over the years, but it never happened. Sometimes the mosquitos are pretty bad here, but not much different from any of the towns nearby. It's not a big tourist destination, though, despite being on the lake. I once saw it on a list of 'Best Kept Secrets in Ontario.'"

"Did you like growing up here?"

He hesitated. "It was fine, but once I was a teenager, it started to feel too small, plus I always felt...different. The town isn't entirely white, but it's still mostly white."

"The other kids used to make fun of my lunches," Lily said. "I was the only Asian kid in my grade. They called me 'Rice Girl.' I knew my food tasted better, but I wanted to fit in, so I pleaded with my mom to make me bologna sandwiches. She refused. When I went to university at Western, there were more people who looked like me, and then I moved to Toronto."

He nodded. "I reinvented myself when I came to Toronto for university. I was determined to be cool for once."

"You weren't the popular and charming quarterback in high school?"

"Nah. I had some friends, but..." He leaned closer. "Don't tell anyone in Toronto. I don't want to ruin my reputation."

His mouth was almost touching her ear. She couldn't think clearly.

She leaned away from him and changed the topic. "There

weren't a lot of books about kids like us, either. A few, but not many. I read a lot of the Baby-Sitters Club books. Claudia Kishi—I thought she was great."

Lily felt a moment of embarrassment for admitting her love of that series, but then decided she didn't care, and Nick didn't make fun of her.

It was nice to talk to someone who'd grown up in a place similar to Ingleford. Tara, on the other hand, had grown up in Toronto, and her experience had been very different.

"When did your family come to Mosquito Bay?" Lily asked.

Nick toyed with a lock of her hair. "My grandparents settled here when they arrived from Hong Kong in the sixties. My dad was seven."

"I like your family," she said, but mortification overtook her as soon as she'd spoken. "Though I didn't like it when your grand-mother caught us. What was I thinking, Nick?"

"That I'm completely irresistible?" The corner of his mouth kicked up.

She huffed out a laugh. "No, I wasn't thinking at all. I let you kiss me and feed me a Nanaimo bar when your family was just in the other room! In fact, I let you feed me a Nanaimo bar in a totally blasphemous fashion."

"Blasphemous?"

"Like I said, you're supposed to eat the three layers together. Why else did I spend all that time assembling them? If everyone ate Nanaimo bars the way you do, I could have served a bowl of the crust, a bowl of the filling, and a bowl of chocolate."

"Deconstructed Nanaimo bars. Intriguing."

"Totally improper."

"Go out with me, Lily," he murmured. "Let me take you on a date back in Toronto."

She looked at him for a moment, then decided to be completely honest. "I like you, but we lead very different lives. You enjoy going out and partying until four in the morning—"

"I usually shut it down before four. I'm in my thirties now. Two or three is late enough."

"You know what I mean. You live in another world, with your fancy job and your penthouse and your commitment to one-night stands. Me, I occasionally meet up with my friends, but often I'm curled up alone watching a movie on a Saturday night."

"The night we met, it sounded like you were trying to get out of your comfort zone."

"My ex-boyfriend told me I was boring."

"You're not boring." He placed his hand on her cheek, and she melted a little beneath his touch. "You fascinate me."

"Why?"

"You just do."

"Terrible answer."

"Let me take you on a date."

"But you're all about one-night stands, by your own admission. Your brother said as much, too. Yet it sounds like you want more than that?"

"I do."

It baffled her. If someone was going to make Nick change his ways, surely it wouldn't be her. She was an ordinary woman.

"I don't know exactly what I want," he admitted, "but I do want to see you again and go on a date with you."

He smiled at her. It was dark here, darker than walking on the Toronto streets at night, but she could still make out his smile, and oh, it did things to her. Nick was so freaking attractive. She'd hardly been able to take her eyes off him at dinner.

On one hand, going out with him felt like she was playing it safe, as she always had, venturing back into something that might be a relationship.

On the other hand, it felt dangerous to do that with a man like Nick.

"Alright," she heard herself say. "I'll go out with you next weekend, but first, I want you to prove you're serious about me as more than a one-night stand, because I still find it hard to believe."

"What do I have to do?" He leaned forward.

Ooh, her plan was evil. She nearly cackled.

But why was she doing this? She and Nick could just have a fling. Casual sex with no commitments.

Except she knew her feelings would get involved, and it would crush her when it ended. Plus, he was talking about dates, not just sex, and she couldn't help worrying that she wasn't good enough for him.

So she needed some reassurance.

"If you're that serious about me," she said, "then come to my family's Thanksgiving dinner tomorrow."

"To eat Kentucky Fried Chicken and apple pie?"

"Exactly." She felt a little embarrassed about her family's Thanksgiving plans. His family had put out quite a spread, and hers ordered fast food.

But she liked their traditions, and KFC for Thanksgiving had been her father's favorite.

"No problem," Nick said smoothly. "In fact, I'll bake something for dessert."

Her phone buzzed, but she ignored it. "If you like."

"I insist."

He pulled her onto his lap and wound his arms around her waist. There was no family to interrupt them now, and her heart beat quickly in anticipation.

He was about to set his lips to hers when her phone started ringing.

"Oh my fucking God," she said.

Nick laughed.

"Why won't it stop?" How did she answer a phone call? She was drawing a blank. Her proximity to Nick had totally fried her brain.

Finally, she was able to answer the phone.

"Lily," her mother said, "I thought you would be home by now. Are you driving? You shouldn't answer the phone while you're driving."

"I'm still in Mosquito Bay."

"Ah, it's going well! I knew you and Greg would be perfect together. Not that I've ever met him before, but—"

"Actually..." Oh, how did she put this? She couldn't lie, not if her mother was friends with Nick's family, plus she'd asked him to come over. "Actually, I'm getting along well with Greg's brother, Nick. I've invited him over for Thanksgiving dinner tomorrow."

"Greg's brother? I don't understand."

"We already knew each other in Toronto and—"

"You invited him for Thanksgiving?"

Lily had to move the phone away from her ear because her mother was yelling. "Calm down, Ma. Is it okay that he comes over?"

She wasn't sure if her mother was shocked that Lily had easily switched from one brother to the other, or embarrassed that someone else would join in their KFC traditions.

"Of course, " Ma said at last.

Lily spoke to her mother for a couple more minutes as Nick slipped his hands under her sweater and ran them over her stomach, nearly making her miss what her mom said on multiple occasions.

At last, she ended the call, and as soon as she did, Nick's hands were on her breasts.

"Now where were we before my grandma interrupted?" he murmured.

They weren't leaning against a brick wall this time. They were in a public park, but it didn't feel as illicit as being at the side of a man's family's house when she was supposed to be his brother's date.

Nope, everybody knew the truth now. She didn't know exactly where this was going, but there were no secrets anymore.

Nick circled his thumb over her nipple, and she arched against him and felt his erection between his legs. What would it be like to have sex here, in a park by Lake Huron?

No, that was a little too much even for New Lily, who'd picked up a random guy at a bar, then somehow managed to have Thanksgiving dinner with his family.

They kissed for a while. Long, luxurious strokes. He knew how to make her feel so damn good, and when he kissed the base of her neck just...like...that...she was barely even able to breathe.

"Alright," she said when she could take it no more, "I need to leave if I'm going to get home before midnight. It's an hour drive."

"Mm, just a little longer."

"You're a terrible influence."

"That's my goal."

She laughed and kissed him one last time.

"Until tomorrow," she murmured.

7

When Nick came downstairs the following morning, he was greeted to a horrifying sight.

Well, "horrifying" might be a bit strong, but it was a sight he didn't really need to see.

His mother was sitting on the counter, her legs wrapped around his father's waist, and they were kissing. A pot of oatmeal was cooking on the stove.

This happened nearly every time he went back to Mosquito Bay. He and Greg would usually stay over for a night or two, and his parents would forget that they no longer had the house to themselves.

"Oh, Smoochie-boo-kins," his mother murmured.

At least, that's what it sounded like, but Nick could have heard incorrectly.

"Ahem," he said. "You're not alone in the house this morning."

Dad stepped back. "Oh, hi, Nick."

"Don't look so scandalized," Mom said. "Old people kiss, too."

"I'm very much aware of that."

An image of him and Lily in their sixties, kissing in the kitchen, popped into his mind.

Nick shook his head. He was getting way ahead of himself. He'd only just decided he wanted something more than a one-night stand, and for him, that was a pretty big deal.

Besides, he'd always been certain he *didn't* want to be like his parents.

But for a moment there...

"You deserve it," Dad said, grinning, "after your grandmother caught you making out with Lily last night."

"She shrieked as though someone had been stabbed," Mom said. "Not that there's been a stabbing in Mosquito Bay in, oh, forty-two years."

"I thought it was thirty-seven years."

"No, I think—"

"Okay, okay." Nick held up his hands. "Enough!"

"Will you have breakfast with us before you leave?" Mom asked.

"Actually, I'm going to stick around a little longer than usual. I won't leave until this afternoon, and then I'm going to Lily's family's Thanksgiving dinner."

Mom and Dad looked at each other.

"Oooh," they said, speaking in unison, as though they'd been together for over forty years. Which they had.

"You and Lily, eh?" Dad slapped him on the back. "And you're meeting her family? This is going fast."

"She's gone through the hardship of meeting my family. Seems only fair."

"Hardship?" Mom clasped her hands to her chest, as though she'd heard terrible news. "*Hardship?* We're nice people."

"Well, sure," Nick said, "but these situations are always awkward. Especially since she came here as Greg's blind date. Anyway, I'm sticking around until this afternoon, and I said I'd bake something for dessert. Maybe those butter tarts you used to make? Or date squares. Actually, you know what? I have lots of time. I'll make both."

Dad turned to Mom. "He really likes her."

Mom just laughed. "You? Baking? You've never baked before, have you?"

"No," Nick said, "but it can't be too hard, once you have the recipe."

"Can you even cook? Do you use the kitchen in that fancy condo of yours? Or are you storing your suits in the oven?"

"Thanks, Mom. Now, where are those recipes, and when does the grocery store open?"

Nick was starting to get the hang of this baking business. He was on his second batch of butter tarts, having burnt the first batch, but this batch was going to work out perfectly, he knew it.

He should have set the timer on the oven the first time, but he'd figured he would notice when it was ten thirty on the kitchen clock, and he would have, except...

Well, the kitchen was a little full.

"Baking is not a spectator sport," he said to his family for the third time.

"Wah, what are you talking about?" Ah Ma asked. "I watch baking and cooking competitions on the television all the time."

"I did not sign up for a baking competition." Nick gritted his teeth. "I just want to bring something nice to my date's family dinner."

"Ah, you are calling her your date, not your girlfriend?"

"I don't like labels."

"Mm, sure, Mr. Fancypants," Mom said.

"Mr. Fancypants!" Zach said. "That's a good one."

"Don't you guys have anything better to do?" Nick muttered.

"No, we really don't," Zach said cheerfully. "What could be better than watching you bake butter tarts for your true wuv?"

Nick did not dignify that with a response.

Zach made smooching noises in the air.

Nick still didn't say anything.

This was the problem with Mosquito Bay. Everyone was all up in everyone else's business, and his family drove him nuts. As soon as he'd mentioned baking, Mom and Dad had called up Zach, Ah Ma, and Ah Yeh and invited them over to watch, despite his protests. Even Greg was watching him bake, though he wasn't saying anything, only occasionally smirking.

Nick shoved the second batch of butter tarts into the oven.

"Look," he said, wiping his hands on the apron that his mother had insisted he wear, "there's nothing weird about a man baking. Dad bakes occasionally, and he does most of the cooking. Ah Yeh is a better cook than Ah Ma."

"Oh, there's nothing weird about a man baking," Dad said. "It's the fact that it's *you* baking."

Everyone nodded in agreement.

"What if it was Greg?" Nick asked as he reached for the container of dates.

Mom shook her head. "Not nearly as exciting."

"But you," Zach said, "with your fancy suits and fancy penthouse and fancy drinks—"

"Thanks for your great description of my life."

"Though I remember Greg baking for Tasha," Zach continued, "and you and I did watch."

"That's right," Nick said. "We watched him make cookies for Valentine's Day back in high school."

Greg grunted.

"I saw Tasha's parents the other day," Mom said. "They told me she's doing well."

Greg grunted again and crossed his arms over his chest.

Excellent. The attention had shifted to Greg. Nick started on the date squares, mixing flour, oatmeal, sugar, baking soda, and salt together in a bowl.

"Why did you drag me here?" Ah Yeh complained to Ah Ma. "I

can watch someone bake on the television, no need to leave the house! Or I could be ordering things on Amazon."

"Silly man! We have everything we need. Why buy all this stuff when we already have one foot in the grave?"

"Don't talk like that," Dad said.

"And watching our grandson bake is more exciting than those TV bakers!"

"It really isn't." Nick was now combining the oatmeal and flour mixture with the butter. He was supposed to do this "until crumbly," according to the recipe. Hmm. "Do you think it's crumbly?" he asked his mother.

Which was a mistake. Four people immediately reached for the bowl, ready to put their fingers in and check the consistency of the dough. Or batter.

What was the difference between dough and batter? Did this qualify as either?

Nick had no idea, and he wasn't about to put the question out to his audience.

Fortunately, he managed to move the bowl before everyone could touch it, just as the buzzer on the oven went off. He pulled the muffin pan out of the oven, happy to see the tarts didn't look burnt this time.

"I will help taste test," Ah Ma said.

"No, I will do the honors," Zach said.

"I'm going to have a nap." Ah Yeh headed toward the living room.

"Nobody is trying any of this batch of butter tarts," Nick said. "If you want a butter tart, you can have one of the burnt ones, which were ruined because you're all distracting me."

"I don't want a burnt one," Ah Ma said. "Only the best for me! I am old. One foot in the grave, remember! I must check that the filling is the perfect consistency. It should be a little runny, you know."

"I don't like it runny," Nick protested.

As he finished making the date squares, his family continued to argue about the consistency of butter tart filling. Finally, the date squares were out and cooling, and his family had gotten tired of talking about butter tarts—and, fortunately, had only consumed two between them.

Nick tried a bite, too, and decided they were quite good, though they weren't the best butter tarts he'd ever tasted. That honor belonged to Happy As Pie, one of the bakeries he'd visited in Toronto. He was a bit annoyed, because he wanted the very best for Lily, but considering this was the first time he'd ever baked—and he'd had to contend with his family's interference— he was pretty proud of himself, prouder than he'd been when he'd closed that last deal at work.

Not as proud as he'd been when he'd given Lily all those orgasms last weekend, but still.

He imagined feeding her a butter tart. Breaking off a piece of the crust and popping it in her mouth, then having her lick the filling from his finger. Perhaps she'd be scandalized by the idea of eating the filling and crust separately. Perhaps she'd kiss him afterward and slip her tongue between his lips.

Nick shoved those thoughts aside. He wasn't leaving for Ingleford until four o'clock, and for the next few hours, his main goal was not to let his family drive him crazy, and not to get himself too worked up by the thought of Lily eating dessert.

He had his work cut out for him.

"Nick," Ah Ma said, "you are an expert baker now. Maybe you can even make your own wedding cake!"

"Ah Ma!"

"No, no, of course, you cannot make that yourself. I will do it for you."

"If you try baking something that fancy," Ah Yeh said, "you will surely burn down our house!"

"You're getting ahead of yourselves," Nick said. "I still have to survive dinner with her family. Nobody's getting married anytime soon, despite your boneheaded attempts at match-making yesterday."

He didn't admit, however, that he was grateful for the match-making shenanigans because he'd gotten to see Lily again.

And he supposed having an audience in the kitchen wasn't the end of the world.

8

LILY, her mother, and her sister were sitting around after lunch, drinking tea.

"How did you meet Nick in Toronto?" Ma asked.

"We went on a date last weekend," Lily said. That was accurate enough, wasn't it?

"Then why did you agree to meet Greg yesterday if you were already dating a man?"

"We had been on *one* date, that's all. You can date multiple men at a time, you know, until you decide to be exclusive."

"Hmm," Ma said. "I don't know."

Marla laughed. She was having entirely too much fun with this, enjoying the fact that her antics weren't the topic of conversation for once.

"Did you sleep with him yet?" Marla asked as she took out the apple pie that had been purchased earlier that day. She pulled out a knife and was about to cut herself a piece, but Ma jumped up and grabbed the knife out of her hand.

"No! We must keep the pie looking nice for Nick."

Marla rolled her eyes and helped herself to some cashews instead. "Well, Lily? Are you going to answer my question?"

"I don't know why you think I slept with him."

"Right, because you're the *good* sister. You'd never do anything like sleep with a man after one date."

"Not that there's anything wrong with that," Lily said. "It's the twenty-first century and women can do whatever they like. They shouldn't be judged."

"You definitely slept with him," Marla said, returning to the table.

Lily did not want to lie, so she said nothing.

Marla grinned. "If you've only gone out once, why did you invite him over for dinner?"

"Seemed only fair. I had to meet his family, so he gets to meet mine."

"Sounds petty. I like it."

"I also want Nick to prove he's serious."

"Testing a guy. I like that, too."

"I'm trying to remember what Rosemary told me about Nick." Ma paused. "He is an advertising executive? I think this is correct."

"He has a penthouse." Lily wasn't sure why she'd felt the need to mention that—it made her feel a bit inferior. She had a sip of her tea.

"Ah," Marla said. "It has been confirmed. You went to his place."

"No," Ma said. "Lily could know that without actually going there."

"True, she could, but I think she went to his place."

"I don't see why this matters," Lily said. "Nick and I are dating, and he's coming here for KFC tonight. That's all you need to know."

But she was second-guessing herself. Maybe having him come to Ingleford wasn't the greatest idea after all.

Too late. She'd already invited him. Though she didn't have to cook, she had a list of things to do in preparation—mostly cleaning—and hopefully the house would look as nice as possible.

She couldn't help the nervous excitement flickering in her belly at the thought of seeing Nick again.

He'd show up, wouldn't he? What if he changed his mind?

~

Nick parked on the street outside a modest brick house in Ingleford. He picked up his plastic containers of butter tarts and date squares—which he'd cut into rectangles because he was a rebel—and climbed out of the car.

He was nervous, if he was honest with himself, and he wasn't used to being nervous about anything in his personal life. For work, occasionally, but not for things like this.

Then again, he'd never met a woman's family before.

He knocked on the door, and a moment later, Lily opened it, looking lovely in jeans and some kind of flowing red shirt. He quite liked her in red, and it reminded him of the day they'd met.

"You came," she said.

He was about to lean in to kiss her, but then another woman skidded into the front hall. She was wearing a band T-shirt and jeans with carefully-placed holes. She studied him in silence for a moment before her face broke into a smile. "Good job, Lily. He looks like Henry Golding."

"That's what I thought the first time we met." Lily turned back to him. "Welcome."

"I'm Marla," said the other woman. "Lily's younger, less uptight sister."

"Marla!" Lily hissed.

"But seriously, good job. This one looks like much more fun than Douglas."

Douglas must be her ex. Hmm.

A middle-aged woman stepped into the hall and approached him with her hand outstretched. "You must be Nick. I am Lily's mother."

"A pleasure to meet you, Mrs. Tseng," he said, hoping he wasn't laying it on too thick.

How was one supposed to act in these meet-the-family situations?

"You brought dessert," she said, eyeing his container. "Lily said you were baking, but I didn't believe her."

"Oh, come on," Marla said. "Men can bake. Just because Dad was allergic to being in the kitchen doesn't mean men can't bake."

They were quiet for a moment, and Nick wondered about Lily's father, but then he looked at her face, and he knew. He just knew.

He slipped off his shoes and followed Lily and Marla into the kitchen while their mother went to get the fried chicken. Lily took his container of sweets and put it on the table, and Marla immediately grabbed a date square. Lily gave her a look.

"What?" Marla said. "I'm hungry, and apparently I'm not allowed to start eating the apple pie." She bit into the date square, and before she finished chewing, said, "Damn, these are good."

"Thanks." Nick smiled. "Do you live in Ingleford?"

"Me? Ha! No, I live in London. For now. I'm a bartender."

"Cool," he said, not sure what the appropriate response was.

"And *you* are dating my sister. I'm not sure why. She's a bit stodgy."

He was taken aback. "Lily is..." Dammit, he was at a loss for words. It was hard to put everything into one or two sentences, especially ones that were appropriate to say in front of her sister. "Definitely not stodgy," he said at last.

Marla barked out a laugh, and he covered Lily's hand with his own.

Dinner went reasonably well. They ate fried chicken, which

he hadn't had in a while. The last time had been at one of those Taiwanese fried chicken places that were popping up in Toronto. Maybe he could take Lily to his favorite. Not for a nice date, of course, but if they needed some late-night sustenance, like last weekend.

Mrs. Tseng seemed to like him well enough, thankfully, and she spoke of Lily with great pride. As she should.

After fried chicken, they ate apple pie and butter tarts and date squares, and everyone complimented his baking skills. Lily's moan when she bit into her butter tart was the highlight of the meal, though the way she daintily ate her fried chicken was pretty cute, too.

Note to self: bake for Lily again.

After dinner, she suggested they go for a walk. She led him to a park just off Main Street, and they sat on one of the benches. It was almost like the night before in Mosquito Bay. Her thigh was pressed against his, and when he ran his hand over her leg, she made a sweet little gasp.

"Your father…" he began.

"He passed away three years ago."

"I'm sorry, Lily."

"At first, doing all the holidays without him felt wrong. They weren't happy, certainly not that first year. But now…" She sighed. "It's okay, but I still miss him. He loved KFC Thanksgivings." She pulled out her phone. "This is the closest you can get to meeting him."

She played a voicemail of him wishing her happy birthday and asking her to call back. A short message, but Nick understood why she kept it. Such things could mean a lot after you lost someone.

"That's the only one I have," she said, her voice wobbly.

Nick wrapped his arms around Lily, then pulled her into his lap because he wanted her as close as possible. He kissed her, trying to make everything better for her, though he knew he couldn't. But he wanted to, so badly.

He hadn't known her for long, but her feelings mattered very much to him.

He pulled back so he could see her dark eyes. "Are you heading to Toronto tonight?"

"No, I want to spend more time with my mother. I'm sorry."

"Nothing to apologize for."

"I'm going back tomorrow afternoon."

"When you get back to the city, come to my place. Sound like a plan?"

He needed to be with her again. Alone—not in public, like they were now.

When she smiled tentatively, he pulled her back toward him and set his lips to hers once more, losing himself in the feel of her.

He couldn't make everything perfect for her, but he'd give her what he could.

An hour later, Nick was ready to head home to Toronto, except for one small thing.

He was kissing Lily against the passenger door to his car.

His arms were wound around her, and she wrapped one leg around him, trying to get closer. He was surprised she was making out with him in front of her family's house, but he wasn't complaining.

Earlier, their kisses had been gentler, deeper. Now, it was more desperate. Frantic. He loved all the different kinds of kisses they shared and wanted to experience more with her. He liked variety, but he was discovering he could have that with one woman.

When he squeezed her ass, they both groaned.

He had to step back before this went any further.

"Tomorrow," he said, panting. "I'll see you tomorrow."

A lot had happened since the night they met, and it would be different this time.

He couldn't wait.

LILY COULDN'T THINK STRAIGHT on her drive back to Toronto that holiday Monday. Normally, she'd be planning the next day in her head, making a mental list of all the things she had to do.

But not today.

No, today she could think only of Nick.

Nick Wong. She knew his last name now.

In fact, she knew a lot of things about him. She'd met his family and saw how he acted around them. He'd met her family. She knew he baked pretty great butter tarts.

She also knew he ate Nanaimo bars in a horrifying way. He always broke off the top chocolate layer and had that first.

Oh, the humanity!

Yet, despite the travesty he'd committed with a Nanaimo bar, she couldn't stop thinking of him, and she ached between her legs, desperate to be with him again. Properly. Somewhere where no one could interrupt them.

When she got to her apartment, she changed into a dress, then texted him to say she was on her way. As she walked to the door of his penthouse—she couldn't believe she was seeing a guy who had a penthouse—she started swaying her hips.

Nick opened the door, wearing dark jeans and a light purple linen shirt—how did he look so good in that? He looked good in everything.

But right now, she had a hankering to see him naked.

He didn't speak, just pulled her toward him and kissed her hard. She fumbled with his shirt, pulling it over his head as the door closed behind them, and ran her hands up and down his gorgeous body. She pressed her lips to his neck and inhaled his clean, soapy scent, then unbuckled his belt and unzipped his jeans.

My God, they hadn't even *said* anything. She was just filling her senses with his body, touching him everywhere she could.

At last, he spoke. "Is being fucked over the counter on your list? Because it's on mine."

"Which list is that?"

"The list of places I want to screw you. It's quite long...ah."

She was touching his cock now, reveling in his reaction. Her power. She'd never felt this kind of power before. Sure, men had wanted her physically, but never quite like this, and never a man like him.

He pulled away, and before she knew it, he'd bent her over the counter. He lifted up her skirt and shoved her panties down her legs. The air was cool against her slick, heated flesh.

And then the warmth of his mouth on her. He was on his knees behind her, licking her, circling his tongue over her clit.

Then he was gone, and she whimpered in need.

But she could hear him opening a foil packet, and a moment later, he was easing himself inside her. "Tell me if you need me to go slower," he murmured against her neck, growling once he was all the way inside.

She was still wearing her dress. Her stilettos—the same ones she'd worn last weekend. Her panties—well, they were down around her ankles.

This wasn't the kind of sex Lily was used to having, but God, it was good.

He pushed into her again and again. "You're not stodgy at all."

She couldn't help but laugh.

"You're beautiful." He kissed her neck. "Fun." Another kiss. "Maker of delicious Nanaimo bars. Writer of lists."

"Nick?"

"Yes, love?"

"Shut the fuck up."

His chuckle was close to her ear, and he started moving faster inside her; she met him stroke for stroke.

"You're also extremely fun to corrupt," he said.

Yes, this was extremely fun, though she would argue about his use of "corrupt" if she were able to think straight. But she couldn't, not now.

He reached around to fondle her clit, and when she started racing up the last stretch toward her orgasm, he withdrew.

"Nick!" she protested.

"I have other plans for you, don't worry. I'll get you off soon."

He picked her up and carried her into his bedroom, with its large bed and dresser, all in neutral colors…and a large mirror. He positioned her directly in front of the mirror and stood behind her. He slipped the straps of her dress down her arms, followed by the cups of her bra.

"Don't shut your eyes," he whispered. "Watch yourself."

He unclasped her bra and tossed it to the ground. Her breasts popped free, and he massaged the tips between his fingers.

She'd never watched herself in the mirror like this before, and she couldn't help feeling a bit embarrassed at the hard, pink-brown nubs of her nipples, the swell of her breasts. All that bare flesh.

He unzipped her dress and pulled it over her head, then helped her step out of her panties. She was wearing only her heels now.

She watched him kiss her neck and shoulders, closing his eyes as he slipped his hand between her legs and parted her folds. She watched his finger disappear inside her, and oh, God, yes, that was good. With his other hand, he squeezed her breasts and brought her nipple to an even tighter peak.

It was hard to believe this was her, but it was.

Like a sex goddess. That was how he made her feel, and she could see how she was driving him mad, his desperate mouth pressing all over her, his erection pushing against her from behind.

Nick sat down on the bed, grabbed her ass, and brought her down on his cock.

"Fuck!" she said, and nearly covered her mouth in embarrassment afterward. Sure, she swore around people she was comfortable with, but not like that. Never so loudly.

"Now move," he commanded, and she did.

She continued to watch them in the mirror as she rode him. He was behind her; it was mostly herself that she could see.

She touched her breasts, kneading them, plucking the tips. Then she slipped one hand between her legs and touched her clit.

The woman in the mirror gloried in her own pleasure, in her sexuality.

And that woman was *her*.

She rode him, faster and faster, her finger moving quicker on her clit, and when she finally reached the peak and let go, it was like nothing she'd ever experienced before. She sagged against him afterward, like a rag doll, and he pushed into her a few times and came with her name on his lips.

"Lily."

No one had ever said her name the way he did. Like there were so many subtle flavors in it—in her—that she'd never been aware of before.

He wrapped his arms around her and held her close, her bare back against his muscled chest, as she caught her breath.

She continued to look in the mirror, but now she only paid attention to him, to the light perspiration on his forehead, the slight muss of his hair, the way he touched her as if he was in awe of her and wanted to keep her safe at the same time.

"Thank you," she said, lifting herself up from his lap.

"Darling, you don't need to thank me for sex."

"But that time, it was all for me."

"I enjoyed myself too, don't you worry."

He spun her around so she was facing him and not the mirror. Her legs were wobbly; it felt like there was no ground beneath her feet.

"I'm sure you'll find a way to make it up to me," he said with a wink.

There was an odd feeling in her chest, and she could do nothing but lean over and kiss him. His lips were soft but demanding, leading her exactly where she wanted to go. His arms went around her waist and he held her firmly, kept her from falling over.

It was everything.

～

"I have to tell you something," Lily said later, when they were lying in bed together.

They were eating date squares, and there were several things wrong with this situation.

First of all, they were eating in bed. They would get crumbs in the sheets, surely. She had told Nick of her concerns, but he'd just said to add "eating in bed" to her list of new experiences.

Second of all, he'd cut the date squares—which had been more like rectangles to start with—into triangles to mess with her.

Thirdly, it was close to dinnertime. She should not be eating dessert right before dinner, but that's what was happening.

"What is it?" Nick asked, licking a crumb from the side of his mouth.

"If we're doing this—me and you, I mean—I don't want either of us to see other people." The pain of imagining him giving another woman what he'd just given her... It was too much for her to bear. She knew some people would be fine with it, but she wasn't one of them.

"Of course."

"Of course?"

"I accept your terms," he said. "That's what I'd assumed you'd want."

"And I'd expected you to...I don't know, but you seem to have this sophisticated life of debauchery, for want of a better term, that involves lots of sex."

"My family was calling me 'Mr. Fancypants' when I was baking."

"Mm. I like that."

"I like 'sophisticated life of debauchery.' Good term. And you're the only woman I want right now. I'm more than happy to only have sex with you, don't worry."

He frowned, as though he didn't know what to make of this. But he'd agreed to it, and he'd actually come to Ingleford for Thanksgiving with her family. Plus, he'd baked for her.

She felt a touch naïve, but she trusted him, even though she didn't know quite where this would go, even though she hadn't known him all that long. Although she still had some lingering doubts about whether they really belonged together—they seemed so different—when his arms were around her, she could push those aside.

She laughed.

"What is it?" he asked.

"I'm *terrible* at one-night stands. My first attempt turned into a relationship."

And she couldn't be happier.

Nick didn't usually have trouble sleeping, but that night, he found himself lying awake, listening to Lily's breathing.

Exclusive. She seemed to think that meant they were in a relationship. She'd been pleased, and he hadn't had the heart to question it. He liked making her happy.

But in his brain, "exclusive" and "relationship" weren't equivalent, and he couldn't help feeling a bit uncomfortable with it all. Sleeping with only one woman was one thing, but a relationship… He'd wanted to meet her family to show he could do more than a one-night stand, yes, and he wanted to spend more time with her, but now he felt a little in over his head.

"So, what have you been up to?" Trystan O'Brien punched Nick lightly on the shoulder.

It was an unseasonably warm October day, and they were sitting on the patio of a downtown watering hole, full of men and women in work clothes. It would likely be the last patio day of the year, and so when Trystan had texted him at five, asking if he wanted to grab a drink, Nick had agreed, rather than staying at the office late like usual.

He considered his answer. He wouldn't lie to Trystan, but his friend would not be impressed with the truth.

"I met someone."

"You...met...someone," Trystan sputtered. "I don't understand."

"I was at Lychee, the Saturday before last."

"I remember. You said you couldn't meet up with me because you were getting laid."

That hadn't been quite how Nick had put it, but yes.

"I overheard a woman say, 'Why is it so difficult to have a one-night stand?' and offered to help with her problem."

"Sounds good so far."

"Then last weekend, my parents arranged dates for me and my siblings for Thanksgiving dinner."

Trystan started laughing. "Desperate to get you guys all married off, are they?"

"Lily—that's her name—was supposed to be Greg's date, but we snuck off together, and my grandma caught us kissing."

Trystan was still laughing.

"Then I went to her family's Thanksgiving. I even made dessert."

"Back up. I missed a few steps. Why did you go to her family's Thanksgiving?"

"To prove I want more than a one-night stand."

Trystan covered his face with his hands and shook his head. "Goddammit. You have a girlfriend now."

Part of Nick wanted to protest at the term, but he didn't.

"Am I going to lose yet another friend to a woman?" Trystan asked.

"You're not losing me as a friend."

"You know what I mean."

Yeah, Nick did.

"Now Saturday will be date night, and on Sunday, you'll go out for brunch." Trystan said the last word quietly, as if it was too horrifying to say in a louder voice.

"What's wrong with brunch?"

"It's the first step on the road to hell."

"Eggs benedict, gourmet waffles, and mimosas are that bad?"

"It starts with brunch," Trystan said morosely. "Next thing you know, she's got a drawer in your dresser and calling you Smoochie Bear."

That reminded Nick of when he'd come across his parents in the kitchen. *Smoochie-boo-kins.* He pushed the unfortunate memory aside.

"And then," Trystan continued, "you're buying her a ring and moving to the suburbs, or back to Mosquito Bay."

Now *that* made Nick shudder.

He'd left Mosquito Bay at eighteen and vowed never to move back. He couldn't imagine Lily wanting to move to Mosquito Bay or Ingleford anyway. She seemed like she belonged in Toronto.

Still, Trystan had made his point.

The thought of a relationship had always made Nick itch. It seemed suffocating, like living in Mosquito Bay, and it felt like the first step to becoming his parents. He loved his parents, despite their fondness for meddling, but he'd known since high school that he wanted a life that was very different from theirs. His parents' lives had always seemed so small and confined, and he had big dreams.

And he'd been living a good life in the city up to now. He didn't want anything that would stop him from being true to himself and reaching his full potential.

He swallowed his unease with a sip of wine.

Despite his fears, Nick was looking forward to his date with Lily on Saturday night. He'd made reservations at Boreal, a Canadian bistro downtown, mainly because of the dessert menu. In fact, he was unreasonably excited about it. Like, the sort of excitement he'd usually feel about a big party—that was how he felt about Lily seeing the dessert list.

Actually, he was excited just to see her.

One of his friends had texted him this afternoon about going to a club tonight, and he'd barely felt any regret about not being able to go.

When he arrived at the restaurant five minutes early, Lily was already there. She sat at a table, her chin resting on her hand, looking out the window. He stood there for a moment, overwhelmed by her loveliness. She was wearing a black shirt that draped in an interesting way, and her hair was wavy tonight, and she was his. There was no chase, no flirting—well, there would be flirting, but it was different now.

Lily turned away from the window, and her face lit up when she saw him. No woman had looked at him quite like that before.

"Hey, Nick." Her eyes traveled down his body, then back to his face. "You look good."

"Oh, this old thing?" he said, tugging the sleeves of his blue suit.

She laughed, and he took a seat across from her.

She was so composed and put together, and he very much liked her look. But he also liked it when she was disheveled and sex-crazed as he fucked her in front of the mirror.

That was the thing about knowing someone for more than a night: you got to see many different sides of them.

He liked all sides of Lily Tseng.

They had a lovely meal together, with a small charcuterie board to start. She ordered the pappardelle with braised lamb, and he ordered the venison with wild mushrooms. They had a reasonably quiet table, tucked into a corner by the window. The lighting was a little dim, and a candle flickered between them.

It was romantic.

He'd done a good job picking this place, even though romance wasn't something he knew much about.

Lily ate her pappardelle delicately. She twirled each wide noodle with care, and she never dared to speak when she had food in her mouth.

He had other things he wanted to do with that mouth.

When the server cleared their plates and asked if they wanted to see the dessert menu, Lily said "no" at the same time as he said "yes."

"Let's take a look." He squeezed her hand.

The server came back a moment later and set a small menu in front of each of them.

"This dessert cocktail looks good," Lily said. "Coffee liqueur and maple syrup and other delicious things. Maybe I'll get one of those."

Maybe she wouldn't see it. Maybe...

"Oh!" She started laughing. "They have a deconstructed Nanaimo bar. I can't believe it! Wait a second... You knew this was on the menu, didn't you? That's why you brought me here."

Busted.

"I did."

He'd never had inside jokes with a woman before, things that were only funny between the two of them. The familiarity made him a little uncomfortable, but her expression was one of delight. Lily's smiles were often a bit restrained, but not now. Not for him.

He couldn't help smiling back at her.

They ordered the deconstructed Nanaimo bar, of course, and Lily ordered the coffee and maple cocktail. She hesitated, probably because of the cost, but he assured her it was no problem.

The dessert came on a long rectangular plate. There was a piece of brown crust in a circular shape, next to a dollop of creamy filling, which was next to a small piece of chocolate. Each component was then repeated, the entire thing covered in chocolate shavings.

"This is wrong," Lily muttered, in a way that suggested she was actually quite pleased. She lifted a forkful of the creamy filling to his lips and he ate it, wishing they were sitting next to each other and he could just lean over and kiss her. Then he broke off a piece of the crust with his fork and fed it to her.

"Mm," she said. "But you know what would be better?"

She scooped up tiny amounts of crust, filling, and chocolate onto her fork.

"You're constructing the deconstructed dessert," he said. "That's against the rules."

"Is it?" She raised an eyebrow. "I had no idea."

"I thought you were a rule follower."

"Most of the time, but then I met you."

They had what he could only describe as "a moment." Everything melted away, even the constructed deconstructed Nanaimo bar on Lily's fork. It was just her and him, and nothing else mattered.

And then, all of a sudden, the world existed again, but it seemed brighter and more brilliant than before.

Lily smiled at him, a little shyly, before sliding her fork into her mouth.

Oh, God. He wanted to kiss her and take off that gauzy black shirt, and he didn't want to let her out of his bedroom until brunch.

It was a little scary, but there was no denying it. He wanted her, and he was terrifyingly glad that she was in his life for more than a night or two.

He helped himself to some of the custardy filling and smiled back at Lily.

This was one date he would never forget.

The next morning, they lay naked in bed, tangled up in the sheets after a round of sex, and Nick wasn't itching to get rid of Lily so he could go about his day and get some work done. No, he was content to be here with her, content to have her lazily trail her fingers over his skin.

Abruptly, she dropped her hand and got up—and he wasn't complaining because he had a nice view of her naked ass as she went to his dresser, picked up a picture that was hiding behind a bottle of cologne, and came back to bed.

"When was this taken?" she asked, pointing at teenage Nick in the family photo.

"I think I was sixteen. It was before Greg went off to university."

She looked between him and the picture. "You look shy! Nick, were you shy?"

"I told you I wasn't cool, didn't I? I was shy, and I hated being different. I felt inferior, got told that girls never went for guys like me and we were supposed to be awkward nerds. Neither of my brothers had that experience—Greg was more or less immune to what everyone else said, and everyone always liked Zach, plus he can pass for being white. But I hated being Asian. Hated my last name. Refused to learn any Cantonese from my grandparents."

He was ashamed he'd felt that way, but he understood how it had happened.

"At last, I got to go to Toronto for school, and I began feeling more comfortable with who I was. I liked being just one more person in a big, diverse city, where nobody knew my family. I started going to the gym, figured out how to project a confidence I didn't feel, and it worked. Three years ago..." He shook his head.

"What?" she asked, setting the picture on the night table.

"I slept with a woman who'd gone to high school with me, who wouldn't have taken a second look at me back then. I'm embarrassed of how proud I was of that, but I did love my new life. Loved that it was nothing like what I would have had back in Mosquito Bay, loved that it was so different from my parents' lives. I never wanted their quiet existence in a gossipy small town, being with the same person for decades..."

Lily worried her bottom lip between her teeth.

Shit. She probably wanted to get married one day and grow old with someone, even if she had no thoughts about the two of them getting married anytime soon.

He glanced at his alarm clock—it was ten thirty. He wanted to do something that would make her smile.

"Let's have brunch," he said in an upbeat voice. His conversation with Trystan popped into his mind, but he pushed it aside.

"How do you feel about pancakes? There's a place nearby that's supposed to have the best pancakes with blueberry compote, but I've never been."

"I will gladly eat pancakes with you, Nick, but they better not be deconstructed."

"Don't you worry." He kissed her lips. "I'm sure they will be perfectly constructed."

IT HAD BEEN three weeks since Thanksgiving, and it had been a very good three weeks for Lily. She'd spent at least one night with Nick every weekend, and several weekday nights with him, too. He texted her at lunch every day. He was surprisingly sweet and thoughtful for a guy who was all about one-night stands.

But somehow, she was special, and he was doing this with *her*.

Still, she had the occasional doubts. He might seem content with what they had for now, but she wasn't convinced he wanted anything long-term, especially after what he'd said when she'd found the old photograph of his family.

Plus, he'd made himself into a man who was smooth and sexy and determined, and she couldn't help feeling a little insecure. If her ex thought she was boring, surely a guy like Nick would eventually come to that conclusion, too. He was a guy who liked variety.

And yet.

The other night, they'd been at a swanky restaurant together. The group of women at the next table had been checking him out, even though he was clearly on a date, and although they were attractive, he hadn't given them a second glance.

No, when he was with Lily, she felt like the only woman who mattered.

Sometimes she wondered if she should be rushing into this when she'd planned to be single for a while, but she pushed those thoughts aside because this was so much fun.

He took her to elegant restaurants and upscale bars. She had to buy new clothes so she didn't appear out of place standing next to Nick, who always looked so fine—she didn't want it to seem like he was way out of her league.

He also brought her coffee in bed and told her about his childhood. She got to know the guy behind the flashy image that everyone knew; he didn't seem to hold anything back from her. She even talked to his mother and grandmother on the phone.

It was good. It was great.

It was just too soon to know if it could go anywhere.

But for the first time in a long time, she was genuinely having fun. She'd never been a person who had lots of fun, but after her father's death, she'd retreated into her routine. Had made herself lists with items like "eat breakfast" and "wash dishes" because crossing out those small things at least gave her something.

Now, however, she could be the responsible career woman during the day and go out with Nick at night.

"Let's go dancing," he said on a Friday night, when they were sitting in his living room.

It was easy to imagine that Nick enjoyed dancing and would be quite good at it, but Lily... Well, this might be a problem.

"I don't dance."

"Surely you dance."

"Not much, and being on a dance floor, surrounded by people who don't look like complete idiots, is intimidating."

"You're good in bed, so you must be good at dancing. It's a fact."

She laughed. "I don't think that's how it works."

He looked at her for a moment. "Okay, no dancing tonight,

but tomorrow, one dance—here, at my place—before I leave for the night."

"Yes," she whispered.

Tomorrow, he was going to a charity gala, and she wasn't going with him. He'd told her that he'd love to bring her and surely she'd look lovely all dressed up, but the tickets had sold out months ago, so he had to go alone.

She still hadn't worked out whether she was disappointed or relieved; he seemed disappointed, though.

Just then, his phone rang.

"Sorry, it's my mother," he said before answering. "Hi, Mom... Yes, of course... You already texted me, and I replied, didn't I?... Okay... She is... Sure." He handed the phone to Lily. "She wants to talk to you."

She put the phone to her ear. "Hi, Rosemary, how are you?"

"Lily, I wanted to tell you that I got Shelly Sanderson's coconut lemon square recipe."

"Um, okay?"

"Not that you know who she is, but she makes the best coconut lemon squares and always brings them to the Canada Day picnic, and somehow she left her recipe book in the library. I returned it to her, of course, after I copied that recipe. I don't want anyone to know I have it, but I sent it to Nick, okay?"

Lily held back her laughter. This seemed very...small town. She didn't know what else to call it.

"Nick is supposed to make them for you," Rosemary continued. "If he doesn't, call me and I will have words with him, okay?"

"Okay."

Lily wasn't sure whether Rosemary heard that, however, because there seemed to be a tussle on the other end of the phone. A minute later, a different voice was speaking to her.

"Lily, it's Ah Ma. Nick will make you coconut lemon squares this weekend."

Someone was yelling in the background, presumably Rosemary. "I already told her that!"

"Yes, I heard," Lily said, stifling a laugh.

"Has he proposed yet?"

Ah Ma spoke loudly, and Nick must have heard. He grabbed the phone back from Lily. "We've only been together for a month... Yes, you told me... Stop interfering with my love life... Go bother Greg instead!"

This went on for a while, and Lily couldn't help but smile, though the mention of a proposal had, admittedly, made her a touch uncomfortable.

When Nick got off the phone, shaking his head, he said, "I'll make you coconut lemon squares on Sunday, don't you worry."

He didn't say anything about the rest of the conversation, which was probably for the best.

～

The next evening, they danced in Nick's living room. He'd asked Lily to wear her red dress, and so she had. He was wearing a tux, and he looked marvelous, of course. Incredibly dashing. She couldn't take her eyes off him, but all they had was this one dance, and then he would leave.

It reminded her of that scene in *Beauty and the Beast*, except she wasn't wearing yellow and he was no beast. But it was the closest she'd ever come, and it was just the two of them, no one watching her not-so-smoothly move across the floor.

She was falling for him. Oh, God, was she ever falling for him. And that scared her.

At the end of the dance, he pressed a kiss to her lips, and she nearly melted against him and begged him to take her to bed. But he had to go to the charity gala, and she was meeting Tara and Sam, whom she hadn't seen since the night she'd met Nick.

He walked her over to Lychee, where her friends were having

a few cocktails before going out for dinner. Everyone's heads turned to watch them—well, she was positive they were all looking at Nick—as he led her to her friends' table in the lounge area. He kissed her hand, and it was all so ridiculous and over the top, but she loved it.

"Damn," Sam said softly after Nick had left.

Lily jerked her gaze away from the door. "Yeah, I know."

"I thought he was good-looking when I first met him, but *damn*." Sam fanned herself with her hand. "I can't believe you turned your hot one-night stand into something more."

"I can't believe it, either," Lily said, and once she had a cocktail in hand—the same mango and black tea-infused vodka one that she'd had before—she added, "How can this last?"

"Stop it," Tara said. "What's with this lack of self-confidence? You're always poised."

"On the outside, maybe, but I can't help my doubts. He's just too much. He's in a class of his own." Seeing him all dressed up tonight had emphasized that.

"He treats you well, doesn't he?"

"I wouldn't be with him if he didn't. When we're together, everything is perfect, but I can't help worrying. The beautiful playboy who doesn't do relationships is suddenly mine? Like I've tamed him. I shouldn't be thinking about the future yet, but..." She shook her head and had a sip of her drink.

"But what?" Sam pressed.

"His grandma joked about him proposing—or maybe she wasn't joking, I don't know—on the phone yesterday, and it frightened me. Not so much because it was too soon, but because I was disturbed by how much a part of me wanted it, despite the fact that we haven't been together for long. And although our families are a little similar and our mothers are friends, his life is so different from mine. I'm not sure I fit in it."

"Don't overthink this," Tara said. "Have fun and see where it goes."

"I'm not trying to overthink it! But I really like him, and my brain can't help jumping to the future. We're exclusive, but does he even think of me has his girlfriend? I have no idea how serious Nick thinks we are. This isn't what I planned…"

Lily trailed off. She was supposed to be having a fun night out. Time to stop bombarding her friends with her insecurities.

But when she looked at her phone a few hours later, they flooded back.

12

NICK HADN'T EXPECTED to miss Lily quite so much once he was at the gala.

He'd been to a bunch of these events before, and they were always fun. Today, however, he'd spent a full five minutes sulking in the corner with a glass of wine, which wasn't like him.

"Hey, Nick."

He turned. It was a white woman in a purple dress with sequins. Miranda, whom he'd met a couple times before. Last time he'd flirted with her, but she'd told him she had a boyfriend.

There was no denying she was a good-looking woman, but when he saw her now, he didn't feel any lust.

He just wanted Lily, dammit. The worst part was that he'd seen her only a couple hours ago. It wasn't like they'd been apart for weeks.

This was a totally unfamiliar feeling for him.

"Miranda," he said belatedly, giving the woman next to him a smile.

She touched his shoulder, and that was when he knew.

He wasn't accustomed to turning down pretty women, but he wasn't even a little tempted.

"Your boyfriend?" he said when she touched him a second time.

"Not in the picture anymore."

He shoved his hands in his pockets and looked down at his shoes. "But my girlfriend is very much in the picture," he said, surprising himself by saying *girlfriend*.

"Ah." Miranda sounded a little disappointed, but they had a pleasant enough conversation for the next ten minutes.

For dinner, Nick was sitting next to Trystan. The appetizer was something a little fussy but delicious. Nick didn't care, though, because Lily wasn't here to share it with him.

"How's your girlfriend?" Trystan asked with a smirk.

"She's well." Nick paused. "We've had brunch now. Twice."

"I told you, man. Brunch is how it starts. Next thing you know, you're moving to your hometown and chauffeuring a pack of kids in a mini-SUV."

"You have a rather fatalistic view of things," Nick murmured, but this time, he wasn't disturbed by Trystan's dire predictions.

Not because they no longer sounded terrible to him. There was still no way he was going to move to a town like Mosquito Bay or Ingleford. But he'd focused on making his life the exact opposite of his parents', on making people see him as the opposite of how the other kids had seen him in high school.

There were reasons he'd done that. He'd found their small town suffocating, and he'd thought being in a relationship would feel that way, too. He hadn't wanted to be tied to anyone.

Yet belonging to Lily, even though she was more of a "lists and rules" person than he was—that didn't feel suffocating or make his world smaller. Rather, it felt like she'd opened up a new world for him.

One with deconstructed Nanaimo bars and lazy mornings and brunch.

One with an awful lot of sex, it was true.

One with the adventure of learning one person intimately.

She got to learn every part of him, too, more than what he showed most of the world.

His parents had been happily married for over thirty-five years, and now he wondered if he might like a life like that after all, but in Toronto.

Even at this fancy event, there was a wonderful ache in his heart. He missed her, and he wouldn't trade it for anything.

He loved her.

He hadn't been looking for this, and yet he'd found it anyway.

Nick left earlier than he normally would, returning to his place around midnight. The lights in his bedroom were on, and Lily was in bed, wearing pajama pants and a low-cut tank top. He'd given her a key so she could come back here after her night out with her friends.

He didn't say anything, just smiled at her.

When he climbed onto the bed and crawled toward her, she returned his smile hesitantly, and he couldn't help wondering why it wasn't her big grin.

"I was..." She shook her head. "You sure look good in that tux."

Then she was kissing him, tearing off his jacket and throwing it on the floor, followed by his tie and shirt. He should hang them up, he really should, but in the end, he left them on the floor.

He pulled Lily's tank top over her head; she wasn't wearing anything underneath. When her bare chest met his, it felt so good, so right.

She unbuttoned his pants, slipped her hand into his boxer briefs, and started pumping him up and down. He needed to touch her, too. He slid his hand under her clothes and ran his fingers over her wetness, loving her response to him.

Normally after an event like tonight's, he'd be having sex, but with a woman he didn't know well, not like his Lily.

His. Yes.

He peeled off the rest of their clothes, then cupped her ass and pressed her against him.

"I really missed you tonight," he said, looking deep into her eyes. He had to make her understand.

"I missed you, too."

She rolled them over so he was on his back, and she took his cock in her mouth. He hissed out a breath. She bobbed up and down, occasionally looking up at him from beneath her pretty eyelashes.

He'd had many women in this bed over the years. He'd enjoyed all of them, but now, he only wanted Lily, could think of no one but her.

She lay down on the bed. "I need you."

Nick rolled on a condom and pushed into her, not wanting to delay any longer.

He moved inside her and kissed her everywhere he could reach. She felt amazing, and he was incredibly lucky that he got to be with her all the time. How had he gotten so lucky?

He licked his finger and circled it over her clit, in the way she liked best. He knew exactly what she liked now, and he loved that. Loved, too, that they could have many different kinds of sex. They'd had that not-so-one-night stand, and he'd fucked her in front of the mirror and watched her discover a side to her sexuality that she hadn't known existed.

Now, she was giving him a kind of sex he'd never experienced before.

Sex with someone he cared for so very much.

She trembled beneath him, close to her orgasm. She never screamed when she came, but her face would open up...just like that.

He came with her, holding her tightly against him.

Yes, this was what he wanted, more than anything.

∼

Something was wrong when Lily woke up the next morning. She tried to sit up, but her body wouldn't obey, and her head felt like shit.

She hadn't drunk that much last night, had she? No, she'd had two cocktails fairly early in the evening, and by the time Nick returned, looking so damn handsome in his tux, she couldn't feel them anymore. They'd had sex before going to sleep. She'd meant to talk to him last night, but she hadn't been able to help herself from jumping him.

Nick wasn't in bed now, but just the thought of sex was unappealing. Her body ached and her head felt like it was stuffed with cotton and her throat was sore. She was definitely sick. Physically sick.

But her heart also ached. She remembered looking at the hashtags for the gala on social media. She'd found lots of pictures of well-dressed people. Nick was in a few of them, looking like he was exactly where he belonged.

She knew she didn't belong in that life.

There was a picture of him standing next to a gorgeous woman in a deep purple dress. Lily had Googled her and discovered she was a high-powered businesswoman.

For now, Lily was a novelty for him, but that would end eventually, and her chest caved in at the thought. This was even worse than being sick.

She collapsed back against the pillow.

A little while later, Nick came in. He was carrying a tray with coffee and—were those the coconut lemon squares that his mother had told her about?

Neither interested her right now. Usually she loved her morning cup of coffee, but not today. Coconut lemon squares weren't normal breakfast food, but of course she would have eaten them if she had any appetite whatsoever.

"What's wrong, Lily?" he asked, setting the tray on the night table.

"I'm not feeling well," she mumbled.

"Oh, no." He put his hand to her forehead. "You have a slight fever."

"I'm not in the mood for coffee and coconut lemon squares, sorry."

"What do you want? I could make wonton soup. I have some wontons in the freezer. Tea? Hot water bottle? Do you need any painkillers?" He looked at her earnestly.

"Wonton soup would be great."

She dozed for a while, until Nick tiptoed into her room with the tray again. This time, it held a large bowl of soup and a glass of orange juice.

He sat on the edge of the bed. "Do you need me to feed you, or can you do it yourself?"

"I'm not *that* sick. I can do it."

He handed her the orange juice. "Vitamin C. You know, I was in China for a business trip once, and they'd heard that North Americans like orange juice for breakfast, so they served Tang. And since it was China, they'd heated it up. Warm Tang."

She laughed at that. Not as much as she usually would, but still.

He did make her laugh, and he was being so sweet right now, looking after her and keeping her company when surely he had better things to do. He had a big job, and he went on business trips to the other side of the world.

Then she berated herself for thinking this was a big deal. All he'd done was bring her a small meal in bed when she wasn't feeling well. It was a natural thing to do when you cared for someone, but perhaps Douglas had taught her to have low expectations when it came to men.

She was still afraid, but maybe she should just talk to Nick.

"I have something to tell you. I..."

She stopped when she heard someone pounding on the door.

13

WITH A SIGH, Nick got up from the bed and headed to the door.

He knew exactly who it was.

This happened once or twice a year. His family, bored in Mosquito Bay, would spontaneously decide to drive to Toronto and show up for a visit.

Last time, a woman had just been leaving his penthouse, and that had been…interesting.

This time, there was a sick woman in his bed, and he wanted to focus on her, not his family.

He opened the door.

Mom, Dad, Ah Ma, and Ah Yeh shouted, "Surprise!"

He pinched the bridge of his nose. "You know it's not my birthday."

"Of course we know. Don't be silly," Mom said. "We're taking you out for dim sum! Greg will meet us at the restaurant."

"This isn't the best time. Lily—"

"Lily can come with us!" Ah Ma said gleefully. "We will ask her lots of questions. Make sure you have been treating her well."

"Lily is sick," he said. "She's in my bedroom."

"Oh, no," Mom said. "What does she have? Is it the flu?"

"You must not give her anything cold," Ah Ma said. "No ice water! Warm water is best."

"I just made her soup."

"I want to see her," Mom said. "Make sure she's doing okay."

"Me, too," Ah Ma said.

Dad shook his head. "I don't want you to catch anything, Ma. You should stay away from sick people."

"Aiyah. How do you think I got so old? I am invincible!"

"You are eighty-seven. You are not invincible."

"I am eighty-eight!"

"No," Dad said, "you're eighty-seven."

"Eighty-eight. Lucky age!"

"I thought you said you had one foot in the grave?"

This was giving Nick a headache. "Look, could you please quiet down?"

Ah Ma marched into his place, not even bothering to take off her shoes, and went straight to his bedroom. Having been here several times before, she knew exactly where to go.

"Lily!" she said when she reached the bedroom door, Nick right behind her. "You are sick, I hear? Good thing Ah Ma is here to take care of you."

"I'm fully capable of doing it myself," Nick said.

"Wah, is that cold orange juice I see? Why you always serve juice cold?"

"Because it tastes weird when it's warm."

"I will make jook."

"No," Ah Yeh said. "I make better jook than you."

"I can cook chicken noodle soup," Mom suggested.

Lily looked exhausted, and she'd been about to tell Nick something important when his family barged in.

Goddammit.

"No, no, it's okay," Lily said. "You said you were going to have dim sum? Go ahead. I'll be fine here for a couple hours."

"We will bring him back to you soon!" Ah Ma promised. "Then I will take care of you."

"No," Dad said. "You're old. People should be looking after you, not the other way around."

"Fine." She stuck her nose in the air. "Carry me!"

"I'm not carrying you!"

"Please," Nick said, "let's allow Lily to finish her food in peace and maybe get some more sleep. I'll go out for dim sum, but I won't stay long, okay?"

"Are these coconut lemon squares?" Mom was already in the kitchen. "You made them this morning? They look fresh."

"I did."

"Coconut lemon squares are not good for sick people," Ah Ma said. "Too much sugar."

"Unless *you* make them," Ah Yeh said. "You used salt instead of sugar."

"Too much salt is bad, too."

"Obviously! They were inedible."

Once Nick had finally herded his family out the door, he returned to Lily. "Are you sure you're okay if I go out for an hour or two?"

"Yes, don't worry. I'll be fine."

"Text me if you need anything. You can tell me whatever you need to tell me when I get back. I'm sorry about this."

Lily alternately fretted and slept as she waited for Nick to return from dim sum with his family. They appeared to have the uncanny ability of arriving just at the wrong time.

She was about to text Tara when she heard the door open.

Her heart kicked up a notch, like when he'd returned from the charity gala last night. Except now she was sick and filled with more self-doubt.

"Hey," he said as he walked into the room. "How are you doing?"

Often she felt a spark of lust when she saw him, but not today. Her body was in no mood for anything but staying in bed and shuffling to the kitchen and bathroom.

But she smiled because she couldn't help it when she saw him. He'd made her feel safe from the very first night he'd taken her home.

The thought of losing him, the thought that she might not be enough for him...

He sat down on the bed and clasped her hands in his.

"I don't want to give you my germs," she said.

"I don't care."

He might care if his body felt the way hers did right now, but she didn't say that.

"I saw lots of pictures of you at the gala," she began. "You looked like you were on the red carpet at the Oscars. So polished, probably paying a thousand bucks or more for your ticket. And I'm an ordinary woman. I'm not rich; I'm not even interesting. I don't belong in your world. When it was just for a night, I could push that aside, pretend it was no big deal, but now..." Tears pooled in her eyes, but she didn't let them fall.

"Lily," he murmured, wrapping his arms around her. "Oh, Lily."

"When we're together, it's wonderful, and you've always been good to me. And yet..."

"I'd never even had a girlfriend until I met you."

So he did think of them that way. Still...

"Maybe," she said, "you wouldn't have one now if you weren't jealous that I'd been set up with your brother." The words were bitter in her mouth, but they came out anyway.

"I admit I was jealous, but even if the circumstances had been different, I can't stay away from you. After our first night, I kept thinking about you. Last night at the gala, more than anything, I wished you were there with me."

He stretched out on the bed next to her and held her more tightly.

"I just worry," she said quietly, "that someday you'll get bored of me."

"I will never get bored of you."

"My ex broke up with me because he found me boring, which is why I made a list of new things to try—including a one-night stand. I told you that, didn't I?"

"Your ex is an ass," Nick said, with quite a lot of passion. "Truly, I could never find you boring. I think you were just stuck in a bit of a rut."

She nodded. "It was tough after my dad passed away."

"You did what you had to do to get through it, and for you, that meant following a tight routine and never stepping outside your comfort zone. There's nothing wrong with that."

"Plus, I've always been the well-behaved daughter. The one who didn't get in trouble. And now..." She trailed off as she realized something. "With you, I feel like myself. I do. I just can't help worrying that your life has gotten less snazzy and fast-paced with me in it."

He sat up and took her hands in his. He looked into her eyes like she was the only thing that mattered. "I don't want my life to be exactly as it was before. It's not the same with you in it—and that's a good thing. I like what I have with you."

She managed an inelegant sniffle. "You're serious about us? You're not afraid of long-term relationships?"

"I admit I was a bit uncomfortable with the idea a few weeks ago, but not now." Nick cupped her face in his hands and swept his thumbs over her cheeks. "I love you, Lily. I always knew I didn't want the life my parents had in Mosquito Bay, and I did my best to make sure my life was nothing like theirs. But now, what I want more than anything is to be with you, and please never call yourself boring because it's not true, not at all. I want to learn every little thing about you. I'm fascinated by the strange way you eat Nanaimo bars—"

"I eat them like a normal person! None of your one-layer-at-a-time crap."

"—and by the way you eat fried chicken so daintily."

"I do not!"

He smiled. "You totally do, and it's cute. I'm fascinated by the noises you make when I'm inside you—and the way you're blushing now. I love how you're so careful and aware of everything around you but completely uninhibited in my arms. There's a freckle on the back of your earlobe, did you know that? I love that, too. And you've already met my family and haven't run away screaming. I want to have lots of new experiences with you, and although I'm never going to be the man who has a quiet life in a small town—"

"Don't worry, I don't want that either."

"I know." He paused. "I don't need the whirlwind that I've been living for the past decade, and to be honest, when I look back on it, it seems like a rather shallow life. I want exactly what we have together. Please don't feel like you're not good enough just because of my money and 'snazzy' life. That means nothing compared to what I feel for you, Lily, and it certainly doesn't mean we don't belong together. God, no. I've been lucky in life, and if I lost all that but had you, I would still count myself lucky."

He slid his hands to her shoulders and looked into her eyes. She couldn't doubt the sincerity in his words, in his touch.

"To be honest," he said, "sometimes I think *I'm* not good enough for you, especially with my lack of experience in this area. Try not to let those feelings overwhelm you. I'll reassure you whenever you need it, and we don't have to go to galas if they make you uncomfortable."

Lily nodded. She was doing a strange combination of hiccupping and sobbing, and he didn't tell her to stop, just handed her a tissue.

She wasn't at her best. She tried to look put together most of the time, but now she was sick and wearing pajamas, and he'd declared his love for her all the same. Much of the past few weeks had been full of exciting new experiences—well, not all of them were new, but they felt new because she was doing them with Nick Wong.

But he didn't just want her in the busy moments. He wanted her in the quiet moments, too. He wanted all of her.

"Although my past doesn't show my ability to commit," he said, "I am definitely committed. Here, I got you something as proof."

He picked up a container she hadn't noticed before. It was emblazoned with the logo of the dumpling place they'd gone to that first night.

She laughed.

"I believed in love before," he said, "but I never thought it would be part of my life, and now... Well, I wasn't even tempted to eat these on the walk home, that's how much I care for you."

"You weren't tempted? What are you, a monster?"

He chuckled. "Okay, maybe I was a little tempted."

Lily wasn't sure she'd ever loved any gift as much as she loved these soup dumplings. Soup dumplings were pretty amazing on their own, but these were extra amazing because they'd come from Nick and they were just for her.

"I'm not sharing." She placed a protective hand over the dumplings.

"You don't need to."

She opened the container and took the pair of chopsticks he handed her. God, these smelled good. She didn't have a huge appetite today, but her stomach rumbled, and as she looked from Nick to the soup dumplings and back to Nick, her insides turned to...well, soup.

"I love you, too," she whispered. "I was just scared that you didn't feel the same way and that I was foolish for giving my heart to a guy who was supposed to be a one-night stand. I'm sorry for being insecure—"

"You don't need to apologize for anything. I'm glad you told me, and I will make sure you never forget how much I care."

"I can't believe I'm sick for such a romantic moment."

"The kisses and sex can wait until another day, don't worry."

"You know what? Lemon is good for sick people, isn't it? I think I might fancy a coconut lemon square, Mr. Fancypants."

He laughed before getting up. He returned a minute later with a coconut lemon square—

Wait. It was actually two coconut lemon triangles. He'd cut the square in half.

Silly Nick.

It was a side of him she hadn't seen right away, but she quite liked it. The side of him that had wanted to take her to Boreal specifically for its deconstructed Nanaimo bars. She chuckled at the memory.

He sat down on the bed and positioned her so she was sitting between his legs. He wrapped his arms around her as she devoured her food, and she was so full of love that she even let him have one of her dumplings.

The next day, she was completely better. Love and soup dumplings and coconut lemon triangles must have worked their magic.

While her boyfriend was in the shower, she wrote "fall in love with Nick Wong" on her list, then immediately crossed it out because it had already happened.

～

The following Saturday, Nick and Lily spent a quiet hour wandering the greenhouses at Allan Gardens. Lily suspected this was the sort of thing Nick never would have done in the past, but here they were.

Later, they went to Lychee together, and this time, they sat in the restaurant instead of the lounge. This time, the man sitting across from Lily wasn't someone she'd just met, but someone she knew well, someone she was looking forward to knowing even better, someone she was looking forward to building a life with.

This time, Operation Get Laid Tonight was a sure thing.

And this time, Nick didn't profess his talent for one-night stands.

Instead he said, "Being with you, Lily Tseng, is my specialty," and she believed him with all her heart.

After all, he'd brought her soup dumplings, and that was a pretty big sign of love.

IT WAS DECEMBER 23, and Nick was back in Mosquito Bay with Lily. He wouldn't normally have come back this early—usually he'd arrive on Christmas Eve and return to Toronto on Christmas Day—but this time, the two of them were spending a few days here. For whatever reason, being in his hometown didn't make him quite as uneasy as it had in the past.

Not that he would ever move back here, of course.

Instead, Lily was planning to move into his place in Toronto sometime in the next few months, and he couldn't wait. They already spent so much time together, and he wanted to have her there on a permanent basis.

Last Christmas, he would have laughed at the thought of being in a committed relationship, but now, it felt right. It felt like what he was meant to do.

It had been almost three months since he'd met Lily, and she'd changed his life. Not that he regretted how he'd lived before, but this was better, even if Trystan was disappointed in him for giving up his bachelor lifestyle and going out for brunch regularly.

He turned to Lily, who was snuggled up next to him on the sofa, and smiled.

As always, the sight of her made his heart soar.

"Dinner's almost ready." Dad came into the living room, where Nick, Lily, Zach, Amber, Ah Yeh, and Ah Ma were sitting. There were no blind dates today. Not yet, anyway. Or maybe the blind dates would show up on Christmas Eve—it was tough to say.

Nick's family was thrilled that he and Lily were together, and they were trying to claim credit for the match, even though they'd set Lily up with Greg, not Nick.

Speaking of his older brother...

"Greg still isn't here?" Dad asked.

Nick shook his head, then glanced out the window. "It's really coming down out there."

The storm wasn't supposed to have started yet, but it had been snowing pretty hard for a while now, and his brother was out on the road. Hopefully he was almost here.

Just then, Nick's phone vibrated.

"It's from Greg," he said slowly as he read the text. "He says the 402 is closed and he had to stop at a motel for the night...and he's with Tasha? I don't understand."

"He's driving Tasha back from Toronto for the holidays," Ah Ma explained. "They will be staying at a motel together? Oh, this is great news!"

Nick stared at his grandma as understanding dawned.

More matchmaking games were afoot in his family, and he wondered if his parents and grandparents were secretly capable of controlling the weather.

It wouldn't surprise him.

But for now, his brother was safe, and Nick was with Lily. He was looking forward to eating the Nanaimo bars they'd made earlier. Maybe he'd ask her to lick out the creamy filling and eat all three layers separately. Maybe he'd kiss her afterward.

Well, he'd most certainly do that.

It would indeed be a wonderful holiday.

A SECOND CHANCE ROAD TRIP FOR CHRISTMAS

BOOK 2

MEET GREG & TASHA...

Greg Wong hates when things don't go according to plan, so he defi-nitely doesn't appreciate it when his mother insists he drive Tasha Edwards back to Mosquito Bay for the Christmas holidays. He likes peace and quiet when he's in the car, and that's the opposite of what he'll get with Tasha, his high school sweetheart. The first woman he ever loved.

Not that he has feelings for her now. Of course not. Though while he's trying not to smile at her laughter and terrible singing, he can't help noticing how beautiful she is.

And then his plans veer further off course when a snowstorm forces them to spend the night in an unheated motel room with only one bed...

"I HAVE A SPECIAL REQUEST," Greg's mom said.

Greg Wong sighed and put the nature documentary on mute. He was pretty sure he would not like his mother's request.

"What is it?" he asked, clutching the phone to his ear.

"I want you to drive Tasha Edwards back to Mosquito Bay for the Christmas holidays. You're getting off work early and leaving Monday afternoon, right?"

It took Greg a moment to find his voice. "Yes."

But he hated it when people changed his plans on him. He loved plans. He made meticulous plans whenever he could.

"Wonderful!" Mom said. "She'll meet you at your condo at three, okay?"

"Why am I driving her home for the holidays?"

"I met her mother at the grocery store the other day—they had an amazing sale on prime rib, so we're going to have a roast when you get home on the twenty-third, what do you think? And she mentioned that Tasha's car had broken down and she hadn't gotten around to buying a new one yet. Since it's hard to get to Mosquito Bay without a car and you're already making the drive from Toronto, I figured, why not?"

Greg took off his glasses and pinched the bridge of his nose.

Dear God.

He'd been looking forward to driving back to his hometown alone. His plan was to listen to CBC Radio, enjoy the solitude, and prepare himself for his boisterous family.

Now it was being snatched away from him.

Instead, he'd be spending hours in the car with his ex-girlfriend.

There were no hard feelings between him and Tasha, though. He'd known her since they were children, and she was the first girl he'd ever loved. They'd started dating in high school when they were sixteen and parted on amicable terms when they were in university, after nearly three years of dating.

God, it had been fifteen years since they'd been together. A lifetime ago.

He hadn't thought he'd still be single at thirty-four, but he found the whole dating business difficult and usually spent Saturday nights at home, watching Hockey Night in Canada and working on his model railway, which wasn't a great way to meet women.

So when his parents had set him up with a woman at Thanksgiving, Greg—unlike his siblings—hadn't minded. Lily was nice, but before he'd really gotten to know her, it became apparent that she and his brother Nick had a history, and now they were in a relationship.

And Greg suspected that the main reason his mother was asking him to drive Tasha home was because she wanted to set them up.

"Mom, I'm not getting back together with my ex."

"Who said anything about that?" Mom said, but she wasn't fooling him. "I just want you to drive her back for the holidays, nothing more."

He grunted.

There was no good reason to refuse. If Tasha met him at his

condo, it wouldn't be inconvenient for him at all, and her parents' house was only three blocks from where his own parents lived. *I want to listen to CBC Radio in peace* wasn't the sort of excuse that people understood, and if he said no, his mother would keep bugging him about it. She'd call him every few hours until he agreed. When she got an idea in her head, she wouldn't let go of it.

Best to just accept it.

He was driving home for Christmas with his high school sweetheart.

~

On Monday December 23 at 3:01, Greg was sitting in the lobby of his building, waiting for Tasha. She should have been here sixty-two seconds ago.

Not that he'd hold being a minute late against anyone, but she'd just sent him a text from Davisville Station, which meant it would take her another twenty minutes to get here.

Hmph.

Tasha was usually on time. She wasn't one of those people who was always running late—like his sister—but she wasn't as obsessive about time as he was.

At least, that's what she'd been like before. He supposed he didn't really know her anymore. He'd seen her only a handful of times since their break-up—all at get-togethers with mutual friends—and the last time had been five years ago.

Greg was particularly anxious about the time today. He wanted to get out of the city well before five, not only because of the traffic, but because a snowstorm was supposed to hit later this evening. He wanted to be in Mosquito Bay by then, eating prime rib and listening to his family squabble.

Except Tasha was screwing up his plans, dammit.

Finally, at 3:27, she entered the lobby of his building, a big smile on her face. She pulled off her toque, and her braids tumbled about her face, and oh God, what was wrong with him? His heart was beating quickly—had he developed a heart condition?

No, this fluttering was just what happened when she was around. Apparently his body was still conditioned to respond this way, even though he hadn't seen her in years.

She'd been very pretty as a teenager, and she was very pretty now as a woman. She looked different, though. He couldn't explain exactly how, but she did.

She grinned even wider when she saw him. "It's good to see you, Greg."

His brain suddenly emptied, and he was unable to do anything but grunt.

Tasha didn't seem bothered by his lack of clear speech, however. That wasn't surprising—she'd always been able to interpret his grunts, even when he wasn't sure what they meant. It was one of her superpowers.

"You're late," he said gruffly.

"I'm so sorry. I got tied up at work. I told my boss I was leaving early, but we were trying to finish something up before the holidays and…well, what are we waiting for? Let's go!"

Greg had a feeling this was going to be a very long trip.

He just hoped the traffic and weather co-operated.

Tasha really was sorry about being late. She'd wanted to get out of the office at a good time, excited about seeing her parents for Christmas, but she took her job very seriously. It was the best one she'd had since she'd graduated.

As an aerospace engineer, she was used to being surrounded by men, and at her last workplace, she'd felt like she was always left out and passed over for things, but this job was good. She did aerodynamic modeling at a company that specialized in wind tunnel testing for buildings. It wasn't what she'd initially thought she'd do with her degrees, but she enjoyed it. Though it was a quieter office than she'd prefer—not much chit-chat around the coffeemaker or anything like that—everyone was kind and respected her.

Greg was an engineer, too. As he took her suitcase, she looked at his right hand and saw the iron ring on his pinky, just like hers.

She followed him into the elevator and down to the parking garage.

"Thank you so much for driving me back to Mosquito Bay," she said.

He grunted in acknowledgement.

Well, he really hadn't changed much, had he?

Except he'd filled out a bit since he was a teenager. Even in his winter jacket, she could see the difference.

"I could have taken the train," she continued, "but it's a long ways for my parents to go into London to pick me up, and you're driving to Mosquito Bay anyway, so it's not like you have to go out of your way. Though if it hadn't been for me, you'd have left half an hour ago."

"Yes."

She hurried to match his long strides. "Like I said, I'm sorry."

"It's fine."

He clearly wasn't happy, but apologizing again wasn't going to help.

"Nick lives in Toronto, too, doesn't he?"

"Yeah, he's some kind of hotshot executive."

She laughed. "Nick? Really?" Greg's brother, the one closest in age to them, had been a bit awkward in school.

"Yeah. And he was quite the playboy, up until a few months ago."

She struggled to wrap her mind around that. "What happened a few months ago?"

"He met a woman. Fell in love. You know." Greg stopped in front of a red Camry. "Get in. I'll put your suitcase in the trunk."

"My car is a Camry, too!" she said, then sighed, deflated. "Well, it was. It's gone now. My dad got it for me second-hand after I finished undergrad. Much older than your Camry, but I loved it."

He popped open the trunk and gave her a look.

"Oh, right! I should get inside!" She hurried to the passenger's seat and sat down. "Okay, I'm ready."

He sat down next to her and started the car without a word.

She had a feeling this was going to be a very long trip.

2

GREG WAS in the car with the woman he'd once thought he'd marry, and she was driving him bananas. First she'd been late, and now she was talking. A lot.

Truth be told, he'd liked that about her before. He'd always found it difficult to string together more than a couple sentences and had admired how easy it was for her. He'd liked how she could keep the conversation going without too much effort on his part, and if he'd wanted, he could always kiss her to make her stop talking.

But not now. Because he was driving.

Plus, that wasn't the way things were between them anymore.

It had been over a decade and he was totally over Tasha. Of course he was. But since they hadn't spent any time alone together since breaking up, it was weird to be in his car with her, just the two of them.

His car.

When they'd dated, they hadn't owned cars. They hadn't had careers. Now, they were proper grown-ups.

Yeah, this was just plain weird.

It was a blast from the past, and it felt all wrong.

"...anyway," Tasha was saying, "let's liven things up a little."

Those were some of Greg's least favorite words in the English language, right up there with any phrase involving the word "party."

The absolute worst? Surprise parties.

Greg liked to prepare himself for long periods of forced socialization. He'd had only two days' notice for this driving-Tasha-back-to-Mosquito-Bay business. It wasn't enough, and his careful plans to get to his hometown before the snowstorm hit were crumbling. There was already a snowflake on his windshield, even though the snow wasn't supposed to begin for another hour.

The radio was telling him about the many traffic problems around the city and warning of the impending storm and—

Wait a second. Why had "Deck the Halls" started playing in the middle of the forecast?

"*Fa la la la la,*" Tasha sang, "*la la la la!*"

No. This couldn't be happening. Where was his beloved CBC Radio One?

"Come on, Greg!" she said. "Where's your Christmas spirit?"

He growled in frustration.

"*'Tis the season to be jolly...*"

It was impressive, really. She still knew exactly how to push his buttons.

"Did you pair your phone with my car's Bluetooth?" he asked in horror. "I need to listen to the traffic report."

"No, you don't. The traffic sucks. You don't need a report to tell you that."

"I have to know which route to take."

"I've got Google Maps open on my phone. The 401 is still moving, it's just slow."

"If you hadn't been twenty-seven minutes late, we wouldn't have hit such heavy traffic."

She shrugged. "Don't worry so much."

She was right. He did worry too much at times. But he couldn't help being afraid that he'd have to spend twice as long in the car with her, and by the time he arrived, the last bite of his mother's roast would have been eaten.

That would be terrible.

Of course, it wasn't the worst thing that could happen. The worst thing, God forbid, was that they couldn't make it home. Tasha wasn't thinking about that possibility—she'd always been an optimist—but he was already picturing them dead in a ditch, having slid off the icy road and down a cliff. Not that there were cliffs along any of his planned routes, but still.

His imagination was running away with itself. Most people probably thought Greg had a terrible imagination, but it was really quite active.

He took a few deep breaths, but with the noise in the car, it was impossible to calm himself down. The current song was "Holly Jolly Christmas," which he thought was incredibly stupid.

The next song was no better: "The Twelve Days of Christmas." Who would willingly listen to every verse of this song?

His ex-girlfriend, apparently. She was singing along and seemed to be enjoying herself.

Alas, she didn't have a good voice. It was unfortunate, given how much she enjoyed singing. She was smart and talented, skilled at many things, but this was not one of them, and her voice hadn't improved over time. He couldn't help a fond smile but quickly schooled his features into a frown.

"Can we please go back to CBC?" he asked.

"So you've become a CBC Radio junkie," she said. "Isn't their average listener, like, a sixty-five-year-old white man in a sweater vest?"

"It's informative. I learn lots of things by listening to the radio."

"Mm-hmm."

"What? I do."

Why, the other day he'd heard a fascinating twenty-minute segment about snails on *Quirks and Quarks*.

"I shouldn't be surprised," she said. "Listening to CBC Radio seems like the sort of thing you'd do. You were always a bit of an old man, even when you were sixteen."

He shrugged.

She didn't seem to intend it as an insult—Tasha wasn't a mean-spirited person—and there was lots of truth to it.

Just wait until she found out about his model railway.

"I have refined tastes," he said, lifting his nose in the air for effect.

She snort-laughed, and—against his will—his lips twitched.

They twitched again when she sang about maids a-milking, loud and out of tune. It hurt his eardrums, but it was kind of adorable and—

No! What was wrong with him? He didn't like this, not one bit.

Finally, the horrid song about turtle doves and swans a-swimming was finished, but the next song was even worse.

"All I Want for Christmas Is You."

He couldn't take it anymore.

"Shut that off," he said through clenched teeth.

"What's wrong, Mr. Grinch?"

"I don't like Christmas music."

"I seem to recall something to that effect."

Dammit, this woman drove him mad.

"Please?" she said. "You know I love Christmas music. Things have been so busy at work, and I haven't gotten to listen to it much this year."

"Fine. But not this song. Anything but 'All I Want for Christmas Is You.'"

All Greg wanted for Christmas was a little peace and quiet and some roast beef.

Not Tasha.

She skipped ahead to "Silent Night," which wasn't so awful. He still didn't like it, but it didn't make him grind his teeth.

"I remember now," Tasha said. "Why you hate Christmas music, especially that song."

He grunted.

She touched his shoulder. "I still have the necklace. I don't wear it anymore, but I never got rid of it."

In high school, Greg had worked in the summers—once pollinating corn, and once at the nearby provincial park—but he hadn't worked much during the school year, aside from a little tutoring.

Except for December of his final year of high school.

He'd gotten a seasonal job in Sarnia so he could buy Tasha something nice for Christmas. He'd hated every minute of that retail job. The worst part was that Christmas music was playing all the damn time, and every third song, for whatever reason, had been "All I Want for Christmas Is You."

He hadn't minded the song before that. He really hadn't. But when you were subjected to it every ten minutes during an eight-hour shift...well, it got to you. You started fantasizing about strangling Santa Claus and Rudolph and stuff like that.

But despite the temptation, he hadn't quit that job, and he'd saved up enough money to buy a necklace from The Bay, the one he'd had his eye on. She'd adored it—as he'd known she would—and he'd thought it was all worth it.

To be honest, he missed feeling like he would do anything for a woman because he loved her so much.

They'd been young, but he'd loved her.

It had been quite a while since he'd felt like that about anyone. Tasha, however, wasn't the solution to his lack of love life. They'd already been together, and it hadn't worked out.

Besides, despite some common interests, they were too different.

Case in point: he'd prefer to spend their road trip listening to

CBC like an old fogey, and she'd prefer to play "The Twelve Days of Christmas" and sing off-tune at the top of her lungs.

And sure, he could admit that she looked nice in her sweater and had a lovely smile, but he refused to admit that her enthusiastic singing was even a little bit charming.

No, he would most certainly not do that.

Tasha sighed and reluctantly turned CBC Radio One back on, though she couldn't suppress a small smile as she recalled Greg's reaction to her singing "Deck the Halls."

He hadn't changed at all, and yet at the same time…he had.

As he focused on the road, she snuck a glance at him. There were fine lines at the corner of his eye—those hadn't been there before. Earlier, she'd noticed two lines between his eyebrows. His features were a little more angular, and now that they were in the car and he'd thrown his winter coat in the back seat, she could get a better look at the rest of him. He was definitely more solid than before. His bicep looked rather nice actually, and she wondered how it would feel if she wrapped her hand around it.

Stop it, Tasha!

Sure, she still found the man attractive. They'd dated for a long time; that was hardly surprising. But it was nothing more than that.

"Thank you again for driving me home," she said.

He grunted.

"It's really nice of you. I guess our moms ran into each other at the grocery store and—"

"Yeah, I know." His voice was clipped. "And my mom called me this morning and made a point of saying you're single. She's clearly hoping we'll get back together."

"What? No."

"Trust me. That's what she wants."

"But that's ridiculous," Tasha said. "First of all, I don't believe in second chances at relationships. Getting back together with an ex never turns out well. Second of all, we dated a *long* time ago. Fifteen years."

He grunted again. "Yes, I'm aware of that."

"I'm surprised you're not married, actually. I can imagine you cuddled up by the fireplace with a woman, each of you wearing a sweater vest and drinking a single glass of wine while you listen to CBC. Sensible presents wrapped under the Christmas tree. Maybe a French press or a fancy screwdriver. A model train if you feel really daring."

His gaze was focused on the road. "It might interest you to know that I have an elaborate model railway in my den."

She couldn't tell if he was joking. Greg's sense of humor did occasionally make an appearance. He'd say something ridiculous in such a calm voice that you'd believe it.

"Really, I do," he said. "I'll show you pictures and you can laugh at me."

She chuckled. Now that she thought of it, a model railway wasn't ridiculous at all. It fit him—and his detail-oriented brain—perfectly. She imagined this sweater-vest-wearing lady buying him tiny buildings and trees to go alongside the railway, and Greg being so overcome with love that he gave her a single peck on the cheek.

No. Greg hadn't been that restrained as a lover. He'd been passionate. Thorough.

Tasha's cheeks heated and she pushed those thoughts aside. She was probably misremembering a lot of things. After all, it had been many years.

For five minutes, she listened to someone on the radio talk about the weather, but dammit, she kept thinking of him kissing her, and that wouldn't do. They didn't suit each other, and sure he was handsome, but there were other handsome men, ones who grunted less and actually liked Christmas music. Crispin, for example.

Tasha always looked forward, never back. She tried not to think too much about the past, and Greg was firmly in her past. The only time she'd broken her own rule and given an ex a second chance, it had failed spectacularly. She'd seen it fail many times for her friends, too.

Nope, no matter what his mother thought, nothing was happening between them.

She let him enjoy the rest of the scintillating weather report, then put on "Wonderful Christmastime."

Greg's lips thinned, but he didn't speak.

"Come on, get in the spirit!" she said.

"You know me. 'Spirited' is the last thing anyone would say about me."

She suppressed a laugh.

She couldn't help wanting to needle him. She wouldn't play "All I Want for Christmas Is You," but she'd play all the other songs in her Christmas folder. And to annoy him further, she started singing along.

He mumbled something that sounded suspiciously like, "Damn infernal racket."

It was snowing quite a bit now—more than a snowflake here and there. Perhaps it would take five hours to get home rather than three, but that was okay. Greg might be a Grinch, but she was having a grand old time with her Christmas music, and once she got home, there would be hot chocolate with her parents in the living room, accompanied by the fragrance of the Christmas tree. Though she couldn't imagine living in Mosquito Bay—and not just because there were no jobs for aerospace engineers—she enjoyed going back to see her family. It was nice to have a small town to visit, away from the bustle of the city.

"Jingle Bell Rock" was next, and she sang along to that, too, until a memory popped into her brain.

She'd once stripped to this song for Greg.

They'd been in their first year of university, home for the holidays. Her parents had gone out for the day, so she'd taken advantage of that and asked Greg to come over. She'd only gotten about halfway through the song before she'd burst into laughter. He'd tackled her, and they'd laughed together before having sex on the floor.

Tasha couldn't listen to this song anymore.

She flipped to the next one: "Do They Know It's Christmas?"

"Yes, Goddammit," Greg said a minute later. "I know it's Christmas. I don't know how I could bloody forget it's Christmas, what with all the music I've had to endure on this trip." He shook his head. "Do you remember that movie with the green ogre? We watched it together once."

"Shrek. You two have a lot of similarities. The resemblance is rather uncanny."

He shot her a look. "You're like the sidekick in that movie. The donkey. The one who's very annoying."

"Gee, thanks. Why can't I be the princess instead?"

They'd been moving slowly, but now they came to a stop on the highway. They hadn't even gotten to Waterloo, and it felt like they'd been in the car for hours. It was already dark.

"People drive like idiots in the snow," he said. "If only you hadn't been late, we could have gotten out before the heavy traffic."

"I think the traffic would still have been bad if we left at three."

"Not as bad as it is now." He gestured to the windshield with one hand. "The snow wasn't supposed to start until later. Why couldn't the meteorologists have done a better job predicting this? Why couldn't the snow have waited until we were closer to Mosquito Bay? Dammit, I'm not sure we'll even get home tonight."

"You've sure spoken a lot in the past minute. What a novelty."

He didn't reply, just tightened his grip on the steering wheel.

"It'll be fine," she said.

"Nothing is going according to plan."

"When does life ever work that way? Don't worry, we'll get home tonight."

"Nick will have already eaten all my prime rib," Greg grumbled.

"Such a tragedy. Why do you have to be so negative?"

"I'm looking at the situation realistically."

Tasha turned off the music and let him listen to the radio in peace. She sent a text to her best friend, Monique. *My ex is annoying me. Trust me, there's no chance of us falling in love again.*

Thank God, Monique said. *But still. Be careful.*

Monique had been concerned when Tasha had told her that she was going back to Mosquito Bay with her high school boyfriend. Last year, Monique had hooked up with her boyfriend from grad school, and it had ended even worse than the first time. He'd promised he'd changed, but he hadn't.

I won't do anything stupid, Tasha said. *I promise.*

She closed her eyes for a few minutes and listened to the news.

And that's when she really started to worry.

The top news story was the snowstorm, which was packing much more heat—or, err, snow—than meteorologists had predicted earlier. The list of delays, road closures, and accidents was alarming. She checked Google Maps on her phone, and it was showing nearly their entire route in red.

Perhaps Greg had a point.

This wasn't simply driving back to Mosquito Bay in a little snow.

This could be bad.

And she was trapped in a car with her ex.

On the plus side, Greg had always been a careful driver.

Though he might freak out, he was actually good at performing under stress and he prepared for everything.

So while the situation was less than ideal, and she didn't look forward to spending several more hours with him, she acknowledged that it could be worse.

She could be in a car with a different ex-boyfriend. Like Lance.

She shuddered at the thought.

"Cold?" Greg asked.

She shook her head. "I'm fine."

"Alright." He didn't sound convinced, but he let it go.

"...particularly bad near London and Strathroy," said the voice on the radio.

Great. That was exactly where they were heading. London, Ontario was about two hours from Toronto—on a normal day—and Mosquito Bay was to the northwest of it.

After sending her parents a quick text to let them know where she was and that she would be late, Tasha closed her eyes once more and leaned her head against the door. She tried to think of sugar plums and shortbread cookies.

It didn't work. Her mind kept coming up with pictures of blizzards instead.

3

IT'S GOING to be okay. It's going to be okay.

Greg took a deep breath and repeated the words to himself again.

It's going to be okay.

Sure, he could barely see two meters in front of the car, and the wipers were swishing frantically across the windshield, but they were still slowly moving, and there weren't near as many cars on the road out here. Most people were sensible enough to stay off the roads.

If only he'd done the same.

But he'd been convinced they could outrun the storm. Nobody had predicted it would be this bad.

And if Tasha hadn't been late...

He should stop fixating on that. It might not have made a huge difference in this weather.

He grabbed a protein bar from the console and had a bite. He would offer one to Tasha, but she'd been asleep for the past hour.

Good.

He didn't need to listen to more horrific Christmas music, or hear her chatter when there wasn't much to say.

Well, he supposed there was a lot to say. A lot had happened in the past fifteen years. But what was the point of catching up with someone who wasn't going to stay in your life?

Better that she sleep so he could concentrate on the road.

Though she did look quite pretty. She'd put on a white toque, and her braids peeked out from the bottom. Her eyelashes fluttered against her dark cheeks.

Yes, he'd glanced at her once or twice before quickly turning back to the snowy road.

And then she snored.

It brought a smile to his lips.

He quickly wiped it away. What the hell was wrong with him?

Despite all the years that had passed, apparently he'd retained a strange affection for her snores. She'd never snored a lot, but on one occasion, it had woken him up, and then he'd watched her sleep in his arms.

There was definitely something wrong with him. Perhaps he needed some caffeine. As a general rule, he didn't drink coffee after six o'clock in the evening, but this was going to be a long night, and he didn't want to fall asleep at the wheel.

Though with all the adrenaline coursing through his veins, there probably wasn't much danger of that, but coffee would make this terrible drive more pleasant.

He continued forward at a slow pace. They had exited the 401 and were now on the 402. Normally, this would be an hour or less from Mosquito Bay, but in a snowstorm, it was anyone's guess. It could be hours from here. He'd switched from CBC to an all-news channel.

"...closed just west of Strathroy..."

Dammit! Was the 402 closed west of Strathroy? That wouldn't be surprising, not in these conditions. But the radio was on low, so as not to disturb Tasha, and he hadn't heard clearly.

He turned up the volume, and a few minutes later, the radio host repeated the closure.

It was indeed the 402.

Greg blew out a breath.

It's going to be okay. It's going to be okay.

But he'd have to take the next exit. He could try driving on back roads to Mosquito Bay, but that probably wouldn't be a good idea. Mosquito Bay was still a ways away, and those roads were likely in poor condition. And it was dark.

He glanced over at Tasha again.

He didn't want anything to happen to her.

They should stop for the night. If he remembered correctly, there was a little motel only a kilometer or so from the next exit. He could get them each a room. Not ideal, but it was for the best.

He blew out another breath as he got off the highway and made his way north. He was starting to worry he'd been wrong about that motel when the orange neon letters came into view: Sugar Maple Motel.

It looked like it had been built fifty years ago and not updated since. Still, better than sleeping in the car.

His heart was thumping too quickly. He was supposed to be in Mosquito Bay tonight, eating dinner with his family. They were too loud and they drove him mad, but he loved them anyway.

Except now he was stopping at a motel for the night with Tasha, a situation he had not prepared for at *all*.

A week of mental preparation for this would have been nice. Better yet, a month.

He tapped her shoulder. She mumbled something inarticulate, her eyes still closed, so he did it again.

"Are we there?" she asked.

"No, the 402 is closed. We'll have to stay at a motel for the night."

She was wide awake now. A range of emotions passed over her face, and then she pressed her lips together. "Okay."

He was already forming new plans in his mind. Hopefully

there was food at the motel, but there probably wouldn't be much. However, he had water, protein bars, and snacks in his trunk, so they'd be okay. Tasha might want to hang out for a little while and talk, and he supposed he could put up with that. Then they could head to their separate rooms by ten o'clock. He'd do some reading and go to bed well before midnight; she'd probably listen to some more Christmas music. There was no point trying to get up early tomorrow, since it would take a while to plow the roads, but Greg would get on the road by mid-morning and be home by lunch.

Yep, that was his new plan.

Oh, and he'd have to text his family to inform them of this unfortunate delay.

He pulled his down jacket tightly around him to protect himself from the brutal wind, then headed to the motel, Tasha behind him. When he opened the door to the motel office, chimes tinkled above the door.

"I'm so sorry," said the woman behind the desk. According to her nametag, her name was Clara. She was white, a little younger than his own mother, her brown hair heavily streaked with gray. "We're full."

Oh, no.

Lots of people must have already stopped here due to the storm. His new plan was crumbling before his eyes.

"Are you sure?" Greg croaked. "There's nothing at all?"

Clara hesitated. "Well, we do have one room."

"Great, we'll take it."

"But the heat stopped working earlier in the day, and the repairman won't be here to fix it until tomorrow. I'll give it to you for half price."

When they'd set out on their road trip five hours ago, this was not where Greg had expected to end up. In a crappy motel, thankful there was one room available, even if it had no heat.

"That's fine," Tasha said. "We can manage."

"It's nasty out there tonight, eh?" Clara asked as she pulled out the key for their room. Yes, this motel had actual keys, not key cards. "Terrible storm. Poor Bobby is trembling in fright." She gestured to a Shih Tzu, lying on the thin carpet.

In Greg's opinion, "Bobby" was a terrible name for a dog.

A few minutes later, they hauled their suitcases to the door of their room, the wind whipping the snow around them. It really was unpleasant out here.

Some part of Greg's brain—the highly delusional part—was thrilled with this situation. He'd get to spend the night in the same room as Tasha, who sure did look cute all bundled up. He pictured her undressing, sliding her hand down his body. They'd had a lot of fun together, back in the day...

Nope, not happening. His imagination needed to calm the fuck down.

He put the key into the lock and turned. The door opened, and he flicked on the lights. It wasn't warm in here, but at least there was no wind.

However, there was only one bed.

4

TASHA RUBBED her eyes and looked again.

No, her eyes hadn't been deceiving her. There really was only one bed.

Once upon a time, this would have been a luxury for them. A night alone together in a motel room with a queen-size bed? Even without any heat, that would have been exciting.

They'd spent some nights together in university, but not a ton, and it required sharing a twin bed, which hadn't exactly been comfortable since Greg wasn't a small guy.

Yep, eighteen-year-old Tasha would have *loved* this situation.

But now, a queen bed wasn't a luxury to her—she had one at home—and Greg wasn't her boyfriend. Now, a queen bed didn't seem big enough.

She looked over at Greg. The look of horror on his face nearly made her laugh.

She wasn't looking forward to spending the night in a motel with him. He wouldn't want to listen to Christmas music or even talk. He'd probably just grunt and scowl a lot.

But although she hadn't spoken to Greg much in years, she trusted him, and he'd gotten them there safely, and eventually they'd make it to Mosquito Bay. Sure, he could be irritating at times, but he wasn't a bad guy.

She'd have to make the best of it. That's what she always did.

She marched into the room and took off her boots and winter jacket, which she hung in the small closet. She didn't remove her toque or her big sweater—thank God she was dressed for this weather—and climbed into bed.

"Aren't you coming?" she asked Greg, who was still standing by the door.

"I...I just..."

It was kind of cute to see him stammer.

"I don't bite," she said. "I promise."

He didn't look convinced, just stood there in brooding silence.

"There's only one bed!" he blurted out at last.

Her lips twitched. "Yes, I'm aware, but it's a big bed. Don't worry, you won't catch any Christmas spirit from me."

"I like Christmas. I just don't like Christmas music."

"*Jingle bells, jingle bells...*" she began singing.

He visibly shuddered.

"Don't worry," she said. "I won't do any more singing tonight." But she hadn't been able to resist teasing him one last time.

"Thank God," he muttered.

"Instead, we'll have a long, heart-to-heart conversation until two in the morning."

He looked equally horrified by that prospect.

They would have enjoyed that sort of thing when they were younger, though. Sure, she would have done three-quarters of the talking, but he'd have been a willing participant.

"Just kidding," she said. "I'm going to call my mom and tell her where we are."

He nodded before coming to sit beside her on the bed. The mattress dipped under his weight, and she exhaled unsteadily. This was how close he'd be to her, all night.

He must have noticed her response, because he said, "I could sit at the table until bedtime, if you prefer." He gestured to the crappy wooden table and two chairs by the window.

"No, stay here. It's more comfortable."

He grunted in acknowledgement.

She set her purse on the night-table and fished out her phone. *Shit.* She'd missed two calls from her parents while she was sleeping and sorting out the motel situation. She immediately gave them a call.

"Tasha!" her mother said. "Where are you?"

"I'm sorry. You were probably worried sick. We're in a motel near Strathroy. We won't make it home tonight."

It ached to say those words. She'd resolved to make the best of this, but she really wished she was at home with her parents, cuddled up under a blanket while watching a movie and drinking hot chocolate.

She should try to make it home more often. She loved living in Toronto and wouldn't have it any other way, but the downside was that she was far from her parents, and they were getting old. Tasha's parents had had her later in life; they were a good ten years older than Greg's parents.

She'd wanted to have children earlier than her mom had, but she was now thirty-four and single.

She took a few deep breaths. No, she wouldn't let this get her down. A new year was starting soon—a new year of opportunities. She had a good career, the one she'd dreamed of since high school, and a condo. Her car had died, but she would get another one soon. She wasn't rich, but she was comfortable. She had a decent life, and she had to believe the right man would come around soon. There was always hope.

And maybe she'd already met the right man. She'd gone on a few dates with Crispin, and they'd been pleasant enough. Perhaps it would just take time for her to feel that spark.

"Thank God," her mother said. "It's quite the storm out there."

"Unfortunately, there's no heat in our room." Tasha wrapped one arm around herself and pulled her toque lower on her ears. "And we—"

"Wait a second. You said 'our room.'"

"We have to share a room because it's the last one, and it only has one bed. But it's okay. Nothing we haven't done before, right?"

Greg got up and headed outside, presumably to get something from his car.

On the other end of the phone, her mom was laughing. "It's a sign!"

"No, Mom, it's not a *sign*."

Her mother was still laughing. She was such a romantic.

Though she hadn't been thrilled when Tasha and Greg had started dating in grade eleven. She hadn't wanted anything to get in the way of Tasha pursuing her dreams.

But Greg, who'd always seemed older than his years, had won her over. He was not the kind of guy who got a girl into trouble or discouraged her ambitions, as her mother's first husband had done.

And now that Tasha had an established career and was over thirty, her mother kept talking about signs and romance all the time.

Which was fine.

But Greg was her ex-boyfriend, and Tasha always looked forward, never back.

"I always liked him," Mom said.

"No, you didn't. You thought he'd distract me."

"Silly of me. I should have known my girl would never get distracted."

Tasha couldn't help but smile.

"It's so cold outside, and when you're huddled up under the covers together, who knows what will happen?"

"Mom!" Tasha wasn't smiling now.

"Rosemary was clearly hoping that you and Greg would get back together when she suggested he drive you home for the holidays. I wasn't thinking of that, just thought it would be convenient for you, but now—"

"Alright, Mom. Enough with the matchmaking. Nothing is going to happen between us."

"You say that, but—"

"Mom!"

"Okay, okay, I'll stop," Mom said. "Guess what I made? Gingerbread cookies."

Tasha's tummy rumbled. She hadn't eaten dinner yet. In fact, she hadn't eaten in nearly nine hours. Hot chocolate and gingerbread sounded delicious.

They talked for a few more minutes, and as soon as Tasha set down her phone on the table next to the bed, a mug of hot chocolate appeared beside it.

She rubbed her eyes. She must be hallucinating. Or she'd gained special powers and had conjured up the hot chocolate just by thinking about it.

That would be a useful skill, but it seemed unlikely.

No, she must be hallucinating.

She reached for the mug, just in case.

It was real. Totally real. She had a sip, and though it was fairly ordinary hot chocolate, it was especially good because she was freezing right now. It warmed her from the inside.

"Figured you could use something hot," Greg said.

She whipped her head around. He was sitting in bed next to her, his legs crossed at the ankles. His glasses were on his nighttable, next to a steaming mug, though it looked like he was drinking tea, not hot chocolate. He'd always been a big tea drinker. She used to tease him about it.

"It's delicious." She looked around the room and saw an electric kettle on the table, which she could have sworn wasn't there before. "Where did that come from?"

He chuckled, a soft sound that made her smile. "I had the kettle, mugs, tea, and hot chocolate in my car."

"Why?"

He shrugged. "Part of my winter survival kit. Plus, it's useful to have a kettle in my bedroom when I visit Mom and Dad, so I don't have to talk to anyone if I want tea. Going down to the kitchen is an arduous affair."

She couldn't help but laugh, though she was still wrapping her mind around the fact that he traveled with all those things. "What else do you have in your car?"

He gestured toward the chairs. There were two sleeping bags, an extra blanket, a couple hats and gloves, and... Oh My God.

"A space heater!" She could kiss him.

She covered her mouth and looked away. She shouldn't be thinking like that. This was Greg Wong, after all.

And this was such a *Greg* thing to do. To be prepared for the unlikely event of staying in a motel with no heat.

"You have any food in your car?" she asked.

He held out three bars: a granola bar, a protein bar, and a Coffee Crisp. "Appetizer, main course, and dessert."

She'd never been so happy to see a granola bar in her life. And a Coffee Crisp!

"You travel with Coffee Crisps in your car?" she asked, gesturing to the yellow wrapper of the chocolate bar. These were her favorite, but not his.

He shook his head. "There's a vending machine in the motel office."

Oh. He'd gotten it just for her. Because he remembered.

This, too, was such a Greg thing. He'd always quietly looked after her in little ways.

"Do you have food for yourself?" she asked, suddenly worried he'd given it all to her.

"I ate a protein bar while you were sleeping in the car, but I have more, don't worry." He held up a granola bar and some trail mix. "You talked to your mother?"

"Yeah, I assured her that I'm perfectly fine and not freezing to death in a snowstorm. Did you talk to your family?"

"I texted my brother." He cocked his head in the direction of his phone.

Greg *texted*. It seemed all wrong.

To her, Greg was the past. When they'd been together, neither of them had a smartphone. Texting wasn't really a thing yet.

"Remember how much time we used to spend on MSN Messenger?" she asked.

He smiled faintly. "I do."

Back when they were at different universities, it was the main way they'd stayed in contact. Daily conversations on MSN Messenger before they went to bed. Weekends together maybe once a month. Toronto and Waterloo weren't all that far apart, but there was always so much schoolwork to do, so much going on, and it had been hard to see each other.

"I'm going to get changed," she said.

She dug around in her suitcase, then went to the washroom to take off her bra and change into her flannel pajama pants. She looked in the mirror afterward and found herself wanting to touch up her make-up.

Stop it, Tasha. It's just Greg.

Yes, they were sharing a bed in a snowstorm, but tomorrow they would go back to their regularly scheduled lives, without each other.

And that was fine. It was what she wanted.

She texted Monique again, telling her that they'd had to stop at a motel, but Tasha emphasized, once again, that there was no danger of her falling in love.

She didn't mention the Coffee Crisp or the hot chocolate, though.

5

WHEN TASHA CAME out of the washroom, she was still wearing the same cream-colored sweater, but she had plaid pajama pants on now.

It was the opposite of revealing, but Greg's jeans suddenly felt a little tight.

He should not be lusting after Tasha, but he couldn't help being attracted to her, even all these years later.

They'd been in the same class throughout elementary school. There was only one class per grade in Mosquito Bay, and he was the only Asian kid and she was the only Black kid in their year. He hadn't talked to her—or anyone else—much, preferring to sit in the corner and work in silence. He'd been a very serious child.

High school was bigger than elementary school, since kids from a few of the nearby towns were bussed to Mosquito Bay. He'd spent much of grade ten math admiring her from the back corner, and in grade eleven, they'd been in physics together. When they'd had to do their first ticker tape lab, she'd turned to him and asked with a bright smile if he'd be her lab partner. He'd smiled and croaked out a "yes," already half in love with her.

She had smooth brown skin and a lovely smile. Nice ass, maybe a little bigger now—and he wasn't complaining.

Stop it, Greg.

He should not be looking at her ass.

They were just sharing a bed, nothing more.

She climbed under the covers, and he went to the washroom to change into his pajamas. When he returned, she was chewing on her protein bar—and his gaze immediately latched onto her lips.

He turned away and picked up his e-reader. Hopefully, she would get the point and realize he didn't want to talk.

For half an hour, he read and she did something on her phone. Although he couldn't forget that she was sitting next to him in bed, it was still comfortable, somehow.

"We never did this before," he said, surprising himself by talking. It was rare for him to break the silence. Tasha was the talkative one, but she'd respected his need for quiet for the thirty minutes, which he appreciated.

"Did what, you mean?"

"Sit quietly in bed together. Whenever there was a bed..." He trailed off, his cheeks heating.

"Please, continue." She smirked.

"We were all over each other," he said hoarsely.

The silence now was distinctly *un*comfortable. She seemed to be checking him out, or was that his imagination? Surely Tasha had better options than him, even if she was single at the moment.

But for a few seconds, he allowed himself to recall what it had been like to be a horny teenager rolling around in bed with her.

"We only ever had a twin bed," he said. "A queen, even in a cheap motel without heat, would have been a luxury."

"That's exactly what I thought when we stepped inside the room."

"Sharing a queen-size bed? Piece of cake." He made a dismissive gesture with his hand.

This, of course was a lie. He was very much aware of how close she was. It would be so easy to reach out and touch her.

He wouldn't.

"We could have rolled over to change positions without toppling onto the floor," Tasha said. "Definitely a luxury."

They were both quiet again. He was thinking about all the sex they'd had, and he wondered if she was thinking about that, too. He wouldn't flatter himself and assume she was. She'd probably had much better sex in the intervening years.

After all, they'd been each other's firsts. First *everything*. It had been a year before they'd had sex—over Christmas holidays when they were both seventeen—but there had been an awful lot of fooling around before that, whenever they had a chance to be alone.

They wouldn't have wasted an opportunity like this one.

"Why did you ask me to be your lab partner?" he asked suddenly.

"You were smart, and I wanted a good mark without having to do all the work myself."

"Mm." He set aside his book, figuring he wouldn't get much more reading done tonight, and he was okay with that.

"And I was right. We had the two highest marks in the class."

She'd beaten him by a couple percent in grade eleven physics, but he'd gotten the higher mark in grade twelve.

"I can't believe I worked up the nerve to ask you on a date," he said. "I'd wanted to do it for months before I finally managed to get the words out."

"You stuttered. Do you remember that?"

"I most certainly did not stutter."

"You did! It was cute."

"I don't think 'cute' was quite what I was going for, and I doubt anyone has described me as cute in decades."

She laughed. "You sound so offended by the thought."

He responded with an exaggerated sniff.

Which made her laugh again.

Greg knew he wasn't a particularly funny guy. He was positive everyone thought he was less funny than his brothers. But he'd always been able to make Tasha laugh—rarely a belly-aching laugh, but a quiet chuckle. He was glad he could still do so.

She tore open the wrapper of the Coffee Crisp and took a big bite. He was pleased he'd been able to get one at the poorly-stocked vending machine in the motel. Personally, Greg didn't much care for candy bars—they were overly sweet and terrible for you. He wasn't a huge dessert person in general, although there were a few things he liked.

But in grade twelve, she'd told him her locker combo, and he never used it unless she specifically asked him to grab something for her, except for the handful of times he'd snuck in to put a Coffee Crisp and a note on the top shelf in her locker.

She'd always rewarded him with a big kiss afterward.

Geez, it had been a long time since he'd thought of these things. So strange to be in bed with her after all this time.

"Is Coffee Crisp still your favorite?" he asked.

"Yeah, but I don't have them much anymore. Haven't had one in months, actually."

Just then, the wind howled outside, and Tasha shivered. Before he knew what he was doing, his arms were around her. It felt good to hold her again.

And then he realized what he was doing and immediately sat back.

"Sorry," he mumbled.

"You scared of the wind?" she teased.

"No, I'm not scared of a little winter weather."

"You built me that snow fort, remember? So we could have a place to be alone together."

He'd certainly not forgotten about that.

They'd only gotten to spend a couple weekends together in

their first term of university. Having two and a half weeks back in Mosquito Bay for the holidays seemed like heaven.

Except their families were *always* home, and the cars were often in use.

Then there had been a big snowfall, and he'd done a little research online about making structurally-stable snow forts. He'd built quite an elaborate one, though he didn't put a roof on it, afraid it would collapse—he used a tarp instead. And then he'd brought her to the park at the edge of town, asked her to close her eyes, and led her inside.

She'd been delighted.

For three days, they'd spent a lot of time in the snow fort. They could make out in peace and quiet, and he'd bring a big thermos of tea to keep them warm. But then a bunch of kids had knocked it down.

It was a pleasant memory, as were most of his memories of their time together. They had completely opposite personalities, but they'd fit together well, and when she got on his nerves, he'd still felt an annoyed affection for her. He just hadn't let himself reminisce in a long time, because after their break-up, it had been too painful.

Their relationship had gone out with a whimper, not a bang. No big fight. Neither of them had met someone else.

But it was hard to maintain a relationship when you were going to university in different cities.

When they were in their final year of high school, she'd dreamed of studying engineering science at U of T, with the plan of specializing in aerospace engineering in third year, and he'd hoped to do systems engineering at Waterloo, which was known for its co-op program.

They'd both gotten into the programs they wanted, and they'd talked about it a lot, but neither of them had felt like the other person should make sacrifices so they could be together. Conventional wisdom said you shouldn't make your decision about university based on where your boyfriend or girlfriend was going.

So they hadn't.

Many people also said you shouldn't marry your high school sweetheart.

Greg's parents had started dating in high school, though, and secretly, he'd thought he and Tasha would end up together, like his parents. Sure, he constantly heard about how these strong emotions were just a teenage thing, blah, blah, blah, but he hadn't believed that.

"No other man has ever built me a snow fort," Tasha said.

"Or gotten you stranded in a crappy motel near Strathroy."

"You're not blaming that on me being twenty-seven minutes late?"

He shrugged. If he was honest with himself, he didn't actually mind being trapped in a motel room with Tasha Edwards, much to his surprise.

"Do you like living in Toronto?" she asked. "I do. It's all that I wanted it to be, and it's hard for me to imagine living in a small town now."

"I like it. I plan to stay." He'd first started thinking about moving to Toronto back when he and Tasha were together—he thought he'd go to school in Waterloo, then move to Toronto with her, since she'd always dreamed of living in the big city. Once he graduated, there was no girlfriend in the picture, but he got an offer for a decent job in Toronto, and so he stuck with that part of his plan. He'd been there for over a decade now, and it was hard for him to imagine living elsewhere, too.

His phone rang, and he picked it up.

"Greg!" said a loud voice.

"Hi, Ah Ma."

"You kiss yet?"

Well, his grandmother had certainly gotten straight to the point.

He scrubbed a hand over his face and glanced over at Tasha. He imagined putting his arms around her again and—

"No," he said curtly, very much aware that Tasha could hear anything he said. She was texting now, a slight smile on her lips.

"You are sharing a room, I hope?" Ah Ma asked.

It was so weird. When you were a teenager, your parents and grandparents were always trying to prevent you from having a little alone time with your girlfriend. When you were thirty-four and they feared you'd never get married, they were desperately trying to throw you together with your ex.

"Yes," he said.

"There is only one bed? When I read romance books, this is what always happens."

"Yes."

She cackled, then turned away from the phone and said loudly, "They have to share a bed!"

Great. Now everyone in his family would know his business.

There was silence on the other end of the phone for the moment, and then a male voice spoke. "You need any advice on how to make a move?"

It was Nick, who was two years younger than Greg, and, admittedly, much more well-versed in the art of seduction.

But Greg did not need advice from his brother, and he was not trying to seduce Tasha.

"Mind your own business," he snapped.

Tasha chuckled. Her face was framed by her long braids, and God, why was that toque with the pom-pom so cute on her?

"You still like her?" Nick asked.

Greg grunted.

"I'll take that to mean, 'Yes, absolutely, I want to jump her bones.'"

"Stop being so crude."

"You definitely want her."

"Nick…"

There was a pause on the other end of the phone before another voice said, "I ate all of your prime rib. Mm, was it ever good."

That was Zach.

Annoying little brothers. Why did Greg have two of them? And why did everyone in his family feel the need to speak to him on the phone so they could make more or less the same comments? It was a waste of time when he could be...well, not kissing Tasha, but quietly reading next to her or having a pleasant conversation. Preferable to dealing with his family.

His stomach rumbled at the thought of that prime rib. That granola bar hadn't been nearly as satisfying.

"Tell Tasha I say hi." Zach spoke in a singsong voice, clearly amused by the situation.

This was another comment that was best responded to with a grunt.

"You know, women like when you talk to them," Zach said.

"My specialty is listening," Greg said.

"And grunting."

"Grunting is very useful. It expresses a wide range of emotions."

Next to him, Tasha doubled over in laughter.

"Do you grunt a lot when you have sex?" Zach asked.

"I am not talking about my sex life with you," Greg replied.

Tasha's cheeks looked a little flushed now. He imagined her underneath him...

No, not happening.

"Okay, okay," Zach said. "I'll be good."

"Yeah, right," Greg muttered.

"Lily made Nanaimo bars and Mom made cheesecake, but it's all gone now."

Truth be told, Greg didn't particularly like Nanaimo bars, but he wanted some damn cheesecake. It was his favorite dessert. His mom had given him the recipe, but his never turned out quite as good. Besides, what was the point of making a whole cheesecake when you lived alone? He didn't need that much cheesecake.

"Thanks for making me hungry," he said.

"You're welcome," Zach said cheerfully. "Anytime. Dad wants to talk to you now."

Their father's voice came over the phone. "Glad you're safe. It looks nasty out there."

"It is," Greg said.

"You know, the cheesecake was *really* good."

Okay, that was enough. "I'm getting off the phone now. See you tomorrow."

Greg ended the call and shook his head.

"'Grunting is very useful and expresses a wide range of emotions,'" Tasha said in a fake deep voice.

"Thank you." He kept his expression stern, but admittedly, he enjoyed when she teased him.

She looked down at her phone.

"What are you doing now?" he asked.

"Talking to the guy I'm seeing."

He couldn't help the jealousy that coursed through him, but he shouldn't be jealous. Sure, he could appreciate that Tasha was a good-looking woman, and he still liked spending time with her, but that was all. She wasn't *his*; she could date whomever she liked.

"We've just been on a couple dates," she said. "Nothing serious. He's not my boyfriend, and we're not spending the holidays together. But he's a good guy."

Unsure what to say but feeling he should acknowledge her words, Greg grunted.

See? It really was a useful sound.

"You seeing anyone?" she asked, putting aside her phone.

"Nah," he said. "Not for a while now."

"Oh." She paused, looking thoughtful. "Are you—"

Before she could finish her question, the lights went out.

6

TASHA TRIED the lamp next to the bed.

Nope, nothing. As expected.

She couldn't help it. She burst into laughter.

The situation was so ridiculous. She was sitting in bed with her high school boyfriend, whom she'd hardly seen in fifteen years, as a snowstorm raged outside. There was no heat, and now, no power.

Across the bed, Greg's laughter rumbled, causing a pleasant vibration in her chest.

"You okay?" he asked.

"Yeah," she said. "I'm fine, though I guess the space heater won't do much for us now."

"Do you want one of the sleeping bags or the extra blanket?"

"Actually, yeah. The extra blanket would be good."

The mattress shifted as Greg got up. Soon, it dipped again as he climbed back in bed, and in the dark, she was acutely aware of his nearness.

For some reason, it felt like the sleepovers she'd gone to in elementary school. The lights were out, and they could giggle and talk about their secrets.

He placed the blanket over her, and she pulled it up to her neck.

"So, you haven't dated in a while," she said, returning to their conversation. "Like I told you, I'm surprised you're not married. You're the sort of man that a woman would settle down with— stable, kind, good job—versus the kind of man she'd have a hot fling with when she's young."

"You dated me when we were young."

Oh. She realized how it had sounded. "Not that we didn't have fun together. Not that the sex wasn't good. You're just husband material. I mean it as a compliment."

"I know."

She could hear the smile in his voice.

"So tell me." She was suddenly quite curious. "How many relationships have you had since we broke up?"

"Three. All lasted more than a year."

That sounded like Greg. He wasn't the kind of guy who'd bounce from one woman to another, and he wasn't scared of commitment.

"None of them were quite right, though," he said. "They didn't last as long as we did. And I'm terrible at meeting women. That involves, you know, socializing." He made a sound of displeasure. "I know that, since I'd like a relationship, I should put myself out there, but I'm not great at it. And online dating…"

"What's wrong with it? That way, you don't actually have to speak to someone right away. Just swipe right and send a message."

"I feel like I don't understand the social conventions. I tried, but very few women contacted me or replied to my messages, the rare times I sent them. Perhaps my profiles could have used some work."

"Ooh, I could help you with that!"

"Get in line," he said. "Nick, Zach, Amber, and Ah Ma have already offered their assistance."

"I'm not sure you should be taking online dating advice from your grandma."

"My thoughts exactly."

"How old are your grandparents? My mom sees them about town on occasion."

"Eighty-eight and eighty-nine."

She looked away for a moment, though she couldn't see him in the dark anyway. Her grandparents would be over ninety if they were still alive. She missed them.

Greg's hand settled on her shoulder, just for a second, before he withdrew. "I listed my interests as CBC Radio, model trains, birdwatching, stamp-collecting, and documentaries."

She couldn't suppress a fond smile. It was so *Greg*.

"You should have added 'baking.' That would interest some women." He'd baked for her a bunch of times. Chocolate chip cookies and other things. All delicious.

"I'll keep it under consideration. But online dating made me nervous and uncomfortable, so I let myself take a break. And most women our age seem to be in a relationship."

Except her.

"Someday, though," he said, "I'll try again."

She could hear the yearning in his voice. When they were younger, he'd talked of getting married and having a small family. She knew it was still what he wanted; Greg wasn't someone who changed his mind about such things.

He wouldn't want four children like his parents had, but he'd want one or two. They'd drive him crazy and mess up his ordered life, something she knew he secretly enjoyed.

There was a pang in her heart. She still cared for him, and she wanted him to have everything he desired.

She pictured them in the kitchen together, making cookies for their two small children, then shook her head.

He was part of her past, not her future.

When she got sad about her dating life, she reminded herself that tomorrow was another day, and sure, her biological clock was ticking, but she still had a little time. That was how she kept her spirits up, kept putting herself out there again and again.

Always forward, never back.

Why, there was already a nice man who liked her.

"Perhaps," Greg mused, "the problem is that I never ask women to come upstairs and see my model trains."

"Like asking a lady to come upstairs and see your etchings."

"Precisely. Or 'Netflix and chill.'"

She laughed, imagining him asking a woman, very seriously, to watch Netflix and chill.

"So, model trains, eh?" she said, finding that rather adorable for some reason. "You spend your free time listening to CBC, painting little trees and figurines, and watching your little train chugging through your model mountain?"

"How did you know there was a mountain?"

"Oh, I just do."

Because she still knew him.

Sure, he had a proper job now and he'd gotten some new hobbies, but fundamentally, he was the same.

If he asked her to come up to see his model train, she'd probably say yes, and he'd undress her with extreme care...and afterward, he really would show her the model train.

"What about you?" he asked. "I thought you'd be married by now, too."

"Why did you think that?"

He made some inarticulate noises, then said, "You're smart and beautiful. Then and now." He spoke as though it was an indisputable fact.

She hesitated. "I wish it had happened, but it didn't. Sometimes, I feel like it's greedy to want a career *and* a family—"

"Nobody tells men that they can't have it all, and we get praised when we take our own kids to the park. You can want it all, too."

"I want what my parents have."

"Me, too." He paused. "This guy you were texting—did you meet him online?"

"Yeah. He was the first guy who hadn't opened with a dick pic in a depressingly long time. His name is Crispin."

Perhaps she shouldn't have told Greg that. It felt weird.

Crispin was an outgoing man who worked in sales. They'd had fun on their dates, and the kissing had been good, but they hadn't gone any further. She'd texted him earlier, after Greg had given her hot chocolate and a Coffee Crisp, to remind herself that she had other options. Maybe Crispin could be the one, or...

"Maybe I have unrealistic expectations when it comes to dating," she said.

"Expecting men not to send you unsolicited dick pics is very reasonable."

It was weird to hear "dick pic" in Greg's sensible voice.

"It's much more than that. I want to just *know*."

"I understand."

When he was on the phone with his family, he'd said his specialty was listening—in response to what, she wasn't quite sure.

But, yeah, he was a good listener. You always felt like he was giving you his undivided attention, seriously considering whatever you said, no matter how trivial or silly. And while he liked when things made sense logically, he accepted that not everything worked that way.

He'd told her once that half the reason he loved her was because she was pretty and smart and fun...and many other adjectives. The other half, he didn't think he'd ever be able to explain. It simply was.

Not knowing what to say now, she asked, "Do you really birdwatch?"

He didn't question the change in topic. "Yeah."

"I don't think I'd have the patience."

"That's fair."

They were quiet for a moment in the darkness of their cold hotel room, and then there was a very loud squeak next door, followed by more squeaks in a slow, steady rhythm.

~

The people in the next room were having sex. Greg was certain of it.

And here, on the other side of the wall, he and Tasha were having a conversation in bed in the dark, and it couldn't help feeling intimate.

He couldn't deny it: he wanted to make the bed springs squeak with Tasha, too. Not just because it had been a long time since he'd had sex, but because it was *her*.

The bed springs next door continued to squeak. Tasha laughed, and Greg joined her.

"Why did we break up?" he asked suddenly.

"We were drifting apart. It was hard to maintain a relationship when we went to different schools."

He knew that, but he'd wanted to hear her answer. "What if I'd gone to U of T with you?"

"I couldn't have asked you to do that. You wanted the co-op program, and you wanted systems engineering."

"And I couldn't have asked you to give up what you wanted, either. But what if—"

"Greg," she said. "Don't."

"Maybe we should have tried harder."

But they'd been in university, and that had been their priority. Focusing on school had seemed like the right thing to do.

And he'd felt like he was a yoke around her neck, preventing her from fully enjoying the university experience. The high school boyfriend who'd outstayed his welcome, even if they still cared for each other. She should be meeting other guys, having lots of new experiences, not spending her limited free time talking to him on MSN Messenger. In the end, he'd been the one to suggest breaking up, but it had been mutual. They'd both agreed it wasn't working.

Perhaps it wouldn't have turned out any differently if they'd gone to the same university.

Squeak, squeak, squeak.

"*Oh, Ethel*," said a muffled male voice.

Tasha laughed. "Ethel isn't a name you hear much anymore, is it?"

"It was my great-grandmother's name," Greg said.

"Can you imagine giving a little girl that name?"

"Many old names have become popular again."

"Yeah, but not 'Ethel.' Or 'Bertha.'"

"This is true."

"*Herbert!*" said a not-so-muffled female voice from the other side of the wall.

So the people next door were Ethel and Herbert. Charming.

"How old do you think they are?" Tasha asked.

"I bet they're two sixteen-year-olds who snuck off during the snowstorm."

"Ethel and Herbert, the coolest kids in school."

"No, with names like those, they're probably in their eighties. Perhaps they were heading out to visit their adult children for the holidays, and they stopped when the weather took a turn for the worse and decided to make the best of the power outage."

"I hope I'm still having sex when I'm eighty-five."

"Same here," he said. "I just hope I'm not so loud about it."

"I don't think there's much danger of that. You were never loud."

For half a minute, all he could hear was the squeak of the bed springs and his own breathing.

And then another, "*Oh, Herbert!*"

Greg felt a strange fondness for this older couple having sex in a dark motel room, though he wished they'd do it a little more quietly.

He also couldn't help wishing that he and Tasha hadn't drifted apart. Maybe they could be stuck in this motel as a married couple, with a small child sleeping between them.

He shouldn't think about it, but he did.

What if...

"*Ethel!*"

"*Oh, Herbie!*"

The squeaking got even louder, and Greg was more uncomfortable than amused, though he was also thinking about doing exactly the same thing with Tasha.

What would it be like to sleep with her now? Would it be as good as he remembered?

Was his memory faulty?

"*Yes, just like that. Herbieeeee.*"

This was followed by a few bangs.

Dear God.

On the other side of the bed, Tasha chuckled, low and husky. Goddammit, he wanted her.

"I hope nobody busts their hip," she said.

"I hope they stop this infernal racket soon," he muttered.

She shifted toward him and put her hand on his shoulder. "You sound like an old man." But she said it with affection, and he didn't mind at all.

Tentatively, he reached out and ran his hand over the curve of her hip.

In response, she cupped his jaw with her hand. He could feel her breath on his cheek.

And then he kissed her on the lips. Just once.

Tasha wasn't as gentle. She yanked him on top of her, and when he pressed his lips to hers again, she thrust her tongue into his mouth.

Greg's body came alive in a way it hadn't for years. He was

aware of every place they were touching. Her legs between his. Her breasts against his chest. Of course, there were a couple layers of sweater between them, but still.

She arched against him, pressing against him *there*.

He growled as his cock hardened, then shifted his lips away from hers and kissed his way down to where her jaw met her neck—she'd always been particularly sensitive in that spot.

And she still was.

"Greg," she whispered, much more quietly than Ethel next door.

He loved hearing her say his name when she was underneath him.

He shifted his mouth back to Tasha's and tasted a hint of Coffee Crisp, something he'd tasted on her lips before.

"Ethel!"

"Herbieee!"

This was followed by more banging and squeaking.

Greg could feel Tasha's smile against his lips. He smiled back before cupping her ass and bringing her more firmly against him as he continued to kiss her.

It had been many, many years, but it still felt right.

Familiar, though not quite the same.

Tasha started grinding her hips against his, and he slipped his hand under her sweater and shirt, smooth skin meeting his fingertips.

He shuddered. He wanted more. He wanted—

Suddenly, they were bathed in light. What on earth was going on?

Oh, right. The power had been restored.

Greg looked down at Tasha, her braids fanned out on the pillow, her sweater pushed up, one hand gripping his shoulder.

He was making out with his ex-girlfriend.

And he'd known what he was doing, but it felt like he hadn't *really* known until now.

Tasha looked even more stunned. When he rolled off her, she shifted away from him. He missed her body heat, and not just because it was cold in the room.

"*Ethel!*"

"*Herbie!*"

A couple more bangs and it seemed to be over.

Strange that a presumably-elderly couple having sex next door during a power outage had encouraged Greg to kiss his ex. The world worked in odd ways.

He couldn't bring himself to regret it, though.

Tasha, however, still looked stunned.

"Are you okay?" he asked, not letting himself reach for her.

"Me? Oh, yeah, I'm fine. Just worried about Ethel's hip. Anyway, I'm going to head to the washroom to wrap up my hair and brush my teeth, and maybe we can go to sleep soon?"

"Sure. Of course. Yeah."

Why was he sounding like a loon?

Tasha padded across the room, and Greg lay back in the bed, feeling like his world had been knocked slightly off orbit.

He wanted to kiss her again. He wanted to lose himself in her.

But he didn't think she wanted the same thing.

7

TASHA COULDN'T SLEEP.

She blamed it on the howling wind and the unheated motel room. She had fuzzy socks and a big sweater and several blankets, and she still didn't feel warm enough. She was even contemplating putting her toque back on, over her silk scarf.

No, she shouldn't lie to herself.

The reason she couldn't sleep was because Greg was lying next to her.

They were sharing a queen-size bed. There was a healthy distance between them, but she was quite conscious of his presence.

And he'd kissed her.

All those years ago, she'd been the one who'd kissed him first. He'd asked her on a date. It was May, and, stammering, he'd suggested a picnic.

She smiled at the memory. How many sixteen-year-old boys would pack a proper lunch—not just a bag of chips and some pop —in a wicker basket and bring it to the park by the lake? He'd made a pasta salad, and there was also a baguette and two types of cheese—cheap marble and cheddar, but still—and juice and chocolate. More than once, he'd leaned forward, and she'd thought he was going to kiss her, but he didn't.

So, finally, she'd taken matters into her own hands.

She wanted to kiss him again tonight. She wanted to do more than that, in all honesty.

It didn't have to mean anything. She'd simply found herself in bed with a handsome man from her past who could kiss the daylights out of her; they could have their fun while they were trapped in the snowstorm, then head their separate ways tomorrow.

She never got involved with an ex-boyfriend, not since Lance, but they wouldn't be getting involved.

No, they'd just have a bit of fun.

Liar.

Tasha shoved that stupid voice out of her brain. It didn't know what it was talking about.

Next to her, Greg rolled over and sighed. Apparently, he couldn't sleep, either. Hopefully it was because he, too, was thinking about their kiss.

Or possibly he was planning his next birdwatching expedition. It was hard to know.

Damn, why did she find his hobbies so endearing?

And, like, kind of sexy?

Perhaps because he was so unreservedly himself. Like in high school, when he'd never tried to fit in.

"I can't sleep," she said.

"I can't sleep, either."

Greg was thorough and detail-oriented, and it wasn't surprising he'd remembered the spot just below her jaw that she liked. He could also be rather intense, like in his hatred for Christmas music—though she could have sworn his lips had quirked up when she was singing—but she'd experienced that intensity focused on her, and there was nothing else like it.

She couldn't suppress a shudder.

"Are you cold?" he asked, his quiet, concerned voice coming through the darkness. "Do you want one of the sleeping bags? I don't think this building has very good insulation, in addition to the lack of heating. Or...never mind."

"Or, what?"

"We could cuddle." He cleared his throat. "Share body heat. You know."

"Maybe after."

"After what?"

"We have sex. If you're interested."

There was a long silence.

Yes, he'd kissed her, but maybe she'd miscalculated.

"If you don't want to, that's fine," she said in a rush. "I just figured we might as well. It wouldn't mean anything, of course, but I haven't had sex in a while, and I know we can make each other feel good, and that kiss was pretty great, wasn't it?"

Oh, no. She was babbling, and she couldn't see his expression.

And then he was on top of her, and she melted into the soft mattress.

"I'm interested," he said.

"Oh." She released a breath. "Well, then." She paused. "Shit, I don't have any condoms."

"Don't worry. I do."

Of course he did. He was prepared for everything. It only stood to reason that a guy who had two sleeping bags, a kettle, and a space heater in his trunk would also have condoms.

The mattress shifted, and she missed his weight and heat on top of her, but it wasn't long before he returned.

"I have two requests," he said.

"Yes?"

"I'd like to turn the light on so I can see you."

She wasn't usually self-conscious about her body, but Greg had seen her naked when she was young and thin and had a flat stomach.

"Tasha?" he said softly. "Is that okay?"

"I don't look like I did when I was nineteen. I've gained at least twenty-five pounds."

"So have I."

"But yours is mostly muscle." She bet he had a regimented fitness routine. That seemed like Greg. She couldn't wait to touch him all over.

"You've been checking me out, have you?"

"Yeah, when you were whining about Christmas music."

"I wasn't whining."

"Fine. Making your displeasure known in a non-whiny way."

"That's better."

"You can turn on the light," she said, "and you can touch me anywhere you want, but don't completely remove my sweater, because I'm cold."

"Anything else?" He wasn't much of a talker in the bedroom, but he'd always wanted to know how she felt and what she wanted.

"No, but you said you had a second request?"

"Yes. You can say my name, but please be quieter than Ethel and Herbie."

"That sounds soooo difficult, because I'm sure you'll make me feel soooo good."

"Tasha," he said sternly.

Ooh, she'd missed his stern voice.

"Okay, I'll behave," she said.

He flicked on the lamp by the side of the bed. "No, you won't." His dark eyes were intent on her face, and her breath came faster. "But I like it that way."

"Take off your clothes," she commanded. "All of them."

"As you wish."

"Unless you're going to be too cold."

"I'll be fine."

He pulled his shirt over his head, and she swallowed hard. He really did look good.

He smirked as she lay there admiring him, and then he stripped off his pajama pants and boxers in one smooth move. She couldn't help staring at his cock, long and heavy between his legs.

He lay on top of her again, and her sweater rode up as her arms went around him, exposing a slice of her skin to his.

"How are you so hot?" she murmured.

"May I ask which meaning of the word you're using?"

Well, both, but... "There's no heat in the room, and yet you're warm."

He tugged off her pants. His warmer legs tangled with hers, and she gasped as he rocked his hips. "I'm going to heat you up."

His hands slipped under her sweater and cupped her breasts. He rubbed the tip of one nipple between his fingers. As his mouth descended to hers, she couldn't help but imagine him doing this with other women. Being naked in bed, using his adorably stern voice on them.

No, it seemed wrong. He was hers. She'd found him first.

You're dating Greg? Her friends hadn't understood the appeal. Sure, he was decent-looking, but wasn't he a little weird?

She'd felt like she was in on some great secret.

She pushed aside her thoughts of the past, as well as her jealousy. It had been many years, and she doubted Greg had had a ton of sexual partners, but of course he'd had some—he'd had three relationships, after all.

Besides, she wouldn't have wanted him to be celibate...and perhaps he'd picked up some useful skills in that time.

She giggled as his head disappeared under her sweater. He brought the tip of one nipple into his mouth and swirled his tongue around it. Then he did something with his mouth that defied description, but it felt amazing.

His head reappeared, and he shifted up her body.

"How are you doing?" he asked.

"I'm good. Very good."

When they were younger, they'd been eager but also hesitant; it was different now. She brought her hands down to his firm ass and gave it a squeeze, not at all ashamed that this was what she wanted to do.

His palms slid over her nipples then her belly, smoothing a path down her legs, then back to her ass, and all the while he kissed her mouth in a heated yet deliberate way.

He still had a little too much control for her liking. She'd always delighted in making him lose himself, when he was normally such a sensible, measured person.

She wiggled her ass and spread her legs so his cock rubbed against the juncture of her thighs. He grunted.

She hadn't heard this particular grunt in a while, because he only made it when they were in bed together. Or in a parked car, or in a snow fort. It was the one he made when he was turned on.

She was an expert in his noises.

He continued to run his warm hands all over her cooler skin —she'd forgotten how large his hands were—and every part of her body tingled in the wake of his touch.

"How long has it been for you?" she asked suddenly.

"Oh, about four years. Since my last relationship ended."

"Four years?"

"Yes." His eyes danced with amusement. "Surprised?"

"Let's hope you're not rusty."

"I don't think you have to worry about that," he murmured.

"It's been four months for me."

"Mm."

"What does that mean?"

"Nothing. Just an acknowledgment of your words." He paused. "No judgment. I wanted you to have lots of, uh, experiences."

Before she could reply, he cupped her mound over her underwear. Not a particularly pretty pair, as she certainly hadn't expected this to happen.

He held her gaze, and when she nodded, he slipped them off and tossed them somewhere among all the blankets on the bed. Then he rubbed two long fingers over her entrance, groaning as he pushed them inside her. "You feel so good, Tasha."

She was practically trembling, and he wasn't even moving his fingers. Why wasn't he moving his fingers?

She circled her hips, desperate for more, and he laughed softly in her ear.

"Yes," he said, "be greedy."

And with that, his head disappeared under the covers. He licked over her slit, nice and slow.

She nearly jumped off the bed. Dear God, his mouth was incredible.

He continued to lick her as he leisurely thrust his fingers in and out, and she could hear her moisture as he moved. He nuzzled her inner thigh, his stubble rubbing over her sensitive skin.

Ohhh.

"Any complaints about my rustiness?" he asked, his words muffled by the blankets.

"No. None at all."

And then he was eating her out as though he was a starving man who hadn't eaten a meal in, well, four years. She gripped the comforter and bucked against his face, close but not quite there. And he would know that, because over the time they'd been together, he'd learned how to read her well, learned how to give her the best oral sex.

Except...what was that move? He definitely hadn't done that before.

It was sort of like... Oh, fuck. She didn't know. It just felt really good.

He lifted his mouth from her, ever so briefly, and parted her folds with his thumbs before diving back down for more.

Her grip on the comforter tightened, and she emitted a tiny squeak.

"Greg..."

He redoubled his efforts, his tongue swiping over her entrance then circling faster over her clit, and when he slipped his finger inside her and curled it, she shrieked in pleasure. She clutched his head through the blankets, holding him against her as she came.

Oh, *God*.

He threw off the blankets and crawled up her body, a crooked grin on his face.

"If you haven't done that in four years," she said, "that's a crime. Your tongue is magnificent."

She could see her moisture on his lips—and all over his chin—and she was glad he'd turned on the bedside lamp.

"Do you want more of my magnificent tongue?" he asked.

"I do believe I would."

She'd barely finished speaking before he dove back between her legs, with single-minded focus on making her feel good. At first, he was gentle, knowing she was sensitive right after she came, but then he was pumping his fingers in and out of her channel as he feasted on her. Her skin felt like it was sparking with energy, and it all coalesced into one big ball that exploded within her.

This time when he slid up her body, he pressed against her, his cock rubbing her slit. She wanted—needed—to feel it inside her; she felt achingly empty without him. She squirmed, but she couldn't move much. He was heavy, and she loved being pinned underneath him.

Now he was feasting on her neck. It felt amazing but...

"Fuck me," she said.

"Gladly."

She was gratified to see his hands shaking as he rolled on the condom. He ran the head of his cock over her entrance a few times before he adjusted himself and began to push inside. She wrapped her legs around his waist and urged him on, bucking her hips up to meet him.

He put his hand on her hip and stilled her.

"Tasha." He hissed out a breath. "Tasha, Tasha. I..."

Unable to say anything coherent, he dipped his head and kissed her as he slid the rest of the way inside. He stayed there for a moment, showering her with open-mouthed kisses, before rocking his hips against hers. It was tender at first, but achingly intense, and despite the mind-blowing oral sex, she'd been unprepared for how good this would feel. How right.

Like it was meant to be.

Taking advantage of the large bed, she tilted her hips to the left, and he rolled himself under her, his hips slamming up to meet hers. After pushing up her sweater, she cupped her breasts in her hands and circled her thumbs over her nipples.

"Yes." His gaze was riveted on her chest. "You're so..." He slammed his hips up again. "Sexy."

That was exactly how she felt.

They moved in tandem before she lowered her chest to his and picked up the pace. He thrust into her and touched his tongue to his finger. When he pressed it against her clit, she came almost immediately. Underneath her, he growled, clutching her against his body as he finished.

～

Well. *Well.*

It had been a long time since Greg Wong had had sex, so it wasn't surprising that it had been explosive, and he'd nearly lost his mind as soon as he slid inside the woman.

But that woman was Tasha Edwards, and he knew it wouldn't have been quite like this with anyone else.

He returned to the bedroom after disposing of the condom and put his clothes back on. Normally, he wouldn't have bothered, but sex didn't change the fact that there was no heat, except for the little provided by his tiny space heater.

He wrapped Tasha in his arms, and she snuggled back against him.

This felt like a luxury. To simply have her in his arms again.

"I missed you," he said suddenly. It was as though having sex with her had cracked something open inside him, something he'd forced closed long ago.

She hesitated. "I missed you, too."

The words hung between them for a long time.

"Look at us," she said after a while. "Snuggling together in a queen-size bed, without having to worry about any parents interrupting us. Without the sound of people funneling beer in the next room. We really are adults."

He smiled against her neck. God, he really had missed her. She'd said the sex didn't mean anything, but it didn't feel that way to him.

She started singing "Jingle Bell Rock," and he wasn't even bothered by the Christmas music. He felt dopey and relaxed, and he was content to lie here with her.

"You once did a strip show for me to 'Jingle Bell Rock,'" he said.

"I did."

All the memories of their relationship were flooding back. He hadn't allowed himself to think of them in years, but they were all there, waiting for him to want to remember.

"Do you have any regrets about us?" he asked when she finished the song. "Like, do you regret having sex when we did? Or staying together until second year? Or—"

"I don't have regrets. It's not a useful way to live life."

He supposed that fit with her optimistic, always-look-to-the-future attitude, but he made a frustrated sound. "People say that, but I think it's impossible not to have regrets."

"I don't have any regrets about you, I promise."

She turned in his arms and faced him.

He did have regrets about the two of them. He regretted that they'd broken up when they did, that they hadn't tried harder to make it work.

And yet, he'd felt like he had to let her go so she was free to experience all the world had to offer. So she could be with guys she hadn't known since kindergarten, guys who wouldn't prefer to stay in their rooms on a Saturday night and watch a documentary, but who would go out to socialize and maybe do stupid things like keg stands.

Tasha stroked her hand down his thighs.

"I'm not nineteen anymore," he said hoarsely. "It'll take more than five minutes before I'm ready for another round."

She laughed quietly, her breath against his neck.

This was definitely not how he'd imagined the day going when he'd woken up this morning. No way had he thought he'd be snowbound in a motel with Tasha, snuggling after a fantastic round of sex. But even though this hadn't been part of his plans, he was happy it had happened. Very happy.

Sure, sometimes she drove him up the wall, but it was easy to be with her, and he didn't often feel at ease with people.

Tasha cuddled closer against him. "I'm definitely all warmed up now."

"So am I."

"You were hot to begin with."

"Why thank you."

After turning off the lamp, he closed his eyes and drifted off to sleep.

[8]

TASHA CRACKED OPEN AN EYE.

The room was no longer completely dark. Light filtered in through the thin curtains and highlighted the fact that yes, this was a crappy motel room.

Her nose felt like an icicle. Still no heat.

Yet she'd awoken with a smile on her face because she'd had pretty great sex last night.

Greg.

OMG. She'd slept with Greg, and it had been fantastic.

What had she been thinking?

She threw back the covers and started to get up, but then Greg opened his eyes and mumbled, "Stay," so she did. It was warm and cozy next to him under the blankets.

Still, she was freaking out.

She'd suggested no-strings-attached, meaningless sex. She had casual sex on occasion to satisfy her needs. Nothing to feel guilty about.

The problem? It hadn't simply been sex.

No, it had been pretty freaking amazing sex.

She'd enjoyed sex with her last two boyfriends, though she'd found herself thinking, *It wasn't as good as it was with Greg.* Then she'd figured she was probably just looking at her first relationship with rose-tinted glasses. It had been more than a decade. The sex hadn't actually been that spectacular, right? After all, they were each other's firsts.

But she'd had sex with Greg last night, and it *was* that spectacular. The best she'd ever had. Maybe even better than it had been fifteen years ago. Someone should give that man's tongue a prize.

The *real* problem wasn't that the sex had been amazing, but that it had felt particularly intimate, and she'd loved it when he held her afterward. Like there was nowhere else she'd rather be than a crappy, cold motel room, as long as he was the one holding her. When he'd admitted he'd missed her, she'd said it back, and it had sent a curl of warmth to her heart. And when she thought about how he'd brought her hot chocolate and a Coffee Crisp, she grinned.

Yep, she had feelings for him.

Maybe they'd never gone away. Or maybe they had and just came back.

It didn't matter. When she looked at his glasses resting on the night-table and his argyle sweater thrown over a chair, she felt a surge of affection.

Oh, no. Did she want to get back together with her ex?

No, she couldn't.

She always looked ahead to new opportunities and experiences. Living in the past just held you back, and there was always a reason an ex was an ex. No need to revisit it.

She'd had sex without feelings before. Why couldn't it have been like that with Greg?

He wrapped his arms around her and nuzzled her neck, and ooh, that felt good. How come everything he did felt so wonderful?

She reminded herself of Crispin, who liked to laugh and respected her boundaries.

Dammit, the bar was so low. That was the problem.

Expecting men not to send you unsolicited dick pics is very reasonable, Greg had said, and she chuckled at the memory.

Really, she didn't understand why he didn't do well with online dating. Compared to all the jerks out there, he was practically a saint.

She sat up.

"What's the rush?" he murmured. "I'll get you home by noon, don't worry. Might as well wait under the covers for now and give them a chance to clear the roads."

His warm mouth pressed against her collarbone, then her neck.

"Look at you." She forced a laugh. "Yesterday, you were so eager to get on the road, pissed that I was twenty-seven minutes late, and now you want to lie in bed and *snuggle.*" She said it with fake disdain.

"Yes, I'm always DTS," he said. "Down to snuggle."

She laughed for real.

Greg had always been a cuddly person, though it seemed counter to his personality. Surely this wasn't just with her, but with other women, too.

She pushed that thought aside. She didn't want to think about his girlfriends.

Though maybe that would help her move on.

"Tasha," he said, serious now. "Do you regret last night?"

"No regrets, like I said." She gave him a peck on the lips and hopped out of bed. "I need a shower. Hopefully there's warm water."

He looked at her for a moment, his face carefully blank. "Okay. I think there's a Tim Hortons nearby. I'll get us some breakfast and see what the roads are like. You still take your coffee the same way?"

She nodded and forced back the tears.

He remembered how she took her coffee. Really, it was nothing.

But he also remembered how she liked to be touched, and so many other things. It was just the way he was. He was careful and kind and remembered little things.

Dear God, how had this happened?

Breakfast sandwiches, coffee, and Timbits.

Simple. He could do this.

Greg stepped out of the motel room and into the bright sunshine reflecting off the snowbanks. He'd have to dig out his car first. That might take a while. Fortunately he had two shovels in the trunk—all part of his winter preparedness kit.

A door creaked, and an older white man walked out of the next room. He looked a little older than Greg's parents, though it was hard to tell as he was wearing a big parka.

Oh, God. This was *Herbie*.

Greg knew what sounds this man made in the bedroom. At least, he knew the tone of voice Herbie used when he said, "Ethel."

This was wrong, so wrong.

And Herbie may well have heard the bed springs creaking in Greg and Tasha's room last night, maybe even some of Tasha's noises. She hadn't been too loud, but the walls were thin.

"Hello, *Greg*," Herbie said with a wink. "Have a good night?"

Well, at least Tasha hadn't called him "Greggie," but it was like finding yourself naked in a classroom. Not, of course, that this had ever happened to Greg, but he'd had dreams—nightmares, really—of that situation.

Someone else may have been able to breezily reply, *Pretty good, Herbie. And you?*

But Greg was not that smooth.

Herbie laughed. "Big storm last night, eh?"

"Yes."

"Me and the wife, we were heading to Hamilton to see our daughter, but we had to get off the 402 during the storm."

Herbie prattled on for a few minutes, and Greg was unable to drag himself out of the conversation. Then a woman stepped outside and linked her arm with Herbie's, and Greg was hit with an unexpected surge of longing.

He wanted to be like them one day. A couple in their seventies, heading out to spend Christmas with their adult children. An older couple who still had very enthusiastic sex. He couldn't look Herbie and Ethel in the eye, but he couldn't help wanting what they had.

With Tasha.

It was impossible to imagine being with anyone but Tasha now.

He mumbled a hasty goodbye, headed to his car, and pulled out a shovel. He shoveled like mad, hoping the physical exertion would drown out his thoughts.

But it didn't.

The crack that had opened within him last night had widened.

He wanted to be with Tasha. Not just for one night in a heat-free motel room. Not just for a few months or years.

He wanted to be with her for always.

Perhaps he'd never stopped loving her; perhaps he'd merely managed to repress those feelings so he could move on with his life, and whenever they'd manage to pop up again, he'd forced them back down, telling himself he was just nostalgic for his teenage years. Once or twice, he'd picked up the phone to call her, then convinced himself he was being silly. Besides, she hadn't bothered to contact him; surely she'd moved on to better things.

But it was now startlingly clear why his other three relationships hadn't worked out. Why he hadn't bothered dating for the past few years.

He'd never been able to imagine far into the future with another woman like he could with Tasha; for him, no one could compare to her. After last night, he knew it wasn't foolish nostalgia. They were good together. They really were. He belonged with her; he knew this with a certainty he'd never had before.

At nineteen, he'd had trouble believing she'd pick him if she could see what else was out there, but now she was thirty-four and still unattached. If she chose him now, after fifteen more years of life experience... Well, that would be different.

There was one big problem, however.

He didn't think she wanted him.

Sure, she'd cuddled up against Greg last night and said she missed him, but this morning, she'd been eager to leave the comfort of the bed and had shown no interest in having sex again.

She'd said she didn't regret it—and maybe she didn't. She'd clearly enjoyed herself. But she didn't seem thrilled about the current situation, and there was no reason to think she'd be interested in anything more. After all, she'd stated, just yesterday, that she didn't believe in second chances for relationships.

Besides, even though she didn't have a husband or boyfriend, she had that Crispin guy, who probably even liked Christmas music.

That asshole.

Half an hour later, Greg finally had his car cleared off, and, with some difficulty, he managed to get it out of the parking lot and down the road to the nearest Tim Hortons. He bought two breakfast sandwiches, a double-double (for Tasha), a black coffee (for him), and a box of ten Timbits.

He was about to head back outside when his phone buzzed.

"Hey, Greg!" Nick said when Greg picked up.

He set down his order on a table and rubbed his forehead. This was just what he needed.

"Why are you calling?" Greg asked.

"Gee, thanks for the warm hello."

"You know I prefer texting."

"I figured this would be more efficient."

"Does everyone in the household want to talk to me again?"

"Yeah, something like that."

Greg grunted in frustration. "I'll be home in a couple hours. You can all bother me then."

"Don't worry. I'm sure that'll happen, too."

Nick got off the phone, and then a different voice said, "So, Greg, did anything happen last night?"

"Mom. Please. I'm starting to worry that you can control the weather, and that's how I ended up trapped in a motel room near Strathroy with my ex-girlfriend, next to two septuagenarians having wild sex."

He didn't know why he added that last part. His brain really wasn't working today.

Mom laughed. "Your grandfather wants to talk to you."

A moment later, Ah Yeh said, "I discovered that you can buy model trees on Amazon. Just the right size for your train set. Should I get cedars or palm trees, or the set of mixed trees? There are dozens of options, actually."

"I have all the model trees I need, thank you," Greg said.

Eventually, he managed to end the call, then took his food and coffee out to the car. He put on CBC Radio, just because there was no one to tell him not to, even though it was only a short drive.

When he returned to the motel, Tasha was dressed in a blue sweater that was slightly more form-fitting than the one she'd worn yesterday. She immediately grabbed the Timbit box and popped one of the donut holes in her mouth.

"Mmmm," she said.

He looked on, horrified.

"What?" she asked.

"I got you a breakfast sandwich, but you're eating dessert first."

"I don't think appetizers, main courses, and desserts apply at breakfast. Breakfast is a free-for-all." She grinned as she dumped two creams and sugars into her coffee.

He had a sip of his own coffee and smiled. He would never eat a donut before his breakfast sandwich—that just wasn't the way he did things—but he appreciated that she didn't follow such rigid rules.

"I'm surprised you bought donuts," she said. "I figured that was too indulgent for you, especially at Christmas. I know there's a ton of dessert at your family's house this time of year."

He shrugged. "You like them. So I got some."

The smile slid off her face and she was back to looking like she had earlier this morning, when she refused to stay burrowed under the covers with him.

"What's wrong?" He yearned to reach out and caress her cheek, but he kept his hands to himself.

"Nothing's wrong," she said brightly, then turned to look out the window.

He studied her profile. She really was the prettiest woman he'd ever known.

He loved the faint wrinkles and stretch marks, the fact that her body wasn't exactly the same as it had been before. She could pass for being younger than thirty-four, but she was a little different from her teenage self, and he liked being able to see that time had passed. She was still *Tasha*, but now she had the career she'd worked so hard for. He'd have to ask her more about her job on the ride back.

She'd also admitted she wanted a relationship, and he wanted to give that to her.

Except she didn't seem keen on being with him for more than a night.

"Did you talk to Crispin this morning?" he asked, unable to keep the edge out of his voice.

"No." She held up a Timbit and changed the topic. "I dare you to eat one of these before your breakfast sandwich."

He grimaced.

"Oh, come on. It's just a donut. Live a little."

It seemed she was bent on torturing him again: she had his least favorite Timbit in her hand.

"Powdered...sugar," he stammered.

Greg hated powdered sugar. It probably had something to do with a little incident that happened when he was three years old. His grandfather—his mother's father, who'd been dead for a dozen years now—had taken him to a bakery in a nearby town, and somehow he'd ended up with a large donut covered in powdered sugar. Not just a little donut hole—no, a full donut. Greg had gleefully bitten into the donut and waved it around in the air...and started crying when the powdered sugar got all over his favorite sweater. Most kids probably wouldn't have been bothered, but Greg had always been concerned with neatness and order, even from a young age, and he'd thrown a temper tantrum in the bakery.

Anyway, he still hated powdered sugar because it was messy. This particular donut, he knew, had jelly inside. That was tasty, but the powdered sugar he could do without.

At the same time, he kind of wanted to eat it now, before his sandwich. Show Tasha that he wasn't a total stick-in-the-mud.

"Alright," she said. "No powdered sugar. Sour cream glazed instead." She held up another Timbit, once that was mercifully less messy. "I dare you to eat one sour cream glazed Timbit before your breakfast sandwich."

Everything in him tensed at the thought of eating dessert first. It went against the rules, and Greg loved the rules.

Though he missed having a little chaos in his life.

His childhood had been too full of chaos. He was the oldest of four, and his parents hadn't exactly run a structured, ordered household. There was always one catastrophe or another, someone shrieking in his ear.

But his life in Toronto had gotten a little boring, to be honest.

"Sour cream glazed is the best one," Tasha said, shaking the Timbit.

"I thought birthday cake was your favorite."

She shrugged. "People change."

Well, yes, and Tasha changing her Timbit preference didn't fundamentally change who she was, whereas him eating a jelly donut covered in powdered sugar, while wearing a pristine argyle sweater, seemed a little more of a stretch.

"Pass me the jelly one," he said.

She raised her eyebrows and handed it over.

Greg held it close to his face. Geez, this was one messy fucker of a donut. Nothing should be dipped in powdered sugar—or cocoa powder, for that matter—and it seemed like this particular donut had an extra-generous amount of powdered sugar.

He was going to eat this. He had to. Somehow, it seemed like eating this little donut symbolized something important.

All in one bite—that was probably the best way to minimize the mess.

He looked down at his sweater, which he didn't want to get dirty before nine in the morning. It was, in fact, his favorite sweater. He wasn't sure whether it was weird for a thirty-four-year-old man to have a favorite sweater, but he did.

And then he had an idea.

TASHA DIDN'T UNDERSTAND what was going on.

Greg was staring at the donut as though it contained the solution to climate change. Then one corner of his mouth quirked up, and his expression changed from thoughtful to mischievous.

She was a sucker for that look.

He put the Timbit down.

Huh? If he wasn't going to accept her challenge to eat a donut before his breakfast sandwich, then why the playful look?

He slid his thumb and finger into his mouth and sucked off the powdered sugar, holding her gaze the whole time, before wiping his hands on his corduroys.

Next, he pulled off his sweater and collared shirt and threw them on the bed.

What on earth was happening? He was going to get hypothermia in this freezing room.

Well, that was a bit of an exaggeration, but...

"You'll be cold," she said.

"For thirty seconds. I'll survive."

She dropped her gaze from his eyes to his chest. He looked

quite nice without a shirt, a light dusting of hair covering his muscled chest. "Are you trying to seduce me again?"

"Again? You're the one who propositioned me last night."

"You kissed me first," she said accusingly.

"After you touched my face."

"If you're not trying to seduce me, why are you half-naked?"

"So I can eat this donut without getting powdered sugar all over my sweater." He spoke as though this was the most sensible thing in the world.

"I offered you a sour cream glazed donut. Why didn't you eat that one?"

"I decided to live dangerously."

And with those un-Greg-like words, he popped the whole Timbit into his mouth.

There was zero mess. He hadn't needed to remove his shirt, not that she didn't appreciate the view.

He wiped his fingers on his chest, right above his nipple. "You want a taste?"

"I thought you weren't trying to seduce me."

"Maybe I changed my mind."

"Nah, doesn't sound like you. I bet this was part of your plan all along."

She couldn't help herself. She leaned forward and swirled her tongue over his nipple. He made a strangled noise in his throat—he'd always had sensitive nipples.

When he kissed her mouth, tasting of sugar and jelly, she dragged him back to bed.

"Holy smokes, it really did snow a lot," Tasha said as they stepped outside. It was like a winter wonderland out here. "Must have taken a while for you to clean off your car. You should have asked me to help."

Greg shrugged. "You were showering. It's no big deal, though it would have been easier had it been drier snow." He picked up a clump of snow in his bare hands, formed a snowball, and tossed it on the ground. "I'll pay for the room, and then—"

"No. We took your car. You bought the gas, plus you provided breakfast and dinner. I'll pay for the room. It's half-price, anyway."

"Very well."

Ten minutes later, they were on their way to Mosquito Bay. The roads weren't great, but at least it wasn't snowing anymore and there were no visibility problems. The sky was a brilliant blue, and Tasha ought to be happy.

She was going home for Christmas. She'd been looking forward to this for weeks. But as she looked out over the snow-covered fields, there was an emptiness inside her.

Their road trip was only supposed to be three hours. Certainly no more than four or five. Instead, they'd had to spend the night in a motel during a snowstorm.

Yet she was sad it was coming to an end. Her time with Greg was almost over.

No more arguing about Christmas music. No more pillow talk when the power was out. No one to bring her a Coffee Crisp and kiss behind her ear and go down on her under the covers.

She shook her head. This was ridiculous.

They were listening to CBC now, and Greg's gaze was firmly on the road—as it should be. She looked at him in profile, his glasses perched on his nose.

God, why did she find him so attractive? There were a few strands of gray at his temples, and those made her smile. Why?

He was stubborn and serious...except when he wasn't, and did silly things like take off his shirt to eat a donut. He was the same Greg he'd been in high school and university...except not quite. He'd grown up. They'd both grown up. And apparently grown-up Tasha was still wildly attracted to Greg Wong.

Being with him didn't *feel* like she was living in the past, but she couldn't start something up with him again.

Or could she? Maybe?

She pulled out her phone and texted Monique. *I slept with him. Twice.*

Tasha! I told you...

I know, I know.

Oh, honey. What were you thinking? Now I don't want to wish bad sex on you, but I kind of hope it was like kissing a frog. Or toad. Or salamander.

Glad you know your amphibians.

I do my best.

The sex was good, Tasha said. *It was more than sex, actually. I might want him back.*

There. She'd admitted it. Now Monique would talk some sense back into her brain.

No!! her friend said. *After Lance, you swore you'd never get back together with an ex, remember? You told me not to get back together with Joey, and I wish I'd listened to you. We broke up for exactly the same reasons the second time. You don't want to make the same mistake twice, like me.*

Tasha didn't consider her long-ago relationship with Greg a mistake; as she'd told him, she had no regrets. But Monique was right. You learned from what happened and moved on. Reuniting with an ex never ended well.

We're going out on New Year's Eve, Monique said, *and we're going to meet cute guys. No assholes or exes. Unless you're still seeing Crispin?*

Oh, Crispin. Tasha couldn't go out with him again. Being with him was nothing like Greg. Greg was wonderful, and the woman who ended up with him would be lucky indeed, but he wasn't for Tasha. She needed to listen to her friend and let this go.

However, as they got closer and closer to Mosquito Bay, she couldn't bear the thought of being separated from him. It was only ten thirty. They could stay together a little longer, couldn't they?

But what could they do?

Ah. She had it. The ground was covered in snow, and it was good packing snow.

She turned to Greg. "Want to build a snow fort?"

Greg hated when people changed their plans on him.

The plan had been to drive back to Mosquito Bay and drop Tasha off at her parents' house, then go home to his obnoxiously loud family.

He wanted to see his family. He did.

He just wasn't in the mood for them right now.

No, he'd do anything to spend more time with Tasha. He was glad she'd suggested a snow fort. It sounded perfect, even if they were too old for this. Building a decent snow fort would take a while.

"Sure," he said. "Let's do it."

When they entered Mosquito Bay, instead of continuing along Main Street, he drove to the park overlooking the water and parked nearby on the street. Then he texted Nick. *Won't be home for a couple more hours. Don't worry. We're safe.*

Then he turned off his phone, expecting an avalanche of texts in response.

"Alright," he said. "Are we going to build a snow fort shaped like an igloo? Or just something with high walls, like the one I made for you in university?"

He couldn't believe he was doing this. Usually if Greg spent so much time with one person, he started to go a little nuts, but he didn't want to be separated from Tasha again.

She'd freaked out this morning, but maybe this snow fort business was a sign that she was changing her mind about him.

He couldn't help but hope.

She smiled at him, and it hit him right in the chest. Goddammit, how had he gone so long without her?

"We won't make it very big," she said, "but tall enough so no one can see inside. It'll be like Rapunzel's tower."

"Why don't you want anyone to see inside?" He waggled his eyebrows.

"Oh, no reason." She was already climbing out of the car, but she winked at him over her shoulder.

For a long time, they worked in silence, starting with the base of their snow tower and building upward. He enjoyed simply being in her presence, doing something with her. It was a bright winter day. Cold, but not frigid, and it didn't bother him at all, as long as he got to be with her, and perhaps make out with her inside the snow fort afterward.

"Greg," Tasha said suddenly, "are you humming 'Winter Wonderland'?"

He realized in horror that he was, indeed, humming a Christmas song.

But he just shrugged and kept on humming.

At long last, their snow fort/tower was ready. Greg grabbed one of the sleeping bags from his car. He threw the sleeping bag into the snow fort first, then crawled in. Tasha followed him and rolled their giant snowball door in front of the entrance.

They were all alone, surrounded by snow.

"It's smaller than the snow fort you made in university," she said. "How long did it take you to build that one, all by yourself?"

"A long time."

Tasha was sitting next to him, both of them with their knees bent, their sides touching—there wasn't much space in here. It was quite cozy.

He wouldn't have it any other way.

He unzipped the sleeping bag and put it over them like a blanket before wrapping his arms around her. Most of her skin was covered by winter clothes, but he kissed her where he could. Her ear, her nose, her temple. He pushed her scarf down and kissed the top of her neck. And with every kiss, he thought, *I love this part of you...and this part...and this part. I love that you drive me crazy. I love that you've accomplished what you set out to do in life. I love that you didn't compromise your dream for me.*

She kissed him, too. His cheek, his nose. Fortunately, he'd already safely stowed his glasses away.

They were in their own little world, blue sky and sunshine above them, and he didn't ever want to leave, even if it was cold. Because as long as they were here, it was just the two of them; the rest of the world didn't matter. As long as they were here, she would be in his arms.

He sucked on her bottom lip, and then they were kissing each other as though their lives depended on it, her mouth so sweet against his; faintly, he could taste the donuts they'd indulged in earlier, and he smiled.

He wanted all kinds of kisses with her. Inside-a-snow-fort kisses. Goodnight kisses. Hello kisses. Goodbye-I'm-leaving-for-work-and-I'll-see-you-this-evening kisses. Please-stop-listening-to-CBC-programming-so-we-can-fuck kisses.

But what if this was all he'd have?

She fumbled with the zipper on his pants, then slipped her hand inside and wrapped her hand around the length of him. Her face was so close to his, watching him. Could she tell how he felt?

She pumped him harder, and he bucked his hips.

He needed to touch her, too.

When he slid his fingers inside her, she was warm and wet for him. Even after all this time, even when they were outside in the snow, she wanted him, and he was in awe of it. He stroked her slowly, the catches in her breath magnified in the little snow tower.

"How are we going to do this?" she asked.

"How are we going to fuck, you mean."

"Yeah." She giggled. "I love when you say that word."

"Do you? I can use it more often." He paused. "I think *fucking* would work best with you on my lap."

She pushed her pants and underwear down to her knees. It wouldn't be possible to get them any further off. Plus, it was cold.

But they had each other's body heat.

He rolled on the condom he'd stashed in his pocket, and she lifted herself up on her knees and lined up the tip of his cock with her entrance. Slowly, she sank down on him, and he tipped his head back and groaned.

Christ, she felt amazing.

He opened his eyes, and her face was right above his. Her lips parted in pleasure as she began to move.

Even if she walked away when this was over, he'd always feel inextricably linked to her.

He'd always belong to her.

He kissed her as she sank down on his cock again and again, her arms wrapped around him, her mitten-covered hands on the back of his neck. There was too much clothing for his liking, but still, they were together.

He took off his glove, licked his finger, and circled it over her clit. Their breaths came faster and faster. When she shattered, he held her tight and he pumped into her a few more times, finding his own release inside her.

They hadn't talked on the walk back to his car, and they hadn't talked during the short drive to her family's house.

Now, they were sitting in the driveway, their time together coming to a close.

"Tasha," he said, "I had a good time with you these past twenty-three hours and six minutes. Would you..." He swallowed. He couldn't manage to say everything he felt, everything he wanted, so he went with, "Would you want to see me again while we're both in town for the holidays? Go out for coffee and Timbits at Tim Hortons, perhaps?"

She met his gaze before looking down.

"Maybe," she said at last.

It wasn't a no, but not quite what he'd hoped for. Even as he felt a heaviness in his chest, he couldn't help wanting to make her smile. "You know who I met when I left the motel room to go to Tim Hortons? Herbie."

To his delight, she did smile.

"He called me by my name," Greg continued, "without me introducing myself."

She kissed him one more time, and then she left.

"Tasha!" Her mother threw her arms around her the minute she stepped in the door. "You're finally here."

"It's so good to see you, Mom."

Tasha tried to sound upbeat. After all, she really was happy to see her mother. It had been more than two months, though they talked on the phone several times a week.

When Tasha was younger, people had often commented on her resemblance to her father, but as she got older, she looked more and more like her mother—the shape of her features, the warm undertones in her skin. Her wide smile.

"You look like you're freezing," Mom said. "Did that boy's car not have any heat?"

"Oh, there was heat," Tasha said.

Mom raised her eyebrows.

Tasha shrugged. "I'm going to make hot chocolate. You want some?"

They sat by the fire, drank their hot chocolate, and caught up on what had happened—well, some of it. But Tasha couldn't help feeling cold on the inside, and there was nothing she could do about it, no matter how many hot beverages she drank.

Maybe having sex in a snow fort wasn't such a great idea after all.

"Where's Dad?" she asked.

"He's at Lawrence's, trying to fix their car."

Tasha had two older brothers, her father's sons from his first marriage. Her parents had met when they were in their mid-thirties, both of them divorced. Her mother's first marriage had been to her high school sweetheart, who'd discouraged her from trying to go to med school like she'd wanted. Instead, she'd become a nurse, which he'd considered a more suitable career for his wife.

That was why her mother never wanted Tasha to compromise her dreams for a man. Why she'd been worried about Tasha having a serious relationship in high school, although she hadn't forbidden her from dating.

"We had a good time together, Greg and I," Tasha ventured at last.

"Did you, now. What, exactly, did you do?"

Tasha looked down at her nearly-empty mug and tried to hide her smile. "He wants to see me again while we're both in Mosquito Bay for the holidays."

"And you said?"

"Maybe."

"Hmm."

It was irritating when her mom did that.

"What?" Tasha asked.

"If you had a good time together," Mom said slowly, "then why don't you know if you want to see him again?"

"Because he's my ex! It ended once before."

Mom didn't say anything, just sipped her hot chocolate.

"I'm thirty-four," Tasha said. "I don't want to waste time on having a little fun. I'd like to settle down."

She thought she'd have someone by now. Instead, people would kindly pat her on the back and tell her that she'd find a man soon enough. They might also tell her to lower her expectations. Or try harder.

And she wanted to tear her hair out in frustration. Had these people seen what the dating market was like? Even finding a half-decent guy seemed like a miracle, never mind someone who gave her a spark.

Which she had with Greg. Oh, she definitely did.

"You think I should give him another chance?" she asked.

"It doesn't matter what I want," Mom said. "It's what you want."

Tasha groaned, and her mom laughed.

"We fight all the time," Tasha said.

"But do you really?"

"Well…" She supposed her mom had a point. They hadn't fought about the big things, the important things. They bantered about stupid shit like Christmas carols. And all couples fought sometimes—even her parents. There was nothing wrong with that. "But I can't get back together with an ex. Everyone knows that doesn't turn out well, and it was a disaster for me and Lance. Why should I think this is different?"

"Why did you and Greg break up the first time?"

"Because we were going to different schools and drifting apart. I also didn't like the idea of having only been with one guy, you know? I was nineteen, and I thought I should get more experience."

"But all of that's changed now. You have jobs in the same city."

"Still, I can't help thinking that if it was meant to be, we would have figured it out the first time."

Though it was nothing like Monique and Joey. He'd screwed up, she'd broken up with him. Then later she forgave him and let him have another chance, and he'd screwed up again. It was a similar story with Tasha and Lance. She'd needed him to change, and he hadn't.

Greg had changed a little over the years, but he was still basically the same—and in his case, that was good. He'd always treated her well.

Tasha shoved her hands into her hair. "I don't know."

"I don't, either," Mom said, "but you shouldn't refuse to consider him just because second chances have failed in the past."

Perhaps her mother had a point.

A lot of things had worked out well for Tasha. She loved her career now. The work environment at her previous job hadn't been ideal, but she was happy with her current job, and she had good friends in Toronto.

Everything had worked out except her love life.

She didn't let herself have regrets. Look forward, never back. That was how she lived. Part of the reason for this was that after her break-up with Greg, she'd wallowed for several weeks, replaying all of their time together in her head, wondering if they'd done the right thing. Then she'd picked herself up and moved on with her life, and she'd started to feel more like herself again.

Still, she'd thought of Greg over the years. In fact, she'd found herself thinking, *It wasn't as good as it was with Greg* many times—and not just about sex. And every time, she'd assumed she was wrong.

But now, they'd spent almost twenty-four hours together. Now, she knew she hadn't been kidding herself.

It really was good with Greg.

She'd told herself they were too different, they weren't compatible. And yes, they were opposites in some ways, but saying they weren't compatible would be a lie. A lie that she'd told herself so she could move on.

But maybe, in this case, looking to the past was the best way forward.

~

As soon as Greg opened the door to his childhood home, everyone descended on him.

"What took you so long?" Nick asked. "Were you off making out somewhere?"

"So, how'd it go, lover boy?" That was Zach. "Did you have a good time getting trapped in that snowstorm?"

"I made the snowstorm happen!" Ah Ma said. "I have magic powers!"

Dad rolled his eyes. "Ma, surely if you had magic powers you would use some of them to improve your cooking."

She sniffed. "They are very *specific* magic powers. For love."

"Greg," Mom said, "why didn't you bring Tasha here for a little visit?"

"She wanted to see her family."

Perhaps he spoke a little irritably. Everyone was giving him funny looks now.

"You know," Nick said, putting one arm around Lily's shoulder, "I'm an expert at relationships now. If you need any advice, just ask."

"A two-and-a-half-month relationship does not make you an expert," Zach said.

"I have been married over sixty years!" Ah Ma raised her hand in the air. "I am the true expert. Plus, I have magic powers. Please, tell your ah ma what happened." She gestured to her ear. "You can tell me, no one else. I will keep your secret!"

"You are terrible at keeping secrets," Dad said. "What about the time—"

"Enough," Greg howled, and everyone stared at him, not used to hearing him speak so loudly. "I asked if I could see her again, she said maybe, end of story. Now, please leave me alone."

"I'll heat up some food for you," Mom said.

Finally, a suggestion he actually liked.

He spent ten minutes eating his grandfather's famous noodles while his family jabbered around him. Normally, he would enjoy his food—Ah Yeh's noodles were delicious. But right now, he just wanted to take off his sweater and eat another donut covered in powdered sugar.

Jesus. He really was losing it.

Afterward, he stalked upstairs to his childhood bedroom and closed the door. There wasn't much in his old room. Just the furniture remained. All the *stuff* had been cleared out long ago.

Except for one red gift box in the bottom drawer of the dresser.

He pulled it out and sat down on his bed as he looked at the contents.

For Valentine's Day in their final year of high school, Tasha had gotten him a box of valentines. Not just one or two—no, she'd gotten him fifty valentines, all with handwritten messages. It must have taken her ages.

He couldn't bear to throw them out, but he hadn't wanted them with him in Toronto. So he kept them here.

It had been many years since he'd looked at them, but now he took them out, one at a time. There was a *Lady and the Tramp* valentine, another with a cute puffin, one with a terrible chemistry joke.

"Whatcha doing?" Nick asked, waltzing into the room without knocking.

A man couldn't get a minute's peace around here, could he?

"Nothing," Greg muttered, shoving the box under the quilt.

"Sure doesn't look like nothing."

"Things Tasha gave me in high school, that's all. None of your business."

"Fine, fine. I won't pry into your life."

That didn't sound like his family.

He waited for Nick to try to grab the box, but it didn't happen.

"I was jealous of you in high school," Nick said.

Greg snorted. "You? Jealous of me?"

"Yeah, why not? You weren't cool—"

"Gee, thanks," Greg muttered, but Nick's words were just a statement of fact. He had never been cool, not one bit.

"—but you didn't care what anyone else thought, and you had a girlfriend."

"Did you have a crush on Tasha?"

"Nah, I was just envious that you got a girl's attention."

Right. It was hard to remember that back in the day, Nick hadn't been popular. High school was so long ago now.

Greg and Tasha…also so long ago.

But he didn't want to be with her simply because he had fond memories of the past. They'd spent time together as adults now, and he'd enjoyed every minute of it, even when she'd insisted on singing "The Twelve Days of Christmas."

"You slept with her, didn't you?" Nick pulled up a chair and sat on it backward.

Greg grunted.

"I'll take that as a yes."

"Why don't you take it as a none-of-your-business?"

Just then, the door opened again, and their father stepped into the room.

"If you want to have a party," Greg muttered, "could you please do it somewhere else?"

"He's moping over Tasha," Nick said.

"That's what I figured." Dad took a seat on the bed next to Greg. "I liked you and Tasha together. You complemented each other. I thought you'd be like me and your mom."

Greg grunted again.

"You know," Dad said, "we didn't date continuously from the time we started going out in grade eleven. At one point, we took a break for several months."

Greg had to admit he was a little intrigued by this.

"We were eighteen," Dad continued. "Not quite sure what we wanted. There was another guy who was interested in her…

Anyway, that didn't last. I'm just saying, when you fall in love when you're so young and you don't really know yourself yet, it can be tricky. I still think it could work out for you."

"Hmm."

"Sometimes it's useful to speak actual words," Nick said.

"I can't think clearly while I'm talking."

Nick and Dad were quiet for a minute. It was still difficult for Greg to think properly when he wasn't alone, but yes, he did want to see Tasha again. Desperately. He loved her; he loved who she'd become.

"So tell me what happened," Nick said, breaking the silence. "The weekend went well, and you casually asked if you could see her again, maybe meet up for coffee?"

"That's right," Greg said. "She said no."

"Not that there's anything wrong with what you did—"

"Glad it meets your approval."

"—but you aren't the most eloquent person," Nick finished. "Maybe you need to really show her how you feel. Not sexually, though."

"Thanks for the clarification."

"Like, show her that you don't just want to grab coffee together, but you want more. Because you do, right?"

"Yeah." So much more.

"And, like, you're both getting old. I mean, you're thirty-four—"

"I know how old I am."

"And she's probably looking to settle down, maybe have kids. It's different from when you were teenagers."

Zach walked into the room. "What are we talking about?"

"Trying to find something nice for Greg to do for Tasha."

"Excellent. Maybe you could set up a special model train for her. Like, make it go through a love forest. Or love mountain."

"Um," Greg said.

Tasha would probably think it was cute, but it would take far too much time to get all the materials and set it up. He needed a better idea.

She'd said she didn't believe in second chances for relationships, but he had to try one last time. Tell her how he truly felt. Put it all out there.

"What about a really big cookie?" Nick suggested.

"That's your genius idea? Just one big cookie?"

"Everyone loves cookies. You baked a few times for Tasha, I remember."

"You could go birdwatching together," Zach said, "and, uh, find a really great bird for her. Or put up a banner under the sign for Mosquito Bay."

"No," Nick said. "Too public. He won't go for that."

Mom and Amber entered the room.

"What are we doing?" Mom asked.

Greg pinched his forehead in frustration, then walked over to the window and looked outside. The blue sky and sunshine were gone. Instead, it was overcast, and it looked like it could possibly snow again—and more snow was just what they needed.

Though he had an odd affection for snowstorms now, having been trapped in one with Tasha Edwards.

All that snow gave him an idea.

"I know what to do," he said, turning to his family, "but I'm going to need some help."

Everyone nodded.

His family drove him batshit crazy, but he could always count on them.

"Okay, here's the plan."

~

It was almost midnight. Tasha's parents had gone to bed.

As a child, she'd bounced with excitement on Christmas Eve, looking forward to Santa Claus's arrival and wishing for the best presents. She'd always tried to stay up late so she could see Santa and his reindeer, but she'd never made it.

Now, she was holding the gold necklace that she'd stashed in her ballerina jewelry box many years before. There was no other jewelry in the box, just the necklace.

The one that had made Greg hate Christmas music.

For two years, she'd worn it every day. She would squeeze her fist around it when she suddenly, inexplicably, felt a wave of longing for him during a lecture or lab.

Just like the way she longed for him now.

She wrapped her hand around the pendant and made her Christmas wish.

ON CHRISTMAS MORNING, Tasha was eating pancakes with maple syrup and drinking her second cup of coffee when there was a knock at the door.

"I'll get it." Her father started to stand, but he wasn't as spry as he'd once been.

"No, I will." Tasha jumped up, hoping it was Greg.

But it wasn't.

The man looked a bit like Greg, but he was a couple inches shorter and wasn't wearing glasses. Plus, his smile was all wrong.

"Nick?" Tasha said. She hadn't seen him in years.

"Hey, Tasha."

Why was Nick on the doorstep?

"Is something the matter?" Her words came out in a rush.

"No, everything's fine. I just have something to show you. Can you come with me now? Or if you want to spend Christmas morning with your family..." He peeked inside and waved at her parents.

"I'll go."

She gulped down the rest of her coffee, hugged her mom and dad, put on her winter clothes, and headed outside with Nick. It was a nice morning, like it had been yesterday. Partly sunny with some clouds in the sky. Not much wind coming off the lake.

Nick led her down Main Street, where the lampposts were decorated with wreaths, then down another street, toward Lake Huron.

Compared to Toronto, it was a tiny speck of a town. Neither of her parents were from Mosquito Bay, but it was in between her father's old auto shop and the hospital where her mom had worked. It was also not far from where her father's ex-wife had lived, so it was easy for him to see his sons.

Tasha hadn't minded growing up here, though she hadn't looked like most of the other kids. But she preferred her life in Toronto, only coming back to visit her family.

"Where are we going?" she asked Nick, hugging her arms around herself.

"Almost there," he said.

She refused to hope too much, but she had a feeling...

They entered the park where she and Greg had made the snow fort yesterday. There were a bunch of kids sledding on the hill, a few kids making a snowman, and some people standing around, looking at—

What on earth?

Their little snow tower was now part of the most magnificent snow fort she'd ever seen. It was like a castle.

Her gloved hand came up to her face. "He did this for me? How long did it take?"

"Oh, he didn't do it all himself. He had help. We spent most of yesterday outside. My whole family, aside from my grandparents. It's Greg's design, and we had to listen to him be a control freak all day." Nick was smiling, though. They kept walking toward the snow fort, until they reached a little doorway, not tall enough to walk through. "Go inside and turn right."

She gave Nick a hug, then did as he said. She got down on her hands and knees and crawled into the snow fort. The short entryway was covered, but other than that, there was no roof. The walls to the right were at least six feet tall, though. She continued crawling, her heart beating rapidly, and when she turned the corner, she saw Greg.

He was sitting on a sleeping bag, and there was a little picnic basket next to him. In the snow fort he'd built just for her.

"Come here," he said.

When she knelt beside him, he pulled a thermos out of the basket and poured her some hot chocolate. The steam curled in the cold air.

"I have something to tell you," he said, "if you'd like to listen, that is."

She nodded.

He looked very serious, despite the fact that he was wearing a red down jacket and gray toque and sitting in a snow fort. He opened a tin of homemade chocolate chip cookies and handed one to her.

She took a bite. It was delicious.

"I..." He took off his glasses and scrubbed a hand over his face. "Okay. Here it goes." But he didn't say anything more. He seemed to be quietly freaking out.

He pulled a sheet of paper out of his pocket. Had he written a speech?

Something swelled in her chest, and she smiled at him encouragingly.

"I want to clarify what I said yesterday," he said, tucking away the paper. "I asked if I could see you again while we were both here for the holidays, but you should know that I want a lot more than that. We only had twenty-three hours and six minutes together, after fifteen years of hardly seeing each other, but it was enough. Enough to remember all the things I love about you. Enough to learn how you've changed, and how you haven't. I want to know every detail of the life you've created, Tasha, and I want to be a part of it. I want another chance at a relationship.

I'm not just a kid anymore, and..." His voice turned hoarse. "I'm serious about you. I do want to get married and have children together and all that stuff we used to talk vaguely about when we were nineteen. It's easy for me to picture us being together when we're as old as Ethel and Herbie."

She couldn't help a small smile.

She could picture it, too.

"On one hand," he said, "I'm angry we wasted so much time apart, but maybe it was necessary for me to be sure of who I am and what I want. We were quite young when we dated, after all." He paused. "I hope you feel the same way, but if not, I understand."

Two nights ago, she'd told Greg that she wanted to just *know* she had the right guy.

And now, she did.

He was the one for her.

That had been her Christmas wish: to figure out if she loved Greg in a way that would last. Her thoughts about second chances had been changing since her talk with her mother yesterday, but now...

Tasha was overwhelmed by her feelings. They had returned in full force, stronger than before, with a decade and a half of experience behind them. There was no way this could be wrong, not when it felt so perfect.

She set down her hot chocolate on a flat patch of snow, then reached into her jacket and held up the necklace she was wearing. For a moment, she simply looked at him and smiled. It felt like she was smiling from every inch of her body.

"I feel the same way," she said. "You know, I once got back together with an ex, and it didn't go well—we still had the same problems as before. I swore I'd never do it again. A couple of my friends got back together with their exes, too, and those relationships didn't work out, either. That's why I was reluctant to start anything with you. But it's different for you and me—I don't think it's foolish to say that. Before, we weren't quite in the right place in our lives for each other, but that's changed, plus we know ourselves better than we did as teenagers. I'm positive we can deal with any challenges that come our way. When I..." Now it was her turn to have trouble getting the words out. It had been many years since she'd said these words to a man. To her family, sure, but this wasn't the same.

So many years of wondering whether she'd ever meet the right guy, and it turned out she'd known him since kindergarten.

"When I was younger, I couldn't appreciate how special and rare this is, but I do now. I love you, Greg."

His arms came around her. "I love you, too."

There was a frustrating amount of fabric between them. Unfortunately, it was necessary, given the freezing temperature, but she was still glad he'd done this here. In a snow castle.

If someone had told her last week that on Christmas morning, she'd be romanced by Greg Wong in a snow castle, she wouldn't have believed them.

She pressed her lips to his. Unlike their very first kiss, in this very same park, she now knew what she was doing. She'd kissed many men in the intervening years, and that didn't make this mean less; it made her more certain that he was the right man. She'd truly never felt like this with anyone else.

His mouth moved over hers, urgent and firm, and she kissed him back with equal fervor, trying to get as close to him as she could with all their winter clothes in the way.

She'd never expected her future to involve embracing the past.

But she couldn't be happier.

"I'm glad I was twenty-seven minutes late on Monday," she said. "If I'd been on time, it might have all happened differently. Maybe we wouldn't have needed to spend the night in a cold motel room." She paused. "No regrets."

No regrets about the past couple days. No regrets about

walking away from each other all those years before—she wouldn't let herself think about the what-ifs, only look forward to their future together. Perhaps Greg was right: they'd needed that time apart.

She kissed him again. So simple—her lips and tongue moving over his, but it was exquisite. She would get to do this again...and again...and again, and that filled her with warmth.

"I'm planning to stay in Mosquito Bay until the twenty-eighth," Greg said, "since I have more than a week off. Will you let me drive you back to Toronto? You can play all the Christmas music you like."

"No, I won't torture you like that. We can listen to CBC Radio for half the trip. Hopefully, we won't get stuck in a snowstorm this time, and when we get to your condo—"

"Perhaps I could ask you to watch Netflix and chill?"

She couldn't contain her laughter.

It was Christmas, and she was in love, and she was so full of joy.

"Or I could ask you to come upstairs and see my model train?" he suggested.

"I *would* like to see it. I'm curious." She picked up her hot chocolate and had a sip. "I'll come upstairs, see your model train, then head home on the subway."

"That's a terrible plan."

"Or maybe I could stick around for half an hour and you could make me a cup of tea."

"I suppose."

"Or you could bend me over the table where you keep your model train—"

"I don't like that idea at all," he said.

"Why not?"

"I don't want anything to happen to it, and surely you would mess it up. You have a tendency to, ah, move around quite a bit when you come. Better to bend you over the couch or the kitchen counter."

"I can accept those alternatives." She winked at him, then reached for another chocolate chip cookie. It was the best cookie she'd ever tasted.

"Greg!" someone shouted from outside the fort. "What is happening in there? Did you make up and kiss?"

Tasha assumed that was his grandma.

"Yeah, can we go home now?" That was probably Amber, Greg's younger sister, who'd been in elementary school fifteen years ago, but she'd be grown up now, too.

"Have you guys been standing out there the whole time?" Greg asked, but probably not loud enough for his family to hear.

"We're all good!" Tasha shouted. "You can leave now, thank you!"

There was round of applause, as though more people than just Greg's family had been standing around the snow fort, and Greg ducked his head in embarrassment.

"Dear God," he muttered.

"I just want everyone to know that I made this happen," Greg's mom said. "I'm taking full credit for this match."

"I spent hours out here yesterday freezing my ass off and listening to Greg boss me around." This must be Zach. "I want some credit, too."

"Same here," Nick said.

"Alright, we hear you," Greg said, loudly this time. "Now you can leave us in peace. I'll see you at dinner."

There were sounds of boots crunching through the snow, and then it was quiet once more. A red cardinal chirped from a nearby tree. Tasha might not know as much about birds as Greg, but she could identify a few.

"I'm having Christmas dinner with my family," he said, "and I'm sure you have plans with yours. But I still have a little time before then."

"Hmm. What could we possibly do with all that time? I have no idea."

"Don't you?" he murmured as he set aside her hot chocolate and gestured her inside the sleeping bags. He'd zipped two together.

Ooh, this was cozy.

He slid a camping pillow under her head. He was prepared for everything. Then he shed his winter jacket and climbed into the sleeping bags with her. His leg brushed against hers, and that nearly made her breathless.

"Who knew that being thirty-four would means lots of sex in a snow fort?" she said.

"Oh, are we having sex? I thought we were going to snuggle."

"We'll snuggle afterward."

And that's exactly what they did.

At ten o'clock that night, Tasha was cuddled up with Greg on the couch in her parents' living room. Greg had come over after dinner, figuring her parents' house would be quieter than his, now that her brothers and their families had left. As fun as the snow fort had been, it was nice to have some time together indoors.

Tasha had texted Monique earlier, and Monique, though she grudgingly admitted the photos of the snow fort were impressive, was aghast that Tasha was getting back together with her ex. Tasha was confident she'd made the right choice, though, and she was also confident Greg would win her friend over soon enough.

Greg clasped Tasha's hand, and their iron rings—which they both wore because they were engineers—rubbed against each other.

He lifted a gift box out of a bag he'd brought with him.

"Is that what I think it is?" she asked, one hand coming to her mouth.

He nodded. "You kept your necklace, and I kept these."

She'd been such a romantic that for their first Valentine's Day together, she'd given him an entire box of valentines.

He opened the box, and she picked up the first one, a heart that said, *Will you be my valentine?*

She smiled and set it down. "Will you be mine for Christmas, Greg?"

"There's nothing I want more."

GREG WOKE up to someone sliding her hands over his chest, and he smiled. He loved waking up next to Tasha.

It was January 25, one month since Christmas, one month since he'd declared his feelings for her in a snow fort in Mosquito Bay. The snow fort had started to melt when the weather warmed up a few days later, but their relationship was a different matter.

"Good morning," she murmured. "When do we have to leave?"

It was Chinese New Year today, and they were going back to Mosquito Bay to have dinner with his family. Tomorrow, they would visit hers.

He checked the clock. It was eight.

"No rush," he said. "Although if it takes as long to get there as last time, we won't make it for dinner tonight."

"True, but I don't think there's any danger of that."

Yes, since there was no snow in the forecast, their drive should be fine.

The past month had been wonderful. Familiar and new all at the same time. They frequently spent the night together, and waking up with her never got old.

They were planning to move in together soon. Likely, she would move into his place, and then they would look at buying a house, hopefully by next Christmas.

They were making plans for their future together, and he loved it.

When her hand slipped under his shirt, he grunted. A grunt of pleasure—as Tasha would know. Perhaps they could stay in bed a little longer before they got on with their day.

"Zach's bringing a girlfriend," he said. "Did I tell you?"

"No. I didn't know he was seeing anyone."

"I didn't either, until yesterday. It's lucky for him, though. My family had talked about setting him up again. Actually…"

Now that Greg thought about it, perhaps Zach didn't have a girlfriend and had just convinced a woman to come as his date so his parents wouldn't set him up with anyone. Perhaps this was a *fake* girlfriend.

Greg considered the possibility for a minute, then dismissed it.

No, a fake girlfriend for Chinese New Year seemed a bit extreme. His imagination must be running away with itself again.

He turned over so he was facing Tasha and grinned.

Usually, he hated it when people changed their plans on him, but rekindling his relationship with Tasha hadn't been in the plans, and he was very glad it had happened.

Now, his plan was to be with her for always.

And maybe have a little fun in this warm, queen-size bed before they got on the road.

A FAKE GIRLFRIEND FOR CHINESE NEW YEAR

BOOK 3

MEET ZACH & JO…

After his family's matchmaking extravaganza at Thanksgiving, high school teacher Zach Wong is terrified of what his parents might do for Chinese New Year. Surely they'll try to set him up yet again, especially now that his older brothers are in relationships. Zach, however, has no interest in dating, not since his fiancée left him.

The solution? Find a fake girlfriend to avoid his parents' matchmaking.

Jo MacGregor, the town dentist, is the obvious choice. They both live in Mosquito Bay and have been friends for years, ever since they bonded over broken engagements. A few kisses and dates around town, and everyone will believe they're in a relationship. No problem.

Except their fake relationship is starting to feel more and more real…

BOUQUET OF FLOWERS IN HAND, Zach Wong exited the grocery store and headed down Main Street. It was a crisp winter day in early January. The sun had shone brightly earlier, but now it was dusk and there was a cool wind off Lake Huron.

He passed the doctor's office, the dentist's office, and the pottery shop, which inexplicably had survived for a decade despite the lack of tourism in the sleepy lakeside town called Mosquito Bay. Next, there was the elementary school, the diner, the bakery, and two units that had been vacant for nearly a year.

A few people were coming out of the Tim Hortons as he walked by.

"Zach! Haven't seen you in a while." Al, a bartender at Finn's, slapped him on the back.

Zach's brothers didn't want to live in Mosquito Bay, didn't enjoy being in a community where everyone knew each other and there was only one bar, but Zach liked it here.

"I guess it's been longer than usual," Zach said. "You weren't working last Friday, right? How's the family up in Owen Sound?"

"They're doing well. My old man broke his arm, though. Fell

off a ladder when he was putting up Christmas lights." Al nodded at the flowers. "Who's the lucky lady?"

Zach just smiled and shrugged.

He talked to Al for a couple minutes, then walked onward, passing Wong's Wok, the restaurant his grandparents had run for decades. A typical small-town Chinese-Canadian restaurant. The new owners weren't named Wong, but they'd kept the name, not wanting to replace the sign. There was a sheet of paper in the window that said, "Now serving pad Thai." That was new, too. There had been no pad Thai back in his grandparents' day.

Finn's was next door. Like Wong's Wok, there was no one named Finn there anymore, but the name had endured.

Zach turned off Main Street and walked by Great Lakes Bed and Breakfast. It was another five minutes before he reached his destination. Though the front door was never locked, he rang the doorbell anyway. His mother answered.

"For you," he said, handing her the bouquet as he stepped inside.

"How lovely!" Mom enveloped him in a hug. "Thanks, Zach."

"Where are my flowers?" Ah Ma, his grandmother, asked as she shuffled into the hall. "Ah, I see. They are mums for your *mum*. It is not fair that there are no flowers called ahmas. They would be a bestseller! The biggest tropical flowers. Bright pink."

"No, they'd be poisonous," Ah Yeh said, coming up behind her. "Just like your cooking."

He stepped to the side as his wife attempted to swat him.

"My cooking isn't poisonous!" Ah Ma said.

"You gave me food poisoning."

"One time, forty years ago. You are always holding that over my head."

She tried to swat Ah Yeh again, but he moved out of the way. They chased each other around the house, though it was hardly at a fast speed, as they were both close to ninety. It was more like watching two tortoises run a race.

Zach chuckled. He enjoyed being able to see his family at least once a week. His brothers, Greg and Nick, lived in Toronto and he usually only saw them at holidays. Amber, his little sister, had moved to Stratford, which was an hour away. But Zach had stayed. Well, he'd gone away for university, but he'd come back after finishing teacher's college.

"Stop it!" Dad entered the front hall. He looked at his parents and shook his head. "One of you will fall and break a hip, and that's the last thing we need."

"No, I am strong. Big muscles." Ah Ma stopped chasing her husband and attempted to flex her arm.

Dad snorted, as did Ah Yeh.

"Dinner is almost ready," Mom said. "How about you put the flowers in the vase and set the table, Zach?"

Ten minutes later, he was digging into his roast chicken, potatoes, and green beans. Sunday night dinners with his family had become a tradition in the past few years. He and his grandparents would go to his parents' house, and his mom and dad would cook. Occasionally Amber came, too.

"So, what did you do for New Year's?" Mom asked.

"Did you kiss anyone at midnight?" Ah Ma made smooching noises. "Did you go to any big parties?"

"I was at Finn's," Zach said. "Nothing exciting."

"You didn't answer my first question," Ah Ma complained.

He laughed. "No, I didn't kiss anyone."

Ah Ma shook her head. "Greg and Nick have girlfriends now. But *you*." She pointed her finger at him as though accusing him of a heinous crime. "You have not dated since Marianne, right? I keep my ears open. Nobody has said anything about you dating. We set you up with Diana, and that did not go well, but we—I mean *you*—can try again!"

Zach felt a ball of tension in his stomach as he recalled Thanksgiving. His family had decided that since Zach, Nick,

Greg, and Amber were all single, it would be a great idea to set them all up on blind dates.

Although Zach's wasn't exactly a blind date, was it? He'd known Diana since childhood. Their families were friends, and Zach had been particularly good friends with Diana's older brother, Sebastian.

Regardless, it had not gone well, though Nick had made out with Greg's date and they were still together. At Christmas, Greg had convinced the family to help him make a snow fort for his high school girlfriend, and now they were a couple again, too.

Zach was happy for his brothers. If that's what they wanted, it was great.

But Zach had been in love once, and it hadn't ended well. In fact, it had ended with a diamond ring getting tossed in his face.

So, no, thank you. He wasn't interested in going through that again. Why keep doing something that brought you pain?

He'd spent many long nights at the bar, not drinking himself into oblivion, but simply because he wanted to be somewhere other than the house he'd rented with Marianne.

The one bright spot in all those late nights at Finn's?

He'd become good friends with Jo.

His engagement had ended more than four years ago, but Zach remembered exactly what it had been like. He didn't need a repeat.

His family, however, seemed keen on him being in a relationship. There had been Thanksgiving's matchmaking extravaganza, and many comments since. *Oh, do you know Lizzy, who works at Tim Hortons? She's Magda's daughter, and I thought we could set you up... Wasn't Lizzy cute in her corn-cob costume at the harvest festival?*

And now, the mention of New Year's reminded him of the next big family dinner.

Chinese New Year.

Would his family try to set him up with another woman? Unfortunately, the odds seemed good. True, there were no matchmaking efforts at Christmas for Zach, but he had a feeling they were biding their time and the next family holiday would involve unwanted matchmaking for him and possibly Amber.

"What is going on, Zach?" Ah Ma asked. "You are deep in thought. It is not like you. You are acting like Greg."

"Oh, nothing," he said. "Just trying to prepare myself for work tomorrow."

He shared pleasant conversation with his family and listened to Ah Yeh describe his latest finds on Amazon.

But once dinner was over and he was walking home, he started thinking about Chinese New Year again. He couldn't bear more matchmaking with his mother's bridge partner's cousin's daughter, or the corn-cob costume lady who worked at Tim Hortons. He was happy with his life as it was. He enjoyed his job as a high school science teacher. He had lots of friends. He played in a hockey league on Monday nights. He had his family.

No, it wasn't the exciting life that Marianne had wanted, but he liked it. He didn't need a replacement for his ex-fiancée.

He did, however, need to take preventative measures to ensure he didn't have to suffer through more matchmaking at the next family holiday. Thanksgiving had been a shit show.

What would dissuade his family?

Well, the most effective thing would be if he already had a girlfriend. His family wouldn't set him up with anyone then. He didn't want a real girlfriend, but maybe he could get a fake girlfriend?

He wasn't sure where the idea had come from, but once it popped into his mind, it wouldn't leave.

A fake girlfriend would be the perfect solution to his problem. He'd bring a woman to dinner on Chinese New Year—a woman of his choosing who knew the whole thing was an act.

Zach had a bunch of female friends, but most of them were married or in relationships.

However, there was one woman who would play the role perfectly.

~

"What would you like?" Dr. Jo MacGregor asked. "An elephant, a horse, or a dog?"

"A dog!" Six-year-old Savannah bounced in the dentist chair.

"A pink one or a yellow one?"

"Yellow!"

Jo pumped air into the yellow balloon then twisted it into the shape of a dog. She handed it to the little girl.

Savannah frowned. "It's just like the horse you made me last time."

"Savannah!" said the girl's mother, Kyla. "What do you say when someone gives you something?"

"Thank you," Savannah said with a world-weary sigh.

The girl was right. Jo's dog was identical to her horse, but nobody had complained. Until today.

Jo suppressed a laugh.

Fortunately, she was a better dentist than balloon animal artist, but usually the kids enjoyed the balloon animals.

"If you use your imagination," Jo said, "I'm sure you can see that it's a very nice puppy."

Savannah squinted at the balloon animal. "I see it now!"

Having finished with her last patient of the day, Jo went over a few things, then returned home for a quick dinner before going out to the town's bar.

She had plans every Friday night at Finn's. It was the highlight of her week, and she'd been thinking about it all day, as she'd looked in people's mouths and filled cavities and made unimpressive balloon animals.

"Here's your Guinness." Al set a pint in front of her.

"Thank you," she murmured, then returned to staring out the

window, waiting for her friend as she sat at their usual table near the front. Sometimes he was a bit late, if he stopped to chat with someone on the walk over, but never more than ten minutes.

And there he was now, wearing his blue parka, a toque pulled low over his ears. He waved at her from outside and she waved back, trying to tamp down the giddy feeling in her chest.

Really, it was embarrassing that she felt like this around him. She was a thirty-three-year-old woman, for God's sake, not a schoolgirl.

How many of his students had crushes on him? She couldn't help wondering.

"Hey," she said as he walked up to the table.

Zach Wong took off his toque, revealing his perfect dark brown hair. It was a little long and floppy, with a slight wave. Hugh Grant hair, she called it. It was unfair that his hair didn't get messed up when he put on a winter hat. Hers, on the other hand...

"Let's sit at the back today," he said. "I have something to ask you."

A handsome man was inviting her to the dark corner of the bar. Her heart beat a touch rapidly, even though she knew it didn't mean *that*.

"Sure," she said with a smile, gripping her pint as she followed him. When she was sitting down, she asked, "What is it?"

"Well," he said, "the Lunar New Year is coming up soon."

"That's in February?"

"This year, it's January twenty-fifth. I'm afraid my family is going to invite a date for me, like at Thanksgiving. So I was wondering..."

He rested his elbow on the table and leaned closer to her. She inhaled his piney scent.

Dammit, this attraction was so *inconvenient*.

She'd known Zach since they were kids, but not well—she'd been three years ahead of him in school. Then one day four years ago, they'd both been drinking away their heartbreak at the bar, and they'd bonded over their broken engagements.

They'd become friends, and two years ago, Jo had developed this inconvenient crush on Zach. Inconvenient because it was quite clear he had no interest in another relationship.

Many times, she'd told herself that she should stop meeting him for drinks, and maybe then she'd finally rid herself of these stupid feelings.

Except every week, they met at Finn's. She couldn't help herself.

She had a successful dental practice, which she'd taken over from her father after his retirement. She owned a cute little house on the edge of town. She could cook. She could garden, and she grew the best tomatoes on the block. She was pretty good at many things.

And yet...

"I want you to come to my parents' house on Chinese New Year," Zach said, "and pretend to be my girlfriend."

A burst of laughter escaped Jo's lips, and with it, unfortunately, a mouthful of dark beer. It landed on Zach's sweater.

Oh, God. She'd spit beer on Zach Wong.

"You want me...to pretend to be your girlfriend?" she asked as she grabbed a handful of napkins and started frantically dabbing at his sweater. She could feel his muscles underneath, and mmm, that was nice.

She leaned back. She should probably let him clean himself off.

"Yes," he said, "I want you to be my fake girlfriend so my family won't set me up with anyone for Chinese New Year."

"Well, there's a sentence that's never been uttered before in Mosquito Bay." Her cheeks flamed. "I'm so sorry. About the beer, I mean."

"It's no big deal." That was Zach, never fazed by anything. "So, will you do it?"

"You think your family will believe we're together?"

"Why wouldn't they?"

"Won't it be a little suspicious if you suddenly show up with a girlfriend when you haven't mentioned a girlfriend before?"

"Good point." He drummed his fingers on the table. "We'll have to go on dates in the next few weeks. Do something other than drinking at the bar every Friday. Then my parents will hear about it through the gossip vine."

"Yes!" Jo said, with perhaps a little too much enthusiasm.

She couldn't help it. Zach was asking her on a date!

True, it was a fake date, but still. Exciting times.

God, she was pathetic.

She had a sip of her beer and managed not to spit it on anyone this time, which she counted as a win.

She would be Zach's fake girlfriend; she couldn't help herself from agreeing. But while they were pretending, she must absolutely not give away her feelings, or that might be the end of their friendship. Jo had a small circle of friends, and she didn't want to lose one.

Would he want to kiss her as part of their act?

Her hands flew to her mouth.

"Are you having second thoughts?" Zach asked.

"No, it's fine. I'll do it."

"Thanks." He raised his pint, and she clinked hers against it. "I owe you."

"Yes, you do," she said good-naturedly.

They drank their beer in silence for a minute before Al came around and talked to Zach about hockey. Normally, Jo would join in, but today, she was lost in thought.

She was going to get exactly what she wanted.

Pity it would all be fake.

2

"MORE FLOWERS FOR YOUR MOTHER?" asked the cashier at Foodland.

"Not this time." Zach smiled at her and she flushed.

He knew his smile was powerful. It didn't make every woman drop to her knees, but when he wanted to fool around, he had little trouble finding a partner. He certainly hadn't been celibate since Marianne ended their engagement, but it wasn't like he was sleeping his way through all the single women in town.

"Who's the lucky lady?" the cashier asked.

This time, he shot her an enigmatic smile before exiting the grocery store. He had many different smiles, all for slightly different purposes.

Zach drove the short distance to Jo's house in his old Ford Focus and knocked on her door. Strangely, his heart was thumping a little quickly, like he was nervous.

But he was just spending the evening with a friend.

No, he definitely wasn't nervous. There was no reason to be.

The door opened, revealing Jo. She was wearing dark jeans and a brown sweater that hugged her curves. He'd likely seen her in this sweater before, but it looked really good on her. Her light brown hair fell in waves, and she wore silver earrings of some sort.

"You look nice," he said, swallowing.

She fidgeted with her hair. "Nobody's around now. You don't have to pretend." Her eyes lit up. "You brought me carnations. They're my favorite—how did you know?"

To be honest, Zach hadn't even known they were carnations. He'd just seen the pink flowers and figured she'd like them.

He shrugged. "Lucky guess."

"Matt never got me flowers, even though I told him exactly what I liked."

Matt was, frankly, a douche canoe. Not that Zach had ever met the man, but from the bits and pieces Jo had shared about her ex-fiancé over the years, it had become apparent that the guy had never deserved Jo.

Which was why she'd ended the engagement. Because she'd realized she deserved better.

After Jo put the flowers in the vase, Zach drove the two of them to Cardinal's, the nice-ish restaurant on the outskirts of town. The server, Jacob, a former student of Zach's who was maybe nineteen now, seated them at a table by the window and kept tripping up over the list of specials.

"We have a pizza today with fresh rainbow trout. Or sardines. I mean, anchovies. We also have ravioli stuffed with...peppers? It started with a 'p.' No, it wasn't peppers...pumpkin, maybe? Shit, I'll go check. It's my second day on the job" His face paled. "Sorry for saying 'shit.' Dammit, I did it again!"

Jo smiled at him kindly. "Don't worry. I'm going to order the mussels, no matter what the specials are."

"Oh, uh, there's a mussel special, too. Our regular mussel entrée has white wine, but I think the special one is cooked in ale?"

"Probably. They used to have that as a special every two weeks when I worked here."

"You used to work at Cardinal's, Dr. MacGregor?" the kid asked.

"Yeah, in my last year of high school. The first day, I spilled seafood marinara all over a lady from out of town who was wearing a white silk blouse."

The kid chuckled.

Zach smiled at his date trying to make their server feel more at ease. Jo wasn't as outgoing as he was, but she was good at this sort of thing.

"What would you like today, Mr. Wong?" Jacob asked.

"You can call me Zach, now that you've graduated."

Jacob looked at him as though this was a horrifying suggestion, even weirder than rainbow trout on pizza. Which surely someone had tried before, but Zach didn't like seafood on pizza.

"I couldn't call you that," Jacob sputtered. "You're Mr. Wong."

"Okay. Mr. Wong, if you prefer."

After they placed their orders, Jacob left and silence descended on the table. It was strange to be at a nice restaurant with Jo. When he saw her, it was usually at the bar.

"I find it weird being called Mr. Wong outside of school," he said.

"Yeah, I understand. I find it weird being called Dr. MacGregor outside the office. Dr. MacGregor is my father."

"For me, I think it's partly because I don't look like I should have a Chinese last name. I like my name, and people from Mosquito Bay know my family and don't question it. But students who are bussed in from other towns, other teachers... sometimes they ask, and it's awkward. Nick and Greg look more Chinese than I do. I look a bit like a white version of my dad. Does that sound strange?"

Jo considered this for a second. "I don't know what it's like, of course, but I understand what you're saying."

Occasionally, people could tell Zach wasn't entirely white from his appearance. It was awkward when people played guessing games about his background and thought it was fun.

He didn't talk about this stuff much, but there were other things he'd talked about with Jo that he didn't normally share. Although Zach had continued to act like his fun, relaxed self most of the time after his broken engagement, he'd talked to her about it a little. About his heartbreak, how he was hurt that the life he wanted was too boring and unfulfilling for Marianne, even though she'd initially been happy to move to Mosquito Bay.

Still, it was Marianne's right to feel that way, and he was glad she'd ended it before they'd started planning the wedding.

Facebook—the rare times he used it—told him that she now lived in Toronto, and she appeared to be enjoying herself there. Like Nick, she seemed to belong in the big city.

He was happy for her, but it had hurt. He'd—

"You know who you look like?" Jo asked suddenly, bringing him out of his thoughts.

"Who?"

"Keanu Reeves."

"You think I look like Keanu Reeves?"

"Yeah, a little. Did you see *Always Be My Maybe*? He was hilarious in that."

Zach shook his head.

"But you look more like Matrix-era Keanu Reeves. You don't think so?"

"That's a big compliment. I'm not sure I can accept it. Are you saying you think I'm sexy?" He waggled his eyebrows.

Jo's mouth fell open, and she paled.

Shit.

"Sorry," he said. "It's not—"

"Here's your bread and wine!" Jacob said.

Zach's red wine nearly sloshed onto the white tablecloth, but

Jacob managed to catch it just in time before he scurried to another table.

Jo reached for her wine and had a gulp, then grabbed a piece of bread.

"Again, I'm sorry," Zach said. "I don't want to make you uncomfortable."

"No worries." She plastered on a smile. "It's fine."

He could tell it wasn't, but also that she didn't want to talk about it.

She took a sip of her wine—a sip, not a gulp this time—and fixed her hair.

She really did look lovely tonight, but she wasn't for him. This was pretend, and she was his friend. He wasn't sure if she was willing to give a relationship another go—she hadn't talked about that recently—but he wasn't.

His life was fine the way it was.

~

You think I'm sexy?

Dear God, it was a miracle Jo hadn't done more than open her mouth wide in horror.

She did think Zach was very sexy, and he looked gorgeous in the black dress shirt he was wearing tonight. He looked a bit like Keanu Reeves, it was true, but why had she felt the need to tell him that?

Zach had been playing around when he made that comment about being sexy, but could he tell the truth from how she'd reacted?

She didn't think so. Still, it had made her jittery, made her feel like maybe he could read her mind, and oh, wasn't that a horrifying thought?

But now everything was back on track. She was eating her mussels and slathering her bread with butter and dipping it in the juices, and it was all delicious. This had been her favorite meal when she'd worked here over a dozen years ago, and Cardinal's hadn't changed much over the years. They served good food, but they'd never been on the cutting edge of trends, and the dining room hadn't been updated since she was a teenager.

Across from her, Zach was cutting off a piece of his medium-rare steak, which, in her opinion, was the perfect way to cook a steak, and oh God, why did she keep finding more things to like about him?

Though she usually prided herself on being upfront and honest, her secret crush on Zach was the exception. Only Tiffany knew. Jo was determined that no one else would ever find out.

After they'd finished their meals, Jacob came over to clear their plates and recite the day's desserts. Jo really hoped today was Fudge Brownie Day.

"We have two desserts," Jacob said. "Tiramisu and fudge brownie sundae."

"Did you say fudge brownie sundae?" Jo asked. After all, Jacob had messed up the anchovy pizza special earlier.

"Yeah."

"Not just fudge brownies with whipped cream?"

"No, fudge brownie sundae. It's new. Fudge brownies with vanilla ice cream, peanut butter ice cream, whipped cream and chocolate sauce. Or fudge sauce? I don't know."

Jo wasn't quite sure what the difference between chocolate sauce and fudge sauce was, but that was a minor detail.

It sounded amazing.

Sure, it would be quite sweet and terrible for her teeth, but a woman had to have a few indulgences in life.

And sure, she could probably eat it all by herself, but she was on a "date" with Zach Wong, and sharing a fudge brownie sundae would be a very datish thing to do.

"What do you think, sweetie?" she said, the endearment

popping out of her mouth before she could think about it. "Should we share it?"

"Sounds good." He turned to Jacob. "One fudge brownie sundae."

"Coming right up," Jacob said.

Once he'd left, Zach said, "If you call me 'sweetie,' what should I call you?"

"Darling." She'd dreamed of him calling her that.

"Darling it is."

They talked quietly for a few minutes, until a high voice shouted, "Dr. MacGregor!"

A little girl scampered toward their table. It was Savannah, wearing a purple party dress.

"I named my puppy Alfred," Savannah said.

Jo smiled at her. "That's a good name for a dog."

"But Alfred wants a friend. Can you make me another balloon dog now? Please?"

"I'm sorry. I don't have any balloons with me."

"Oh." Savannah twisted her mouth, then started back toward her family's table.

She'd only taken two steps before she collided with Jacob.

Who was, of course, carrying a fudge brownie sundae, cherry on top.

Jo saw it happen in slow motion.

"Zach!" she cried.

Unfortunately, there wasn't enough time for Zach to move out of the way before the fudge brownie sundae toppled off the tray. Chocolate sauce and ice cream spilled all over his hair and shirt, though he managed to catch the glass dish before it landed on his crotch.

Oh, dear.

Zach, however, quickly recovered his composure. He held out his arms, looked at his ruined shirt, and said, "Want some ice cream, darling?"

～

Jo sat in the passenger's seat of Zach's car as he left the parking lot. Cardinal's had quickly brought them a new sundae and comped their dessert and wine, and now their so-called date was over.

They didn't say anything for a minute or two, and then Zach started to laugh. It was a contagious sort of laughter, because soon Jo was laughing, too.

"People will definitely...be talking about our date," Zach wheezed.

"Which is exactly what you wanted."

"I didn't ask to have an ice cream sundae decorate my shirt."

"You could start a hot new trend."

"Cold trend, you mean." He glanced over at her, and her heart skipped a beat when he smiled like he didn't have a care in the world.

Whereas if Jo had been on the receiving end of the spilled ice cream, she wouldn't have been a happy camper. After all, she was wearing a nice sweater for her first date with the man she'd had a crush on for two years.

Now, one of Jo's domestic skills—along with growing great tomatoes and making really good French toast—was her ability to remove any stain. But still. Although she wouldn't have gotten angry about the spilled sundae, she might not be able to laugh about it yet.

"At least my shirt is black," Zach said. "Hey, you want to come over and watch the end of the game?"

Watching Hockey Night in Canada was something they'd occasionally do together on Saturday nights. It was part of their friendship, along with Friday nights at Finn's.

Dinner at Cardinal's, on the other hand, was something different, and Jo had enjoyed it very much, despite the unfortunate ending. Zach picking her up and handing her a bouquet of carnations—that was the stuff of her dreams.

And now they were back to Jo and Zach, friends in heartbreak.

"Sure," she said, trying to hide her disappointment.

"Better go to my place so I can get changed. I'll walk you home later."

The Leafs were winning three to two against the Bruins when Zach flipped on the television at the start of the third period. Jo curled up on the couch as he went upstairs. She tried to focus on the hockey game, rather than picturing him without a shirt, but it was a lost cause.

If only she could drizzle chocolate sauce on his bare chest, maybe garnished with cherries and whipped cream for good measure, and lick it off...

Stop it, brain! It's not going to happen.

Zach was a good friend, and he'd never shown any interest in her. There was no reason that should change now, just because they were faking a relationship.

After the game—the Leafs won—Jo still didn't want to leave.

"Let's watch *Always Be My Maybe*," she said to Zach. "Since you've never seen it and that's a travesty."

They started the movie, and though Jo very much wanted to watch it, she soon found herself getting sleepy. Maybe she was crashing after all the sugar in that sundae. She curled up against the arm of the couch...

~

Something didn't feel right.

Jo opened her eyes and jolted up as she took in her surroundings.

She was on Zach's couch, covered in a fleece blanket, and sunlight was filtering through the curtains.

It was morning.

She'd spent the night at Zach's.

"Hey." Zach stepped into the living room with two cups of coffee in hand.

"What time is it?" she asked, her voice raspy.

"Nine."

"Shit, I have to get home. I'm supposed to be at my parents' house for brunch at ten, and I need to shower."

"You can shower here."

"But I need a change of clothes."

"Of course. Just drink your coffee and you can be on your way."

"No sugar?"

"No sugar. I know how you like it."

Frankly, Jo kind of liked sugar in coffee, but it wasn't necessary and she was trying to limit her sugar intake, especially after all the ice cream she'd consumed last night—that sundae hadn't exactly been small.

She took the mug from his outstretched hand and her fingers brushed against his, which was as much touching as they ever did.

"My neck hurts," she said.

"I would have moved you from the couch, but I didn't want to disturb you."

He'd thoughtfully put a blanket over her, and he'd made her coffee the way she wanted it. The only time Matt had made her coffee, it had been weak and overly sweet.

She needed to stop comparing men to Matt.

Her ex hadn't cheated on her or stolen from her or threatened her. Nor had he done any of the other things that women wrote to advice columns—or posted on Reddit—about.

She used to read those columns to convince herself that Matt was a good guy and she was lucky to have him. But then she'd noticed a pattern. Women would describe all the horrible, jaw-dropping trash their husband or boyfriend did, then end with, "He's a good guy and maybe I'm being too hard on him." Basically, "My husband kills unicorns, but he cooks dinner once a month." Women were taught to be forgiving and lower their expectations.

Whereas when men wrote in, they'd say something like, "Occasionally she eats food with raw garlic and her breath smells." Or, "She gained ten pounds and my new twenty-year-old assistant at work is hot and smiled at me once."

It was rough in the dating world. Matt wasn't the worst guy out there, true, but he'd neglected their relationship and never prioritized her, and she'd realized it was better to be single than to have what she did with him.

Jo shouldn't swoon over a cup of coffee. It was just coffee. Except she, pathetically, swooned over nearly everything Zach did.

"Thanks," she said. "Is your nosy neighbor still out working in his garage every morning?"

"He is."

"So he'll see me leave your house on a Sunday morning and draw conclusions. It'll be good for our story."

Zach's mouth curved into a stunningly attractive smile. "It will indeed."

～

"I hear you're dating Zach Wong," Jo's mother said over brunch a couple hours later.

Well, that was fast, though Jo couldn't say she was surprised.

"I am," she said. "Where did you hear that?"

"Shelly. She said you were at Cardinal's last night, and the waiter spilled an ice cream sundae all over Zach. How long have you been seeing him?" Mom lifted a forkful of salad to her mouth. She seemed a touch hurt that she'd had to learn about her daughter's date from Shelly Sanderson.

"Not long," Jo said. "That was our first official date." For once, she allowed herself to sound dopey and in love when talking about Zach. No acting required.

"I'm glad you're finally dating again," Becky, Jo's sister, said before dropping some quiche on the baby asleep in her arms. "Oops."

Becky was two years younger than Jo. She'd been married for more than five years and had three children; the older two were currently squishing bread rolls at the other end of the table.

"Yes, I'm glad, too," Mom said.

Jo's family had been bugging her about her love life. Not because they thought she was a failure for being single at thirty-three and having a broken engagement. It was more that they were all happily married and couldn't imagine it any other way. They meant well, but Jo's situation seemed to baffle them. Her parents had met when they were twenty; Becky and her husband had been twenty-one, in their final year of university. Dating in your thirties—in the age of Tinder and other apps—wasn't something they knew anything about.

As Jo looked around at her family, all excited to hear that she'd begun dating again, she made a resolution.

She'd spent two years in love with Zach, and he was never going to want another relationship, that much was obvious. Two years was a lot of time to waste on a man who wouldn't love her back.

Sure, there were lots of crappy men out there, and sure, Mosquito Bay wasn't a big town, but she wasn't restricted to the men in Mosquito Bay, and maybe she'd get lucky, like the other members of her family.

It was possible, wasn't it?

She would not settle, like she had with Matt. She would keep her expectations firmly intact, thank you very much, and hope she found a guy similar to Zach, but emotionally available, or whatever you called it.

She'd enjoy her "dates" with Zach Wong, but that was only temporary.

After January 25, she'd do her best to finally move on.

3

"BY THE WAY, I HAVE A GIRLFRIEND." Zach spoke nonchalantly as he dug into his fried rice, but he couldn't help smiling as he antic-ipated his family's reaction. He was at his parents' place for Sunday dinner, along with his grandparents and Amber.

Sure enough, his announcement had quite an impact.

"You do?" Ah Ma said, practically shouting.

"How wonderful," Mom said. "Who is she?"

"Jo MacGregor."

"You two have been friends for a while, haven't you?"

"Yes, and we decided...well...that we have other feelings for each other, too." He wasn't his smoothest today.

"Invite her next Sunday," Ah Ma said. "I will make her a nice meal."

Dad gave his mother a look. "You will scare her away with your horrible cooking."

"I tease! You knew I was teasing, Zach, didn't you?"

"I'm not having her over next Sunday," Zach said. "She can meet everyone at Chinese New Year the following weekend, when Greg and Nick are in town."

"Not that we haven't all met her before," Mom said, "but usually she's examining my teeth when I see her."

"I will get out my list of questions!" Ah Ma said gleefully. "Sixty-nine questions to ask future granddaughter-in-law."

Zach choked on his rice. For multiple reasons.

"What is wrong?" Ah Ma asked.

"Sixty-nine questions," Amber said. "That's, um, an awful lot."

"Sixty-nine. It is a good number, isn't it? It always makes people laugh when I say it, so I think it must be a good number."

Zach and Amber looked at each other.

"Um," Zach said.

"Do you want to tell her?" Amber asked.

"No, thank you."

"What are you not telling me?" Ah Ma demanded. "What is wrong with sixty-nine? Is it some weird sex thing?"

"I don't know if I'd say *weird*..." Dad began.

"Ah, it is a *normal* sex thing?"

"It's perfectly normal," Mom said.

Zach was having flashbacks to the sex-ed talks his parents had given him when he was a preteen. He supposed he was grateful for those, but he didn't really want to think about that now.

"In fact," Mom continued, "Amber came home from school one day—I think she was eleven—and asked me what it was."

Everyone looked at Amber, and Zach couldn't help smirking, just a tiny bit, at his sister's discomfort.

"You told her?" Ah Ma said. "Why won't you tell me?"

"You can look it up on the internet," Dad said.

"I don't know how to use the internet."

"I do," said Ah Yeh, who had been silent up until this point.

"All you know how to do is order things we don't need. You know what arrived yesterday?" Ah Ma pointed at her husband but looked at her son. "An avocado slicer, an egg slicer, and a cake decorating set. Why do we need those things? He doesn't even like boiled eggs. Or cake."

"I like cake." Ah Yeh crossed his arms over his chest. "I just don't like that dry vanilla cake you buy from the grocery store."

"Wah, that is the best. So cheap!" Ah Ma said. "But this is just a distraction from my question. What is sixty-nine? I don't want to use the internet to find out."

"Yeah, maybe it's best you don't use the internet for that." Dad looked pointedly at Ah Yeh. "You might find porn, and I don't want to have to fix your computer because you got a virus from looking at porn again."

"I don't know what you are talking about," Ah Yeh said.

On the plus side, no one was talking about Zach marrying Jo now—Ah Ma's comment about her being a "future daughter-in-law" was the main reason he'd choked on his rice.

But when he got home, he'd have to scrub this conversation from his brain.

Tuesday evening, Zach sat in Wong's Wok, waiting for Jo to arrive.

The reason for this choice in venue was simple: the new owners of Wong's Wok—though Zach should probably stop thinking of them as "new," seeing as they'd run the place for twenty years—were friends with his family, and they would almost certainly tell his parents or grandparents that Zach had been here with Jo. Though he'd already told his family about his "girlfriend," they hadn't heard it from any other source—surprisingly, no one had told them about the ice cream sundae incident. This would make it look more real.

Jo walked into the restaurant a few minutes later. She removed her winter coat and toque, then sat across the table from him and smiled.

For a moment, Zach was unable to speak. He was transfixed

by her smile. Good advertising for a dentist to have a nice smile, he supposed.

Then he moved his gaze lower. She was wearing a sweater that graded from light blue at the top to dark blue at the bottom. It showed more cleavage than her usual clothes, and those buttons sure were tempting.

Stop it, Zach.

He would not ogle his friend.

"Hey," he said at last, trying to sound casual.

"Hey, Zach. How's your week been?"

"A bit rough waking up for early morning basketball practice." He coached the senior boys' team. "And..."

Why couldn't he find his words? This wasn't like him.

But Jo really did look good today. She'd looked good on Saturday, too, but he hadn't found himself stunned into silence.

What was wrong with him? He'd seen her many, many times over the past few years. Why was it different now that they were supposedly in a relationship? They'd both known it was fake from the start.

He shook his head to clear it, then looked around the restaurant. There were red lanterns and other decorations on the walls for the upcoming holiday.

"Should I bring anything when I come to your parents' house for Chinese New Year?" Jo asked. "The red envelopes—how do they work? I'm sure I could get some online."

Zach wasn't sure how most people celebrated Chinese New Year, since he knew so few people of Chinese descent. He didn't know which things his family did were "normal" and which were just his family—other than Picitonary—and what would vary depending on where you were from in China.

He felt like he should be aware of these things, but he'd grown up in a small town where more than ninety-five percent of the people were white, like Jo. His father had spent most of his life in the same small town.

"You don't have to bring red envelopes," he said. "They contain money, and they're given to the younger generation. My grandparents and parents give them to us. I don't know when we'll become old enough for that to stop, but it hasn't happened yet, and none of my siblings have kids."

"Okay," Jo said. "Is there anything I can bring food-wise?"

He shook his head. "You don't need to."

"I feel like I should."

"Some fruit, if you like, but it's not a big deal, don't worry."

"I want to make a good impression on my fake prospective in-laws." She smiled at him again, and he felt a strange jittery sensation in his stomach.

He reached forward and took her hand in his. "Thank you for doing this. I know it's a hassle."

"It's not a hassle to occasionally have dinner together and accompany you to a family event."

He always felt comfortable with Jo, content when they were together. Not that anyone would notice the difference when he was with her, since that was the sort of image he always projected; it was what people expected of him.

But sometimes, that image was a bit of an act.

With her, though, it never was.

"Zachary!" Mrs. Tan came over to their table. "Long time since you came here."

Zach felt a touch of guilt. He came to the restaurant maybe once a month, though perhaps it had been two months now.

"Dr. MacGregor." Mrs. Tan smiled at Jo. "I have appointment next week. Hope I have flossed enough! Are you two…" Her gaze traveled from Jo to Zach, then down to the table, where his hand was still covering hers.

Huh. He'd completely forgotten about that, as though it felt natural to hold her hand.

"Yes," Jo said, beaming at Mrs. Tan before shooting him a

lovesick gaze. She really was a good actor. He hadn't expected that of her.

Zach ordered egg rolls and chow mein; Jo ordered ginger beef.

"It's been my favorite since I was little," she told him after Mrs. Tan left. "I've never seen it at another Chinese restaurant."

"It was added to the menu in nineteen seventy-eight," he said. "After The Trip."

"The Trip?"

Apparently he'd never told her about this before. "The restaurant was open six days a week from the time my grandparents came here in the mid-sixties. They'd never taken more than two days off until The Trip—it was the only family vacation they had after moving to Canada."

Zach had heard tales of The Trip many, many times. From his grandparents, his father, and his aunt. Everyone remembered it a little differently, and they'd regularly reminisce about it at family meals. At some point he'd become sick of hearing about it—couldn't his family think of any other stories to tell?—but he smiled at the thought of telling Jo.

"For years, Ah Yeh planned this trip," he said. "A cross-country road trip out to Alberta. He'd seen pictures of Lake Louise in a magazine once, and he'd wanted to go to Banff ever since. Along the way, he planned to stop at every Chinese restaurant he could find. Research, he said. He called it a business trip, which made Dad and Aunt Cheryl roll their eyes. Anyway, in nineteen seventy-eight, before my father's final year of high school, they closed down the restaurant for a full month and finally went. Ginger beef was on the menu at many of the Chinese restaurants in the Prairies, and it seemed popular. Ah Yeh talked to the owners at every restaurant. They were usually happy to chat with someone else who was Chinese, and he convinced one of the cooks to show him how to make it. My grandpa did the cooking at Wong's Wok—my grandma is terrible in the kitchen, and she ran the front of the restaurant."

"Is ginger beef from a particular region in China?"

Zach shook his head. "It was supposedly invented at the Silver Inn in Alberta in nineteen seventy-three. A Chinese-Canadian dish."

"So it's not authentic?"

"Don't get my grandfather started on 'authenticity,'" Zach said. "These small-town Chinese restaurants in North America are kind of their own type of cuisine, adapted to fit the tastes of the people in the area. Egg rolls, General Tso's chicken, and such. In the Prairies, they have ginger beef, and in Thunder Bay, they have a rib dish. My grandparents put that on the menu, too, but I think the Tans took them off. In Newfoundland—my grandparents went there after they retired—chow mein is made with cabbage because it used to be difficult to get the noodles there, so they had to make changes."

It was interesting how these immigrant families, many with limited English skills, had managed to make these businesses survive. Though whenever his dad talked about The Trip, he sounded like a cool teenager who didn't want to be trapped in a van with his family for half his summer vacation. Zach's father had recently started dating his mother, and they'd been devastated at the thought of spending the summer apart.

"So, yeah," Zach said. "That's why there's ginger beef on the menu."

"Were your grandparents upset that neither of their children wanted to take over the family business?"

"They encouraged my dad and my aunt to go to university, to get good degrees so they wouldn't have to work at a restaurant. Running Wong's Wok was hard work—they were *always* there, except for that one trip out west. Still, I think they were a little disappointed they had to sell the restaurant out of the family, even if they never said so." His father was a pharmacist, and Aunt Cheryl worked in finance on the other side of the country.

Their food arrived a few minutes later, and Zach didn't immediately take a bite. Instead, he watched as Jo speared a piece of deep-fried beef, covered in dark sauce, with her fork and popped it into her mouth.

"Mmm," she said, and for some reason, it made blood rush to his cock.

What was wrong with him? It was just Jo eating. Nothing special.

A drop of sauce clung to the corner of her lip. He was about to reach over to wipe it off, then decided that would be too intimate. He pointed to the corner of his own mouth. "You have some sauce...there."

She swiped at the other corner of her mouth.

"No, on your left side."

She swiped the sauce off and wiped it on her napkin, but he wished he'd gotten a chance to suck it off her finger instead. His body didn't seem to have gotten the message that this relationship was fake. He needed to have a few words with it in his stern teacher voice.

"Thank you for telling me the history of it," she said. "I never knew." Then she got a gleam in her eye. Why, it was almost a *wicked* gleam—which wasn't like Jo at all. "Can you make this for me at home, sweetie? Afterward, I'll..." She gave him a suggestive wink.

She was just playing around, acting the part. But his body responded nonetheless.

"I'll ask my grandfather to teach me," he said hoarsely. "Just for you, *darling*." He emphasized the last word as Mrs. Tan walked by.

"Everything good?" Mrs. Tan asked.

"Delicious, thank you." Jo smiled.

"Ungh," Zach said. "I mean, it's delicious."

"You haven't started eating," Jo pointed out.

"Yes, but I know it's going to be delicious."

He finally had a bite, and it was, indeed, good. He and Jo ate in companionable silence for a while, and then she mentioned the Leafs. It was the sort of thing they'd usually talk about. There were no wicked gleams or winks.

When Mrs. Tan brought out the bill with two fortune cookies on top, Zach reached for it before Jo could.

"I'm paying," he said.

"No, you paid last time."

Before he knew what was happening, Jo had grabbed the bill. She took out her credit card and held it out to Mrs. Tan.

"I insist," Jo said, turning back to him.

Well, he supposed he could allow her this, even though he really ought to be paying because he was the one who'd roped her into this fake relationship.

After Mrs. Tan left, they each took a fortune cookie. Zach opened up the package, snapped the cookie in half, and pulled out the fortunes. Plural.

"I got two." He and his siblings had considered that good luck back in the day.

The first fortune: *You will find romance in unexpected places. Lucky numbers: 7, 10, 28, 63, 45*

"What does it say?" Jo asked.

He shifted the small slip of paper to the middle of the table and turned it around. Jo leaned closer. Her hair smelled faintly of vanilla, and he wanted to bury his head in it.

Probably that fortune was getting to his mind.

The second fortune said: *Don't be stupid. Lucky numbers: 18, 23, 2, 78, 6.*

What did it all mean? That he would find love somewhere unexpected—frankly any kind of love and romance would be unexpected at this point—and he shouldn't be stupid about it? Or would it be stupid if he found romance in an unexpected place?

Well, in truth, it would be stupid to pay attention to the fortunes in a cookie.

He popped half the cookie in his mouth as Jo opened hers up. When she read her message, her eyebrows shot up, and then she started laughing.

"What is it?" he asked.

She held up the fortune so he could read it.

Brush your teeth. Lucky numbers: 69, 23, 45, 1, 15.

Zach couldn't help the strangled noise that escaped his throat when he saw the number 69, recalling the conversation with his family, then quickly pushed it out of his mind and focused on the first part of the fortune.

"It's like the fortune cookie gods know I'm a dentist," Jo said. "Terrifying, isn't it?"

"Or maybe they could tell that you haven't been brushing your teeth."

She looked affronted. "Of course I brush my teeth. How dare you!"

After tossing her fortune on her plate, Jo ate her cookie, and Zach found himself staring at her mouth again.

Hmm. This really would be an unexpected place to find romance…

He quickly dismissed the thought.

"You and Jo MacGregor, eh?" Shawn Little walked into the room where Zach taught grade ten science at the end of the day. The students had just filed out the door, and Zach was tidying up a few things.

Shawn taught phys ed and health. He was Zach's closest friend at Mosquito Bay Secondary School, and Zach had planned to tell him the truth. Just Shawn, no one else.

He beckoned his friend closer to the lab counter.

"It's a ruse," Zach said. "We're pretending we're together so my parents and grandparents don't get up to more matchmaking, especially with Chinese New Year approaching."

Shawn lifted his eyebrows. "You went to all the effort of getting a fake girlfriend to avoid their matchmaking plans?"

"I don't think you understand how annoying it can be."

"Well, no. My mom comments about my single status, but I can't say I have any experience with my family finding me a surprise date for Thanksgiving." Shawn slapped Zach on the back. "I hear your neighbor saw Jo sneaking out of your house the other morning. Are there any benefits to this fake relationship?"

"No," Zach said, rather harshly.

Though he was now thinking about him and Jo in bed together, much to his annoyance.

Don't be stupid.

That's what his fortune cookie had told him, and it was good advice, even if it had come from a questionable source.

Zach would not be stupid.

4

Jo walked into Finn's and sat at her usual table. She waved at Becky, who was by the bar with a group of friends, and then a minute later, Al came over with a pint of Guinness.

"Waiting for your boyfriend?" he asked.

"No, I…" Jo began.

I don't have a boyfriend.

Except as far as everyone knew, she *did* have a boyfriend, a boyfriend she was very much in love with.

Too bad it was one-sided.

"Zach will be here soon," she said with a smile.

"You two have been friends for a long time," Al said. "What happened? What changed?"

Good question. Jo and Zach had never discussed their how-we-started-dating story.

"It began last Friday," she said, having no idea where she was going with this. "After we left Finn's, he walked me home, and it started snowing…"

"…and you know when you suddenly see someone in a new way?" Zach came up behind her and put his hand on her shoulder. "Well, to be honest, that had never happened to me until last week. Jo looked so pretty, snowflakes in her eyelashes, and before I knew what was happening, we were kissing."

Oh, if only.

If only they had kissed. If only he could see her differently.

Al brought Zach his usual beer. Zach held up his pint, and Jo clinked hers against his.

"Cheers to us," Zach said as he took a seat.

Jo attempted a smile, but based on Zach's concerned expression, she hadn't succeeded.

"What's wrong?" he asked, once Al had walked away.

She couldn't tell him the truth, but he was her friend, and perhaps she could tell him part of the truth. "I didn't want another relationship after I dumped Matt—"

"He wasn't good enough for you. I'm glad you dumped that asshole."

The corners of her mouth quirked up. "I'm glad, too. But lately, I've been thinking that I'd like to date again."

Zach looked at her over his pint of beer, not at all distracted by the Friday night noise of the bar, the laughter from the pool tables at the back.

She liked how he could make her feel like she was all that mattered.

"It's hard, though," she said. "There aren't a lot of options in Mosquito Bay. I could use a dating app and try to find someone in one of the nearby towns, but..."

But I'm in love with you, and I don't know how to move on.

She would, though. Somehow, after Chinese New Year, she'd try again. She'd put aside this pathetic crush on Zach and do her best. Or maybe she'd have to go on dates with other men even if she still had a crush on him, and *that* would help her move on.

"I know it's silly," she continued, the words pouring out of her now. Quietly, though; she didn't want anyone to overhear. "But Becky was always the pretty sister, the one everyone loved. The one who always had a boyfriend. I was the smart one, the athletic one, though some people told me that I could stand to lose a few pounds. And sometimes, I was envious. Then I felt guilty. I knew I should love myself as I am, but I struggled with that when I was with Matt. I thought I couldn't expect any better than a guy who didn't mind having me around."

Zach shook his head. "You deserve much more than that."

She nodded. She shouldn't be insecure, but probably most women felt this way at some point, right?

"Say it," Zach said. "'I deserve so much more than that good-for-nothing douche canoe.'"

"Douche canoe? What does that even mean?"

"That a bag isn't big enough to contain the guy, so a canoe is needed?"

She snorted. "You're making this up."

"No, it's a thing people say, I promise."

"I don't know if I'd call Matt a douchebag—or canoe. He was just…"

"As useful and affectionate as a potted fern?"

"Yeah, something like that. He wasn't evil; he just put me at the bottom of his priority list."

"Douche canoe," Zach said solemnly. "And I will always be here so you can rant about the not-so-fantastic guys you meet online, but I'm sure you'll find the right guy eventually."

Why can't you be the right guy?

"You don't want to try again, right?" she said.

"Nah, I like my life the way it is."

"You don't believe in love for yourself?"

"I don't know what I believe, but it's not something I'm looking for. If you want it, though, I want you to have it."

Oh, God. It had been a mistake to have this conversation with Zach. This was too much.

"And just so you know…" Gently, he slid his hand up her cheek and into her hair. His large hand caressed her; she could melt into his touch.

"You're very pretty, and I hope you find romance in unexpected places."

His eyes were focused intently on hers, and though he looked serious, there was still the unruly lock of hair over his forehead, the hint of a smile at his lips. He was looking at her in a way he'd never looked at her before, but he was still *Zach*, and she yearned to be with him.

Maybe he wanted her a little, too.

Wishful thinking... Or was it?

Her heart was hammering in her chest, and somehow, it felt like it was connected to his. She leaned forward and—

"Dr. MacGregor, hiiii!"

A young woman stumbled into Jo. Jo reached out her hands to steady her and tried not to curse at the interruption.

"Hey, Kyla," Zach said easily, as though he hadn't been about to kiss Jo. "Having a good night?"

"These sure are strong. Or maybe it's because I hardly drink anymore. My tolerance isn't what it used to be before Savannah was born." Kyla held up her drink, and a little sloshed over the edge of the glass.

"Let me get that for you." Zach wiped the glass with a napkin.

"Thank you!" Kyla touched his shoulder—she seemed to be an affectionate drunk. "I'm sorry about what happened at Cardinal's. I told Savannah, *no running in restaurants...*"

He laughed it off. "It didn't hurt, and the stain came out. It's all good."

"But it was your first date, wasn't it?"

"And now we have a memorable story."

"You can tell it to your children," Kyla said with a hiccup.

Becky—she'd been in the same year in school as Kyla—came over and put her hand on her friend's shoulder. "Let's order fries. I think you need some food."

"Poutine! We should have poutine." Kyla turned to Jo. "My ex has Savannah for the first Friday night in months, and I'm going to have fun!"

Becky smiled. "I'll let you get back to your date, Jo."

Zach placed a hand on Jo's knee—and Becky definitely noticed—before he held his other hand up in a wave as Becky and Kyla walked away.

"Sorry," he said suddenly, removing his hand from her knee. "Was it okay that I touched you? Both now and a few minutes ago when I touched your hair?"

"I'm your girlfriend," Jo said. "Of course you can touch me."

"I don't have to. I can lean in close, whisper in your ear..." And then he did just that, his voice soft and low. "I can make it look like we're intimate without physical contact, if you prefer."

Well, she liked this whispering business, but she liked the touching, too.

If only Kyla hadn't interrupted them.

"Zach," she said, "you were about to kiss me, weren't you?"

He scratched the back of his neck. "Uh, yeah. As part of our act."

Her heart deflated, though she wasn't completely convinced he was being honest.

"I won't do it again," he said.

She hoped that wasn't true.

5

WHAT AM I DOING?

Zach backed his car out of the garage on Sunday morning and drove along the quiet streets to Jo's house on the other side of town.

There was a new skating trail through the woods, about forty minutes north of Mosquito Bay. Usually Zach only skated when he was playing hockey, but the idea of skating on something more than sixty meters long was appealing. The whole track was over a kilometer, which sounded nice. And romantic.

And so he'd asked Jo to go with him this morning, and she'd agreed.

Part of our act, he told himself.

Except this was different from going to Wong's Wok or Cardinal's, where they'd inevitably run into other residents of Mosquito Bay. It was possible they'd encounter no one they knew on this excursion.

You just want to see her again.

Well, they were friends. Wasn't that reasonable?

But you saw her on Friday night, and you usually only see each other once a week.

He told himself that he was just trying to get into the role.

Zach wasn't in the habit of lying to himself, however, and in truth, he'd felt like there had been a spark between them the last two times they'd met up. His hands tightened on the steering wheel as he remembered sliding his hand over her cheek.

He couldn't help himself; he wanted to do that again.

He pulled up to Jo's house, and she scampered out the door and into the passenger's seat.

"Hey." She was wearing a white toque and her usual blue parka, and she grinned at him.

He couldn't help returning her smile.

They started driving north. It had snowed yesterday morning, and sunlight reflected off the snowy fields, but the roads had been cleared. A cold day—well below freezing and a bit windy.

"You been to this place before?" Jo asked.

He glanced at her. Her brown eyes held excitement, even though they were simply going skating, something they'd both done many times before.

"No," he said, "but I thought it would be the perfect thing to do with my girlfriend."

They arrived at the skating trail around ten thirty and paid the rink attendant. Based on the lack of cars in the parking lot, it appeared they were alone. Probably had something to do with the bitterly cold weather.

They laced up their hockey skates in the little hut. It wasn't heated, but at least it offered protection from the wind.

Jo got her skates on first and tossed an "I'll race you" over her shoulder before she pushed open the door to the hut.

Zach finished tying up his skates in a hurry and followed her out. She was already whipping down the ice in long, smooth strokes, and he had lots of distance to make up.

That was no surprise. He'd played hockey with Jo; he knew she was an excellent skater.

As it turned out, he couldn't catch her. He managed to get

close at one point, but then she whizzed past him, and when he reached the beginning of the trail, she was waiting for him.

"I win!" Her cheeks were pink and her toque was slightly askew, and it was just the two of them...and hell, she looked good.

Usually, Zach was a talker, but right now, he didn't talk.

He took Jo's gloved hand and raised his eyebrows. She nodded before she started skating again, not quite as fast as before, and he skated with her, holding hands.

It was a novelty, skating through the forest like this. The bare branches of the deciduous trees and the green of the conifers were covered in a layer of fluffy snow. Large flakes of snow started falling slowly from the sky, and Jo tipped her head up and smiled.

It was peaceful.

They kept skating, hand in hand, around the track.

He remembered what she'd told him the other night, about wanting another relationship, even after all that had happened.

He hoped she'd get what she wanted. He was her friend after all.

But dammit, if some part of him didn't tense at the thought of her skating hand in hand with another man.

It had been a long time since he'd felt like this.

After the fifth loop, Jo came to a stop near the hut. She was about to step through the doorway, but he took her hands and pulled her close, as if in a trance.

Once again, he raised his eyebrows, and once again, she nodded.

He kissed her.

Her mouth was welcoming, hot compared to the air around them. She curved her arms around him and pulled him even closer. It was fortunate that she was only a couple inches shorter than him, or they wouldn't have been able to make this work.

And boy, was it ever working.

She moaned softly as he took her mouth in his again and again, and when she slipped her tongue between his lips, he nearly swore.

But he didn't, because he didn't want to break the spell they were under.

He touched his tongue to hers; she felt so *necessary* right now, just as necessary as the winter clothes that were protecting them from the cold.

Suddenly, after years of friendship, kissing her was just what he needed.

A snowflake fell on her nose; he licked it off before returning to pleasuring her mouth, each of her precious sighs making his pants a little more uncomfortable.

She leaned into him, and then, suddenly, she was gone.

He caught her before she fell onto the ice.

"Perhaps we should take off our skates," she said, leading him into the hut.

She sat down on a bench and unlaced her skates. After she put her boots on, she took off her toque and unzipped her jacket, exposing her Leafs sweatshirt. Her cheeks were flushed and her hair was wild, some of it slicked with sweat, and he'd never seen anything more beautiful.

Once he'd changed into his boots, she slid across the bench, straddled him, and went right back to kissing him.

Jo was a steady presence in his life, and he'd never imagined she'd be so passionate.

His imagination clearly needed work.

Zach slid his hands under her sweatshirt and T-shirt, and he groaned as he touched her hot skin.

"Okay?" he murmured.

When she nodded, he moved his hands higher, under her sports bra.

This time, she was the one who groaned, and that sent a bolt of lust straight to his cock.

He circled her nipple with his thumb, then tweaked it. She groaned once more, and God, he wanted to hear that sound again and again.

He kissed her neck and cold cheek before making his way back to her mouth. Her sweet mouth would feel so good on—

"Daddy, what are they *doing?*"

Jo scrambled off his lap and fell backward onto the ground, landing on her ass.

"Shit, are you okay?" Zach extended a hand, realizing belatedly that he'd sworn in front of a small kid. Actually, three small children, who were all peering at him curiously.

"They were kissing, you dumb-dumb!" said Kid 2.

"You said a mean word!" said Kid 1.

Zach grabbed Jo's hand and pulled her up, and they scurried out of the hut before they could hear any more.

Once they were sitting in the safety of the car, she glanced out the window and said, "I'm sorry. I shouldn't have…you know."

He took her chin in his hand and turned her so she was looking at him. "Yes, you should have. I enjoyed it."

She gave him a tentative smile, but it wasn't enough for him, so he kissed her again, in a way that would totally scandalize those children and their parents.

"Don't apologize," he said, then started the car.

They didn't talk much on the drive back to Mosquito Bay. Zach was still trying to wrap his mind around what had happened.

He didn't understand it. He'd never wanted to kiss Jo until they'd started this charade.

He shook his head. It was probably just because he hadn't had sex in six months, and he was horny.

Really, that's all it was. And he wouldn't let anything come of it. She was his friend, and that would make things weird.

～

Jo sat at the back of the bakery with her hot chocolate and scone...and a wide grin on her face.

A few minutes later, her friend Tiffany walked in, her two-month-old baby in a carrier.

"So, what's up?" Tiffany asked, sitting across from Jo. "What's this emergency that required me to leave the warmth of my house?"

"I don't understand why you're complaining," Jo said. "You're having a currant scone. Isn't that worth a little trek outside?"

"It's pretty freaking cold out there." Tiffany bounced her sleeping child up and down.

Tiffany and Jo had been friends since elementary school. Their friend group used to be bigger, but the other three women had moved away from Mosquito Bay and only came back to visit family a few times a year, so usually it was just the two of them.

"You'll never guess what happened," Jo said. "We kissed!"

"You and Zach?"

"Who else could I possibly be talking about?"

Tiffany wasn't a fan of Jo's crush on Zach. Not that she disliked him, but she didn't like the idea of pining in secret for someone for years.

"Who kissed who?" Tiffany asked.

"The first time, he did, but the second time, I made the move." Jo flushed as she thought of Zach's hand on her breast...then flushed in embarrassment as she recalled how they'd been interrupted. "We went to the skating trail near Goderich. The first lap, we raced and I won."

"His delicate male ego wasn't bothered?"

"Zach doesn't have a delicate ego," Jo said. "Afterward, he took my hand and we skated together for a while." She couldn't help the smile that came to her face. "Then we kissed."

"I'm guessing by your expression that it lived up to your expectations?"

"Yes."

Oh boy, had it ever.

"I'm impressed," Tiffany said. "I figured it couldn't possibly be that good."

"I think something might actually come of this," Jo said. "Perhaps this fake relationship was just what he needed to see me in a different light."

"Jo, I love you, but I don't think it means anything. Zach's kissed many women. It's not like he's restrained himself since Marianne left him. And he never ended up dating any of those women, did he?"

The hot chocolate tasted bitter in Jo's mouth.

"Sure, he might be attracted to you," Tiffany continued, "but I doubt anything will come of it. I'm sorry, but I don't. You know he has no interest in another relationship—he's told you that."

Jo wasn't surprised by Tiffany's words. Her friend was always the pessimist. Maybe Tiffany wasn't the person Jo should have texted the instant she stepped out of Zach's car.

Or maybe she'd done it instinctively out of self-preservation, like a part of her had wanted someone to knock some sense into her.

But was what Tiffany saying really *sense*?

Tiffany wasn't the one who'd been kissed by Zach Wong. Tiffany hadn't skated through the snowy woods with him, hand in hand.

It had felt like it was more than just physical.

Jo wasn't delusional, was she?

6

IT WAS Chinese New Year at last. The whole reason Zach had gotten a fake girlfriend.

His siblings hadn't arrived yet, and right now, Zach and Ah Yeh were in the kitchen of his parents' house, preparing their evening feast. They would have a whole chicken and a whole fish, as they always did at Chinese New Year, plus noodles and fried rice and turnip cakes. For most holidays, his parents did the cooking, but Ah Yeh was always in charge for Chinese New Year.

Ah Ma was also in the kitchen, sitting at the table, eating the sweet rice cake made of glutinous rice flour and brown sugar.

"Aiyah," Ah Yeh said. "You will eat it all before everyone is here."

"I know. I am so sneaky!" Ah Ma said.

"I don't think 'sneaky' is the right word." Dad sat down beside his mother and helped himself to a piece of cake.

Zach hoped Jo enjoyed herself. He was suddenly nervous about the whole thing. Would she be weirded out by the chicken feet and head?

Would his grandmother really ask her sixty-nine questions?

"This year is very exciting," Ah Ma said. "All grandsons have a date! Last year, there were no girlfriends, and now, there are three. Maybe next year, all three of you will have wives."

Zach stared at her.

"What?" Ah Ma said. "You are not thinking about marriage?"

"Jo and I have been together for two weeks," Zach said. "It's a bit soon."

"But you have known each other for a long time. I think it's not too soon."

"Please don't scare her away," Mom said, walking into the kitchen.

"I am not scary!" Ah Ma said, affronted.

Dad snorted.

Zach put down his knife and turned to his grandfather. "Could you show me how to make ginger beef sometime? It's Jo's favorite."

"Ah, how sweet," Ah Ma said. "He is cooking for her. Very romantic."

Ah Yeh was focused on something on the stove, but he nodded, and Zach told himself that he'd asked about the ginger beef only because it was part of his act.

Jo stood on the doorstep to Zach's parents' house and took a few deep breaths.

This was it. The family dinner.

She wanted to make a good impression on Zach's family, especially since now, there was a real chance…

Well, Tiffany didn't think so, but Jo couldn't completely give up hope.

She hadn't wanted to show up empty-handed, so she'd brought persimmons, having learned that it was a fruit some people ate for Chinese New Year. She'd bought them on her monthly trip into London.

At last, she knocked on the door, and a moment later it swung open.

"Hey." Zach smiled at her.

His hair flopped over his forehead, and she reached up to push it to the side before kissing him on the cheek.

Just acting like his girlfriend, nothing more.

But after that chaste kiss, she couldn't help thinking about the not-so-chaste kiss by the skating rink, and her cheeks turned pink.

He smiled at her again, as though knowing exactly what was going through her mind.

A minute later, all of Zach's family had crowded into the front hall, and he introduced them. "These are my grandparents. My parents, Rosemary and Stuart. My sister, Amber. Nick and his girlfriend Lily, Greg and his girlfriend Tasha."

"It's so nice to meet you all," Jo said. "I mean, to see you again. I've met most of you before. Small town, you know."

Did she sound nervous?

She was pretty sure she sounded nervous.

"I brought persimmons." She held up the small box.

"Ah, good, good!" Ah Ma said. "I like persimmons."

Stuart picked one up. "They're not ripe yet."

"When they're not ripe, they make your mouth feel fuzzy," Greg said. "This is due to the tannins."

Oh. Jo had no idea when persimmons were ready to eat.

"No big deal," Zach said, putting his hand on her shoulder. "They'll be good in a few days. Come in and try some of the nin gou. Chinese New Year cake."

He took her hand, and she couldn't help smiling at the gesture. When they reached the dining room, he picked up a brown rectangle and held it in front of her lips.

Zach was going to feed her. And his grandmother, mother, and sister were looking on.

She took a small bite. It was chewy and not quite what she'd expected, but it wasn't unpleasant. She took a couple more bites and decided it was pretty good, now that she was accustomed to it.

"My husband made it," Ah Ma said. "Am very lucky to have husband who is a good cook. Zach wants to learn to make his ginger beef. Apparently it is your favorite?"

"Ah Ma!" Zach said. "That was supposed to be a surprise for Valentine's Day."

"Ah, sorry. Me and my big mouth."

Jo took another bite of the cake from Zach's fingers.

"Ugh, get a room," Amber said. "I can't believe all of you are coupled up now."

"Perhaps a date for you will arrive any minute," Zach said. "There's still time."

Mom shook her head. "I promised Amber we wouldn't set her up with anyone tonight, but maybe we'll find someone for Easter."

"Oh, God, *no*." Amber glared at her.

Zach fed Jo the last of the cake before planting a quick kiss on her lips.

"Woo-hoo!" Ah Ma said. "You are practicing for wedding ceremony?"

"Alright, that's enough," Zach said. "Now, Jo, I forgot to warn you about an important New Year's tradition in our family. Pictionary."

Jo couldn't help but laugh.

"Usually Amber and I are a team," he continued, "and Greg and Nick are a team. But I think you and I should be a team tonight. Amber's drawing abilities leave a little to be desired."

Amber stuck out her tongue. "I guess I'm the odd one out, since I'm the only one who's not in a couple. I can be the judge."

"You're just glad you don't have to draw anything," Nick said.

"We will kick everyone's ass." Ah Ma lifted her foot and kicked the air. She wobbled, and Stuart caught her.

"Unlikely," Ah Yeh said. "You are terrible at Pictionary."

"I am the best artist! It's not my fault you are so bad at understanding my drawings."

"Your elephant looked like a bear. How could anyone guess that?"

They kept arguing about their Pictionary skills, and Jo was glad that everyone seemed comfortable enough to act like themselves around her. She could totally handle Pictionary. She hadn't played in years, but it sounded like fun.

Zach dragged her into the hallway and rested his hands on her hips.

"How's it going?" he whispered. "You okay? Is it overwhelming?"

"No," she said, allowing herself to wrap her arms around his neck. "It's great."

I only wish it were real.

Dinner was delicious. Jo particularly liked the chicken, plus the turnip cake, which was actually made with a type of radish.

Ah Yeh allowed her to try one of the fish cheeks, which were his favorite; supposedly it was a delicacy. Jo didn't quite understand the appeal, but she didn't dislike it.

After dinner, Zach and Nick cleared the table and brought out more of the nin gou, plus Nanaimo bars, butter tarts, oatmeal cookies, and White Rabbit candies. Zach handed one of them to Jo.

"The rice paper wrapper is edible," he said.

The candy looked a bit like a white Tootsie roll. She popped it in her mouth and quite enjoyed it.

Ah Ma handed out red envelopes to her grandchildren, as well as Lily, Tasha, and Jo. She clucked her tongue as she did so.

"I hope next year there will be no red envelopes. You are all getting too old for this."

"We told you," Nick said. "You don't have to give us money."

"Yeah, you live in a penthouse in downtown Toronto. Why do you need ten dollars?" Stuart said, but he handed an envelope to Nick all the same.

"Younger generation gets red envelopes until they are married." Ah Ma looked at her grandchildren. "I hope next year, everyone is married, and there will be no red envelopes. Except maybe for a baby?"

"You know," Amber said, "we might not all get married."

"Fine. I will stop when you turn thirty-five. Greg, this is your last year."

Greg nodded his head with a grunt.

Jo regarded her envelope, red with gold lettering—not that she could read what the Chinese characters said—and a gold rat, since it was the year of the rat.

"Thank you," she said to Zach's grandmother.

"You will come back next year?"

"I hope so."

"You might change your mind after Pictionary," Amber said.

Pictionary turned out to be quite an operation. They retired to the living room with cups of tea and sat on the couches. Nick got an easel with a whiteboard and set it up in front of the television. Greg placed a small sand timer on the coffee table. Amber made a scoresheet and set it next to the timer.

"So," Zach said, "this is how we play the Wong version of Pictionary, since Jo and Lily are new to this and Tasha hasn't done it in a while. We'll be in five teams of two tonight. Amber will use a Pictionary word generator and show the word to a member of the first team. They will start drawing, and the other member will have one minute to guess the word. If they do, they get a point, then it moves to the next team. We'll play eight rounds, and then the top two teams make it to the playoffs."

"We're the team to beat," Stuart said, putting his arm around his wife.

"It's true," Zach said to Jo. "My grandparents are terrible at this game, but my parents are freakishly good. I'm sure we can do just as well, though."

They picked Scrabble letters to decide which team would go first. She and Zach got an "A."

"Do you want to draw, or should I?" he asked.

They were sitting on one side of the couch, his leg against hers; Tasha and Greg were sitting at the other end.

"Um, I'll draw." Jo stepped up to Amber, who, as the official judge, was sitting on the chair by the whiteboard. Amber pulled up a word generator on her phone and clicked "generate."

Jo's word was "hipster."

She'd expected something a bit easier, but she could do this. She started drawing a man.

"Man," Zach said.

She added a collared shirt with a checkered pattern.

"Lumberjack."

She added a toque.

"Canadian," he guessed.

Finally, she added glasses and a beard.

"Douche canoe?"

She couldn't help smiling, but dammit, he still wasn't getting this? She'd have to add something to show the hipster's interests.

She drew a bottle of beer.

"Drunk," Zach said.

Unfortunately, it was hard to emphasize that it was craft beer, since presumably writing anything on the bottle would be against the rules.

Next, Jo drew a vinyl record and musical notes, then turned to Zach.

"Um. Musician?"

As his gaze caught hers and she gestured for him to keep

guessing, it felt like there was a connection zinging between them.

"Time—"

"Hipster!" Zach said, as the last of the sand in the timer fell.

"Hmph," Ah Ma said. "Not fair, he guessed when the time was up."

"No, it was *almost* up," Zach said. "I got it at the last second."

"I'm the judge, and I say it's fair." Amber drew a single line on the scoresheet. "Point for Team Hipster."

Jo returned to the couch, and Zach settled his arm around her. "Our team names are based on the first thing we draw," he said. "Good job."

He kissed her cheek, and she smiled.

She was determined to get as many points—and kisses—as possible tonight.

Game on.

Stuart and Rosemary were next. Rosemary looked at Amber's phone, then drew the symbol for "male" and a bunch of stick figures below it. All had top hats and angry faces.

Below this, there was a person—a woman?—with long hair and a frown on her face.

Jo had no idea what this word could be.

"Patriarchy," Stuart said.

Rosemary pointed at him and smiled.

How the hell had he gotten patriarchy from that?

Next it was Greg and Tasha's turn. Greg drew first. Whereas everyone else had drawn quick, simple pictures, Greg's was more detailed. It looked like a root vegetable, but which one?

"Carrot," Tasha guessed. "Parsnip. Celeriac. Turnip. Rutabaga. Radish…I'm running out of guesses."

"Time's up," Amber said.

Greg turned away from the whiteboard. "It's obviously wasabi."

"How should I know what that looks like?" Tasha asked. "Why didn't you draw sushi?"

"Then you would have guessed 'sushi.'"

"You could have drawn a little dish with wasabi paste and pickled ginger next to it."

They kept arguing, but when Greg returned to the sofa, Tasha laughed and planted a kiss on his lips, and Jo couldn't help feeling a burst of longing.

Ah Ma and Ah Yeh were up. Ah Ma went to the front and started drawing. Jo tilted her head this way and that, but she had no idea what it was. Next to her, Zach chuckled softly, and it rumbled through her body.

"Garbage can," Ah Yeh said. "Vase. Mug. Teapot. Teacup. Soccer ball."

Ah Ma scrunched up her face in frustration and kept drawing.

"Time's up," Amber said.

"Aiyah, why couldn't you get it?" Ah Ma said. "It was clearly a hot air balloon."

Jo tilted her head again and squinted...and okay, maybe it looked like a hot air balloon, if she really used her imagination.

After the first round, three teams had a point, and two teams did not.

It was Jo and Zach's turn again. When Zach got up from the couch, Jo missed his body heat. He looked at the word on Amber's phone and nodded seriously.

First he drew a rainbow, then an arrow pointing to one of the bands of color.

Ah, he was trying to tell her a color. Clever.

It was the fifth color in the rainbow.

"Blue!" she said.

A ball of joy formed in her chest, though they were just playing Pictionary with his family. But she didn't push the feeling aside. She'd enjoy this night of pretending they were a couple. Of pretending she had what she wanted.

Next, Zach started drawing an odd pattern of swirls. She shook her head, having no idea what that was. Beside it, he drew a finger.

"Blue finger?" she guessed. What on earth could it be? "Blue… fingerprint? Blueprint!"

She laughed when Zach held his hands up in victory.

He sat back down and wrapped his arm around her. She felt gooey, like the filling of a butter tart, and content.

"Mom and Dad, it's your turn," Amber said.

Stuart stepped up to the whiteboard and glanced at his word. When Amber flipped over the timer, he drew an odd shape with a circle in the middle…was that an avocado? Next to it, there was a plus sign, followed by a slice of bread.

"Avocado toast," Rosemary said. "Millennial."

Stuart gave her a thumbs-up.

"I do not understand this one at all," Ah Ma said.

"Two points for both Team Patriarchy and Team Hipster," Amber said.

"Unfair that we have to be Team Patriarchy," Rosemary muttered.

"Well, we can hardly call you Team Millennial. That would be misleading, since you're many decades too old for that."

Rosemary sniffed. "We're not *that* old."

"You could be Team Avocado Toast," Jo suggested.

"I like that," Stuart said.

Jo felt stupidly pleased for getting Zach's father's approval.

But she still wanted to beat him at Pictionary. For some reason, she felt like winning this game, against a happy couple who had been married for almost forty years, would mean something.

Would mean that she and Zach belonged together.

It was foolish, but this was more than just a game to her.

～

An hour later, it was time for the Pictionary finals.

Team Hipster vs. Team Avocado Toast.

Team Lawn Mower—Nick and Lily—had finished third, Team Wasabi in fourth place, and Team Hot Air Balloon in last place.

"Aiyah," Ah Ma said. "This happens every year. We never make the finals."

Zach's grandparents had had a hilariously poor showing, but despite their digs at one another, they seemed to be having a good time.

Jo was gearing herself up for the playoffs, but it wouldn't be easy. She wasn't sure she and Zach could win against a team that had gotten "society" in fifteen seconds.

Seriously. Fifteen seconds!

Jo and Zach were first. Jo drew, and Zach easily guessed "lyrics." Team Avocado Toast wasn't to be outdone, however, and got a point for "extra virgin olive oil."

Zach went up to the whiteboard next. After looking at Amber's phone, he began drawing.

"Airplane," Jo said. It was clearly an airplane, though she doubted that was the word—it would be too easy. "Travel. Vacation. Trip."

Beside the airplane, Zach drew a stick figure lying in a bed, the sun shining above them, a suitcase on the floor beside them.

"Jet lag?"

This correct answer earned Jo a gorgeous smile.

Team Avocado Toast was up. Rosemary guessed "standing ovation" from Stuart's drawing in less than thirty seconds.

"How many rounds are in the playoffs?" Lily asked.

"Four," Amber said. "If there's a tie, we go to sudden death."

Now it was Jo's turn to draw. Her heart was beating extra fast, even though it was only a game of Pictionary.

Her word—or words, rather—was "time zone."

She drew a rough map of Canada and glanced at Zach. He was looking at the whiteboard in puzzlement.

Hmm. Maybe it was a very crude map, but she wasn't accustomed to having to draw their country from memory.

Jo wasn't sure what the time zones did in the territories, but she drew thick lines for the approximate time zone boundaries in the provinces, followed by a clock at three o'clock over BC, a clock showing four o'clock over Alberta, and a clock showing five o'clock over Saskatchewan and Manitoba.

Come on, Zach. You can get this.

"Cross-country," he guessed. "Time. Clocks."

She drew a clock at six o'clock over Ontario, then circled most of Ontario and Quebec.

"Eastern Standard Time?"

She drew another circle around the Central Time Zone—at least, her best guess at where it was. Was she making a mess of this?

"And that's..." Amber began.

"Time zone!" Zach said.

"You got it!" Jo grinned and returned to the couch. "Good job, you."

"No, it was thanks to your wonderful drawing skills."

Jo said nothing, just gestured to the whiteboard, containing her horrible map of Canada. It looked even worse from a distance. Still, he gave her a quick kiss on the temple.

Team Avocado Toast successfully guessed "cheater," and now it was time for the final playoff round. Zach's turn to draw. He frowned when he looked at the word on Amber's phone.

Shit. This was probably a hard one.

Zach drew a wide cylinder, the circular faces horizontal, with a wavy line through the middle—was that supposed to be water? Next, he put a stick figure in the cylinder.

"Tub," Jo said. "Bathtub. Hot tub."

Zach drew another tub of water to the left, except there was no stick figure, and the water line was a little lower. He drew an arrow between the water line in the two tubs. To emphasize that it had moved, perhaps?

Jo wasn't sure what he was getting at, and dammit, she really wanted to win.

Think, Jo. Think.

But she had nothing.

She stared at Zach and willed him to telepathically tell her the word. After all, she was convinced that was how Stuart and Rosemary had gotten some of their words so quickly.

Unfortunately, she got distracted by Zach's forearms. He'd pulled off his sweater and was now wearing just a T-shirt.

Focus.

Zach drew a speech bubble for the stick figure in the tub. Of course, he couldn't actually write any words in it.

Jo looked at the picture again. The water level had increased when the stick figure stepped into the tub. That was displacement. Discovered by Archimedes, right? She remembered learning that in high school science—Zach probably taught it to his students. And when Archimedes had stepped into his tub and suddenly understood displacement, he'd said...

Zach circled the speech bubble.

"Eureka!" Jo shouted.

"Yes!" Zach ran to the couch and lifted her up, and once again, she found herself admiring his arms.

He gave her a peck on the mouth, and now she was admiring his lips.

It had seemed instinctive for him to rush over and kiss her. She couldn't help the way that it warmed her heart.

"You were amazing," he whispered, and that sent tingles through her body.

Rather than sitting next to her on the couch, he pulled her into his lap.

"Get a room," Amber muttered.

Was Jo seducing Zach with her Pictionary skills?

If she'd known this would work so well, she'd have done it ages ago.

Team Hipster had managed to get all four words in the play-offs, but Team Avocado Toast still had a chance to tie.

Indeed, they successfully got "climate."

"I think this is only the second time in Pictionary history that we've needed the sudden death round," Nick said.

Ah Ma patted Jo's knee. "You are so good at this game."

Jo smiled, then walked up to the whiteboard on wobbly legs.

They needed to get this. Somehow, she felt like everything depended on it.

Unfortunately, her word was "shaft."

Shit. The first thing that popped into her head was, unfortunately, not something she wanted to draw in front of Zach's family.

"And...go," Amber said.

Jo stood there for a moment, unsure what to do, before she started drawing a mine shaft.

"Tower?" Zach guessed once she had finished.

She shook her head.

Dammit, this wasn't working. She drew a big "X" through her mine shaft and attempted to draw a shaft of light coming through a window.

"Window," he said. "Sunlight. Morning."

She looked at the time. They were past the halfway point. She needed a new plan.

She *really* wanted to win, and her best chance was to draw a penis in front of Zach's family.

Did she dare?

7

ZACH WATCHED as Jo quickly erased everything she'd drawn.

He had zero idea what this word could be, but he was thrilled that he and Jo were close to defeating his parents. He and Amber had never beaten their parents in the playoffs. Nick and Greg had, but only once, and Zach suspected Mom and Dad had let them win.

Jo, bless her, was the perfect partner who'd gotten more into this game than he'd expected. He'd rarely seen her so animated. It warmed his heart that she fit in with his family.

But it doesn't matter. It's not real.

He pushed aside his momentary disappointment and focused on the whiteboard.

Jo drew a long object with two circles at the base of it. She added some wiggly lines on the balls.

Because…those sure looked like balls, didn't they?

"Cactus," he said, though that made no sense. That was an easy word, and she would have drawn a sensible cactus from the beginning. "Rocket?"

Then Jo drew the head of the penis.

There was no doubt now about what she was drawing.

Everyone else was snickering, but not Zach.

"Penis," he said. "Cock. Balls. Circumcision. Erection."

He couldn't believe he was doing this in front of his parents and grandparents, but he was determined to win this thing.

Jo drew a circle around the center of the drawing, then turned to look at him. Her cheeks were slightly pink, her eyes wide and imploring.

"Shaft!" he exclaimed.

"Yes!" shouted Jo, pointing at him.

"Just in time," Amber said. "I can't believe you went there, Jo."

"Yeah, neither can I."

There was some uncomfortable laughter.

Ah Ma sniffed. "I thought Pictionary was a G-rated game. This is not G-rated."

"The picture isn't quite anatomically correct," Greg said. "For example—"

"I think it's a perfectly good shaft," Zach said.

"Alright," Amber said. "Time to move on. Mom and Dad, if you get this, we'll have to do another round of sudden death overtime. If not, Team Hipster wins."

When Jo came to sit on Zach's lap, he was very aware of a certain part of his anatomy, especially when she wiggled to adjust her position.

Did she know what she was doing to him? Was she wondering if he had a perfectly good shaft?

He couldn't help it; he rather hoped she was.

Amber turned over the timer, and Mom started drawing. There was a man with a beard and a hat. Santa Claus? And now he was drinking a beer?

Zach had no idea what this was, but he wouldn't be surprised if his father still guessed correctly.

Next, Mom drew faces of people laughing.

"Humor? Laughter? Comedy act?" Dad said. "Christmas gone wrong? Drunk Santa?"

Zach stared at the timer and tightened his hold on Jo.

He wanted to defeat his parents, but if he was honest with himself, this was mostly about Jo. About the way she would smile when they won. She was so sexy when she was flushed and excited.

"And..."

"Boxing Day?" Dad said.

"...that's time," Amber said. "Team Hipster wins!"

Jo grinned as though she'd never been happier.

"What was the word?" Dad asked.

"It was 'parody,'" Mom said. "Sorry, I had no idea what to draw. It's hard to show 'parody' when you can't use any words."

"That's okay," Dad said.

Zach wasn't looking at him, though.

He couldn't take his gaze off Jo.

They left at ten o'clock. Zach offered to walk Jo home, like he always did after they went to the bar on Friday nights. But this time, as they made their way across town, there were a couple things different from usual.

First of all, it was slippery.

The temperature had been above freezing for much of the afternoon, and some of the snow had melted, but now the water had turned to ice.

Jo slipped and clung to Zach. To steady her, he wrapped his arm around her body.

The other thing that was different?

He couldn't help wanting to take off her jacket and toque... and more.

They'd made out when they were skating, and he'd replayed their kisses over and over in his head, thinking about what would happen if they went further.

"What was going through your mind," he said, "when you drew a cock and balls on the whiteboard in my parents' living room?"

"Oh, God." She turned away. "I really wanted to win, that's all, and I couldn't think of another way to get you to say 'shaft,' since you didn't get 'mine shaft' or 'shaft of light' from the first two drawings. Your grandma kept giving me dirty looks afterward! I'm mortified."

"Yeah, I figured you just wanted to win."

"I'm sorry."

"It's okay, I like your competitive spirit." He paused. "What else was going through your mind other than winning?"

"Nothing. Nothing at all."

"For example," he pressed, "were you thinking of that particular part of my anatomy?"

"No, your whole family was there!"

The strength of her protest was suspicious, however.

"Mm-hmm," he said. "But my family isn't around now. What are you thinking about?"

"Zach," she said, as though in pain.

"I'll stop right now if you tell me to."

He waited a beat.

She said nothing.

"I think you want to do unspeakably dirty things to my *shaft*," he said quietly.

A strange sound escaped her lips, a mixture of shock and laughter.

No one else was out on the residential street. He stopped walking and pulled her against him, each of his hands holding one of hers.

"May I kiss you again?" he asked.

She nodded quickly and tilted her head upward.

"You're eager," he observed.

"Sorry!" She put a hand over her face.

Jo might have drawn a not-quite-anatomical picture of a penis at his parents' house, but she seemed a touch uncomfortable talking about this stuff. It was cute.

He pulled off his gloves and tucked them into his pocket. Gently, he cupped her cheeks and slipped his fingers under the bottom of her hat.

Then he kissed her, in the quiet of the night, his lips meeting hers over and over. He hadn't thought of doing this with her until recently, but somehow it felt right and *real*, despite the lies they were telling his family.

Jo adjusted herself so that one of her legs was between his, but she lost her balance and knocked into him. He fell backward before he could catch himself, though he managed to land on a snowbank instead of the icy sidewalk.

She fell on top of him, laughing, and kissed him again.

For a moment, neither one of them spoke.

"Jo," he said carefully, "would you want to do this indoors? Maybe on a bed?"

It was the stuff of her fantasies. Jo was walking up the stairs in her house and Zach Wong was following her, his hand resting lightly on her hip.

They were going to her bedroom.

They were going to have sex.

At least, she was pretty sure that's what would happen.

She flicked on the lights in her bedroom and sat on the bed. She should probably strip off her shirt and give him a show, or kiss him against the door, or…something.

But though she could do those things in her imagination, she couldn't do them now.

He sat beside her and pulled her into his lap.

"If you've changed your mind, that's okay," he said.

"No. Not at all. I'm just not very good at initiating stuff. Feeling comfortable with someone new. You know."

Except Zach wasn't "new." She'd known him for ages. They were friends. Maybe that's why she was sharing her inadequacies with him, even though she had a crush on him.

Plus, she'd already drawn a cock in front of his family, so it was hard to feel more embarrassed after that.

"That's one thing I never told you about Matt," she said. "He wished I'd initiate more often. I like sex, but I was always...well. Just a tiny bit awkward about how I look. Not that I think I'm ugly, but my body is more function over form. I can run 10k and play hockey and swim laps, but I hardly look like a model. Anyway, one time, I decided I would try. After dinner, Matt was on the computer, and I told him to join me in the bedroom, with a little wink, you know? I asked him to give me five minutes. I put on sexy underwear and a bra, nothing else, and lay down in bed, waiting for him. After half an hour—"

"*Half an hour?*"

"Yeah. He still hadn't shown up. So I texted him and he didn't reply. He knew how hard this was for me, and he didn't even have the decency to let me know he wasn't interested that night. Then the next week, he asked me again why I didn't initiate."

Zach held her more tightly against him. "That bastard."

He'd called Matt a bastard before, but this time, it was different.

"Anyway," she finished, "that was a few weeks before I ended the engagement. And I haven't been with anyone else since. You're much less out of practice than I am." She shook her head. "Sorry. I'm being weird. I wouldn't blame you if you don't want to do this anymore."

The confused look he gave her was, admittedly, rather gratifying.

"I'm interested, I promise," he said, sliding his hands down to her ass. "Relax and don't worry about anything. I'll take care of you. Just tell me if you ever want to stop, okay?"

"Okay."

He turned on the lamp beside the bed and got up to flick off the main light. It was dim now, the lamp only illuminating part of the room, and it made her feel a little more comfortable somehow.

As he sauntered back to the bed, he pulled his sweater over his head, followed by his T-shirt, exposing his chest. She swallowed as she took in the light and shadows playing over the canvas of his body.

It was nothing she hadn't seen before. She'd seen him in a swimsuit more than once. But this time, he was going to bed with her.

At the back of her mind, she wondered if maybe this wasn't a good idea. He might be physically attracted to her, but he'd never given any indication that he wanted this fake relationship to be not-so-fake, that he harbored anything other than friendly feelings toward her. As far as she knew, he still had no interest in a relationship.

But Jo was suddenly tired of only doing things that were good ideas. The man she craved wanted to be with her tonight, and she wouldn't pass up the opportunity.

"Second thoughts?" he asked. "Want me to cover up?"

"No, that's a terrible idea."

He chuckled as he eased himself on top of her, his chest vibrating against hers. His cock was right *there* between her legs, and he was getting hard. He circled his hips against her, nice and slow, and she groaned. God, that felt nice. When he grasped the bottom of her shirt, she lifted her arms up so he could pull it off, and then he unclasped her bra and tossed it to the side.

She felt a moment of panic that he'd change his mind now, but he didn't.

Instead, he looked at her in awe.

She swallowed past the lump in her throat. She could trust him. He would never make her feel like Matt had.

He started kissing her everywhere. All over her chest, her breasts, her stomach…as though every inch of her was important and deserved attention. She squirmed against him when he pulled her nipple into his mouth and swirled his tongue over the peak. Then he made his way down, and when he got to the waistband of her jeans, he lifted his gaze, and she nodded.

And then he was sliding off her jeans.

Zach was taking off her jeans.

She was nervous, but also excited, and his kisses had helped her relax into the mattress.

He grinned wolfishly when she was wearing just her panties, a pair that was black with a little bow on the front. He slipped his hands under her ass and rolled her over, then pressed his chest against her back. His erection was nestled against her ass, and she moaned as he swept her hair back and kissed her neck before planting a few kisses on her lace-clad ass.

"You're amazing," he whispered, and she smiled into the pillow.

He shucked off his jeans and boxers in one smooth move, and *that* was a sight she'd never seen before.

"What do you think?" He lay down next to her and pumped himself a few times. "Is it a perfectly good shaft?"

She couldn't help the burst of laughter that escaped her lips.

"I don't know," she heard herself say. "I need to touch it first."

Oh my God. Where had *that* come from? It wasn't like her at all.

Zach laughed, his eyes darkening at the same time. He took her hand and brought it down to his crotch.

She very much approved. His cock was hard and filled her hand just right.

She didn't say that, though.

"I still can't tell," she said. "I think I need to put my mouth on it before I can make my final assessment."

He growled low in his throat, and she felt a surge of power.

She was doing this to him.

"Jo..." he said, as he rolled onto his back. "I won't last long."

"I won't take long, then. Just a little lick..." She licked up the underside of his cock and couldn't help squirming as she did so. "And another..." She licked over the head. "And now I'll take the whole thing into my mouth." Her voice shook. "Can't make a proper assessment without doing that, can I?"

He made some inarticulate noises.

She smiled.

Then she took his cock into her mouth and sucked, and he gripped the sheets in his fists.

She released him with a *pop*.

"My expert opinion," she said, "is that it is indeed a perfectly good shaft."

"Just 'perfectly good'?"

"Well, it's quite excellent—does that sound better?"

"I know what would be better." He held her gaze as he pulled off her underwear and tossed them aside. Slowly, he slipped his hand between her legs, and she tensed in anticipation. He slid one long finger inside her and moved it in and out. "God, you're wet."

He still sounded like he was in awe of her.

"For you," she whispered. "Of course I am."

I've wanted you for so long.

He added a second finger, and she could hear her moisture as he moved inside her body. He brought his hand up to his mouth and licked off the first finger, then the second, then his thumb. When he moved his hand back between her legs, he circled his thumb over her clit.

She needed to touch him, too. She reached between his legs and wrapped her hand around his *quite excellent* cock.

"You feel wonderful," he whispered.

Jo had been anxious at first, a little self-conscious, but not anymore.

She ground against his hand. "I need you."

Though he wouldn't know everything that was behind those words, he could give her what she needed at this moment: to feel him within her.

He reached into the pocket of his discarded jeans and pulled out a condom. Her heart raced as she watched him roll it on.

This was really happening.

He held himself above her, and she could barely breathe. He wasn't even inside her yet, and it was already so intense. The way he looked at her. The way it was easy to be naked with him.

She grasped his erection and positioned it at her entrance. He pushed inside, groaning as he filled her.

Yes. Yes. Yes.

"Zach," she breathed.

He was still for a moment, as though this was almost too much for him, too, and then he started to move, pumping in and out.

He would take care of her. He would give her exactly what she needed. She trusted him.

She hooked her ankles over the backs of his thighs, opening herself up even more, allowing him to go deeper.

"Yes, darling," he said.

He kissed her neck, and she arched up against him as he sucked on her skin. He was hitting every perfect spot inside her; she didn't know how else to explain it, but it was like no sex she'd ever had before.

Her imagination hadn't been up to the task of imagining how good it would feel to be with Zach—which was surprising, because she'd spent a *lot* of time imagining it.

When he raised his body off her, she put her hands on her breasts, pushing them up and tweaking her nipples. He tugged the tip with his teeth before he took as much into his mouth as he could.

She bucked against him, on the precipice, so, so close. If only he could...

He touched his finger to her clit, and she shattered almost immediately, shaking mindlessly and crying out his name, losing herself in her climax.

As she came back down, he gentled his thrusts and looked her in the eyes as though she had just done the greatest thing he'd ever seen.

Eventually, his thrusts became deeper, more powerful, and she felt like he was filling every inch of her, out to her toes and fingertips.

"Jo!" he said as his own climax overtook him.

Half an hour later, they were still lazing in bed, recovering. Neither of them had put on any clothes. Jo enjoyed being naked with Zach. Even if he no longer looked like he wanted to devour her, his eyes continued to roam over her, full of appreciation.

Plus, if she put clothes on, he might feel the need to get dressed, too.

And that would be a calamity.

She gathered up her courage. "Will you stay the night?"

"Of course."

She didn't know what would happen tomorrow, but she wouldn't let herself think about that. For now, she would just enjoy going to sleep next to a man with a perfectly amazing shaft.

8

As Zach drifted into consciousness, he became aware of a warm body pressing against his chest. The warm, *naked* body felt wonderful next to his, and he tightened his arms around her.

Yes, he'd woken up snuggling Jo MacGregor.

He felt a moment of panic but told himself to take deep breaths and calm down. Though Zach wasn't usually one to freak out, this was a most unexpected situation, even if he'd been thinking about sleeping with Jo since last week's skating expedition.

Then last night, she'd come over to his parents' house for Chinese New Year. They'd won Pictionary, and she'd horrified his grandmother by drawing a large cock on the whiteboard.

He couldn't help chuckling at the memory.

Then after...

Well.

And now he was snuggling Jo and feeling like all was right in the world, which disturbed him. He'd wanted a fake relationship precisely because he had no interest in a real one.

What was going on?

"Morning." Jo rolled over to face him. There was a bit of makeup smudged under her eyes, and her hair was a mess.

She was just right.

But Chinese New Year was over, and she didn't need to pretend to be his girlfriend anymore.

He couldn't bear the thought, though he didn't care to examine his feelings too closely.

"We never talked about the end of our so-called relationship, did we?" he said casually.

"No, we didn't."

"Wouldn't it be a little suspicious if we broke up right after my family's New Year dinner? They might catch on. Perhaps we should keep doing this for another week or two."

"I think that's an excellent plan."

"You sure you don't mind?"

"I'm quite sure."

She slid her hand down his chest and grasped his erection.

Jo was so much fun in bed. Playful and sexy and eager... He wanted to punch Matt the Douche Canoe for making her feel unwanted and uncomfortable with her sexuality.

But she'd blossomed under Zach's touch last night, responding to everything he did.

He couldn't help feeling a little proud of the way she'd come apart in his arms, and the dopey expression she was giving him now as she leisurely stroked him.

He wanted to touch her, too. In fact, he very much wanted to do something he hadn't had a chance to do last night.

"How about we start the morning off right," he said, "with you sitting on my face?"

She grinned, slow and sexy, and his balls tightened.

Yes, this would be a great morning indeed.

～

"Hey," Jo said.

"Morning." Tiffany sat down across from her. "What's so important that you need a Sunday morning tea-and-scone date at the bakery?"

Jo leaned forward and lowered her voice. "I slept with Zach last night!"

"And it was good?"

"Do I look like I had bad sex?"

Tiffany regarded her for a moment. "Nah, you look like you had amazing sex. I bet everyone in here can tell."

"Tiff!"

"Just kidding."

Jo glared at her friend, then went back to thinking about last night. "It really was amazing," she said dreamily. "He was so sweet and attentive, and he made me feel like I *mattered*, more than Matt ever did. And this morning, he said he'd like to extend our fake relationship a little longer. I said yes, of course, but I wish he wanted a real relationship, and he didn't say anything about that."

"He might just want to get laid again."

"Yeah, maybe he wants to use me for sex." *Using someone* didn't seem like Zach, though. "Or maybe he's trying to figure things out. Maybe he's developing feelings for me."

Tiffany looked at her sadly.

The excitement Jo had felt over having great sex with the man she loved started to fade. Perhaps it was delusional to think he was starting to develop feelings, and if she just waited, it would happen.

It was risky, too. After the intimacy she'd shared with Zach, she could already feel herself getting more attached. Her sky-high fantasies about the sex hadn't been dashed by the real thing, and they'd woken up cuddling, for God's sake.

Jo sighed. She'd allow herself to continue this fake relationship...for now. Zach was right—it would be odd if they broke up right after she met his family.

~

Sometimes when Zach's brothers were in Mosquito Bay for the weekend, he'd invite them over to knock back a beer or two. This Sunday afternoon was one of those days. However, Zach was now regretting his decision.

"I can't believe your girlfriend drew a giant dick in front of Ah Ma and Ah Yeh!" Nick slapped his knee and laughed. They were all sitting on the couches in the living room. "It must have been... what would you say, Greg? Was the dick twelve inches, or longer?"

Greg grunted in response, but the corners of his lips tilted up.

Zach wasn't used to being in a bad mood, but he'd been like this since Jo left this morning. "Thanks, Mr. Fancypants," he said to Nick.

Nick took a sip of his beer. "So you and Jo, eh? How long has this been going on?"

"Two weeks."

"Did something bad happen? You're even grumpier than Greg."

"Thank you," Greg said.

"I'm fine," Zach said in a clipped voice.

Nick drummed his fingers on the table. "I thought you swore off dating after Marianne left you."

"Well, you didn't date either until you met Lily."

"Guess I was waiting for the right woman. Is Jo the right woman? Is she your true wuv?"

Nick was teasing Zach the way Zach had teased Nick about Lily.

Yeah, on some level, Zach felt like he deserved this.

However, he wanted to set the record straight. Just with his brothers.

"Jo isn't my girlfriend," he said. "I just asked her to pose as my girlfriend for Chinese New Year so nobody would try to set me up with another woman. I didn't need a repeat of Thanksgiving, thank you very much. Don't tell anyone, okay?"

Nick scratched his head. "But you two have been dating for a couple weeks."

"Had to make our relationship believable."

"You were sure doing a good job of being affectionate."

Zach shrugged. "I'm a good actor, what can I say?"

"No, I think you're secretly in love with her, and now that Chinese New Year is over, you're mourning the loss of your fake relationship." Nick laughed. "Can't believe you got a fake girlfriend!"

"The possibility actually occurred to me yesterday morning," Greg said. "But then I brushed it aside as too ridiculous. Guess I was wrong."

"It's not over yet," Zach said. "I asked her to extend the act a little longer. It would be suspicious if we broke up immediately after Chinese New Year, right?"

"Aww." Nick put his hands over his heart. "You really do love her."

"No, I don't."

Why was he telling his brothers about this?

Well, he could use some advice, he supposed, though whether he could get anything useful out of Nick and Greg was questionable.

He took a deep breath. "We slept together last night."

Nick grinned. "Ah. She wanted to see if your shaft looked like her drawing."

"I sure hope it doesn't," Greg said. "Or your dick isn't normal."

"Alright," Zach said. "Enough. No more talk about the Pictionary game, okay?"

Nick leaned forward and rested his arms on his knees. "So you slept together. Was it bad? Is that why you're in a crappy mood?"

"It was not *bad*," Zach said.

"Ah," Greg said sagely, nodding his head. "It was the best you've ever had, and that disturbed you."

Zach said nothing.

Unfortunately, his brothers read a lot into that.

"You love her," Nick said. "I was right."

"I don't love her," Zach protested, "but I do want to do it again. I've had a bit of a dry spell lately—that must be the reason."

"It could be. Or maybe you're meant to be together. Personally, I vote for the latter."

Geez, Nick had gotten annoying since he'd started seeing Lily.

"You asked her to continue your fake relationship," Nick said. "I think you're in denial. Next thing you know, you'll be making her soup dumplings and butter tarts and ordering your family to make you a snow fort."

"Hey." Greg crossed his arms over his chest. "I didn't *order* you. You helped willingly."

"Yeah, we were willing to help," Zach said. Greg and Tasha, his high school girlfriend, had always seemed like they belonged together. "But your control-freak side really came out when we were helping you with that snow fort."

"Agreed," Nick said. "You were a pain-in-the-ass."

Greg grunted.

"Back to your problem." Nick turned to Zach. "I still think you're in love with Jo, but you can't accept it yet. And I feel your pain. I've been there before. But you don't need to be so frightened."

"I'm not frightened." Zach was just being logical after the implosion of his engagement.

Greg gave him a not-so-comforting slap on the shoulder.

"I like Jo," Nick said. "She's nice, and she's not afraid to draw pictures of giant dicks in front of your family. Always a winning combination."

God, Zach would hear about that dick pic for years to come.

Although, admittedly, the memory did make his lips twitch. The look on Ah Ma's face had been priceless.

His brothers had been of no assistance today, but that was okay. Zach was sure these weird feelings would disappear soon.

He couldn't help hoping that he and Jo would sleep together a couple more times, though. Another week or two of casual sex between friends, and then she'd be out of his system, right?

[9]

On Wednesday, Zach was marking chemistry exams, but it wasn't going well.

He kept thinking about a different kind of chemistry.

He texted Jo. *Want to come over after dinner?*

She didn't immediately respond. He kept checking his phone every minute, feeling pathetic. She was busy at work, of course. She had an important job. Perfectly reasonable for her not to respond right away.

But to sweeten the offer, he added, *Actually, you can come over for dinner. I'll cook.*

At lunch, she replied, *Sounds good!*

He didn't pump his fist in the air. No, he most certainly did not.

That evening, after much debate, he made chicken alfredo and Caesar salad, cursing himself for not having gotten the ginger beef recipe yet. He also bought one of the currant scones she liked from the bakery.

As they ate dinner, they talked about their days at work, including Jo's attempts to expand her repertoire of balloon animals. It all seemed horribly domestic, but he reminded himself that they were simply friends having dinner together. Nothing weird about that, right?

And afterward…

It turned out to be a very good night.

However, it hadn't gotten her out of his system. But surely another couple times and he'd be happy to go back to being friends, not friends with benefits in a fake relationship.

On Friday, they met at Finn's as usual, but their regular table was taken by some out-of-towners, so they sat at the bar.

He shifted his bar stool close to hers, so his hip pressed against her, and placed his hand on her leg. She looked up at him from beneath her long eyelashes, and God, he wanted her.

Okay, maybe it would take more than a couple times.

This wasn't love, though. Love might not happen instantly, but there was always a spark from the beginning. He'd been in love four times—he knew this. Plus, that's how it had been for Nick and Lily. Greg and Tasha—that was a little different, as they'd known each other for most of their lives.

But he and Jo had known each other for a long time, too.

Except, not really.

He'd known *of* her, but three years was a huge age difference when you were a kid. They hadn't become friends until they'd both ended up here, at Finn's, disappointed by the people they were supposed to marry. They'd been friends for four years now, and okay, he was suddenly attracted to her, but that didn't mean he was falling in love.

It just meant he hadn't had much sex in the past year, and Jo was here, and convenient, and very lovely.

How had he never noticed that before?

As she sipped her Guinness, he watched her throat, which he'd kissed on Wednesday night. She always drank Guinness at the bar. He wasn't a fan, but it was her favorite beer, and now he found that rather charming, like the way she'd slide her hand up her neck and smile shyly at him.

He needed to get them back to their simple friendship.

"You excited for the hockey game on Sunday?" he asked.

"Yeah, we're going to kick their ass," she said, her competitive spirit coming out. "Can't believe we lost last year."

Every year on Groundhog Day, there was a hockey game between Mosquito Bay and the nearest town to the north, Ashton Corners. They charged admission and sold snacks, and the proceeds went to charity. Last year, Mosquito Bay had lost for the first time in five years, and Jo hadn't been happy. She was usually fairly easygoing, but when she really got into something...

"We'll win this time." He didn't care about the outcome much, but he wanted Jo to have what she wanted.

Just because he was her friend, that was all.

Both towns' teams were mostly male, but Jo was one of two women on their team. Suddenly, the thought of her whipping down the ice on a breakaway turned him on.

What the hell?

He wouldn't let himself get too worked up about it. It was just because they were sleeping together. It didn't mean anything.

Alright. Time to return to what had started their friendship: their break-ups. That was a safe topic, and it would remind him of why he never wanted another serious relationship.

"Did you always plan to return to Mosquito Bay after dental school?" he asked. This wasn't directly about his break-up, but thinking about staying or leaving Mosquito Bay made him think of Marianne, as Jo would know.

"I did go off to university with the intention of going to dental school after undergrad. My dad talked about me taking over his practice, and at first, I didn't like the idea. I was determined to do everything all by myself, start over on the other side of the country, or at least on the other side of the province." She chuckled, then said with a shrug, "I was a teenager. But after a few years of living in Hamilton, I tired of city life. My dad was getting old, and I knew how much it would mean to him if I came back to Mosquito Bay. By the time I got into dentistry, that was my goal. A stable job, my family nearby. A quiet life, but I like it."

"Me, too." *I like that you came back here. I like that you're a part of my life.*

He took a gulp of beer and looked at the television above the bar. There was a game on, but he hadn't paid any attention to it until now because he'd been talking to Jo.

"I looked forward to going away for school," he said, "although I didn't spend much time thinking about what I'd do with my life afterward. But a part of me always thought I'd come back, if I was able to get a job in the area, even though..."

"What is it?"

He turned toward her. "My family isn't like most of the other families in Mosquito Bay. There's the Chin-Williams, but they've all left now, and the Lee family that runs the convenience store. The Lams are good friends of my parents, but they live in Ashton Corners. We don't quite fit in. Nick was always very aware of that, and he hated it. For me, it wasn't a big deal—maybe it helps that my appearance doesn't make me stand out as much. Either way, this is my home, and it's not perfect, but I like it. Marianne thought she'd like it, too."

As long as we're together, it doesn't matter where we are, Marianne had said. Zach had been a stupid young man, and he'd believed her. Besides, it wasn't like she'd come from Toronto; she'd grown up in a small city. And Mosquito Bay wasn't isolated, unlike some of the towns up north. Inland from Mosquito Bay, it was farming country, and there were towns every ten or fifteen kilometers. London and Sarnia weren't all that far. Toronto was less than three hours away.

It hadn't been enough, though.

But all his bitterness was gone now. The thought of Marianne didn't cause the pain in his heart that it once had. In fact, he realized this wasn't anything new; he hadn't thought of her much in the last year or two.

Jo nodded and squeezed his hand.

Jo, whose plans for life weren't incompatible with his. She'd grown up here, too, and she'd lived here as an adult for several years. He didn't see her changing her mind about this. Jo was pretty steady, and she knew what she wanted.

And one of the things she wanted was another relationship.

As long as she kept sleeping with him, she couldn't have a boyfriend—unless she was into such arrangements, but he didn't think she was.

Just a little longer. Surely it wouldn't take much longer, and then he'd let her go. He'd encourage her to date and pursue what she wanted.

But for tonight...

He placed his hand on her leg, his fingers gently stroking her inner thigh.

Jo made an inarticulate noise that sounding like "gunhhh."

"Any plans tomorrow?" he asked conversationally, as though he wasn't touching her.

"Some...cleaning," she managed to say. "And..." She shook her head, then hissed, "What are you doing?"

"Oh, nothing." He circled his thumb over the inside of her knee. It seemed to be a particularly sensitive part.

"Zach..."

She was pretending to be annoyed with him, and it was kind of adorable.

But truth be told, he couldn't keep this up much longer.

"Want to get out of here?" he asked.

This time, they went to his house. He recalled how tentative she'd been last weekend, but there was none of that today. It thrilled Zach that she felt comfortable enough to push him up against the front door and pin his hands at his sides.

Her kisses were wet and sloppy and tinged with Guinness, but he didn't mind. She tasted fantastic. Guinness and *Jo*.

His jeans were getting very tight.

He freed his hands from her grasp and dragged down the zipper on her jacket. She was still kissing him as though her life depended on it, as though nothing was more important than this kiss.

And perhaps nothing was.

He needed to touch her. He bunched up her sweater with one hand, and his other hand unbuttoned her jeans and slid inside her panties. He groaned as he encountered her wetness.

"You're so sexy," he breathed.

"You really think that." It wasn't a question; she was just stating it with wonder in her voice.

"Of course I do." He ran his finger over her slit and released a shuddering breath.

Zach shucked off his coat, got down on his knees, and looked up at her. She was still wearing her jacket—though it was unzipped—and her hat and her boots, but it would take too long to remove them now.

He pushed down her jeans and underwear and put his mouth between her legs.

She gripped his hair, and that wasn't unpleasant, not at all.

He hadn't gotten to do enough of this last weekend, but he'd make up for it now. When he gave her one long lick, she threw her head back against the door. Encouraged, he licked her more urgently and slid two fingers inside her tight channel. She clenched around him, and God, he couldn't stand it anymore. With his other hand, he unzipped his own jeans, removed his cock from the opening in his boxers, and started stroking himself as he pleasured her. When he glanced up, she was looking down at his cock, and then, goddammit, she licked her lips.

"Zach…"

He'd never tire of hearing her utter his name like that.

Jo said his name again as her legs slipped out from under her, her back sliding down the door until her ass came to rest on the floor.

And the whole time, he was pleasuring her.

Her hands were in his hair again, urging him on. He moved his fingers faster, in and out, and stroked his dick more quickly, too.

Jo wasn't a screamer, but she gasped and jerked as her climax overtook her. Her head tipped back, exposing the column of her throat; he looked up at her face as he continued to lick her and help her wring every last bit of pleasure from this.

Afterward, she collapsed on the carpet in the hallway, but she didn't have the blissed-out expression that he'd expected. Instead, her eyes roved over him hungrily.

"Take it off," she said.

He didn't know what she was referring to, so he took off everything. His shirt, his pants, his boxers.

She reached for his cock and pumped it a few times. When he pulled a condom out of his pants, she rolled it on.

And then she sank down on him, right on the carpet near his front door.

Had he ever had sex here before?

He didn't think so.

But his thoughts were wiped from his mind as she began to ride him. He loved seeing her above him, like a brilliant goddess. She leaned forward and pressed her breasts against his chest and kissed his mouth.

Possessiveness curled through him. He bet she wasn't like this with anyone but him.

He cupped her ample ass in his hands and urged her on. He buried his face between her breasts and sucked on one.

When he could take it no more, when he felt the need to be in control, he twisted them over so he was on top.

For a moment, though, he didn't move. He just held himself

above her and grinned, and she squirmed beneath him, her pretty brown hair fanned out on the carpet.

"Zach," she said, "fuck me."

Those words, tumbling from her lips...

He pushed into her again and again, each stroke more intense than the last, as she writhed beneath him. When he licked his thumb and pressed it to her clit, her eyes opened wide, and when she pushed up against him one more time, she emitted the prettiest sigh he'd ever heard, and he growled as he found his release inside her.

As he came back down, and they lay there with their arms around each other, just inside the door to his house, he started laughing. He couldn't believe they hadn't been able to wait to get to his bedroom—or at least a couch.

Jo tucked her body closer to his and laughed, too.

He felt a bone-deep satisfaction that he hadn't experienced in a long, long time.

~

When Zach woke up, he was cold, and it was still dark out.

He checked his alarm clock. It was three in the morning.

The reason he was cold? He was naked and didn't have any blankets. Jo, apparently, was a blanket stealer, which was rather charming, actually. He was pleased to learn this detail about her.

Stealthily, he slid over to her side of the bed. She had a strong grip on the blankets, and he had to tug firmly to get them out of her hands.

"Zach," she murmured.

He wasn't sure whether she was conscious or not.

"Why are you taking my blankets." She sounded a little more awake now, but still vulnerable; he felt special for being able to see her at a moment like this.

Not that he could see anything but shadows in the dark room, but he could touch her and hear her.

"I'm freezing," he said. "You're hogging the blankets."

"Am not."

"Are too."

"Oh. So I am."

She adjusted the blankets so he was covered, then snuggled up against him, her front pressed against his back. He was the little spoon.

He enjoyed having her arms around him. And he had blankets on top of him now, so he was cozy and warm. He could stay here forever, cocooned in the darkness with her. He still felt that deep satisfaction from earlier, like he was exactly where he belonged.

After a while, however, Jo wiggled against him and stroked her hand over his chest, and he started to get hard.

He rolled over and slipped his hand between her legs, finding her slick with moisture.

"Yes," she murmured.

As he slid his finger inside her and she moaned, he realized something terrifying.

There was no way he'd be able to "get her out of his system."

It would never be enough.

Zach had fallen asleep soon after their middle-of-the-night sex, but Jo was still awake.

When she'd felt hopeless about her crush before, she used to console herself with the thought that maybe the sex would be bad.

But that was the exact opposite of the truth.

He made her feel sexy, desired, and completely comfortable to initiate things. Why, she'd pushed him up against the door and stuck her tongue down his throat, and that hadn't been weird, not at all. Nor had it been weird when she'd said, "fuck me."

She'd forgotten it could be like this. Both the sex, as well as the quiet moments cuddling in bed together, when it felt like all was right in the world.

Maybe it had never quite been like this for her before.

She was falling even more in love with him.

But he was still Zach Wong, and he hadn't said anything more about what was going on between them. In fact, tonight he'd asked if she'd always planned to come back to Mosquito Bay after university, and she'd figured he was thinking of Marianne.

It didn't seem like he wanted anything close to what she wanted.

And she deserved better, didn't she?

She'd deserved better than the sex she'd had with Matt; she'd deserved a partner who'd actually respond—even if it was to say he wasn't interested that night—when she put herself out there and tried to initiate.

She deserved the sex she had with Zach.

But she also wanted a relationship, and she shouldn't settle for a guy who seemed to have no intention of giving that to her.

She should stop sleeping with him, but the thought of giving up that intimacy made tears prick at the back of her eyes. She liked being able to show him how she felt even if she couldn't tell him. She liked feeling good about her body.

Just a bit longer…and then maybe she should give up their friendship, too.

She hated the thought. Their friendship had been a great comfort to her after her break-up with Matt, the thing she looked forward to every week, even before her crush.

However, she needed to move on, and as long as she kept seeing Zach at least once a week, it would be hard for her to extricate herself.

She needed a clean break.

Next to her, Zach released a single snore, and she laughed through the tears that were now falling down her cheeks. She wanted more nights like this.

She snuggled up close, careful not to wake him or steal the blankets.

Just a little longer...

THERE WERE twenty seconds left in the game. The score was tied at four.

Zach, who'd assisted on Mosquito Bay's second goal, was on the bench next to Shawn, but Jo was on the ice. His eyes didn't follow the puck. They stayed on her.

And then she got a breakaway and he was yelling.

She was going to do it!

When she was a couple meters from the net, she took her shot…

…and scored.

Of course his Jo didn't miss.

His? Well, they'd been fake dating for a few weeks. He supposed he was used to the idea of being with her.

When the game was over and she skated over to the bench, he took off his helmet and greeted her with a kiss. A few people whistled, but he ignored them.

"You were amazing," he said.

"So were you."

"Not as good as you."

She laughed a little, but he could tell she was proud.

They all went out for beers at Finn's afterward, and he kept close to her side the whole time. He didn't want to leave her, but he could only stay for an hour—he had other plans.

When he got back to his house, Sebastian Lam was already there. Sebastian had been back in Ontario since December, but he'd only contacted Zach last week. And he hadn't gone to the hockey game—hockey wasn't really his thing.

Sebastian and Zach were the same age. They'd attended different elementary schools, since the Lam family lived in Ashton Corners, but they'd seen each other all the time as kids and been best friends. Later, they'd gone to high school together.

It had been a few years since they'd seen each other, though, as Sebastian had gone to med school out west and stayed there to do his residency. He'd returned to be a family physician in a small town near Stratford.

"Good to see you, man," Zach said, giving his friend a back-slapping hug.

"Same," Sebastian said gruffly. He was about the same height as Zach, but a bigger, sturdier guy.

They went inside and Zach pulled out a beer for each of them. They sat at opposite ends of the couch in the living room, and for a minute, it was quiet.

They were good friends who'd hardly seen each other in years. Shouldn't they have something to say?

Zach was miffed that Sebastian hadn't contacted him earlier, that he'd had to hear it from his parents, but he wasn't sure he should bring it up. And the biggest thing happening in his life was his fake relationship with Jo, but he didn't know what he wanted to reveal about that.

Though Zach was usually the chattier of the two, it was Sebastian who broke the silence.

"You're probably wondering why I didn't text you earlier," Sebastian said. "Honestly, I was avoiding you."

Zach wasn't sure how to respond.

"Why?" he finally managed.

"Because I hadn't been back for long when I started…well." Sebastian took a pull on his beer. "Seeing your sister."

"You're seeing Amber?"

"Last I checked, you only had one sister."

"Thanks, smart ass. Are you, like, officially her boyfriend?"

"What is this?" Sebastian grunted. "High school again?"

"You know what I mean."

Are you just sleeping together? Is there any kind of commitment?

Sebastian shrugged.

It seemed Sebastian wasn't quite sure what was going on with Amber, just like Zach wasn't sure what was going on with Jo.

Except that wasn't true, right? They were friends who were sleeping together and faking a relationship. It was simple, really. He knew exactly what was going on.

Then why does it feel like I've been pushed into the deep end?

Zach shook his head to clear his thoughts.

"Okay," he said to Sebastian. "You're seeing my sister. You're less of a bastard than her exes, so…cool. You don't know exactly where you stand, but you'll sort it out, I'm sure. You were worried about telling me this?"

Yes, it was a little weird and it would take time to wrap his mind around it. Especially since Sebastian and Amber were such different people. Amber was…not precisely irresponsible, but free-spirited, and more artsy than the rest of them, despite her poor Pictionary skills. Sebastian was nothing like her.

But Zach was fine with this. Truly.

"I figured you'd be cool about it, but Amber wasn't sure." Sebastian paused. "Thanks."

Zach wanted to pry, but he didn't.

"I hear your parents tried to set you up with my sister at Thanksgiving," Sebastian said, a little smirk on his face.

"Yeah, they did. It was a disaster."

Sebastian's smirk widened. "Can't believe your parents found dates for all of you. And Nick is now dating Greg's date?"

Zach nodded.

"Thank God my parents have never attempted anything like that."

"Do your parents know about you and Amber?" Zach asked, then realized what he was saying. "No, of course they don't, or they would have immediately called up my parents, who would have then knocked on my door."

Sebastian chuckled. "Yup, exactly, which is why I don't want you to tell them."

"Don't worry, I won't."

"I'll figure this out soon, I promise."

Zach wanted to tell Sebastian to treat his sister right and all that fun stuff, but he knew it didn't need to be said. His friend was a good guy.

"What's this I hear about you and Jo MacGregor?" Sebastian asked, clearly having had enough of talking about his own dating life.

"We've been seeing each other for a month." Zach looked down at his beer and tried to hide his goofy smile. *Where did that come from?*

He didn't end up telling Sebastian the truth.

For some reason he liked the idea of Sebastian thinking it was real.

"One last Friday, and that's it," Jo said to Tiffany. They were at the bakery, each with a hot chocolate in hand. "You were right. Nothing more is going to happen with Zach. He just doesn't see me that way."

She choked up on the last words. She hated admitting it out

loud. Hated that she'd spent so long in love with someone who wouldn't love her back.

And yet, in the middle of the night when he...

She shut down that train of thought. It wasn't going anywhere productive.

She wouldn't regret the last few weeks, though. Wouldn't regret knowing what it was like to go on dates with Zach and kiss him and wake up with him.

But it was time to move on. She'd allow herself one more night, and that was it.

"Oh, Jo," Tiffany said, squeezing her hand. "I hate that I was right. You know that."

Jo blinked back tears and forced herself to laugh instead. "I can't believe I was in a fake relationship. Doesn't it sound ridiculous?"

Before Tiffany could answer, an older woman approached their table.

It was Shelly Sanderson. Shit. Had she heard what Jo said?

If she had, she gave no indication of it.

"Just want to congratulate you on your fabulous goal in the hockey game, dear," she said before bustling off to the front of the bakery.

When Jo arrived at her parents' house that night, Mom, Dad, and Becky looked at her with sad smiles, even though Jo had scored the game-winning goal against Ashton Corners.

They knew. They had to know.

Jo couldn't help but be annoyed with their pitying looks. *Poor Jo, she's already thirty-three and she can't get more than a fake relationship.*

"Shelly Sanderson overheard you and Tiffany at the bakery earlier," Mom said as she steered Jo into the kitchen. "Apparently you weren't really in a relationship with Zach? You were just pretending?"

Jo nodded. She didn't see the point in trying to lie now. "He had reasons for wanting his family to think he had a girlfriend, and I said I'd play along."

"Why didn't you tell us the truth?"

"It wouldn't be a good fake relationship if lots of people knew it wasn't real, would it?"

Ugh. If only Shelly would go back to making her coconut lemon squares and stop gossiping so much.

"You have a good career," Mom said. "And a house and friends and hobbies—"

"I know," Jo snapped, even though she *never* snapped at her mother. "I have a great life. I just want someone to share it with. I won't apologize for wanting more."

She didn't admit she had a crush on Zach, and she certainly didn't admit how intimate their fake relationship had become.

"Maybe you shouldn't have broken things off with Matt, then," Mom said.

"No, I absolutely should have. I regret not ending it earlier. It's not unreasonable to…"

…to want a man who looks at me the way Zach does.

She would end things with him and put this behind her. She would *not* settle for less than she deserved. Maybe it would take her a long time to find the right guy, but that was okay.

"Excuse me for a minute," she said.

She needed a moment to compose herself, and she needed to do one more thing.

Sorry, I can't see you this Friday, she texted Zach. *Something came up.*

Spending one last night with him would be too painful, and she should start the process of moving on as soon as possible.

Shelly Sanderson overheard me telling Tiffany that our relationship was fake, so if your family finds out the truth, I'm sorry about that, too.

She couldn't bring herself to tell him that their friendship was over. Besides, she owed him more than a text. She didn't see how she could face him this week, though; she needed a little more time.

Jo walked out of the washroom with her head held high.

If she could score that great goal, she could handle dinner with her family and a Friday night alone.

OUCH.

Zach rubbed his cheek, where he'd just been hit with a basketball.

"What's wrong, Mr. Wong?"

"Why aren't you paying attention?"

The senior boys' basketball team came to stand in a group around him. Seven thirty in the morning was too early for this, especially since he hadn't gotten a good night's sleep last night.

In fact, he hadn't had a good night's sleep in a while now, and he constantly found himself reaching for Jo, even though she wasn't there. He wished he would wake up cold, without blankets, because at least that would mean she was in his bed to steal them.

"Lady troubles?" asked one of the boys.

"Apparently he's dating Dr. MacGregor."

"No, they were just pretending, didn't you hear?"

"Enough," Zach said in an unusually stern voice. "I'm going outside for a minute, and when I get back, you guys better be doing drills, not gossiping about my personal life, okay?"

He exited through the doors that led to the parking lot and

breathed in the cold air. It was below freezing, and the snow was falling lightly. It reminded him of the day he and Jo had gone to the skating trail up near Goderich.

Goddammit. Today was Friday, and he always looked forward to Friday night. It was his time to hang out with Jo.

Strangely, though, she'd said she had plans today.

She never had plans on Friday night, except with him.

He couldn't help feeling a bit bereft.

He'd been looking forward to seeing her at the bar, and maybe afterward, they'd go back to his place and have sex, then wake up wrapped around each other and do it again. That was what he'd become accustomed to in the past couple weeks.

And the Friday nights at Finn's—he'd been accustomed to those for the past four years.

Fuck, it was cold out here, though it was nice to feel something other than the pain of not seeing her.

He'd slowly been realizing it over the past week or two, but now, it was crystal clear.

He wished their relationship were real.

Zach hadn't thought love could work this way for him, and he'd done his best to protect his heart ever since Marianne left. But it had snuck up on him.

He loved Jo's intelligence and athleticism. Her laugh, her smile. The way she could make people feel at ease. The way she could be strong and vulnerable with him at the same time.

It had never been "just sex" with Jo.

He needed her back in his life. He needed to wake up with her again and again. He needed to watch her draw more phallic objects in front of his family and score more game-winning goals.

Except he didn't want another relationship. He'd sworn them off—and for good reason.

He scrubbed his hand over his face.

Screw it. He was heading out of town tonight.

~

At nine o'clock that night, Zach was in Toronto with Nick, Lily, Greg, and Tasha. They were sitting around a table at a busy restaurant on King Street, drinking Thai iced tea and eating grabong, a Thai version of deep-fried shredded vegetables. Zach picked up a piece of squash and dipped it in the sauce—he had no idea what was in the sauce, but it was tasty.

"So, what's with the sudden decision to come to Toronto for the weekend?" Nick asked.

"I missed you guys."

His brothers looked at him skeptically.

"You saw us at Chinese New Year," Greg said.

"I know." Zach took a deep breath. "I'm falling for Jo, but I was in denial. You two were right."

"Sounds like it pained you a lot to say that," Nick said. "Hard to admit we're smarter than you, I guess?"

Zach gave him a look. "Yeah. But worse, I swore I'd never fall in love again."

Nick turned to Lily. "He was engaged once, but his fiancée left him."

"She didn't want to live in Mosquito Bay anymore," Zach said.

"I don't blame her," Nick said, "but Jo's made a life in Mosquito Bay. I doubt she has any intention of leaving. It's not the same."

"Still. The idea of having a relationship again, giving someone the power to hurt me that much…" Zach helped himself to more deep-fried squash.

There wasn't any food like this in Mosquito Bay. The only Thai food in town was the recent addition of pad Thai to the menu at Wong's Wok.

But Zach was content to take the occasional trip to the city to enjoy such things. He didn't need them all the time. He enjoyed visiting Toronto, but he wouldn't want to live here. It was too much, and everyone you passed on the street was a stranger.

"A lot of things that are worth having involve risk," Lily said.

"Very true," Greg agreed.

"What if she doesn't feel the same way?" Zach asked.

"You feel like a fool in front of one person," Nick said. "Are you more scared of telling her and being rejected, or of what could happen if you started a relationship and it doesn't work out later on?"

"The second. But also the first."

"I'm not sure you need to worry about that one," Tasha said. "It was pretty clear at Chinese New Year that she had feelings for you. When Greg told me you guys were faking it, I had a hard time believing it. I bet she's been in love with you for a long time, Zach, and that's why it was so easy for her to act as your girlfriend. And you've been unable to see what was right in front of you until now."

He felt a burst of hope. Had Jo really been in love with him before their fake relationship? For how long? Why had she never said anything?

The answer was obvious. She would have known he'd shoot her down.

They'd started sleeping together, but he'd only said he wanted to extend their fake relationship, and now she was trying to step back before she got hurt more.

His heart clenched. He felt terribly for her.

Or maybe she hadn't been in love with him before, and he just liked Tasha's explanation because it assuaged some of his fears.

But even if Jo returned his feelings, and even though he was pretty sure she wanted the same future as he did, what if they broke up?

"That's no guarantee," he said hoarsely as the waitress set his khao soi in front of him. He took a bite of the crispy noodles on top, then dipped his chopsticks into the broth and stirred the beef and noodles.

"No," Nick said, "but like Lily said, sometimes you have to take risks. Which is something you're not great at doing. You live in your hometown. You work at the high school you attended."

Zach enjoyed his simple life, and he didn't like having to defend his choices. There wasn't somewhere else he'd rather live, another career he'd rather have.

Except now there was another person he wanted.

Jo.

His brothers had a point. His life hadn't made him very good at taking risks, and this felt like a huge risk. His last relationship had failed, and his feelings for Jo were quite strong, if he was honest with himself.

"How do I do it?" he asked.

"Well, you could try Greg's snow fort idea," Nick said, "but you'll just have Mom and Dad to help you, not us."

"That's not what I mean. How do you mentally prepare yourself to do something scary?"

God, he felt like a wuss.

"Roller coasters," Greg said cryptically.

"Roller coasters?"

"You liked them when you were young, even though you'd always freak out a bit when we were in line at the amusement park."

"And horror movies," Nick said.

"I wouldn't compare Jo to a horror movie."

"I just mean," Greg said, "that sometimes scary things are great experiences. You have to remind yourself of that. I know you're afraid of rejection and of it not working out, but won't you regret it even more if you never try?"

That was a good point.

"I'm fucked either way," Zach said, but at the same time, hope fluttered in his chest.

"Basically, yeah," Greg grunted.

But Zach looked at his brothers and their partners—Tasha sneaking a shrimp off Greg's plate, which Greg didn't fail to notice, and Nick resting his hand on Lily's shoulder—and felt an intense longing to have the same thing with Jo.

Just her. He didn't want a relationship if it was with anyone else.

There was no guarantee, but he'd gotten through heartbreak once before. It had sucked, but he'd done it. He had to try.

∼

After spending the night in Nick's guest room, Zach drove back to Mosquito Bay. Instead of going to his place, he went to his grandparents' house—the one they'd bought five years after arriving from Hong Kong and had lived in for decades—and parked in the driveway.

He knocked on the door, hoping only his grandfather would be home and he could ask a little favor without too much drama.

Alas, after five minutes, he sighed and had to accept the truth.

Nobody was here, which almost certainly meant Ah Yeh and Ah Ma were visiting Zach's parents. So Zach headed to his parents' house.

"We were just talking about you," Mom said when he stepped inside.

"Good things?" Zach inquired.

Ah Ma marched into the front hall and pointed a menacing finger at him. "You lied to us. You were not dating Jo. You were faking it!"

Oh, dear. The gossip had reached his family.

Zach ran his hands through his hair. "It's true."

"Really?" Mom said. "I was convinced Shelly was wrong."

He shook his head. "No, it's true. I asked Jo to pretend to be my girlfriend because I was afraid of the matchmaking you guys would attempt for Chinese New Year, after what happened at Thanksgiving."

"Yes, we did overstep there a little…" Mom admitted.

Ah Ma, however, did not feel the same way. "Don't worry, I will set you up with four women at Easter to make up for it. I am glad you are not with Jo." She clucked her tongue. "I don't approve of her."

Anger coursed through Zach's veins. "Why not? Jo's great."

"Hmph. She made inappropriate drawings."

Oh. Ah Ma was still upset about the dick pic.

"I thought it was hilarious," Dad said. "Though your mother and I would have won if Jo hadn't drawn such a clear picture of a *shaft*."

"Enough," Zach said. "I'm actually here to see Ah Yeh."

At that, Ah Yeh walked into the front hall. "What is it?"

"I want to learn how to make ginger beef. It's Jo's favorite, and I want to ask her to be with me. For real."

Some part of him protested, reminding him of all the ways this could go wrong.

But he needed to do this. For Jo. And for himself.

"I will help you," Ah Yeh said, "but first you need to go to the grocery store to get a few things."

Zach returned half an hour later with the ingredients, along with flowers for his mother and grandmother. He'd also brought his family a few foods in Toronto that couldn't be found here. Asian eggplants and gai lan, for example.

His parents and grandparents were already in the kitchen.

"Stuart has convinced me that Jo will be good for you," Ah Ma said, "even if she draws inappropriate things if front of your family. I give you my blessing."

"Thank you," Zach said.

"Me, too," Mom said. "I was worried you wouldn't let yourself fall in love again after Marianne. I'm glad I was wrong."

"No, you were right. That's what I thought until recently. But this crept up on me, and Nick, Greg, Tasha, and Lily talked some sense into me."

"Now start cooking," Ah Ma said. "I want to see you cook."

"Is everyone going to watch?" Zach asked. "And provide unwanted comments?"

"I'm afraid so," Dad said.

"It's not a cooking competition." That, of course, didn't deter Zach's family, and Zach understood. He'd had a good time watching Nick bake for Lily last year.

He sighed.

Oh, well. Jo was worth it.

He owed her something special, that was for sure.

JO PLODDED down the sidewalk toward Zach's house. He'd texted, asking her to come over, and here she was.

Perhaps he wanted to make up for last night. Yeah, that was probably it.

But she had plans of her own. She would do what she should have done last week: tell him they needed to stop their Friday nights together at Finn's.

She wasn't sure what kind of excuse she'd use. She didn't want to reveal her feelings. Maybe she'd just say that having sex had made things weird between them?

She couldn't help recalling how it had felt when he dove between her legs and licked her, when he slid inside her… He'd made her feel beautiful again, after Matt had made her feel like she wasn't worth his time. She was thankful for that.

But this had to end.

~

All of the food was ready.

The ginger beef Zach had cooked with his grandfather hadn't

made it home. He hadn't expected it to. He'd let his family consume it, then made a new batch back at his place, as well as gai lan with oyster sauce and some rice. He also had drinks and dessert.

Now he was waiting. He couldn't remember the last time he'd been this nervous, but he was going to declare his feelings for the woman he loved, and he couldn't help it. He just hoped she was interested and it wasn't too late.

He was so nervous that he started reciting the periodic table as he paced the hallway, and then, when he was at silicon—atomic number fourteen—his doorbell rang.

Jo curled her hands into fists, ready to do battle.

But when Zach opened the door, she lost her nerve. An errant lock of hair flopped over his forehead, as it often did, and she itched to touch it. He was wearing jeans and a gray Henley, and dammit, she wanted to pull off his shirt again, but she wouldn't.

She had a mission, and she would not fail.

"I have something to tell you," they both said at exactly the same time.

This was followed by synchronized awkward laughs.

"Let me go first," Zach said.

She nodded. She could delay this another minute or two.

He took her hand and led her into the kitchen. It smelled good in here. There were utensils and empty plates set out on the kitchen table, as well as a vase of mini carnations.

No, she must not let her resolve waver. She'd say her piece, then go home and eat Kraft Dinner rather than whatever he'd planned here. He probably wanted to get her in bed, and as appealing as that sounded, she wouldn't let herself do it again.

But if he just wanted sex, would he have done all this?

She told herself not to get hopeful.

"We're going to play a round of Pictionary." Zach walked to the whiteboard in the corner of the kitchen. The same one that had been at his parents' house.

"Okay." She sat down. She had no idea where he was going with this, but she could give him one round of Pictionary.

He picked up a marker and started drawing. It was pretty clear what it was.

"Eye," she said.

He nodded, then drew something else.

A heart.

Her pulse kicked up a notch.

Lastly, he drew an animal. It was fluffy—a sheep?

"Eye love sheep," she said, even though she was pretty sure it meant something else. But that seemed too good to be true.

He shook his head and held her gaze.

She swallowed.

"Eye love ewe," she whispered.

"Point for Team Hipster." He knelt in front of her, taking her hands in his. "I never thought I'd want this again. I was heart-broken after Marianne left, but there was a good side to the break-up. I found a friend in you. Some people assume the events of life just roll right off me. But you didn't assume that. You understood what I was going through, and you helped me get past it without every Friday night turning into a misery fest. Our nights together were the highlight of my week."

This was really happening. It was an effort for Jo to keep breathing.

Eye love ewe. I love you.

"I said I'd never have another relationship," Zach continued, "because I was afraid of being hurt again. But I've been over my ex for a long time, and I think I was holding onto it because I felt like our friendship depended on us both being single and heart-broken." He squeezed her hands. "I was wrong. And as we went out for dinner and skated hand in hand and won Pictionary because of your incredible drawing skills…"

Jo couldn't help blushing.

"…I realized our friendship was changing. I still want to be your friend, of course, but I want something else, too, though it took a while for me to accept it. I think you may have felt that way about me for a long time—much longer than the past month—but never said anything because you thought it was hopeless. I'm sorry, Jo, for not seeing what we could be for each other until recently, but I do now, and the last month has been the best of my life. You're beautiful, sexy, intelligent, kind, and you have a huge competitive spirit hidden beneath it all."

She chuckled, but at the same time, tears came to her eyes. She was overwhelmed.

"It's been a long time for me," she said hoarsely. "Two years."

"We have a lot to make up for." He wiped away the lone tear that had fallen from the corner of her eye, but he didn't tell her not to cry.

Instead, he walked to the counter and dished out some rice, then—oh my God!

"You made ginger beef!" she exclaimed.

"I had my grandfather teach me, while the rest of my family watched, unfortunately."

"Did they hear the gossip about our fake relationship?"

"They did."

"I'm sorry. I was at the bakery with Tiffany—she's the only one I confided in—and Shelly Sanderson overheard. I was telling Tiffany that I had to let you go."

"And now?" He came to stand in front of her.

"You want this to be real, and there's nothing I'd like more."

She stood up and threw her arms around him. He pulled her close, and then his lips were on hers, tender and needy at the same time. He slipped his hands under her sweater and stroked her skin as he kissed her. Kisses that were full of love.

"I love you," she murmured. "I never thought I'd actually say that to you, but I do."

"And I love you. I was just too stupid to realize it until recently."

"Not stupid. You weren't ready, but you are now, and you were worth the wait."

"Is that so?" He cocked an eyebrow, then pressed himself against her, the winning word from the infamous Pictionary game between her legs.

"Let's eat first," she said.

"Good idea." He returned to the counter to dish out the rest of the ginger beef, followed by a green vegetable. "Gai lan with oyster sauce. I know you like broccoli, so you'll probably enjoy it."

She was sure she would.

He brought over their plates of food, then returned to the fridge. Before sitting down, he placed two bottles of Guinness on the table.

She laughed. "You're drinking Guinness, too? You don't like it."

"Just for today, since it's your favorite." He raised his bottle and clinked it against hers. "Cheers."

As they ate their food—Zach had done an excellent job cooking—they held hands under the table and gave each other dopey looks, and occasionally exchanged a few words. He told her about his trip to Toronto to see his brothers.

"Next time you can come with me," he said, and she grinned, still unable to believe this was happening.

After they finished their dinner, he asked her to close her eyes.

When he set his hands on her shoulders a minute later and told her to open her eyes, there was a giant sundae on the table.

"Are these the fudge brownies from Cardinal's?"

"They are, and there aren't any children to knock it onto the floor. And since we're in the privacy of my home..."

Zach sat down next to her. He dipped a spoon into the ice cream covered in chocolate sauce and held it up to her mouth. She wrapped her lips around the spoon and ate the ice cream, then licked her lips, nice and slow, relishing the desire in his eyes.

Next, she fed him a bite of fudge brownie with ice cream, and he did the same thing, his tongue swirling over his lips in slow motion.

She shifted in her seat before standing up. "My turn to draw."

She didn't erase his "eye heart ewe" but drew another picture at the bottom of the whiteboard. Two stick figures, the one with long hair lying on top of the other. She added a large rectangle— the bed—and a smaller rectangle under one of the stick figure's heads. A pillow.

"Ooh," Zach said. "I know this. Group push-ups? Calisthenics? Surfboarding?"

"That's an odd way to surfboard."

He shrugged before giving her a lopsided smile that suffused her with joy and warmth.

She no longer had to hide how she felt about him.

She'd already had much of what she wanted in her life, but now she had the one person she'd assumed would never return her feelings.

Fortunately, she'd been wrong.

They finished eating the sundae before going upstairs so she could show him *exactly* what those two stick figures were doing in her drawing.

[EPILOGUE]

IT HAD BEEN a while since Zach Wong had gone out with a woman on Valentine's Day.

He'd left school right after classes ended, and he and Jo had driven up north to the skating trail, which had been full of couples.

Now the two of them were having dinner at Cardinal's, sitting at the same table where they'd had their first "date" a month ago. Zach was having the lamb; Jo had ordered the eggplant parmesan. She was wearing a sweater that showed a tantalizing amount of cleavage, and her hair fell in soft waves about her face.

How had it taken him so long to realize how beautiful she was?

He was very glad he'd decided to get a fake girlfriend for Chinese New Year, and even happier that he had a real girlfriend for Valentine's Day.

"I don't know why they're out together for Valentine's," said a woman standing near the door. "Everyone knows their relationship is fake. What's the point in pretending now?"

Across from him, Jo stifled a laugh.

"I heard the whole fake relationship story was actually a lie," another woman said.

"Then how did the rumor start?"

"Shelly overheard Jo MacGregor talking to Tiffany Bauer, but maybe Jo was being sarcastic. Shelly's not always great with sarcasm."

The women headed outside, and their voices faded into the night.

"Well," Zach said, "we gave everyone in town a lot to talk about."

"We certainly did," Jo said.

For dessert, they ordered a fudge brownie sundae. Sure, they'd shared one of these just six days ago, but it was a special occasion.

Although Zach hadn't celebrated Valentine's Day in years, he knew he'd be celebrating it again next year with the woman sitting across from him. They hadn't been together for long, but somehow, he just knew.

She slipped a spoonful of ice cream into her mouth and swirled her tongue around it.

Okay, that was it. Time to get out of here.

But before he could ask for the bill, his mother walked toward him, followed by his dad.

"We didn't think you'd be here," Mom said. "We figured you'd stay in for your first Valentine's Day."

Zach shouldn't be surprised. This was the thing about living in a town where there was only one "nice" restaurant: you were bound to run into lots of people you knew when you were out for Valentine's Day. Including your parents.

Still, he wouldn't trade this life for anything.

"Hi, Jo," Dad said. "Nice to see you doing something other than drawing phallic objects."

Jo choked on her ice cream.

Just then, Zach's phone rang. It was his grandparents. Shit, why were they calling at eight thirty? Was everything okay?

"Zach," Ah Ma said when he answered the phone. "You have been lying to us again."

"What have I been lying about?"

"Silly boy. You know! Sebastian and Amber were together, and you didn't tell me?"

"Wasn't my news to share."

"Of course it was. You hear news like that, you immediately tell your ah ma."

Zach pulled the phone away from his ear. His grandmother was too loud.

"It's Ah Ma," he said to his parents. "Since she's probably going to call you next, you might as well know that Sebastian and Amber are seeing each other, and yes, I already knew, but was sworn to secrecy. For obvious reasons."

"*Were* seeing each other," Ah Ma said. "I think they have broken up now, but I don't know, because nobody tells me anything. *You* didn't tell me your girlfriend was fake."

"That would have defeated the purpose of the fake relationship."

Dad grabbed the phone and said something to his mother in Cantonese, then ended the call and handed the phone back to Zach.

"Anyway," Mom said, "we'll deal with that tomorrow. You two have a nice night."

His parents headed to a table at the far end of the restaurant, and Zach took Jo's hand as they finished off their ice cream sundae.

"Sorry about the interruption," he said.

"No problem." She was laughing.

After he paid the bill, they headed out into the snowy night. She pressed a quick kiss to his mouth, snowflakes in her lashes, and they started back to his house, where they would do something more fun than play Pictionary. No beer at Finn's tonight—he had other plans.

"Hi, Mr. Wong! Dr. MacGregor!" said one of Zach's super-keen grade ten students.

Zach lifted a hand in response.

He kept his arm around Jo's waist as they walked through the familiar streets of Mosquito Bay. This was their home, and they belonged here.

Together.

A BIG SURPRISE FOR VALENTINE'S DAY

BOOK 4

MEET AMBER & SEBASTIAN...

Amber Wong has landed her dream job at the Stratford Festival, and life is looking good. Sure, she hasn't had sex in so long that her condoms have expired, but she'll just pick up some new ones, along with discounted Christmas chocolate, at the grocery store.

And that's where she runs into Dr. Sebastian Lam, the son of her parents' close friends, whom she hasn't seen in years. He's moved back to Ontario, newly single, and... Oh my God. He's really hot.

The attraction is mutual and no-strings-attached sex is the perfect arrangement for both of them, since Amber has sworn off dating after a string of terrible boyfriends.

But what if their families find out they're spending time together and start interfering in their lives? That would be a disaster.

Even worse? If they develop feelings for each other, given a relationship is the last thing Amber wants right now...

VALENTINE'S DAY had not gone according to plan.

Instead, it had been Amber Wong's worst nightmare.

She returned to her apartment only half an hour after she'd left and shimmied out of her little black dress, then put on some fleece pajamas with penguins.

She glanced at the box of donuts *he* had given her. No sense wasting them. She pulled out the crème brûlée donut and took a big bite. The caramelized sugar on top was delicious, but she couldn't fully enjoy it.

Her phone rang.

She let it ring.

When it rang again two minutes later, she picked it up. She couldn't avoid this forever.

"You and Sebastian?" shouted her grandmother.

"Yes, Ah Ma. Did his parents call you?"

"Just ten minutes ago! Then I called Zach. He is at Cardinal's for a Valentine's dinner with Jo, and your parents are there, too."

So, everybody already knew.

Yep, her worst nightmare.

"But I don't understand," Ah Ma said. "Are you still together now? Should I be planning the wedding?"

"We were never really together."

"Aiyah, I do not understand young people these days. Tell me exactly what happened."

No way was Amber sharing any of those details.

"You are no fun," Ah Ma said in response to Amber's silence.

Amber sank onto the couch. Her head throbbed. She just wanted to curl up in a ball and watch baking shows.

"You better come for dinner on Sunday," Ah Ma said, "or I will drink two piña coladas."

Given Ah Ma's last experience with piña coladas—and that time, she'd only had one—this was a rather terrifying thought.

Amber laughed weakly. "I'll think about it."

"You want to get off the phone now and nurse your broken heart?"

"My heart isn't broken."

Ah Ma sniffed. "We will have a big talk when you come on Sunday."

"Maybe. If I come."

"You will be there!"

Amber finally got her grandmother off the phone and curled up in a ball like she wanted. She turned on the television, but she couldn't focus on the show.

Instead, she thought back to the day she'd encountered Sebastian for the first time in nine years...

Several weeks earlier...

AMBER WONG WAS the Queen of Bad Boyfriends.

She even had a cross-stitch that said so.

She took it out of her night table. There was a border of vines and flowers; the letters were blue and purple. *Queen of Bad Boyfriends.*

She'd stitched it in a fit of fury after her last break-up, almost a year ago now. Somehow she'd ended up dating another guy with a weird fetish for Asian women. You'd think she'd have figured out how to avoid these idiots, but no. She'd also managed to date a few cheaters and had more than her share of general douchebaggery. She'd even dated a guy who'd proclaimed, when he was drunk at a party, that women shouldn't have the right to run for public office. Or even vote.

Yet these men always seemed normal and well-adjusted to Amber when she first met them. She wasn't sure why her asshole detector was so bad, but it was.

Finally, at the age of twenty-five, she'd wised up. After

finishing her *Queen of Bad Boyfriends* cross-stitch, she'd made another.

Rule #1: No Dating.

She'd hung it above her bed.

Amber had followed that rule scrupulously for the past eleven months, and she was proud of herself for that accomplishment.

However, there was one serious problem.

Sex.

She hadn't had sex in a year, and it was really starting to get to her. The toys in her night table saw quite a bit of action, but it wasn't the same as being with an actual human.

It was now January 5, and she'd made a New Year's resolution: have sex without dating.

She hadn't made a cross-stitch of that, however.

Back in university, Amber had had a fair bit of casual sex, but it was harder to meet people her age for a hook-up now. She could try an app, but she'd been putting that off, afraid she'd only end up swiping right on men who were total assholes.

At least she wouldn't be dating these assholes, just sleeping with them. Though it would be better to sleep with someone who was a half-decent person.

Amber rifled through her night table drawer. She tossed her collection of sex toys on her comforter, followed by her sexy lingerie, which hadn't seen action in a while. And she didn't expect that to change. Sexy lingerie was a relationship sort of thing, not something she'd wear with someone she was just going to fuck a few times.

Ah, there it is!

Finally, she'd managed to locate her squashed box of condoms. Since, with any luck, she'd be having sex in the next couple months, she figured she should start keeping them in her purse again, just in case.

She ripped three packets off the strip then noticed the numbers printed on the packets.

They'd expired.

She let out a rueful chuckle. She hadn't had sex in so long that her condoms had expired.

It didn't make sense, though. Condoms were good for a few years, weren't they? It had only been eleven months for her... though she'd stopped using condoms with that guy several months earlier.

Hmm. Maybe she had a newer box.

Amber searched through the rest of her night table and came up empty.

Alright. She needed to get condoms. Best to be prepared, and she was going to the bar with her friends tonight—perhaps she'd get lucky. Unlikely, but not impossible.

It was three o'clock and she wasn't meeting Gloria and Roxanne until seven. She'd run out to the grocery store, which had a pharmacy. Surely they'd stock condoms, and hopefully there would be discounted Christmas chocolate, too.

Condoms and chocolate. How wholesome.

Amber lived in Stratford, Ontario. Home of the Stratford Festival and the Ontario Pork Congress, as the sign said. It had about thirty thousand people, so it wasn't huge, but it was much bigger than the town where she'd grown up, Mosquito Bay, which had a population of less than two thousand.

Her apartment was nothing special, but fortunately, it was less than a ten-minute walk from the grocery store. She picked up a basket at the entrance and quickly located the Christmas chocolate. She was able to get cheap Santas and reindeer chocolate, plus some truffles. She also managed to find some candy cane ice cream for less than two bucks.

After that, she headed to the "family planning" section, feeling a little uncomfortable. Even though she was twenty-six and not at all ashamed of her love for sex, there was just something about buying condoms that made her cheeks turn bright red.

It was probably because of what happened the first time she'd tried to buy condoms.

She'd gone to the lone pharmacy in Mosquito Bay. Seventeen years old and ready to have sex with her first douchebag boyfriend. Thankfully, her father worked at the pharmacy in Ashton Corners, the next town over, and not this pharmacy. But as she was heading to the cashier, her grandmother came in, noticed the box in her hand, and screeched, "Aiyah! What are you doing?"

Ever since, Amber had hated buying condoms.

She looked left, then right. No grandmothers or other family members. Excellent. Seeing as her grandmother didn't live in Stratford, it was unlikely, but you could never be too careful.

She knelt down and plucked a box of condoms off the shelf. When she stood up—

"Ow!" she exclaimed as she knocked into someone, who must have been reaching for something above her head.

"Sorry, I'm so sorry," said a low voice.

She rubbed her head as she turned around. The guy was kind of cute. A stocky East Asian man, her age or a little older, with short hair. Even his frown was appealing.

She had a split second to consider that he could help her with her New Year's resolution before she noticed the box of Magnums in his hand.

Amber couldn't help rolling her eyes.

She'd had two boyfriends who'd insisted they needed larger-than-average condoms, but honestly, they were both average size —which was fine. However, with the second boyfriend, the condom had slipped off, and she'd had to take the morning-after pill. After that, she'd insisted on normal condoms.

But what if this man is actually...

Well, whatever. Amber wasn't a size queen; she was the

Queen of Bad Boyfriends. More likely, this guy had an inflated ego.

And then something truly horrifying came out of his mouth.

"Amber Wong? Is that you?"

Oh, God! This handsome guy with the box of Magnum condoms knew her!

She regarded him closely. There *was* something familiar about his features.

"Sebastian Lam?" she whispered.

He nodded.

The Lams had been good friends with her family when they were growing up. Sebastian was the same age as her brother Zach, and they'd been best friends.

Yes, someone who'd seen her play hopscotch and belt out tunes with a hairbrush as her microphone had now seen her put a box of condoms in her basket.

It seemed wrong.

"You've, uh, grown up," he said.

"Brilliant observation. I thought you were out west, doing your residency."

"I finished."

"And now you're working in Stratford?"

"Small town about twenty minutes from here. The doctor retired and I took over his practice, but I live in Stratford."

Sebastian had always been a good kid. His mother had bragged about him constantly, much to Amber's annoyance. He'd been a great student, excellent piano player, and then he'd gone to med school.

Holy shit, when had Mr. Perfect Son gotten so hot?

～

This was wrong.

Sebastian should not find Amber Wong so attractive.

He did some quick math. She'd be twenty-six now. He assured himself there was nothing weird about a thirty-year-old man lusting after a twenty-six-year-old woman. Perfectly reasonable.

But this was Amber. Zach's little sister. The last time he'd seen her, she'd been in high school and he'd been in university. It was hard to reconcile the woman standing in front of him with the girl he remembered. He'd barely recognized her.

Her dark brown hair was in a low ponytail that curled over her shoulder, and her lips were pink and full and lickable. She was still petite, but she had curves that hadn't been there before. Very appealing curves.

"You have a romantic night planned?" He gestured to her basket, with the box of condoms and surplus of chocolate. Surely she'd tell him that she had a boyfriend, making her completely off-limits.

"You think Christmas chocolate and candy cane ice cream on January fifth means I'm planning a romantic night?"

He scratched the back of his neck. "I don't know. But...condoms."

"Useful things to have on hand. Mine expired."

He couldn't help chuckling.

"What about you?" she asked. "What are your condoms for?"

She said it casually, as though it didn't matter at all to her, but her gaze traveled over his body, and stupidly, he puffed out his chest.

He'd had a girlfriend in Vancouver. They'd been together for a few years; she was doing her residency, too, and they hardly saw each other.

Then he'd finished and wanted to move back to Ontario and she...hadn't. She was from Toronto, but she'd wanted to stay out there.

They'd broken up.

Frankly, he hadn't been as hurt as he'd expected, given they'd been together for so long.

That was a couple months ago now. He'd figured he wouldn't bother dating again for a while as he got his life settled in Ontario, but when he'd come to the grocery store for his weekly shop, he'd thought it wouldn't hurt to have condoms on hand.

And then he'd run into Amber.

Nothing would happen, but it was nice to have her looking at him appreciatively.

Sebastian had never gotten vast amounts of attention from women. A little, but not as much as, say, Zach. He was too serious, too quiet, occasionally gruff.

Normally, he'd be getting out of this awkward situation as fast as possible, but for some reason, he stayed. Not because she was pleasant to look at, but...

Okay, maybe that was the reason.

"Best to be prepared," he said with a grunt.

"But Magnums?" she said. "Puh-leeze."

He frowned. "What's wrong with my choice in condom?"

"Men who think they need those almost never do."

Well.

There were *so* many lines he could say in response.

"Is this from personal experience?" he asked.

"Yes. Condoms shouldn't be loose, you know."

"Don't worry, I'm aware of that. These fit...snugly."

Was he flirting with her?

Sebastian was not well-versed in the art of flirtation, but this might qualify as such, even if his tone of voice was all wrong.

"Right," she said skeptically.

That bothered him. Not because she assumed he was smaller than he actually was, but because she thought he was dumb enough to not know what kind of condom he needed.

He'd first had sex when he was twenty, and he'd purchased regular condoms. However, the condom had broken the second time, and after that, he'd invested in some larger ones.

He'd had no problems with broken condoms since then. Nor had any slipped off.

Amber tilted her head and stared at him, as though considering the size of his...member. Wondering if he was telling the truth.

She even licked her lips while looking at his crotch.

And then Sebastian did something so bold, he later couldn't believe it, though the fact that it didn't require him to speak probably made it easier.

He took the condoms out of her basket and dropped in a box of Magnums instead.

"That's presumptuous," she said.

He'd been paying careful attention to her body language. If he'd thought she would have been disgusted, he wouldn't have done it.

He managed a casual shrug. "I know."

"You should also know that I'm not interested in a relationship."

"Neither am I. I just got out of one."

"I have a tendency to date terrible men, so I'm taking a break from dating."

"But you miss sex, and you haven't had it in so long that your condoms expired."

"Yeah."

The silence. It was heavy.

This was not what he'd expected to happen when he'd arrived at the grocery store.

They continued to stand there as a woman walked down the aisle and picked up a bottle of shampoo, followed by some lube, before continuing past.

"That's a good idea." He grabbed a tube of lube and placed it in Amber's basket.

Her cheeks turned a delightful shade of pink, but he could tell she was enjoying this. Which was why he was still here, even though he'd known her since she was a small child.

But she was grown up now, and she could make her own decisions.

"You don't think this is a little weird?" she asked.

"It is," he admitted, but he was getting used to the idea. It didn't feel wrong the way it had when he'd first realized who she was.

She ran her hand over his bicep, which was covered in a gray sweatshirt. He wasn't wearing anything fancy, but her lips parted and she hummed in appreciation.

He definitely wanted to feel her hands on his skin.

He swallowed. "How about this. I'll give you my number, and if you decide you want to find out whether I actually need those condoms..." He glanced meaningfully at the box he'd put in her basket. "Send me a text, okay?"

That would give her some time to think about it—give them both some time to think about it—and leave the ball in her court.

He slid his hand over her neck, just above the neckline of her sweater, and to his satisfaction, she inhaled swiftly.

"You should know that I don't care about size," she said. "I'm not going to be impressed just because you're apparently bigger than average."

He shrugged. "I hear you."

"You sound like you don't believe me."

"Oh, I believe you. I also believe that I have the skills to impress you."

Why was he so cocky right now? It wasn't like him.

Most men probably thought they were better than average at sex, and it stood to reason that many of the men who thought that actually sucked.

But somehow, Sebastian was confident he could make Amber very happy in bed.

"You know," he said, "your ice cream's going to melt if you

keep standing there with your mouth hanging open. You want my number before you head to the checkout?"

She held up her phone, and he entered in his number.

Then he strolled toward the fish counter, whistling.

It was only when he got there that he realized he didn't need any fish.

2

"LET ME GET THIS STRAIGHT," Gloria said. "Your parents are good friends with his parents, you've known him your whole life, and now you're going to fuck him?"

Amber sighed and had a sip of her beer. "Maybe. I don't know."

They were at The Tempest, a bar they'd taken to frequenting recently. The walls were covered with posters of every production of The Tempest that the Stratford Festival had put on.

Amber worked in marketing for the Stratford Festival. It was basically her dream job.

When she was younger, she'd dreamed of being on stage herself. Unfortunately, she couldn't act. Or sing. Or dance. Or play an instrument. She had zero artistic talents whatsoever.

"Look," Gloria said, "I'm not going to tell you not to do this. You've had a long dry spell. But seriously think about it. I can't imagine sleeping with my parents' best friends' son. Dude is an ass."

"Sebastian isn't an ass," Amber said, "which puts him ahead of most of my boyfriends."

"Until today, you hadn't seen him in years. You don't know that, and you don't have a very good instinct for these things."

"That's a little harsh," Roxanne piped up from the corner, speaking for the first time in five minutes.

Roxanne and Gloria were Amber's closest friends, and in the mostly-white city of Stratford, the three of them stood out.

Roxanne, a Black woman with a quiet temperament, was an incredible dancer—she worked part-time at a dance studio. She lived in Waterloo, forty minutes away, where she and Amber had gone to university, but came to Stratford on a regular basis and crashed on Amber's couch.

Gloria—louder and brasher—was third-generation Chinese-Canadian, like Amber, though she wasn't biracial. She currently had a pixie cut and was wearing black fishnets with a short black skirt, black sweater, and bold jewelry. She worked as a costume designer and was a wizard with a sewing machine.

Yeah, Amber definitely couldn't approach the talents of her friends, but that was okay.

"He doesn't have to be the greatest guy ever," Amber said. "I'm just going to sleep with him, not fall in love."

Truth be told, she figured it would be pretty hard for her to fall in love now, after all her shitty experiences. One day, she'd try again, but at present, her "no dating" rule was firmly in place.

A white dude in a trucker hat approached their table. It was clear who his eyes were on: Gloria. "You Japanese or Chinese?"

"I'm Canadian, you punk," Gloria said.

"Hey. All I did was ask you a question. Can I buy you a drink?"

"Nah, I got a girlfriend."

The guy smirked.

"And she owns a boxing gym, so I'd watch it if I were you."

The guy eventually returned to his table of dude-bros at the front of the bar.

"Bet he has some kind of strange Asian fetish." Gloria shook her head. "Probably thought I'd be sweet and submissive."

"Pretty sure you're right," Amber agreed.

"I love being able to truthfully say that my girlfriend owns a boxing gym. I'll keep saying it even after we break up."

Roxanne's eyebrows drew together. "Are you having problems with Syd?"

"Nah, but you never know. We're coming up to the six-month mark, and my relationships never last more than six months." Gloria gestured to Amber's phone. "You got a picture of this guy of yours?"

"He's not *my* guy."

Gloria made a dismissive gesture.

It took Amber a minute, but she found Sebastian's profile on Facebook. There was a photo of him—unsmiling—with trees and a tent in the background.

Gloria looked at it in horror.

"What?" Amber said. "He's decent looking, isn't he?"

"Tent," Gloria whispered. "Camping. He likes...camping."

Roxanne shook with laughter.

Amber laughed, too. Gloria enjoyed playing up her hatred of camping.

Amber turned her gaze back to Sebastian's profile picture, and suddenly, she imagined that mouth on her neck, where he'd touched her earlier.

It would be crazy to date him. The thought of her parents and his parents finding out they were together...that was the definition of hell. But they wouldn't actually be together, and Amber was sure Sebastian was sensible enough not to say anything.

In fact, sleeping with Sebastian really was sensible. Safer than sleeping with a stranger.

And sure, Amber didn't care about size, but she couldn't help being intrigued, plus she hadn't felt chemistry like that with a guy in a while. She'd spent a disturbing amount of time thinking about Sebastian since she'd returned from the grocery store that afternoon, and he was certainly a better prospect then any of the guys in this bar.

Amid all posters of The Tempest on the bar's walls, there was a poster that was out of place: the Justin Bieber one.

Stratford was, after all, his hometown.

So Amber did whatever she, Gloria, or Roxanne did when they had a dilemma and were sitting around The Tempest with their drinks.

She lifted her beer toward the poster and said, "Justin Bieber, what should I do?"

But she was already pretty sure of what she wanted.

On Sunday evenings, Amber sometimes went to Mosquito Bay to have dinner with her family, but this morning, she'd decided that she wasn't up for the hour-long drive and would prefer to spend the time doing other things.

Her family, however, decided to take an impromptu road trip to visit her.

At eleven o'clock that morning, her parents and grandparents barreled into her apartment.

Amber's mother, Rosemary, was white, and her father, Stuart, was Chinese. Her paternal grandparents lived in Mosquito Bay, a few streets over from their son.

"Happy New Year!" Ah Ma said, giving Amber a hug. "You do anything exciting to celebrate?"

"Just hung out at the bar with my friends."

"Did you dance with any guys?" Ah Ma gyrated her hips as best she could.

"No."

"Did you kiss anyone?"

"No."

"Did you get drunk?"

"Not very."

"Amber, I am disappointed in you! You are supposed to be living an exciting life!"

Amber had been the wild child in high school, to the exasperation of her family. Her brother Greg, eight years older than her, was the polar opposite of wild, which had set certain expectations for the rest of them. Nick's wild years had come later, once he was in Toronto. Frankly, Amber didn't think she'd been all that different from Zach in high school, but she was the baby of the family—and the only girl—and anything she did seemed to worry her family more. As a result, they'd received a censored version of her exploits in university, as well as her relationships.

Now that she had a full-time job and lived on her own, they would sometimes ask her to tell them exciting stories, then be disappointed that she'd never been whisked away for a romantic weekend by a star hockey player—or whatever they expected.

In fact, they'd become rather obsessed with her lack of love life lately.

"I got you a scarf on Amazon." Ah Yeh, her grandfather, held up a piece of cream fabric. "It is a Hamlet scarf."

Since she'd started working at the Stratford Festival, Ah Yeh had begun buying Shakespeare-related things for Amber. As a Christmas present this year, he'd gotten her salt and pepper shakers with Shakespeare's face on them.

"Thanks, Ah Yeh." Amber wasn't sure if a scarf with quotes from a Shakespearian tragedy would go with any of her outfits, but she'd make a point of wearing it at a family gathering this year.

"I brought you some beef stew and butter tarts." Mom handed her two containers.

"I made you coconut lemon squares!" Ah Ma raised her hand in the air.

"No, you did not," Dad said. "If you'd tried to bake, you would have burned down the house."

"Wah, I am not that bad at baking!"

"She didn't start a fire the last time she tried to make them," Ah Yeh said, "but she used salt instead of sugar. They were terrible."

"Then why don't you make them?" Ah Ma retorted.

"I did! You don't remember?"

"Hmph. You probably ate them all and didn't leave any for your poor wife."

"You have a bad memory."

Her grandparents continued to bicker until they were all sitting around Amber's small dining room table with cups of tea.

An hour and a half later, her family was out the door, and Amber collapsed onto her couch. She enjoyed seeing her family, but she often felt like she needed a relaxing afternoon at the spa afterward. Alas, that wasn't in her budget.

However, she could think of another activity that was very good for stress relief.

~

Sebastian checked his phone. Still no text messages.

Well, of course there weren't any. If he'd gotten a text, his phone would have vibrated to tell him so, and his phone had never been more than a foot away from him for the past twenty hours.

It was Sunday afternoon. Sebastian had made himself fried rice for lunch, and now he was relaxing with a mug of tea and a book on his recliner.

At least, he was supposed to be relaxing, but he kept checking his damn phone every five minutes.

Even when he wasn't looking at his phone, he was having trouble concentrating on his book. He kept thinking about sliding his hands through Amber's hair. Maybe pulling it a little, if she was into that. He would ask her what she liked.

But it had been almost a day, and he was worried she wouldn't contact him.

And that was fair. They'd known each other since childhood, and it was a little awkward, he understood. He wouldn't blame her if she decided against it.

Still, he was hoping…

Sebastian nearly jumped out of his chair when his phone finally vibrated.

He couldn't help feeling disappointed when he saw that it was his sister. He was about to put his phone back on the table, but then it vibrated again.

Hi, it's Amber. I'm interested. Are you free this afternoon?

3

AMBER CONSIDERED CHANGING into a more revealing top. But she didn't want to make a big deal of this, so she left her sweater on, though she changed from her frayed pajama pants into a pair of jeans.

Her phone rang. Sebastian was here.

Her heart beat a little quickly as she buzzed him in. A minute later, he was standing inside her door, his large frame making her apartment seem small.

Yeah, she definitely still wanted him. It hadn't just been a quirk of her brain that had found him attractive yesterday.

But although Amber had had a lot of sex before, and a decent amount of casual sex, it had never seemed quite as awkward as it did now.

"Hi," he said.

"Uh, hi." She paused and glanced toward the bedroom. "Let's lay down a few ground rules. This is just sex, and under no circumstances will our parents find out about it."

"Agreed."

This seemed so transactional.

Shit, was it going to be too weird?

He scratched his chin. "Is there anything in particular you like or don't like? Any boundaries I shouldn't cross?"

She wouldn't wear sexy lingerie for him, but she didn't think he'd expect that anyway.

"Off the top of my head, no," she said. "I'll let you know if anything comes up. Today, I think I'd like it rough."

"Okay."

"Just don't leave any marks that I can't easily cover with my clothes."

He padded over to her couch and sat down. "Come here."

Hesitantly, she walked over and sat on his lap, straddling him.

He grabbed her ass firmly in his large hands, and she gasped. This was still a bit weird, but in a good way.

He lifted up the bottom of her sweater and the T-shirt underneath and slowly dragged them up her body. She was acutely aware of the fabric sliding over her skin. He tossed her clothes on the floor, then placed his hand at the clasp of her bra. When she nodded, he threw that on the floor, too.

His hands were all over her skin now, as were his lips and teeth and tongue, and the man was *good* with his mouth. As he was feasting on her, he kept one hand on her ass, the other arm on her back with his hand gripping her hair.

"You okay?" he murmured, lifting his head to her ear.

"Yeah. Just keep going."

An infuriating smirk touched his lips. He dove back down and latched onto her nipple, biting it lightly before soothing it with his tongue.

She grabbed the bottom of his long-sleeved shirt. He separated from her just long enough to pull it over his head, and then he was lavishing attention on her other breast.

She pressed herself against him, enjoying the incredible feel of his warm skin against hers. It had been so long. Too long. She'd craved this sort of contact, and...*oh*.

There were multiple layers of clothing in the way and she

couldn't see it yet, but yes, she had the sense that he'd been telling the truth about needing Magnum condoms.

She reached between them and undid his jeans with shaking hands. Why was she shaking? It wasn't like she hadn't done this many times before. He helped her slide off his jeans and boxers, and she rolled to the side to get a better look.

He was long and thick, definitely a little bigger than anyone she'd been with before.

And he would put that inside her.

She squirmed, practically grinding herself against the couch.

She had a momentary fear that he was too big and it wouldn't fit, but she pushed that aside. A ridiculous thought. Of course it would fit.

Sebastian unzipped her jeans and thrust his hand into her panties. She inhaled swiftly as his finger slid over her entrance.

She watched his hand, inside her jeans, moving in and out of her, and then she looked at his body, all gloriously naked. She couldn't decide what she wanted to look at more.

The fact that this was Sebastian, whom she'd known her whole life, somehow made it filthier, in a very good way.

He pulled off her jeans and underwear then returned to fingering her, getting a better angle than before. She squirmed against him in pleasure-filled agony and reached for his cock.

"Please," she said.

It was the first word either of them had uttered in a long time, and he didn't say anything in response, just grabbed a condom out of his jeans and put it on. She positioned herself on all fours in front of him. When he rubbed the tip of his erection over her instead of thrusting inside, she pushed back against him in frustration.

His chuckle, as he began to push into her, was low and—

"Oh. You really are big," she whispered. "Go slow."

The tip of him still inside her, he leaned over and kissed the side of her neck. His body surrounded hers, and it felt good, but when he started to push in deeper...

"Ow."

Dammit, why wasn't her body co-operating? She hadn't had sex in eleven months, and she needed this. She craved it.

Or maybe that was the problem: she wasn't used to this.

Sebastian pulled out. "Where's the lube I tossed in your basket yesterday?"

"Let's go to the bedroom."

She jumped off the couch and walked toward her bedroom, glancing back to check that he was following her. He was, his ample erection encased in latex, bobbing between his legs. She threw herself onto the bed and opened her night table. The lube was right on top.

She got down on her hands and knees again, heard Sebastian slick himself with lube, and then a lubed finger circled her entrance.

The tip of his cock was next.

"Ow."

She couldn't believe this. It wasn't going to fit.

"Keep going," she said, not ready to give up.

"Are you sure?"

"Yes." She took a deep breath. "I know it'll feel good soon."

He pushed in a little more but had trouble getting in any farther.

When he pulled out, she rolled onto her back, mortified. She'd envisioned a hot, quick, and sweaty encounter, but it wasn't going according to plan.

"We don't have to do *that* today. I don't mind." Sebastian glanced over at her bedside table, the drawer still open. "You have a nice collection of toys in here. We could try one?"

Now she was even more embarrassed. He could see her sex toys. She had seven—did he find that excessive? His expression betrayed no judgment, though.

She grabbed her dildo, which was about the size of a small penis, rather than Sebastian's monster cock. It was clear glass with pink ribs. He took it from her hand and peered at it curiously, as though he'd never seen anything like it.

He set it on the comforter. "I'll use it in just a minute."

He climbed on top of her and slid a finger into her again. She wasn't as wet as she'd been a few minutes ago, but she got a little wetter as he continued to fuck her with his finger, then added a second.

And then he kissed her.

She realized, with a jolt, that though they'd been all over each other, this was the first time he'd kissed her on the lips. He tasted faintly of coffee, with a hint of pine, an unexpected but appealing taste. She coaxed his lips open and slipped her tongue into his mouth, and he hissed. He was still turned on, despite everything.

He continued to finger-bang her with gusto. When he stopped suddenly, she whimpered against his mouth.

He sat up and held the dildo to her lips. As she took it into her mouth, desire flashed in his eyes.

"I want to see your lips around my cock," he said.

"Now?"

"No, maybe next time."

Next time? She couldn't think that far ahead.

He crawled backward down her body, took the toy that she'd slicked with saliva, and pushed it inside her. Her body accepted it without difficulty.

"You feel okay?" he asked.

She nodded.

He pumped the toy in and out of her, his gaze riveted on her crotch.

Something about letting a man use a toy on her—during their first time together—was oddly intimate.

Sebastian lay down on his stomach and licked her as he continued to fuck her with the dildo. She squirmed against his face, and when he swiped his tongue over her clit, she grabbed the comforter in her hands and cried out for him.

He crawled up her body, a self-satisfied grin on his face, and kissed her.

She wanted more.

"Let's try again." She bent her legs and spread them as wide as she could.

He removed the toy, and then his stiff cock was at her entrance. This time, he watched her face as he pushed inside. When her breathing hitched, he stopped, but when she nodded quickly again, he kept going, until he was fully seated inside her.

"Good girl," he murmured, and it made her stupidly pleased.

She could feel her body stretching to accommodate him, and there was the tiniest bit of pain as he pumped in and out of her, but it was good this time. He pushed his hands through her hair and tugged her head back, just a bit, allowing him access to her neck. She moaned.

"Yes, that's right," he whispered. "You're taking it. Taking it hard." He pounded even deeper inside her, and she cried out.

He wrapped his mouth around her left nipple and sucked before he pulled out and arranged her on all fours—like the first time they'd tried this—and thrust into her again. As he fucked her, he stroked her clit, sending her over the edge once more in a spiral of pleasure.

Through the haze, she heard him grunt, low and long.

After he pulled out, he held her against his chest, anchoring her to the world as her breaths gradually slowed.

"Is this okay?" Sebastian asked, tightening his arm around Amber.

This was what he'd usually do after sex, but maybe it was against the rules. Too affectionate, perhaps? He didn't want to do anything she wasn't comfortable with.

"Yes." She cuddled up to him. "I miss physical contact."

She didn't care that it was *him*; she just wanted a warm body in her bed. And that was fine with Sebastian, it truly was.

"Has that ever happened before?" she asked. "The not-fitting business, I mean."

"My second girlfriend was a virgin. It took three separate tries before we managed it."

"I'm far from a virgin, though."

She sounded worried that he'd been disappointed in her performance, but nothing could be further from the truth. It had felt amazing to slide inside her...but also to taste her and watch as the toy moved in and out of her body.

"I would like to do it again." He figured it was best to be straightforward about this. "Not today. Another time. If you're interested."

When she nodded, warmth spread inside him. He pulled her closer and planted kisses up and down her neck.

Yes, he would enjoy this arrangement. It was exactly what he needed after getting out of a long relationship. He'd just have to make sure there was *lots* of foreplay, as well as lube. He'd treat her well and ensure she always had a good time. It would be mutually beneficial.

Okay, that didn't sound sexy at all, but it was true.

They lay in contented silence for a few minutes. Then he sat up and started looking for his clothes.

"They're in the living room," Amber said.

He was about to head to the living room, but then he noticed the piece of fabric hanging above her bed. Cross-stitching, he thought it was called.

Rule #1: No Dating, it read.

She really was serious about this no-dating business.

Which was fine.

His gaze dropped to the top of the bedside table, where the

dildo was sitting. It was wet from her moisture, and God, that was nearly enough to make him hard again.

Next to the dildo, there was a collection of crochet birds. He picked up the peacock. Though it was small, it was extraordinarily detailed.

"Did you make these?" he asked.

"Yeah."

"Did you buy a pattern?"

"Nah, just made it up myself."

He looked at the peacock, then back at Amber. "You're very talented."

She rolled her eyes, and dammit, that pissed him off.

"No, really," he said. "You are."

She shrugged. "Nothing like how you can play piano."

"But I can't do this."

She didn't say anything, but she smiled up at him, and he ran his hand down her back.

Yes, he would enjoy this arrangement very much.

4

"WAIT A SECOND." Gloria put down her latte. "You're telling me he was ginormous, but he was actually good in bed? In my experience, the guys with the biggest dicks are also the ones who have no idea how to use it. They think being big is all they need to do."

"Yeah, he was good," Amber said. "And when it didn't fit the first time—"

"*It didn't fit?*"

"Just a little louder." Amber looked around the coffee shop. "I'm not sure everyone heard you."

Gloria laughed. "Sorry. I'm imagining—"

"Please don't imagine."

"Alright, alright."

"Anyway, when it didn't fit, he wasn't frustrated, just gave me an orgasm before trying again." Amber tried not to get lost in her memories of Sunday. Had that orgasm been particularly good because she'd had nothing but self-induced orgasms in almost a year?

"So you're going to keep seeing him?" Gloria asked.

"Yeah."

"And you're not falling in love with him?"

"Definitely not. This is the ideal set-up. Just what I need." Amber paused. "How long should I wait before I text him again?"

Gloria gave her a look, then sipped her latte.

"Seriously, it's nothing more than sex." Though Amber couldn't help recalling how close to him she'd felt when he slid the dildo inside her.

Physically close, that was all.

They'd fucked, nothing more.

Well, they'd snuggled for ten minutes, too, but it didn't mean anything. He'd left right after that.

"I've been sex-deprived for so long," Amber said. "I need to make up for lost time."

"I'd wait another couple days."

After she got out of the shower the next evening, Amber walked into her bedroom and picked up the crochet parrot and peacock sitting on her night table.

Sebastian had said she was talented, and she'd brushed him off. Besides, what did he know about this stuff? But secretly, she'd been rather pleased.

Cross-stitching and crocheting were things she did to keep her hands busy, often while watching baking shows. Things she did just for herself that other people almost never saw.

In fact, with her last boyfriend, she'd always dumped her crochet animals into her dresser before he came over, afraid he'd laugh at her.

But it hadn't occurred to her to do that with Sebastian— maybe because she was so out-of-practice with this sex business —and he'd actually liked them.

She had nothing on Gloria's or Roxanne's talents, but it was nice that he'd been kind.

Her gaze traveled down to the knob of the top drawer of her

night table, and she couldn't help the little moan that escaped her lips.

He'd been kind and filthy and enthusiastic, in his own serious way.

Amber couldn't wait any longer. She sent him a text.

Friday evening, Amber was doing a little cleaning as she waited for Sebastian.

When her parents called, she answered the phone with a sigh, hoping this would be quick, but that was probably too much to ask.

"Hi, Amber," Mom said. "You're coming over for dinner on Sunday, right?"

"I'll be there, don't worry."

"What are you doing tonight?"

Well, obviously Amber wasn't going to tell the truth about that. "Oh, not much. Just staying home and tidying up. Watching TV."

"Staying home on a Friday? That doesn't sound like you."

It wasn't super unusual for Amber to be home on Friday night, even if her family assumed otherwise.

She sneezed as she dusted the small table in the corner of the living room.

"Are you sick?" Mom asked.

"Uh, yeah." Amber hoped that would put an end to any questions about her Friday night plans.

But saying she was sick only led to other questions, of course.

"What are your symptoms?" Mom demanded. "Do you need to talk to your father? He's the pharmacist, after all. Actually, I have some chicken soup in the freezer. Why don't I bring it over right now—"

"Mom, that's really not necessary."

It was unlikely her mother heard, however, as there was some banging on the other end of the phone, and a moment later, she heard a different voice.

Ugh, it was one of those days when she had to talk to every member of her family. Her paternal grandparents were at her parents' place all the time.

"You are sick?" Ah Ma asked. "Did you go to bed with your hair wet?"

"No, Ah Ma."

"Hmm, you don't sound sick to me."

Now that Amber had said she was sick, she couldn't admit she was lying. She let out a weak cough and made her voice a little fainter. "It's not too bad. I'm sure I'll be fine by Sunday."

Dammit, Sebastian would be here any moment. She needed to get off the phone.

"Hi, Amber." That was her dad. "Sorry you're feeling under the weather."

"Thanks." She managed a fake sniffle.

"Make sure you get lots of rest."

"I know."

"And don't listen to anything your grandmother says about wet hair. It's bullshit."

Amber wasn't surprised to hear yelling in the background.

Her mom came back on a minute later. "Are you sure you don't want me to bring soup?"

"Positive. I can order soup here if I need some."

"But it's not the same as your mother's chicken noodle soup."

"Of course not, but it's an hour drive. It's not necessary, and I'm really not that sick."

"You sound pretty sick to me."

What? Her grandmother had said just the opposite two minutes ago. Maybe Amber was playing it up a bit too much now.

She glanced at the clock. "I need to get going. I have, uh, something on the stove."

"Of course. I'll call you in an hour to see how you're doing."

"Mom!"

"Just kidding. Go to bed early and have a good night's sleep. Talk to you tomorrow. Oh, wait. Your grandfather wants to talk to you."

"I—"

"Hi, Amber," Ah Yeh said. "I hope you feel better soon. I just sent you an email with some books about Shakespeare that I thought might interest you."

"Okay, thank you, Ah Yeh. I'll look at them tomorrow." She let out a weird-sounding fake cough. "See you on Sunday."

And finally, she was off the phone.

Thank God.

Sebastian arrived a few minutes later, and this time, there were no awkward hellos. This time, Amber threw herself at him the instant he walked through the door, and he responded by growling and kissing her back...then lifting her up and carrying her straight to the bedroom, where, after lots of foreplay and lube, he slid into her from behind without any problems and fucked her hard until they both cried out.

It was unfair, really, that he got to be Mr. Perfect Son *and* be so good at sex.

Afterward, she snuggled up to him again, relishing the luxury of having a man in her bed. Sebastian was about five-ten, and solid. Not solid muscle, no, but she loved his strength.

"The other day," she said, "I was masturbating, and I thought of you the whole time."

His eyes darkened. "Did you use your toys?"

She nodded.

"Good girl." He paused. "Do you like when I say that? If not, I won't do it again."

"I like it." It reminded her of the fact that she was younger than him, that he'd known her when she was just a girl—and that seemed delightfully wrong.

But it's not wrong now, she told herself.

"I considered sexting you," she said.

"Yeah?" The corner of his mouth quirked up. His smiles were often lopsided, and for some reason, she liked that.

"But I didn't know if you'd be into it."

"I'd be into it." His voice was rough.

"Ooh, you know what would be fun? We could have a code word that either of us can use when we want to sext. Then the other person can reply yes or no, if it's not a good time."

"Bubble tea," he suggested.

"No, that's confusing because you might actually want bubble tea one day. Unless you hate it."

"Of course not. I miss it, actually. It's one of the things I miss about being in the Vancouver area, where I could get any Asian food or drink I wanted."

"But you came back."

"I came back."

His arm was around her, and he was absently—or perhaps not-so-absently—running his hand over her side.

"You didn't want to live in Ashton Corners, though?" she asked.

That was his hometown, fifteen minutes from Mosquito Bay.

"Ha," he said. "Have you met my parents?"

"You think they'd be surprising you with visits every day?"

"Absolutely."

She could imagine it, yeah.

"You wanted to be close but not too close," she said.

"Exactly."

"That's what I wanted, too. Close enough that I can easily

visit, but far enough that I won't run into them at the pharmacy when I'm reaching for a box of condoms. Far enough that they won't barge in with chicken soup the instant they learn I'm sick." She paused. "My mom called right before you came. She was surprised I wasn't going out tonight, and since I didn't want tell her about my plans with you, I said I wasn't feeling well. And then Dad, Ah Ma, and Ah Yeh all insisted on talking to me."

Sebastian laughed. "My parents bought the house next door to them."

"Your parents *what?*"

"The house next door was for sale, so they bought it last year. They did a bit of work on it and *heavily* implied that they wanted me to move there when I was done my residency and work at a practice in one of the neighboring towns."

"By 'heavily implied,' you mean they talked about it constantly during every phone conversation."

"That's exactly what I mean."

What a horrifying thought. Amber was speechless.

Living next door to her parents? She didn't know how Zach lived in Mosquito Bay—and he, at least, was a ten-minute walk away from their childhood home. Much as they liked to interfere, she couldn't imagine her parents buying the house next door and expecting her or her siblings to live there.

But Sebastian's parents? Yeah, she could see it.

Apparently he wasn't enough of a pushover to go along with their wishes. Good.

"Are they still hoping you'll change your mind?" she asked.

"Yes, but they don't talk about it much anymore. I think they know they'll have to sell the house. They did some work on it, and they should be able to make a little money, even though the real estate market in Ashton Corners isn't exactly hot."

Amber started laughing. "I still can't believe it. I mean, I can, but it's just so ridiculous. They bought the house next door!"

"Sure, sure," he muttered. "Laugh at my misery."

She slid her hand up his chest. "We still need to come up with a code word or phrase. How about 'house next door'?"

"Amber..."

"Fine, fine."

"Sonata." Sebastian had chosen a music word, of course.

"Okay," she said. "When one of us texts 'sonata' to the other person, that person can reply 'yes' or 'no,' no questions asked."

They were quiet for a moment, and Amber simply let herself luxuriate in his presence. She loved sex, but she'd always loved the after-sex cuddle and conversation, too, and she was glad she could have that with him.

Eventually, she began stroking her hand over his leg. First his shin, but then she moved higher...and inward.

"Thank God you caught me reaching for a box of condoms," she murmured as she grasped his cock.

He growled and pulled her on top of him, so she was sitting on his face, and circled his tongue over her entrance.

And then they had lots more fun.

That Sunday, after recovering from her pretend illness, Amber went to dinner at her parents' house and imagined, with fresh horror, living next to her family. Her horror magnified when Ah Ma tried to get everyone to tell her what sixty-nine was.

Yep, no way in hell would her family *ever* learn about her and Sebastian.

Besides, if her family found out, his family would know, too... and they wouldn't approve of her. They'd thought she was too wild ever since she'd given their daughter a "dirty" book in high school. And telling them that she and Sebastian weren't *actually* together wouldn't make things better.

Yes, sleeping with him was worth it, but they needed to be careful.

5

SEBASTIAN WAS in the car with Amber, which was, in all honesty, not somewhere he'd expected to find himself. But when he'd texted to ask if Wednesday would work, she'd suggested he come over at six so they could do something first. As in, before sex.

"Where are we going?" he asked again as they drove east out of Stratford, passing through the village of Shakespeare.

"Oh, you'll see," she said airily.

He grunted. He liked to know what he was doing in advance.

Amber was wearing work clothes: gray dress pants, a checkered vest, and a white collared shirt. He'd never seen her dressed up like this before, and it made him even more desperate to get her naked. Except, even though this "relationship" was supposed to be casual sex, they were heading out of town.

"Zach has a girlfriend," Amber said. "Jo MacGregor. She was a few years above you in high school."

The name was familiar, but Sebastian didn't remember this woman.

And the mention of Zach caused a pang of discomfort.

They'd been close friends when they were younger, but they'd drifted apart when they went to different universities, though they'd still seen each other from time to time. Then Sebastian had gone out west for med school, and he hadn't really kept in touch with anyone in Ontario except his family.

He'd planned to text Zach once he was settled in Stratford.

But then he'd started seeing Amber.

"How's Zach doing?" he asked.

"You haven't spoken to him since you got back?"

"No. I feel a little awkward about it. It'll be weird to talk to him without saying anything about you and me. I'll call him, though. Just not yet."

"He's doing well," Amber said. "Teaching science at our old high school—you knew that, right?"

"Yeah."

"Jo is the first girlfriend he's had since his broken engagement. I'm glad he's moved on."

Sebastian nodded, and they slid into silence.

Where on earth were they going? They'd been in the car for thirty minutes now.

Finally, they pulled up to a plaza in Waterloo, near the universities. When they got out of the car, Amber grabbed his hand and led him to the right, then seemed to realize they were holding hands and let go.

He felt a momentary disappointment but pushed it aside.

And then he saw the bubble tea shop.

He wasn't accustomed to bursts of joy, but there it was.

It was partly because he was going to have bubble tea for the first time since he'd moved across the country, but also because Amber had gone out of her way to take him here.

Maybe it was more the second than the first; he didn't examine it too closely.

Before she reached for the door handle, she turned back to look at him.

"Should I not have taken you here?" she asked. "You mentioned missing bubble tea, and I thought...well. I hadn't had it in a while either, and there's a pan-Asian restaurant in Stratford that serves bubble tea, but it's not very good. My friend Roxanne lives in Waterloo and we come here sometimes—it's my favorite tea shop in Waterloo. Of course, there aren't nearly as many here as in Toronto or Vancouver, but this one is good, trust me—"

Sebastian jerked her away from the door, cupped her cheeks in his hands, and kissed her. She squeaked in surprise, but she started kissing him back almost immediately, her arms winding around his neck. One of her hands slid through his hair, and that felt good, too, but not as good as her lips and her tongue stroking his.

"Woo-hoo!" someone shouted.

Amber and Sebastian jumped back from each other. There were a couple teenagers standing nearby. Were those kids even old enough to be in university? Were they drunk, despite it being before seven on a Wednesday evening?

Sebastian took Amber's hand and pulled her inside.

"Sorry for kissing you in public," he mumbled.

Her cheeks were a little pink. Perhaps she was a touch embarrassed—or maybe that flush was just from his kissing skills—but she didn't seem too bothered.

He'd kissed her because he'd wanted her to stop babbling...

And because he'd simply wanted to kiss her.

They ordered their bubble tea, and he handed over a twenty-dollar bill before Amber could get her wallet out.

"Hey!" she said. "You're not allowed to pay."

"Why not?

"This isn't a date. We're friends. I don't want you to get the wrong impression."

"I'm not. We took your car, so I'm paying."

"Fine, fine," she muttered with an exaggerated frown.

They took a seat by the window, next to some kids wearing University of Waterloo sweatshirts. Geez, he felt old. The people around them were all in their late teens and early twenties, and he was the grumpy old guy.

Though he was sitting with the prettiest woman in the tea shop.

"I can't believe you got banana milk tea." She gestured to his cup.

He took a sip and got a tapioca pearl and mango jelly along with the milk tea. "Why not? Banana is delicious."

"Ugh. You were probably one of those kids who liked getting sick so you could have that stupid banana-flavored medicine.

"Amoxicillin."

"Yeah. That."

"I wouldn't say I liked being sick, but if I was, I always hoped I'd have to take it."

She shook her head, as though he was hopeless, but in an affectionate way. "I only like cooked banana. Banana bread, for example, is delicious. But that? Not for me."

Amber had ordered taro milk tea with tapioca, and she looked cute with her lips wrapped around that straw.

She also looked cute in that vest. He'd suddenly developed a massive thing for vests.

"If I remember correctly," he said, "my parents told me you work at the Stratford Festival."

"Yeah. In marketing."

"Do you like it?"

"It's perfect for me. I always wanted to work in the arts, but not actually performing. I had a few jobs in Toronto after I graduated."

"I didn't know you lived in Toronto."

"For a couple years. Did whatever work I could get—which wasn't always related to my degree. A lot of temp stuff."

"Did you like Toronto?" he asked.

"I enjoyed being there, but I didn't want to live there permanently. I guess after growing up in a small town, the big city was a bit overwhelming. My current life suits me just fine."

He was glad she had a career she enjoyed. Not everyone managed that—especially not by the time they were twenty-six. He liked his, but it was stressful at times, especially now that he was running his own practice.

It had been barely a month, though. It would get easier.

But he'd had to give bad news to a patient today, and that was always tough.

Yeah, he'd really needed this time away from home tonight. He felt awkward thanking Amber for it, but he reached over and gave her hand a quick squeeze.

She looked a little baffled.

His phone rang and he checked the display. "It's my mom."

"It's okay, you can get it," Amber said.

He picked up the phone. Probably best to answer, as she might keep calling otherwise.

"Hi, Mom," he said. "I'm kind of busy right now, so if you could keep this short, that would be good."

"What are you doing? Are you still at work?"

"I'm out with a friend."

"Which friend?"

"Not someone you know."

Across the table, Amber laughed, apparently amused that she was a "friend," even though she'd called him that just ten minutes before.

"Come over for dinner tomorrow," Mom said. "I will make your favorite, but I need you to take down the Christmas lights."

"Surely that's not a rush. Christmas was three weeks ago. Can I come on the weekend instead? Another couple days won't hurt."

His mother clucked her tongue. "Tomorrow, okay?"

"Okay. But why can't you or Dad take down the Christmas lights?"

"Your father could break his neck. He is getting old. Do you want that on your conscience?"

"No, of course not."

"Tell me who this friend is. I heard a woman's laughter. Is this friend a girl? Do you already have a new girlfriend?"

"That's just someone sitting at the next table."

"Why are the tables so close together? What kind of place are you at?"

"A bubble tea shop," he said.

"In Stratford?"

"In Waterloo."

"Why did you drive all the way to Waterloo on a work night?" she demanded.

"Look, Mom, I really have to go. I'll see you tomorrow."

He set down his phone and massaged his temples.

"You are such a pushover," Amber said.

He shrugged. "After years of being out of the province and only visiting once a year, I'm now less than an hour away. I feel like I owe them. I can let myself be pushed around a bit, but I draw the line at moving in next door."

"Why did you go so far away for med school?"

"I didn't get into any med schools in Ontario."

She nodded. "I know it's competitive."

He was glad he'd gone to the other side of the country—it was nice to experience something different. But now he was back home. Not Ashton Corners, but close.

He'd always intended to work in a small town. Some towns found themselves without a doctor when theirs retired. At least in southern Ontario, the towns weren't too isolated, but still.

Amber gestured at his toque, which was sitting on the table. "Is it strange experiencing winter again after living in Vancouver?"

"I kind of missed winter, actually."

"You freak of nature. You like winter?"

"I like having four seasons, though I'm not a big fan of hot summer days. Winter is better."

"Ugh, what is wrong with you?" she teased.

When they finished their bubble tea, it was well after seven.

"So, uh." He scratched the back of his neck. "Time to head back to Stratford?"

"Let's grab something to eat in Waterloo first. There's a good Taiwanese fried chicken place near here, or there's a sandwich bar that does pretty decent banh mi. Which would you like?"

"Fried chicken."

"I was hoping you'd say that, but I figured I'd better give you an option." She grinned.

He had a large piece of crispy fried chicken for dinner. Hardly healthy, but that was okay. He would eat well tomorrow.

Even though this was *not* a date, as she'd made clear, he couldn't help wanting to put his hand on her knee. In fact, he couldn't help feeling like they were teenagers on a first date, unable to afford anything fancier than fast food.

It's just lust, he told himself.

Lust and friendship. Yes, that's what it was.

She popped another piece of popcorn chicken in her mouth, and he shifted in his seat. Goddammit, what was it about seeing Amber Wong in work clothes, eating fried chicken, that made his pants so tight?

"What's wrong?" she asked.

"Why do you think something's wrong?"

"You're glaring at me."

"I'm not glaring at you."

"You are." She gave him a look.

"Fine. Maybe I was. You're just so..." He gestured toward her helplessly.

"I'm what?"

"Cute," he said accusingly. "In a grown-up way, of course. The way you eat popcorn chicken seductively...it's cute."

"I'm not trying to be seductive! I'm just eating."

"Sure, sure."

Maybe she wasn't trying, but he seemed to find everything she did seductive.

When they got back to Stratford, it was nine o'clock. He appreciated that she'd taken him out for bubble tea, and they'd had a good time together, but his body had been ready to jump her three hours ago.

Though he'd been itching to remove that vest for hours, now that he had the opportunity, he decided to leave it on.

Sebastian carried her to the bedroom and set her down on the edge of the bed. He sat down behind her, his legs outside of hers, and kissed up and down the side of her neck as his hands roamed over her chest—on top of her clothing. For now.

When she writhed against his cock, he unzipped her pants, then slid his hand inside her panties, finding her warm and wet for him. He brushed his fingers against her clit; she inhaled sharply.

He captured her mouth in his. Unlike their last kiss—in front of a bubble tea shop, of all places—this one was private.

"You taste like fried chicken and banana," she murmured.

"Sounds delicious." He pressed his erection against her back. "I think you like bananas after all, don't you?"

It was horribly lame, but she burst into gratifying laughter.

And now, it was time for her to make other noises.

He got off the bed and knelt before her. He pulled off her pants, then the pink underwear underneath.

As he set his mouth to her, he looked up. She was still wearing her white shirt and that sexy vest, like she was a professional career woman, but her head was tipped back, her lips parted in pleasure, and it was so hot.

He finger-fucked her roughly as he rolled his tongue over her clit, savoring her taste. He took his cues from her sounds. They got louder, and he worked her with his fingers and mouth until she was shrieking out and shaking for him.

When she had come down from her orgasm, he stood up and shifted her up the bed so her head was on the pillow. Then he finally unbuttoned her vest and tossed it on the floor, along with her shirt and bra. Now he had full access to her breasts. He cupped one in his hand and plucked the nipple with his fingers before setting his mouth to it.

She squirmed.

He slid two fingers inside of her as he continued to suck her breast.

She squirmed some more.

"Yeah, that's good," he said. "You like my fingers in your pussy, don't you?"

He glanced up to see her nod, and then he kissed her mouth, giving and taking as much as he could before sliding down her body so his mouth could join his hand.

His cock was rock hard, but he wanted to focus on her. Wanted to get her ready to take him.

Amber came again. She was quieter this time, but she shook and gripped the comforter.

"Sebastian," she groaned. "Please."

"Tell me what you want."

"You know what I want."

"Amber…" he said sternly.

"I want your cock."

Fuck. Not long ago, she'd been driving him around, wearing her proper work clothes, and now she was naked in bed and begging for him.

He reached into her bedside table and pulled out the box of Magnums that he'd tossed in her basket the day they met. After rolling on a condom, he slicked himself with lube, then placed the tip of his cock at her entrance.

"Just tell me if I need to stop," he said.

She nodded, but this time, with lots of preparation, he was able to push inside without much difficulty.

"Good girl," he murmured.

God, she felt amazing, so tight around him. He started moving slowly, using his whole body to coax little sighs from her lips, to make her feel as good as he could. He kissed her neck, her mouth, her earlobe. She was wearing pearl studs to match her work outfit, and he found that hot, too.

She arched up, wrapped her legs around his thighs, and took him even deeper.

"Amber, I'm not going to..."

He touched her clit, and they both shuddered together as he rammed into her with a few quick strokes.

He collapsed on his back next to her, head spinning.

"That was incredible," she said, curling up against him.

He put his arm around her and held her close.

Yeah, it had been a pretty incredible night.

[6]

WHEN SEBASTIAN ARRIVED AT HIS PARENTS' house on Saturday morning, there was already a box of food by the door. No doubt this was for him to take home.

Half the fridge was likely also full of food for him, even though he'd seen them just two days ago. He'd barely had to do any grocery shopping in the last month—except for the time he'd run into Amber.

"Sebastian," Dad said, coming up the stairs from the basement. He was carrying a giant package of toilet paper. "This is for you, too." He placed the toilet paper beside the box. "There was a sale."

Mom hurried to the door. "Don't take off your boots yet!"

Sebastian, unfortunately, had already removed a boot.

"Aiyah." She clucked her tongue. "Okay, put it back on. You need to buy some lightbulbs." She gestured to the light fixture in the front hall. "It is burnt out, and your father bought the wrong ones."

There was a small hardware store on Main Street. Sebastian headed there right away. When he walked out of the store, purchase in hand, his phone buzzed and he reached for it.

The text was from Amber. *Sonata.*

His blood pumped quickly as he pictured her wearing that sexy little vest and pearl earrings...and nothing else. He'd never been turned on by the word "sonata" before.

But.

He was in Ashton Corners visiting his parents. He could not do this right now.

He was about to type out a quick reply when someone said, "Sebastian?"

Sebastian glanced up. There was a middle-aged man coming toward him, and he was the last person on earth Sebastian wanted to see.

"Hello," Stuart said.

I'm fucking your daughter.

Of course, Sebastian didn't actually say that—thankfully, he had better control of his mouth—but stood there speechless.

Sebastian had called his man "Uncle Stuart" when he was younger, but the "uncle" part had been dropped over the years.

Suddenly, the fact that he was sleeping with Amber seemed incredibly wrong, even if they were consenting adults who had a good time together.

Your daughter wants to sext me right now.

"Hi," Sebastian managed instead. "Good to see you."

Stuart chuckled. "You certainly don't sound happy to see me."

Oh, no.

"Uh, just running some errands for my parents, trying to get back in time for lunch!" Sebastian was rattled and his voice sounded weird to his ears.

He talked to Stuart for a minute before hurrying down Main Street.

When he returned to his parents' house, he changed the lightbulb in the hall light fixture. Both his mom and dad found it necessary to supervise, much to his annoyance.

Then he sent Amber a text. *Sorry, I can't. Maybe tonight.*

He was sitting at the kitchen table while his mother finished cooking lunch when she said, "Who is this friend?"

"What are you talking about?" Sebastian asked, tensing. She hadn't seen him texting Amber, had she?

"You know. The friend you were having bubble tea with when I called on Wednesday."

Ah. Sebastian would have to make something up, and making shit up on the spot was not one of his strengths. But his mother wanted details, so he'd give her details.

"His name is Shane," Sebastian said. "A friend from med school. He, uh, lives in Toronto—that's where he's from—but he was in Waterloo for the day and wanted to meet up."

"What is he doing now?" Mom asked. "Residency? Or is he finished?"

"He's doing his residency in internal medicine."

"Is he married?"

What was with this inquisition?

"Yes," Sebastian decided.

"Did you go to his wedding?"

"No."

"Why not? If you are good enough friends to meet for bubble tea a few years after you have finished med school, why weren't you good enough friends to go to his wedding?

"He got married before med school. Before I met him."

"He must have been very young," Mom said.

"Twenty-three."

"Too young. But you are thirty and have no girlfriend!"

An image of Amber in her vest popped into Sebastian's head again, but he pushed it aside. She wasn't his girlfriend.

"I just got out of a relationship," he said.

"You wasted so many years on Lucinda."

"Wasted" was a bit strong. Though at least they were talking about something real now, rather than Sebastian's imaginary friend named Shane.

This was not what he'd expected adulthood to be like.

"Now you should be in high demand," his mother said. "You are a doctor. You are handsome. Maybe I should start looking for someone for you."

Sebastian sighed. He didn't need his mother involved in his dating life.

Wasn't running into Stuart right after Amber had tried to sext him bad enough?

"Please don't do that, Mom," he said.

"Stuart and Rosemary set their children up with dates for Thanksgiving," Dad said. "Diana went as Zach's date."

"I'm guessing that didn't turn out well or I'd have heard about it before."

Mom lifted the lid on the rice cooker. "Zach did not tell you about this?"

Sebastian felt a stab of guilt at the mention of his friend.

Yes, he really did need to call Zach sometime. He had no social life at present, aside from visiting his parents and having bubble tea with his imaginary friend Shane.

And seeing Amber, of course.

"I want one of those," Ah Ma pointed at a cocktail on the waiter's tray.

"I think it's a piña colada," Amber said.

"What is in that? Is there alcohol?"

"Yes. Rum, plus pineapple juice and coconut cream, I believe."

"It looks so cute, with the little umbrella and pineapple slice. Today I am going to be wild and fun like my granddaughter."

Amber's father was working today, and she was having a "girls' day" in London with her mother and grandmother. Ah Ma had seen this on a TV show and decided it needed to happen.

Before driving to London, Amber had attempted to sext

Sebastian, thinking that might relieve some of her stress, but unfortunately, he'd been busy.

And now, here she was.

They were at a new restaurant in downtown London, Ontario, and afterward they'd go shopping at Masonville.

"You should have one with me," Ah Ma said to Amber.

"Okay. But just one. I'm driving."

"You, too," Ah Ma said to her daughter-in-law.

Mom shook her head. "No alcohol for me right now."

"Wah, is this the price?" Ah Ma stabbed her finger at the drinks menu. "So expensive."

"It's fine," Mom said. "It's our special day out. And you are only having one drink, because one drink for you is the equivalent of four drinks for someone else."

Ah Ma shook the lunch menu. "I don't understand this. It is supposed to be in English, but I am not so sure? What is chimichurri? What is tartare? This is too complicated. And why are there chocolates in the mac and cheese?"

Amber looked at the description of the mac and cheese and immediately understood her grandmother's confusion. "They aren't talking about chocolate truffles. Truffles are a fancy fungus."

"*Fancy* fungus! In mac and cheese? What do you mean?" Ah Ma shook her head. "White-person restaurants are weird. I am ordering just for me, right? Not for sharing?"

For decades, Ah Ma and Ah Yeh had run Wong's Wok, a Chinese-Canadian restaurant in Mosquito Bay. They'd been so busy working at the restaurant that they hadn't gotten a chance to eat out very often. Besides, there wasn't much selection in Mosquito Bay. When they were in London, Ah Ma usually wanted to go to a Chinese restaurant, but occasionally she could be persuaded to try other things.

However, she ended up complaining most of the time.

Mom sighed. "Maybe this was a mistake. I should have picked something else, but I wanted to give this place a try."

The server came around to take their drink orders, and it was another ten minutes before they decided on their food. Amber ordered the truffle mac and cheese, which came with a spinach salad. Her mother ordered the calamari. Ah Ma chose the lamb burger with sweet potato fries.

Their drinks arrived soon after, and Ah Ma looked at hers with delight.

"Ah, it is so big! And there is the umbrella." Ah Ma took a sip. "It is a little sweet, but still tasty. Amber, take a picture of me enjoying my tropical vacation!"

Dutifully, Amber snapped a picture with her phone.

When the food arrived, Ah Ma didn't even complain about the portion size, which was a definite sign that she had drunk a lot.

Amber had a bite of her salad, then tried the mac and cheese. It was rich and creamy, and she closed her eyes and sighed in bliss.

"It looks like it is delicious," Ah Ma said. "Let me try." She reached over with her fork to grab a bite of Amber's mac and cheese. "Amazing! This is nothing like what comes from the box. I guess fancy fungus is good after all. Rosemary, I am trying some of yours, too." She helped herself to a piece of calamari. "Not as good as the truffle mac and cheese, but still delicious. Can I have some of your drink, too, Amber?"

"You have exactly the same drink as me," Amber pointed out.

"But yours has a blue umbrella! Mine is pink."

"The color of the umbrella doesn't change the taste of the drink."

"Let me test. It will be like a science experiment." Ah Ma grabbed Amber's drink and had a sip. "I think yours is not as sweet as mine."

Mom laughed. "I think you should eat your own food and

drink. But I'm glad you like it." She turned to Amber. "How's work going?"

"Pretty good."

"How are Gloria and Roxanne?"

"They're good."

"You know, you can add a little variety to your answers."

"Sorry," Amber said, "I was distracted..."

Her grandmother was triumphantly holding three fries up above her head.

"I am a sweet potato queen!" Ah Ma burped. She had another sweet potato fry, then picked up her burger. She took a big bite of it, and some of the condiments came out the other side. "Such a good burger."

The people at the next table were staring at them.

"So," Mom said to Amber, "Greg, Nick, and Zach all have girl-friends. Are you going to bring a date to Chinese New Year, too?"

"No date," Amber said, "and don't you *dare* set me up with anyone."

"Oh, I wouldn't dare."

"Except you did. At Thanksgiving. With one of my exes."

Mom managed an infuriating smile. "Okay, we did. But I promise, I will not set you up with anyone for Chinese New Year. Maybe we could buy you some nice going-out clothes today, though. Something to really get a guy's attention."

"It's not hard to get a guy's attention. The difficulty is getting a decent man's attention. The dating market is harsh, trust me. I'm off dating at the moment."

"You might meet someone when you least expect it. Like at the grocery store."

Amber choked on her mac and cheese. Her grandma stumbled up from her chair and slapped Amber—with surprising strength —on the back, but unfortunately Ah Ma then tripped on the table leg, and Mom barely got a hold of her before she knocked over one of the piña coladas.

Though Amber was most certainly not dating Sebastian, he was a decent guy, and she'd run into him—for the first time in years—in the grocery store. They'd discussed condoms, not apple varieties or cuts of beef, which was likely what Mom had in mind.

At the horrifying thought of Mom learning the Magnum condom story, Amber took a gulp of her piña colada and almost choked again.

"Went down the wrong pipe," she said. "I'm fine."

"Is there something you're not telling me, Amber?" Mom asked. "Did you, in fact, meet someone at the grocery store?"

"Amber has a mystery man," Ah Ma said gleefully. "Who is he? I will find out."

"No mystery man," Amber said.

But apparently she wasn't convincing enough.

"Does he have big muscles?" Ah Ma flexed her arm before biting into the pineapple garnish on her drink.

"What's his name?" Mom asked. "What does he do for a living?"

"I want to be young again!" Ah Ma said. "Having lots of love affairs. Amber, you should enjoy yourself now. Are you using Tinder? How do these things work? We will get you sexy clothes at the mall today for your mystery man. You will be a hot piece of ass."

"Don't tell my daughter she's a hot piece of ass," Mom said, then started laughing. "You're definitely drunk."

Oh, God. Why was Amber's family even more embarrassing now than when she was a teenager?

Why were they doing this in public?

"We will get you a sexy skirt," Ah Ma said. "Or skort."

Amber just shook her head and looked at her plate. She was losing her appetite.

Her mother and drunk grandmother talked about Amber's love life while they finished their food. The waiter came over and asked if they wanted anything for dessert.

"I will have that," Ah Ma pointed at the table next to them. A woman was drinking a fancy coffee beverage, topped with whipped cream and a cherry.

"I think it has booze," Mom said, "and the last thing you need is more booze."

"We could make booze-free coffee garnished with whipped cream," the waiter said.

"Excellent." Mom smiled at him. "We'll each have one."

"Don't forget the cherries!" Ah Ma said. She grabbed the little umbrellas off the empty cocktail glasses and stuffed them in her purse before the waiter cleared the table.

"Why are you taking the garnish?" Amber asked.

"They are cute! Maybe I will put one in my water glass tonight."

"You know you can buy packages of those. I bet Ah Yeh can find them on Amazon."

"Wah, waste of money when there are two right here. Plus, I want to remember this wonderful girls' day out. These will be a memento. For when I called you a hot piece of ass!"

"I think the coffee will sober her up," Mom whispered to Amber.

"Maybe," Amber said. "But you are perfectly sober and still threatening to get me clothes to help me pick up guys."

The coffee sobered up Ah Ma a little, but she seemed particularly sensitive to the caffeine and started talking a mile a minute. She also had to go to the washroom every ten minutes and kept trying to dance, for mysterious reasons.

Thus, the group shopping trip did not go as planned. It ended after thirty minutes, which was for the best, as Mom's and Ah Ma's taste in clothes had almost no overlap with her Amber's. Also, Ah Ma had insisted they go into a lingerie shop, and Amber had needed to explain how thongs worked.

Not how she'd expected to spend the afternoon.

Once her mother and grandmother were on their way back to Mosquito Bay, Amber did a little shopping on her own. She ended up buying a vest rather similar to the one she'd been wearing when she had bubble tea with Sebastian. Just because it was on sale.

Oh, and Sebastian would like it. Whenever she thought about wearing it for him, it brought a stupid grin to her face. Maybe she could wear it with nothing underneath.

Lingerie was a relationship thing to Amber, but a vest was *not* lingerie.

After leaving the mall, she figured she might as well make another stop while she was in London. She went to Glazed, a gourmet donut shop, and enjoyed a red velvet donut—her favorite—as she recovered from seeing her family.

As she licked the cream cheese frosting off her fingers, she thought of Sebastian again. Imagined licking frosting off his long pianist's fingers. Wondered if he'd be free to sext later.

That evening, after a few drinks at The Tempest with her friends, Amber went home, changed into her pajamas, and took her phone to bed with her.

Hey, she texted Sebastian.

She waited. And waited.

Amber organized the top drawer of her night table—the one with the sex toys and condoms—and still her phone didn't buzz.

She picked up her phone to check that she hadn't set it to silent.

No, she hadn't.

She tried not to feel disappointed.

She was about to get up to brush her teeth when her phone finally vibrated.

Sorry about earlier, he texted. *I was in Ashton Corners, and a few seconds after I got your text, I ran into your dad.*

Oh, dear. That sounded as painfully uncomfortable as her day.

I was out with my mom and grandmother. Mom suggested I might meet someone when I least expect it. Like at the grocery store. Ah Ma got drunk on a single piña colada and said she wanted me to look like a hot piece of ass.

You want me to help you forget about it all? he asked.

Please.

I have a question for you first. Want to come over tomorrow night? I'll cook dinner.

Sounds like a date, she replied.

It's not. You took me out for bubble tea and fried chicken, so I can make a meal for you, right? How's 7?

Works for me. Amber's hand drifted over her body, from her breasts to her thighs. *Sonata.* She waited for his reply, her heart thumping too fast.

Where are you? he asked.

In bed. Wearing pajamas.

I want you to lick your finger...

Oh, hell, yes. She'd been waiting for this all day.

She did as he asked and got comfortable under the covers, ready for more.

7

SEBASTIAN WAS NERVOUS.

He shouldn't be nervous. This wasn't a date.

Which had made it difficult to figure out what to cook. Pasta seemed romantic, as did mussels. Fried rice wasn't romantic, but it didn't seem fancy enough

What was it that made pasta more romantic than fried rice? Hmm.

He had a nice chicken dish that he'd made for dates in the past, but he didn't like the idea of making something he'd cooked for a date before, even if this was, decisively, *not* a date. Also, it was a little fussy. This meal should be simple, something that didn't scream, *I spent all day in the kitchen for you!* But also not something that said, *I just tossed any old thing into the frying pan.*

In the end, he'd decided on a lentil-sausage soup. But what if she didn't like soup?

Once, he would have thought that impossible, but his ex hadn't liked soup of any kind, and it had driven him mad. They hadn't been able to go out for ramen or pho.

Perhaps he should have asked Amber what she preferred.

He remembered from their childhood that she hated broccoli,

but that could have changed. Though to be safe, he hadn't made anything with broccoli.

The doorbell rang, and he padded down the hallway to answer it.

Amber looked around after taking off her boots. Sebastian lived in a small house that was a short drive from her apartment. It was clear he hadn't lived here long. Not because there were piles of boxes, but because it was a bit sparse. Like it needed some homey touches. Perhaps she could make him a cross-stitch that said, *Welcome to my den of pleasure.*

"What's so funny?" Sebastian asked.

"Oh, nothing," she said. "It smells good."

He led her to the dining room table, where there were two empty bowls, spoons, butter, and a small pile of crusty rolls. He placed a large pot on a trivet.

"I made lentil-sausage soup with kale," he said, ladling them each a bowl.

They sat in silence as they waited for the soup to cool, Sebastian constantly dipping his spoon into the soup and letting it drip off, Amber tearing her dinner roll and buttering it.

This was weird. Why was this weird?

Was it because just last night, they'd sent each other naughty text messages?

Nah, she didn't think that was it.

She tried some soup.

"It's delicious," she said.

"Thank you." His voice was unsteady.

They'd already slept together and sexted, but she hadn't been to his place before, and they were having a home-cooked meal for the first time. Perhaps he was nervous.

"You wanted to feed me something with sausages, didn't you?"

she said. "Except the sausages in the soup are cut up, so I can't see whether they were long and extra-thick. Were they *magnum* sausages?"

God, she sounded like she was drunk on a piña colada.

Sebastian lifted a spoonful of soup to his mouth, then snorted and put down the spoon. He started laughing as she'd never heard him laugh before. He chuckled a lot, sure, but this was a full-on belly-aching laugh, and she couldn't help the warmth that spread through her body. Though perhaps he was laughing like this mainly because of his nervousness, which was kind of cute, actually...

Friends, she reminded herself. *Friends make friends laugh.*

He squeezed her hand, then went back to eating his soup.

She could get used to this. A nice, casual dinner at the end of a workday with Sebastian.

Friends! she screamed inside her head. *This is friendship, not romance.*

"Amber?" Sebastian said, his eyebrows drawing together. "Is everything okay?"

"Oh, yes, everything is great, thank you!" Her voice sounded a little too chipper, but he didn't comment on it.

After dinner, Sebastian brought out some candy cane ice cream, the kind she'd had in her basket at the grocery store two weeks ago.

Two weeks? Weirdly, it seemed both longer and shorter at the same time.

Everything was going great so far. They'd been having sex about twice a week—and regular sex was exactly what she needed.

She had a generous serving of ice cream, then stood up and slid onto his lap.

"You're wearing too much clothing," she declared.

"Am I?"

"Mm-hmm. I think it's time I did something about it. To thank you for the great meal."

And that was exactly what she did.

It was nine o'clock, and Sebastian had stuff he should probably be doing—dishes, for example—but instead he was lying in bed with Amber, her head resting on his shoulder.

His bedroom seemed boring compared to hers. There were no crochet peacocks on the bedside table, no cross-stitched rules above the bed.

"What's rule number two?" he asked suddenly. "Rule number one is no dating...what's rule number two?"

"Yet to be determined," she said. "I'm keeping my options open."

He pulled her closer. It was a touch drafty in his bedroom, and they were snuggled up under a mound of blankets...and there was nowhere else he'd rather be.

"You said you're taking a break from dating because you tend to date terrible men."

"Yes." She sighed. "I really do. Any type of bad boyfriend you can think of, I've had."

"Cheaters?"

"That goes without saying. One guy claimed he was single but turned out to have a wife and two small children. I also dated a man who thought women shouldn't be able to vote."

"He didn't think women should *vote*?"

"He only said that once. When he was drunk. Went on a rant about how women were too liberal and didn't know what was good for them. I bet that was how he truly felt; he just knew better than to spout those views when he was sober. Then there were a couple of white guys who had creepy Asian fetishes. One thought I should be more in touch with my culture and mocked me for some of the non-traditional food I made. The other thought I should be submissive. When I dumped him, he blamed my lack of meek and polite personality on me being..." She shook her head. "I won't repeat what he said. Slurs against people who are biracial."

Sebastian's hand tightened on Amber's arm, but then he realized he might be hurting her. He let go and soothed her skin with his fingers. "I can't believe you dated those guys."

"I'm incredibly dumb."

"That's not what I meant."

"You don't have to lie. I was young, I liked men, I wasn't too picky. I enjoyed the attention."

"I'm sure they didn't act like total jerks when you first met them."

"No, but I should have known better. Especially when I..." She shut her eyes for a moment. "You can't tell Zach or anyone else in my family, okay?"

"Okay."

"I dated a few men who were quite a bit older than me. Like, when I was nineteen, I dated a guy who was thirty-five. Older than you are now. He made me feel grown-up. I wanted people to see me as something other than the baby of the family, wanted them to take me seriously. It felt like he did. Then he dumped me for someone who was only seventeen." She shifted against Sebastian. "I also dated a professor."

"While he was teaching you?"

"No, afterward. Well, we kissed once when I was taking his class, but it didn't really start until the next semester. I know, I was stupid."

"It's not you. It's him. He was your professor."

"Yeah, it was fucked up. But it felt like I had a dirty little secret, and I loved it...for a few weeks. He was kind of an ass, to be honest, and he had another girlfriend. Anyway, that's why I've taken a break from dating for nearly a year now."

"Have you've enjoyed it?"

"It's been good. More time to spend with friends, crochet, and watch Netflix. I feel like I have a better handle on who I am. Only problem was that I missed sex, but I have that now." She tapped his naked ass.

"Do you plan to date again?"

"Oh, sure. I haven't sworn off dating for the rest of my life. Just figured I could use a long break. Hopefully, when I start dating again, I'll be better at seeing past bullshit."

It seemed like she was pretty good at seeing past bullshit now.

She sounded matter-of-fact and cautiously optimistic that one day, it would work out. He couldn't help being impressed she'd gone through all that and become the person he'd gotten to know over the past two weeks. Fun, joyful, thoughtful, and down-to-earth. He knew she could survive more shit, but he wanted to prevent her from going through it again.

He was about to—jokingly, of course—suggest he vet her potential boyfriends, but he couldn't get the words out. The idea of her being with someone else was difficult to think about.

"None of them were as big as you," she said, "in case you were wondering."

"I wasn't. That would be odd."

"I don't know, men are weird about dick size. Why did I end up dating multiple men who were convinced they needed Magnums but didn't?" She stretched out next to him. "What about you? Have you dated a lot of women?"

"Just a few."

"My dating history must seem rather excessive to you."

"No, I'm not judging."

It made you who you are today, and I think you're amazing.

This was the truth, but he wasn't sure why he was quite so sappy about it.

He didn't say anything else for a few minutes, just enjoyed

having her in his bed. It was getting late, though, and they both had to work tomorrow.

"You want to stay the night?" he asked, surprising himself.

"No, I should probably be going."

He tried not to be disappointed.

8

WEDNESDAY AFTER DINNER, Amber was watching a baking show and working on her latest crochet project when the TV and lights suddenly went out.

No big deal. The power would probably just be off for a few minutes.

She took out her phone and looked at a houseplant forum. She'd joined it on a whim last summer when her fern was dying.

She had yet to make a single post.

She was, quite frankly, terrified to do so. Who would have thought that houseplant enthusiasts would be so vicious? But they were. Someone had posted a picture of their succulent the other day, and there had been a heated debate over what type of succulent it was. Last week, a woman had managed to kill a cactus, and oh my God, she'd gotten destroyed.

Amber, for whatever reason, enjoyed the low-stakes and high-drama debates.

She'd also learned quite a bit about ferns and had managed to figure out what was wrong with hers, but she would never, ever post her own question.

After looking through the houseplant forum, she went to

Instagram. She followed a bunch of bakers who posted pictures of their amazing cakes, and there was a spectacular geode cake today.

Finally, Amber got tired of social media, and her phone battery was running low.

And the power still hadn't come back on.

She looked at the Twitter feed for the hydro company, which confirmed that yes, there was a localized outage, and they expected it to last until midnight, maybe later.

Midnight! It was only eight thirty now. What would Amber do for the next three hours? And what if the power wasn't back on by tomorrow morning?

Maybe she could stay with Gloria.

She texted her friend but didn't get a response, and actually, that was a bit of a relief.

Because now she could ask Sebastian.

She figured Sebastian would be home on a Wednesday night, and he'd let her stay—after all, he'd asked her to stay on Sunday.

She'd said no. Although she didn't have strict rules about not staying overnight with a guy other than a boyfriend, it had seemed a little relationship-y for her comfort.

But now, her power was out. It was only sensible.

She texted Sebastian, and she got a reply a couple minutes later.

Sure, come on over.

Amber could barely contain her grin.

She needed to make sure they focused on sex, with a side of friendship. Nothing romantic about tonight at all. No snuggling up while they watched a movie.

She had better ideas.

～

Amber set down her overnight bag and slipped off her winter boots.

"Hey," Sebastian said, his hands slung in the pouch of his hoodie. "Sorry about your power."

"Are you?" she asked, sliding her hands under his sweatshirt and T-shirt.

She couldn't think straight now that she was touching him, especially not after what she'd done before leaving her apartment. It had been hard to get dressed in the dark, and it had taken a while to find what she needed.

She kissed him hard on the lips, and he growled.

"I have something to show you," she said coyly. "Let's go upstairs."

"Lead the way." His rough voice vibrated inside her.

Once they were in the bedroom, she pushed him down on the bed so that he was lying on his back, his head on the pillows.

Then she stood at the foot of the bed and tossed her sweatshirt on the floor.

He breathed in sharply.

She wasn't wearing anything particularly revealing. Just a skirt, a button-down white shirt with one—okay, maybe two— more buttons undone that was strictly proper. Plus the vest she'd bought the other day. Some minor adjustments and she could wear this to the office.

"You like it?" she asked.

"You look hot." He leaned forward and reached for her.

"Uh-uh. You only get to touch when I tell you to."

The corner of his mouth quirked up. "Okay."

She wasn't entirely sure what she was doing, but she'd wanted to wear something he'd like, and she wanted to be in charge for a little. The other day, when he'd cooked her dinner and they'd talked for a long time in bed, she'd felt like she was losing some control of the situation.

But not now.

They were going to *fuck*.

His gaze raked over her, and he licked his lips.

She got a thrill out of turning him on, more than what she'd experienced with other men.

Discarding that thought, she crawled across the bed toward him, her hands and legs staying on either side of his body.

And...*oh*.

"You okay?" he asked.

"Yeah, I'm fine." She wouldn't tell him why she'd winced, not yet.

He was looking down her shirt—he must have a good view of her cleavage in this position—and she watched his Adam's apple bob as he swallowed. He kept his hands fisted in the blanket when she touched his cheek and kissed him, her tongue stroking against his.

Next, she got to work on his jeans. She unbuckled his belt, unzipped the zipper, and slid her hand over the hot length of him.

He hissed and tore his mouth away from hers.

Oh, just you wait. She'd hardly gotten started.

She moved to his side and took his erection—as much of it as she could—in her mouth.

He gripped her hair and moved her up and down on his cock. When she squirmed, the toy shifted inside her, and she groaned.

Fuck.

She couldn't wait any longer. She rolled off him, removed her skirt and panties...and watched his eyes widen. To give him the full effect, she stood up beside the bed and clenched her inner muscles.

She was wearing a dress shirt and vest, but her tits were almost hanging out, and the end of a dildo stuck out of her.

He looked at her with *very* appreciative shock.

Sebastian was the good son, who'd gone to medical school and hadn't given up on piano lessons but instead got his ARCT.

And here he was, mouth hanging open, pants undone, watching with rapt attention as Amber pumped a toy in and out of her body.

She took a moment to savor the situation.

She felt like she was the bad girl corrupting him, even though that wasn't true. He hadn't had as many sexual partners as she had, but he'd been in relationships and was clearly experienced in making a woman feel good.

And though Amber's life was actually quite respectable now—decent apartment, decent job—in this position, she felt anything but respectable, and it was a great feeling. Empowering.

Yes, with him, she had power. He wasn't some asshole with weird and possibly racist preconceived notions of who she should be. They'd known each other for a long time, but—perhaps because they hadn't seen each other in nine years—she could be who she wanted with him and know he'd see her that way. The way she wanted to be seen.

He yanked off his shirt and crawled toward the edge of the bed. She breathed in swiftly, her attention focused on the swell of his biceps, his erection bobbing between his legs.

And the toy inside her, of course.

He came to sit in front of her on the bed, his feet planted on the ground.

"You," he whispered, "are incredible. That toy looks so fucking pretty in your pussy."

Her skin sparked at his words. She loved when he talked to her like this. When he was filthy, rather than the proper man the world saw.

He grasped the end of the dildo. "May I?"

Filthy, but polite.

"Please."

Slowly, he slid it in and out of her. His gaze was riveted on hers, as though he was memorizing every quick gasp, every flutter of her eyelids.

"God, you're so sexy." His other hand moved over her ass, kneading and squeezing. "Naughty girl." He gave her a light slap.

Then he let go of the toy and unbuttoned her vest, followed by her shirt. These, and her bra, were tossed on the carpet before he returned to sliding the toy inside her.

"Sebastian," she moaned. "I can't…I'm not going to…" Her legs started to quiver.

"Come to bed," he murmured, scooping her ass toward him. She fell on top of him, laughing. "On your elbows and knees."

It wasn't a command. Well, not what *she* thought of as a command. His words were quiet, and not firm—but not weak, either. It wasn't a question—and yet it was. *If it will please you, this is what I want you to do.*

She wasn't in control anymore, and yet she was.

She did exactly as he said, her face toward the foot of the bed, her ass toward the pillows. She sensed him adjusting himself behind her.

"Good girl," he said.

She was acutely aware of every inch of her bare skin; it felt overly sensitized.

"Touch me," she whispered.

Sebastian would touch her soon, but for now, he'd simply enjoy the delectable image in front of him.

Thank God for power outages.

Amber hadn't simply thrown a few things in a bag and come over to his well-lit home. No, she'd put on a special outfit just for him.

The toy he'd used on her the very first time. Sexy work clothes, similar to the one she'd worn for bubble tea, which he'd professed to like very much.

For him.

And for her, of course. He knew she wouldn't be doing this if she didn't enjoy it.

There were so many things he wished to do to her.

"You're face-down on my bed with your ass in the air," he observed. "Is that because you need a spanking?"

He could tell from the hitch in her breath that she liked the idea, but he waited for her to speak.

"Yes," she said.

He wouldn't spank her hard, but God, he was desperate to see his hand hit her ass.

First, he palmed her ass gently, then raised his hand up.

He smacked her.

She trembled.

"Okay?" he asked.

Her head was pressed against the bed, but she nodded.

So he spanked her again. Twice. Three times. Four times.

"Sebastian," she said, begging, but she didn't say for what.

He pulled the dildo out of her and replaced it with two fingers, hissing when he discovered that she was dripping wet. The fact that she was so turned on...it turned him on even further.

"Good girl," he murmured. "So good."

He shed the rest of his clothes and sat behind her. Pressed his mouth to her entrance, fucked her with his tongue, then swirled his tongue over her clit. Again and again.....

"Sebastian!" she cried, her hands gripping the blankets.

Over the past couple weeks, he'd learned that Amber could come a few times in close proximity—usually with clitoral stimulation.

"Another?" he said.

"Yes."

He jacked himself off with one hand while the other thrust the dildo into her body. He loved how it looked coming out of her channel. When he pressed his finger to her swollen nub, she jumped and came immediately, sobbing against the blanket, her knees sliding back until she was lying on her stomach, unable to support herself.

He lay on top of her, pressing kisses over her neck and face. "Do you want more, love? Or are you finished?"

"Let me get you off first. You wanted to see my mouth on your cock, didn't you?"

He could only nod.

She took a few deep breaths, recovering, before pushing him onto his back and wrapping her lips around his erection.

He ran his hand through her hair and murmured, "You're incredible... You're so good at taking my cock... God, yes."

He didn't last long. Soon, his entire body was pulsing with his orgasm, and a shout ripped from his mouth, catching him off guard.

"*Amber.*"

When he found his bearings again, he realized the dildo was still inside her. Her pussy had been full when she'd sucked him off.

Oh, fuck. He jammed it into her again and again as he devoured her mouth and squeezed her breasts and tried to give her all the pleasure in the world.

And when she screamed for him, he was filled with bliss.

Amber felt like she was drunk, though she hadn't had a drop of alcohol tonight.

But she was giddy and light-headed, and she couldn't stop smiling and laughing. She'd had plenty of satisfying sex before, but it had never made her feel quite like *this*.

She nestled against Sebastian. He was grinning too, looking mighty pleased with himself for what he'd done to her. She wanted to kiss him, and so she did, leisurely stroking her tongue into his mouth.

Afterward, she couldn't help giggling again.

Her body, though, was utterly boneless with satisfaction. She'd already gotten up to go to the washroom, and she didn't plan on standing up again for a long time.

"You wore me out," she said.

And she drifted off in his arms.

~

Sebastian was a bit of a morning person, though he would have happily stayed in bed for longer today, tangled up with Amber.

However, they both had to work.

He'd showered quickly, and now she was showering while he made her breakfast.

Coffee was already brewing. Normally he'd have cold cereal during the week, but he figured he had enough time to make French toast. Thankfully, he had the ingredients for this unexpected romantic mid-week breakfast.

Romantic?

For Sunday's dinner, he'd been very careful to make sure it wasn't romantic, but now he was making French toast with maple syrup and strawberries and baked banana, and he was *whistling*.

He wiped his hands on a towel and glanced at the perfect slices of strawberries he'd cut, determined to make sure their plates looked just right. He couldn't help wishing that it wasn't dark out, and that he had a little glass vase of flowers. Daisies, maybe.

Sebastian wasn't used to lying to himself, but he realized he'd been doing a little of that lately.

But no longer.

He was falling in love with Amber Wong.

He certainly hadn't expected this to happen, just after he'd moved to Stratford, only a few months after his break-up with Lucinda.

Yet there it was.

Funny that you fucked a woman with a dildo and it made you realize you were falling in love with her.

Though, frankly, it had started when she drove him to Waterloo to have bubble tea, if not before.

He brought the coffee and mugs to the table on a tray, and he was about to plate the French toast when Amber came into the kitchen. She was wearing black pants, a white shirt—and God, the vest she'd worn yesterday. Her hair was wet, and she had a towel over her shoulders.

"You don't have a hair dryer," she said.

No, he kept his hair quite short and didn't need one.

He made a mental note to buy a hair dryer this weekend.

"I might have thought of it if I'd had more time to pack, but there was the blackout, and..." She shrugged. "The power's back on, supposedly."

"That's good." Though he would have been happy to have her back here tonight.

"It smells great. What did you make?"

He held out a plate with two pieces of French toast and two long slices of baked banana. She hadn't been impressed with his banana milk tea, but she'd said she liked cooked bananas, and he didn't have much other fruit in the house. There were sliced strawberries scattered over the French toast, and a few more in the corner of the plate.

"Sebastian, you garnished it!" She took the plate and kissed his cheek.

He could get used to this. Waking up with Amber, having breakfast with her, seeing her dressed up before she went to work...

Oh, yes. He wanted a whole lot more than this arrangement offered.

Perhaps the fact that she was happy about breakfast was a sign that she might be interested in something more, too.

After all, it wasn't like Amber was completely against dating. She'd just wanted to take a break after all her shitty experiences with men.

Which she'd told him about.

Perhaps that was also a sign that she wanted to be closer to him.

Or it was a sign that they were friends, and her delight over breakfast was just a sign that she was hungry.

Hmm.

He knew he was better than the boyfriends she'd told him about the other day. This had nothing to do with size, of course. He wasn't a white boy with a creepy fetish; he believed in equal rights; he wasn't sixteen years older and in a position of power over her.

Okay, the bar was low, but he knew he'd treat her right.

He sat down with his plate of food and put the pitcher of maple syrup on the table. Yes, he'd actually poured the maple syrup into a small pitcher rather than putting the bottle on the table. He sure was being fancy.

"This banana is good," Amber said. "It's so sweet and melts in your mouth. You used butter didn't you?"

Watching her eat his food was making him a little hard, but he didn't think they had time to do it before work.

"Do you enjoy cooking?" he asked instead, wanting to know more about her.

"I don't mind it on occasion, but I don't like having to think about meals every day. It's one of the things I hate about being an adult—you always have to figure out what to eat for breakfast, lunch, and dinner. I wish someone would do it all for me for a few weeks."

He held himself back from volunteering.

"Actually..." She had a bite of French toast before continuing. "You know what I want to get into? Cakes. I love watching baking shows. I want to make and decorate fancy cakes. There's a class I could take in Waterloo, but..." She shrugged.

"Why not? Is it too expensive?"

"It's more that it seems like a silly hobby, and it's not like I'd ever do it for a living."

"You don't think you'd be good enough?"

"No, I just don't have an interest in doing it professionally. I prefer my current job to working in a kitchen."

"There's nothing wrong with doing things for fun. If you don't want to take the class alone, I could do it with you."

The words had just popped out of his mouth.

And that's how he knew he was really falling in love. Sebastian had no interest in cakes and cake decorating. He appreciated the taste of a good cake, but he'd always thought elaborate wedding cakes and such were silly.

But it sounded fun...if it was with her.

When should he broach the issue of them being a real couple?

Amber had a sip of coffee, then spontaneously burst into giggles, as she had so many times in his arms last night.

"Imagine if our parents found us eating breakfast together," she said.

"Fortunately, my parents are unlikely to surprise me with a visit at seven in the morning."

"But if we did this on the weekend and were, say, having brunch at ten, it wouldn't be out of the question. My parents usually call before they visit, but occasionally they don't. They'd ask lots of questions and would interfere so much. My family is always jumping to conclusions and getting carried away. If my grandma saw us eating breakfast together, she'd probably be planning the wedding." Amber shuddered.

"My parents, too."

"No, your parents hate me."

What?

"Of course they don't," he said.

"Okay, maybe that was a bit strong, but they're not my biggest fans. I work for a theater festival—that's not respectable enough for them. They were perturbed by my so-called wild antics in high school. I'm positive they don't think I'm good enough for you."

"Our parents are good friends. They'd be thrilled."

She shook her head. "Our families can't find out. They'd get the wrong idea—mine would be happy, yours wouldn't—and I don't want to tell them what's actually going on. Your parents would definitely think I was a bad influence."

It was clear she wouldn't be receptive to the idea of a relationship with him.

If they were in a real relationship, they'd have to tell their families eventually. He agreed that their families would be a little annoying, but it seemed like a small price to pay for being with Amber. And in a way, it was nice that their families were already friends. There would be no uncomfortable meet-the-parents-for-the-first-time dinners—because they already knew each other's parents.

He still didn't believe his parents would be unhappy, as she assumed.

Well. Now was not the time to ask Amber about being a couple. He would say something eventually, but not yet.

"LET'S see if I've got this right," Gloria said. "There was a blackout on Wednesday night, I wasn't responding, so you went to Sebastian's and stayed overnight?"

"Yep." Amber sipped her beer. "What else was I going to do until bedtime?"

"You could have hung out at Tim Hortons. Or here." Gloria took off her black fedora and gestured to their surroundings. "You could have spent the evening staring at Justin Bieber." She pointed at the poster on the wall.

"Or I could have had sex. It was an easy decision. What's wrong with a booty call?"

"Nothing," Gloria said. "But you could have returned home to sleep, yet you stayed. Just trying to figure out what's going on."

"What happened the next morning?" Roxanne asked.

"He made me coffee and French toast with baked bananas," Amber said morosely, knowing how her friends would take it.

"He likes you. He definitely likes you."

"No," Amber protested. "He's just a sweet guy, that's all."

"You think he makes French toast for every booty call?" Gloria asked.

"I don't think Sebastian has many booty calls, to be honest."

"Yet he made an exception for you."

"We agreed it's just sex."

"Perhaps he thought that at the beginning," Roxanne said. "But French toast? With baked bananas?"

"And a strawberry garnish." Amber wasn't sure why she mentioned that. It was adding fuel to the fire.

"*He garnished your fucking breakfast?*" Gloria spoke as though this was truly shocking information. "None of my boyfriends or girlfriends have done that for me."

Amber's lips twitched at her friend's vehemence. "Well, they should. You deserve a strawberry garnish."

"Ha!" Gloria said. "You didn't protest and say he isn't your boyfriend."

Oops. She hadn't. It didn't mean anything, though.

"I'm drunk. My brain isn't operating at a hundred percent."

"Oh, come on. You're only on your second pint. You're not that cheap of a drunk."

"Personally," Roxanne said, "I think the baked bananas are a bigger deal than the strawberries. Slicing up strawberries takes a minute. Baking bananas requires more effort."

"But less hands-on time," Gloria countered. "No, strawberries are inherently romantic. If a guy serves you strawberries, he knows what he's doing. Bananas might have been meant as a dirty joke. Like, he wants you to bake his banana."

"What does that even mean?" Amber asked.

"Who knows. I just made it up."

"Anyway," Roxanne said, after raising an eyebrow at Gloria, "this guy definitely has a crush on Amber. On that we agree."

"Yep." Gloria took a swig of her beer. "Amber, this guy wants you for more than your hot body and great skills in the sack. I'm positive."

"And you definitely want him, too," Roxanne added.

"Have you not been listening to anything I've said?" Amber

curled her hands in frustration. "We're fucking, and we like each other's company. I don't want anything romantic."

"Then why have we been talking about this for twenty minutes?" Gloria demanded.

"Hey, this wasn't my choice of conversation."

"But you keep adding interesting details." Roxanne crossed her arms over her chest. "I think you secretly want him, but you're in denial."

"My thoughts exactly," Gloria said. "The reason you keep bringing up all the things he's done—"

"Is because I'm drunk!" Amber protested.

Thank God she had enough presence of mind not to mention the cake decorating class.

"I don't buy it," Gloria said. "You enjoy being teased about this guy because you liiiiiike him."

"Stop it," Amber said, without any force behind her words.

She most certainly did not enjoy all this teasing...did she?

She doubted herself for a moment, then shook her head. Nope, she didn't enjoy it. Time for a new topic of conversation.

"Hey." The voice was lower than either Roxanne's or Gloria's.

Amber turned and saw a man standing beside her, with glasses and a rather cute nerdy look. He ran a hand over his face, as though nervous.

"Hey." She smiled at him.

"I...uh...can I buy you a drink?" He gestured to her nearly-empty pint. "What are you drinking?"

Amber's instincts when it came to men had failed her many, *many* times in the past, but she was older now, and she was convinced she was getting better at this.

And this guy seemed sweet and looked like Chidi from *The Good Place*.

However, she didn't feel even a flicker of interest.

"Sorry," she said kindly. "I have a boyfriend."

"Really, she does," Gloria piped up. "It's not just a line. I mean, the guy's not officially her boyfriend, but she sleeps over at his place—"

"Only because of the blackout," Amber said.

"—and he makes her romantic breakfasts."

"They're not romantic."

"Tell me." Gloria turned to the man. "If you made French toast with baked bananas and strawberries for a woman who spent the night, would that mean you had romantic feelings toward her?"

"Uh, yeah?"

"See, Amber?" Gloria grinned triumphantly. "Told you."

The man returned to his friends on the other side of the bar.

"Do you and Sebastian have any cute nicknames for each other?" Roxanne asked.

"I bet you call him Sebbie, don't you?" Gloria said. "How sweet!"

"I don't think he'd like that," Amber said.

"Nah, I'm sure he'd find it cute if *you* called him Sebbie."

Amber felt her lips curve into a smile, then quickly put a stop to that instinctive facial expression. Her friends would read too much into it.

"Have you done lots of dirty things together?" Gloria asked. "Did you grapefruit him?"

"Um...."

"Didn't you see *Girls Trip*? Is his dick so big that it requires two grapefruits?"

Amber found herself considering the size of an average grapefruit relative to the size of Sebastian's dick...then told her brain to behave. "I'm not dicknifying that with a response."

Gloria slapped her hand against the table. "You said 'dicknifying'!"

"No, I said 'dignifying'."

"Gloria's right," Roxanne said.

"It's the alcohol." Amber nodded at her glass. She was getting sick of all the teasing, and her friends were delusional. "Hey, there's a play I want to see in Toronto next month. Anyone want to come with me?"

"You could bring—" Gloria began.

"No, I'm not bringing *Sebbie*. But you could ask Syd. Things are still going well, right? And you've reached the six-month mark now?"

Amber was pleased things were working out for Gloria. But her and Sebastian? That wasn't the same.

When Amber got home on Saturday after her family's Chinese New Year dinner, she brushed her teeth, changed into her pajamas, and snuggled under the covers, phone in hand.

Hey, she texted Sebastian. *You'll never guess what happened tonight.*

She stared at her phone for two minutes, willing it to vibrate.

What? he replied at last, and she couldn't help smiling.

You know how my family always plays Pictionary at Chinese New Year? Zach's new girlfriend got "shaft," and she drew an enormous picture of a dick. In front of my entire family.

LOL. Were your grandparents scandalized?

Yeah, I think they were.

How did your team do? he asked.

I wasn't on a team. As the only one who wasn't part of a couple, I got to be scorekeeper.

Which she hadn't minded. It meant Zach didn't bug her about her drawing skills.

She suddenly realized she'd spent her entire drive home looking forward to telling Sebastian about a Pictionary game. It didn't mean she *liked* him, but... Her excitement about telling him was disturbing, nonetheless.

Time to make this sexual.

She opened the top drawer of her night table and sent him another text.

Speaking of big dicks...

Wednesday evening, Amber saw Sebastian again.

Thursday evening, she was sitting in front of her TV, watching a baking competition and trying to decide what to crochet next.

Sebastian had liked her little peacock. Maybe she could make something for him. But what would be best? Which animal was his favorite?

Okay, she had to admit that she liked Sebastian a teeny-tiny bit as something other than a friend. She was thinking of doing a crochet project for him, which wasn't the sort of thing she did for Gloria or Roxanne.

But this could never become anything more.

First of all, she was off dating at the moment. Now, it had been nearly a year, and the reason she'd stopped dating was because she was the Queen of Bad Boyfriends—and Sebastian was nothing like her exes. He was a good guy.

He'd made her French toast for breakfast. With baked fruit and a garnish.

He was thoughtful and considerate in the bedroom...in a totally ungentlemanly way. She squeezed her thighs together at the thought of what they'd done together last night. He'd blind-folded her with one of his ties and pleasured her for half an hour, until she was begging for his cock. He'd whispered such naughty things in her ear...

She'd assumed they'd sleep together a couple times and that would be it. Except it had been going on for a few weeks now, and she had no desire to end it. This was exactly the sex she needed.

And, okay, there was that teeny-tiny feeling of romance.

Her friends had a point, much as it pained her to admit it.

Sebastian would not be the bad boyfriend she was afraid of, but was she ready for a relationship? With a Lam?

That was the big problem. She might be interested in dipping her toe back into the world of romance, but with Sebastian, she couldn't simply dip her toe. Their families would make sure of it.

They could avoid telling their families for a little while, but not forever, especially since Sebastian was an honest guy who didn't like keeping secrets.

He'd asked her if he could tell Zach there was something going on between them—because he was seeing Zach this weekend and would feel weird about his friend not knowing—and Amber had said yes, as long as it was vague and Zach swore not to tell anyone else.

She wasn't sure how Zach would take this. He was her older brother, after all, but Sebastian thought it wouldn't be a big deal, and she was trying to believe him.

Their parents absolutely couldn't know, however.

Besides, she only liked Sebastian a teeny-tiny bit, and maybe she should stop seeing him soon, to prevent those feelings from becoming anything more.

No, she wouldn't make him a peacock.

～

Sebastian drove back to Stratford, whistling along to the music in the car.

After visiting his parents this afternoon, he'd stopped by Zach's house in Mosquito Bay and told his friend that he was seeing Amber. To his relief, Zach had been fine with it. This was what Sebastian had expected, although he hadn't been entirely confident.

With Zach, Sebastian had pretended he didn't know where

things were headed with Amber, though that wasn't true. He knew he was falling in love, but he hadn't wanted to say it out loud until he'd spoken to her, and that wouldn't be for a couple more weeks.

Valentine's Day.

Yes, Sebastian had finally settled on a date.

Sure, Valentine's Day might be a little lame and predictable, but he liked the idea of it. It seemed fitting, since her basket had been full of discounted Christmas chocolate when they'd met at the grocery store, that this involved another holiday. Plus, Valentine's Day was on a Friday this year. The timing was good.

Until then, he'd be very sweet—except in the bedroom—and prove he was the guy she deserved.

He just hoped she'd be interested, and he hoped he could reassure her that his parents would like her and wouldn't interfere *that* much.

"YOU WILL NEVER GUESS WHAT HAPPENED!" Ah Ma said.

Amber held the phone closer to her ear as she reclined on her couch. "What?"

"Guess!"

"No, I'm not playing this game."

"Fine, be no fun," Ah Ma said. "Zach's relationship was fake. Jo wasn't his girlfriend."

Amber sighed. "I already knew that." Her mother had called her the other day.

She'd been surprised. Zach and Jo had seemed like a real couple at Chinese New Year. However, she could understand Zach's desire to avoid further matchmaking.

"You already knew?" Ah Ma shouted. "Aiyah. I thought I had big exciting news! But did you hear the rest of the story? They are now together for real. It is like a novel! Maybe you should get a fake relationship and turn it into a real one."

Zach and Jo's story did sound sweet, yes. However, Amber was not interested in doing that herself.

"Guess what I am doing now?" This time, Ah Ma didn't give Amber a chance to respond. "I am having orange juice in a glass with a little umbrella. I use the umbrellas every time I have water or juice."

"You mean the cocktail umbrellas from the time we had piña coladas?

"Yes! That was a great day, wasn't it?"

"To be honest," Amber said, "I'm surprised you remember any of it."

"Silly girl! Of course I remember. I had a piña colada, and it was delicious! Then I went home and had a long nap."

"Do you remember going to the mall?"

"We didn't go to the mall."

"Yes, we went to Masonville. You don't remember because you were drunk. You were trying to get me to wear clothes that would make me look like a hot piece of ass."

"Wah, don't use those naughty words."

"I'm just repeating what you said."

"Hmm," Ah Ma said. "I guess it sounds like something I might say if I was drunk. So, did it work? Do you have a boyfriend now?"

"No boyfriend."

Why did that feel like a lie? It wasn't a lie. Amber had a fuck buddy, not a boyfriend.

"You hesitate!" Ah Ma said.

"No, I did not hesitate."

"Yes, you did. You have a boyfriend! Amber has a boyfriend! This is so exciting! All grandchildren have partners now!"

There was a kerfuffle at the other end of the phone, then Amber's mother said, "You have a boyfriend?"

Amber sighed. "No, I do not."

"Why does your grandmother think you do?"

"I paused for a split second, and she misinterpreted that pause."

"What's his name?"

"Se—I mean, I have no boyfriend!"

Amber was used to lying to her family about her dating life. She carefully controlled the information she gave her parents, grandparents, and three older brothers. No sense making things harder for herself.

But despite all her practice, she'd nearly screwed up just now.

What was wrong with her?

"What did you say?" Mom asked.

"I said I have no boyfriend."

"Okay, I'll take your word for it," Mom said in a completely unconvincing tone.

There was some more banging on the other end of the phone, then Ah Ma was back. "Where did you meet him? At the grocery store? Did you wear sexy clothes?"

God, this was spinning out of control.

Yep, when this conversation was over—Amber had no idea how long it would be—she could use some sex to help her forget.

As it turned out, Sebastian wanted to go out for lunch first. He'd named a wood-oven pizza place downtown that he wanted to try, and Amber's mouth had started watering, even though all her instincts had screamed, "No!"

She loved this restaurant. For half of the year, during the theater festival, it was busy and you needed reservations. It wasn't far from the theaters, and it was popular with the out-of-towners who came to Stratford for a weekend of Shakespeare and other plays.

But at this time of year, they were able to walk right in and get a cozy booth.

It felt like a date. True, lunch was somehow less romantic than dinner, and Sebastian didn't hold her hand under the table, but still. He was wearing a button-down shirt with pale blue stripes, open at the throat, and she couldn't help wanting to climb onto his lap, right here in the booth.

If they had this place all to themselves...

"And for you?"

Oh, shit. The server was here and wanted to know her order. She'd barely looked at the menu, distracted by Sebastian's good looks.

Thankfully, she was familiar with the selections. She ordered the pizza with asiago cheese, three types of mushrooms, and sausage—it was her favorite.

The server left them alone and Amber returned to looking at Sebastian, studying his facial features. He had dark eyes and a slightly wide nose. His jaw was not as square and angular as what she traditionally thought of as ideal masculine features, but somehow, when you put every part of him together, it was perfect.

When she'd seen him at the grocery store, she'd been caught off-guard by his good looks, but now she found him even better looking than she had then.

She nearly reached out to touch his hand, then held herself back.

No, she wouldn't.

This was getting dangerous. It was too much like a relationship. They shouldn't see each other again.

Her heart sank. She'd enjoyed their time together, the bubble tea and the homemade breakfast...

Wait. Why was she focusing on those things? She should be focusing on the sex.

Yes, the sex.

"Has a woman ever grapefruited you?" she blurted out.

His eyebrows drew together. Ooh, he was kind of adorable when he looked puzzled.

Sexy. That's what he was. She shouldn't be calling him adorable.

And God, what was wrong with her? Why was she bringing up the weird grapefruit technique? Damn Gloria.

"Here's how it works." She decided that plunging ahead with this conversation was better than any romantic thoughts. "You slice off the sides of the grapefruit and cut a hole in the middle. Big enough for a dick. So for your dick, it would be, um, kind of a big hole, because you're thicker than average. And yes, I've been with lots of guys, so I know these things."

She was trying to put him off her romantically, telling him about this bizarre grapefruit technique, plus the fact that she'd had lots of partners. But of course the latter didn't affect him; he already knew something of her past and had been fine with it.

"Okay," Sebastian said, still frowning. "You put a grapefruit on my dick. Then what?"

"I twist and squeeze the grapefruit around while I suck on the head of your penis."

Sebastian stared at her in wide-eyed horror. "I assure you none of my sexual partners have ever juiced a grapefruit while giving me a blowjob."

"Would you be willing to do it?"

He said nothing.

"I take it that's a no. Oh well, it was worth a try."

He continued to look at her in horror, and then the corners of his mouth twitched and he let out an enormous laugh.

"How do people come up with these things?" he asked.

"I don't know. Apparently it's quite messy—"

"No shit."

"And rather noisy, too. Here, I'll show you the video."

"Amber, I don't want to watch porn in a restaurant."

"It's not porn. She uses a zucchini or cucumber instead...or maybe it's a dildo. Hmm, I forget. I'll show you later. I'm told there's also a scene in *Girls Trip*."

"Well, if you like, we can watch the movie this afternoon."

No! How was this becoming romantic? She was talking about

juicing a grapefruit on his dick, and he was talking about watching a movie together. He probably imagined them cuddled up with a bowl of popcorn on her couch.

"How about donuts?" she asked, pushing ahead.

"I like donuts."

"Have you ever used them during sex?"

"I'm not seeing how this would work. Unless you mean the hole..."

"It would go around your dick."

"This is something you've done before?"

She shook her head. "Nah. But would you, if I wanted to?"

He picked up her hand and said, in dramatic fashion, "For you, darling, I'd do anything."

He was goofing around. It was fine. It didn't mean anything.

Though "goofing around" didn't really fit Sebastian's personality—he'd become more comfortable with her in the past few weeks, it seemed.

"I still don't quite know how it works," he said.

"And yet you agreed, without knowing the details."

"Foolish of me, I know."

"I'd just...eat the donut off your dick."

"What kind of donut would you use?" he asked.

"Chocolate dip, I think."

"You answered quickly. You put a lot of thought into it?"

"No, I just like chocolate dip. Though something with sprinkles might be nice."

"Is that so?" He stroked his chin, as though taking this very seriously. "Might be messy."

She imagined multi-colored sprinkles all over his navy sheets. He'd probably hate it.

"Better than Boston cream," she said.

"How would that even work? There's no hole in a Boston cream donut."

"Remember the grapefruit. I could cut a hole in it. You need to be adaptable." She patted his hand again.

"And then there would be cream all over my dick."

"Yeah, I suspect that would be inevitable."

"It would definitely be inevitable," he said. "So after you ate the donut—and hopefully didn't bite me—you'd have to lick off the cream."

"Ooh. Sounds dirty."

"But if you're going to put a donut on my dick," he continued, "you might as well go all-out. Chocolate dip? Boston cream? Those are boring. I used to go to a gourmet donut place in Vancouver, and they had pumpkin spice donuts every fall, filled with pumpkin spice custard."

"Pumpkin spice donut dick. I like it."

"They also had a cherry cheesecake one, with cherry jelly and cheesecake filling."

"OMG, you're making me hungry."

"For donuts?" He waggled his eyebrows. "Or...?"

And even though they'd been talking about something utterly ridiculous, Amber couldn't help clenching her thighs together.

"Both," she said.

"I'd take you to that donut shop if it was anywhere near here."

"There's a donut place in London called Glazed. I went there a few weeks ago."

"We could go together sometime."

He was making plans for the two of them, but Amber couldn't keep doing this. She couldn't go out with Sebastian. Their families would drive them absolutely bonkers, and they already drove her bonkers as it was. She'd only be willing to put up with that if she was head-over-heels in love with him, and she wasn't.

She had to put an end to this. Today would be their last time together. It was getting too intimate for her.

"So, what do you think you'd prefer?" Sebastian asked. "Pumpkin spice donut dick, or cherry cheesecake donut dick?"

"A honey cruller would be less messy, and I think it would flatter the shape of your penis. Though the cherry cheesecake would bring out the color."

"Ahem."

Amber whipped her head around. The server was standing at the end of their table, one pizza in each hand. She told herself not to blush. There was nothing strange about these sorts of conversations at lunch, was there?

Okay, maybe there was.

"Thank you so much," Amber said as the server set down her pizza.

Her dining companion covered his embarrassment by drinking his water.

Unfortunately, he choked.

"You okay?" she asked when the server had walked away.

"I'm fine. But perhaps we should keep the conversation a little more PG-rated for the rest of the meal."

"I know, I'm terrible. You can't take me anywhere."

He smiled at her from across the table, and that definitely did not make her heart sing.

No, it did not.

For dessert, Amber suggested they get tiramisu. To go.

Sebastian looked rather concerned.

"Don't worry," she said. "I'm not going to coat your penis in tiramisu."

"After our earlier conversation, I hope you understand my fears."

"Hmm." She put a finger to her chin and pretended to consider it. "Intriguing idea."

"Amber," he said sternly, in a way that made her want to misbehave.

They did end up getting the tiramisu to go, and when they arrived at Amber's apartment, she slid it onto a plate and placed it on her small dining room table.

"Now let me slip into something more comfortable," she said with a wink.

She went to her bedroom and opened up her night table. She pulled out the skimpy red babydoll that she hadn't worn in quite a while. Normally, she wouldn't put on lingerie for a man who wasn't her boyfriend, but she looked stunning in this, and she wanted Sebastian to see it once.

Because this would be the last time.

There would be no experimenting with grapefruit and donuts in the bedroom. No more swapping pieces of pizza at lunch and clutching the table in laughter.

A tear fell from her eye, and she swiped it away angrily.

She would not cry.

They had no future together, and she was starting to get too attached. This was the way it had to be, and she could handle it like an adult.

She strutted out of the bedroom, chin held high, one hand on her hip.

Sebastian's mouth fell open. He stalked toward Amber, his gaze riveted on her.

"You look...wow."

His mouth collided with hers. One hand came up to squeeze her ass; his other hand was in her hair.

When he slid his lips to her neck, she said, "Don't you want to eat your tiramisu?"

"Later."

"You have something else you'd rather eat?"

"Mm-hmm."

"Well, too bad for you. I want my tiramisu." Admittedly, it would be torture for her as well, but she thought it would be worth it.

"Alright." He led them to the table. "Let's make this fair."

He whipped off his shirt and placed it on the chair next to him.

She swallowed.

He looked particularly good without a shirt. Her eyes lingered on his arm muscles, then followed the light trail of hair...

"We'll eat the tiramisu later," she decided.

"Nope, you wanted to eat it now. So we will."

He held a spoonful of mascarpone cream up to her lips. It was rich and delicious.

It was not the most interesting thing in the room.

"Good girl," he murmured, then had a bite of the dessert himself. He licked his lips slowly, almost obscenely, before feeding her again.

She, in turn, fed him a bite.

"Now keep eating," he said, pulling her into his lap so she was facing the table. As she ate the next few bites of dessert, he slid his hands up and down her bare legs and dipped his fingers inside her barely-there thong, which matched her babydoll. She pressed back against his bare chest.

He hissed out a breath when he touched her wetness.

She was supposed to keep eating, though. So she raised the spoon to her mouth, her hand shaking, and slid it between her lips.

He slipped his finger inside her, and his thumb circled her clit.

She gasped.

"I love the noises you make," he murmured. He continued to stroke her leisurely as she swallowed. "You're so fucking sexy." His other hand rubbed the bottom of her babydoll. "Did you buy this just for me?"

She shook her head. "I've worn it for a bunch of guys."

It was the truth, and she didn't want him to feel special. Because this was all they'd have together.

He plunged two fingers deep inside her, and she shuddered.

She rode his fingers, trying to get the right angle, but she couldn't. She groaned in frustration.

"More tiramisu?" He held the spoon to his lips.

"Later. When I can enjoy it properly."

"Why can't you enjoy it properly now?"

"You can be infuriating, you know."

He laughed.

When it was just the two of them, he had a soft, commanding presence. She didn't know how else to describe it. She felt like it was all for her, nobody else was in on this little secret, and she loved it.

He swiped up a small amount of mascarpone cream with his finger and held it to her mouth. She sucked it off, careful to use lots of tongue to drive him wild.

But really. Enough with the tiramisu.

She turned in his lap so she was facing him, her legs wrapped around his waist. The juncture of her legs pressed against his erection, and she groaned again.

How did he feel so good?

How could this be the end?

She unbuttoned his pants and removed his cock through the slit in his boxers, stroking the hard length of him. His size was less intimidating than it had been the first time, but she still required lots of preparation and lube to take him.

He slid his hand into her thong again and worked her into a frenzy. His fingers were no longer enough.

"Sebastian. Please. I need…"

He rolled a condom onto his length, then pulled a small bottle of lube out of his pants—she appreciated that he was prepared.

When he was ready, she raised herself up and pushed her thong to one side. She eased herself down on him, nice and slow, gasping with each additional inch she took of him.

It felt like he was splitting her open, and she would never be able to completely put herself back together.

She didn't care. She kept going.

Finally, his cock was fully inside her.

"Yes, Amber." He sounded in awe of what was happening between them. "You're amazing." He cupped her cheeks and bestowed a single kiss on her lips before shifting his hands to her ass. "Now move."

They thrust together, up and down, in perfect harmony, and she ached. Oh, she ached. This would be it for them.

Why couldn't he be someone else? Someone she hadn't known all her life, someone whose parents were strangers to hers. Someone who wasn't friends with her brother.

What if...

No, it was impossible. She couldn't start something real with him unless she was positive it would last. Otherwise, it wasn't worth the risk. She didn't love him.

But it's already real.

Amber rode him harder to drown out her thoughts. She kissed him long and deep and held him against her. She took his hand and shoved it into her thong, and he immediately began rubbing her clit.

"Was it like this with anyone else?" he asked as he thrust particularly deep inside her.

She shook her head, unable to be anything but honest when they were together like this.

On and on she rode him. Every inch of her skin sparked with energy, and when her breaths came faster, he pounded into her even harder from below, one hand gripping her thigh, the other moving furiously on her clit.

"Sebastian, I'm going to..."

And then it happened. She shook as though she was breaking into a million pieces, and beneath her, he cried out and tightened his hold on her.

He stayed inside her for a moment, and they simply looked at each other. She felt too raw, though, too naked, and she raised herself up and straightened her clothes.

"Let's finish the tiramisu," she said.

If they were in a real relationship, maybe they could get tested and she could go on the pill. They could stop using condoms; she could feel him go soft inside her.

But none of that would happen.

"Friday is Valentine's Day," he said. "I don't have any plans. Want to come over and spend the evening in bed?"

"Yes," she said before she could stop herself.

She'd sworn this would be the last time, but she couldn't seem to keep away, and she was weak after that incredible orgasm. It was too good with him. They laughed and they ate and they talked and they fucked.

But then she imagined her parents barging into her apartment while she was trying to eat a honey cruller off his dick. An embarrassing situation with any guy, but ten times worse with Sebastian, who knew her family, and it was exactly the sort of thing that would happen to her.

Okay. One more night and then she would end it.

For real this time.

~

It was Valentine's Day, and Sebastian was nearly ready.

Amber was coming over at eight. As far as she knew, they were going to have sex and order pizza. Cheap pizza, not the thin-crust stuff they'd had the other day.

But he had different plans.

To start, there was a plate of fancy crackers and cheese, as well as wine.

Next, he had a mixed green salad with pear slices and nuts, which he would toss with the balsamic vinaigrette right before they ate.

Then, they would have mussels. He wouldn't cook those until she got here, but everything was ready to go.

For dessert, there was a box of four donuts. Sebastian had driven to London to get them after work. He hadn't known which flavors she'd like, so he'd gotten a selection. He didn't plan on putting one on his dick; he just hoped she'd see the donuts and laugh.

He loved making her laugh.

As soon as she saw everything he'd prepared, she'd know something was up. So before they ate dinner, he planned to tell her the truth. *I'm falling in love with you and I want to have a relationship.*

He wasn't sure what she'd say, to be honest. It was possible she'd walk out before they even got to dinner, but he suspected her feelings toward him had changed, too. Just from the way she'd been with him last weekend, when they went to a cozy restaurant and had sex on a chair afterward, Amber wearing that stunning red slip. It didn't seem like the sort of sex you had with a friend with benefits, even though she hadn't gotten that slip just for him.

There was a knock at the door.

He frowned. It was five minutes to eight, and Amber was never early.

Or maybe she was as excited to see him as he was to see her?

He walked to the door, trying to be all casual and not show his nerves, but when he turned the doorknob and saw who was standing on his porch, his mouth fell open.

It wasn't Amber.

It was his parents.

Shit.

Shit, shit, shit.

Fortunately, Sebastian managed not to say any of that out loud. He was thirty years old, but it still seemed wrong to swear in front of his parents.

"Sorry, I have plans," he said to his mom and dad. "I told you to call before you visit."

"What is the point of living so close if we cannot stop in and see you?" Mom said.

"I don't live all that close to Ashton Corners. It's nearly an hour's drive."

And part of the reason for that was to avoid these situations.

But apparently he still lived too close to avoid the unexpected drop-in.

"You don't have plans tonight," Mom insisted. "It's Valentine's Day and you don't have a girlfriend. Only couples have plans tonight."

"I have plans," Sebastian repeated. "So you have to go before my visitor arrives."

"Who is your visitor?"

"It's a secret."

Bad call. Now his mother was even more intrigued.

"It must be a girl, don't you think?" she said to his father. "He was lying to us about not having a girlfriend."

Sebastian pinched the bridge of his nose. "I was not lying to you."

"Maybe you are having other single men over?" Mom suggested. "Like a Bro-entine's Day? Let us see what you are preparing."

She ducked under his arm and entered the house.

Sebastian sighed and followed her into the kitchen.

There was a bottle of white wine in an ice bucket. The table was set. There were even candles.

"Looks like a date to me," Dad said. "Your date is a woman, yes?"

Sebastian nodded.

"Ha! You nodded. You agreed you have a date!"

"Yes, I have a date. She's not technically my girlfriend, but we've been seeing each other for a little while. Now, can you please leave? Having my parents here when she arrives would spoil the mood."

"We brought food." Mom lifted up two plastic bags that Sebastian hadn't noticed before. "I need to put it away."

"I'll deal with it," Sebastian said.

"No, I can do it." Mom was already opening up the fridge, and she noticed the box on the counter. "You bought donuts for her! You know, a good chocolate cake would be more romantic. Why donuts?"

Obviously Sebastian wasn't going to mention his conversation with Amber.

He shrugged. "She really likes donuts."

"Tell me more about her. What is her job? Where did she study? Where is she from?"

"She'll be here any minute. Can you please leave?"

He'd been nervous before, and now he was very agitated.

Of course, if everything went well, he'd tell his parents about Amber eventually, but he wasn't ready for that yet—not here, not like this—and without a doubt, she wasn't, either. She'd made her thoughts on family interference clear.

"We're not going anywhere," Mom said as she put a bag of bok choy in the crisper. "I want to meet her. See if she is good enough for you."

"Please, Mom. She's shy. She won't appreciate being ambushed like this. I'll bring her over soon, okay?"

"Hmph."

"Why do you have grapefruit?" Dad asked, holding up the two grapefruit from the fruit bowl on the counter. "I thought you hated grapefruit."

"I changed my mind."

"Or does *she* like grapefruit?" Mom asked. "Grapefruit is breakfast food. You are thinking she will stay overnight? She is not even your girlfriend."

Once again, Sebastian hadn't actually intended to use the grapefruit for any weird sex acts, just as a joke he shared with Amber, but his cheeks flamed.

"Mom." He grasped her hand and started leading her to the front entrance.

Just then, there was a knock on the door.

Shit, shit, shit.

"Ah, I am going to meet her!" Mom pulled her hand out of Sebastian's grasp and hurried to the door. She wrenched it open. "Amber, what are you doing here?"

Sebastian's mother was here.

Oh, God, no.

"Hi, Auntie Cecilia. Uncle Randall," Amber said, out of instinct. "Haven't seen you in a while."

She was certain Sebastian hadn't invited his parents over, since he looked as desperate to get out of this situation as she was. His mom and dad must have turned up unexpectedly.

Cecilia glanced between Sebastian and Amber, and then her gaze lingered on Amber. Amber's long coat was undone, and underneath, she was wearing a little black dress and high black boots.

She looked like a woman who planned to have sex tonight.

"What are you wearing, Amber?" Cecilia asked. "That barely counts as a dress. It is a shirt!" She turned to Sebastian. "Amber is your mystery woman. *Amber?*"

"Yes, Mom," Sebastian said, pulling Amber inside. "Now can you please leave?"

"She is the one you are making a romantic dinner for?"

Amber's head snapped toward Sebastian. "What are you talking about?"

"It was supposed to be a surprise," he muttered.

Well, this was certainly a big surprise for Valentine's Day.

It was all wrong. A romantic dinner was the last thing she needed. She'd just wanted to order fast food and fuck one last time.

And now she had to deal with his parents. What terrible luck.

She wanted to sink into the floor.

"Mom, you're making a mess of this," Sebastian said. "Could you leave now so I can talk to Amber alone?"

Cecilia clucked her tongue. "I do not approve of you being with Amber."

"Why not? You're friends with her parents. I thought you'd be thrilled—a little too thrilled."

"Look at her." Cecilia gestured to Amber's barely-there dress. "She is dressed like—"

"Don't say it, Mom!"

It was the first time Amber had ever heard him raise his voice.

"She is not good enough for you," Cecilia went on. "Rosemary and Stuart let her get away with too much. Yes, they are friends, but that doesn't mean I approve of all their parenting methods. Did you know her grandmother caught her buying condoms when she was only seventeen? And she used to give Diana dirty books when they were teenagers."

That had happened a grand total of once.

"You are a doctor," his mother continued. "She went to *Laurier*."

No surprise that Amber's university hadn't been prestigious enough for them.

Amber wanted to talk back, but she couldn't manage it. Cecilia was a family friend, someone she'd been taught to respect.

Randall placed his hand on Cecilia's shoulder. "You have made your point. Let them talk by themselves."

He didn't disagree with anything his wife had said, though.

"Mom." Sebastian's hands were clenched at his sides. "I don't want you to ever, *ever* talk like that." He reached for Amber. "I lo—"

"Nice to see you again!" Amber chirped, waving at his parents.

Sebastian had been about to declare his love for her, hadn't he?

No, she couldn't take it.

Cecilia sniffed, and then she and Randall headed outside. Finally.

Sebastian turned to Amber and wrapped his arms around her. "I'm so sorry. I'll make sure she never says stuff like that again. I promise."

"How would you manage that?"

"Threaten to stop talking to her."

"And you would mean that."

"Yes," he said, "I would."

Admittedly, a part of Amber was thrilled at the firmness in his voice. He was Mr. Perfect Son, but apparently he was willing to throw his parents' approval away for her.

"I told you she didn't like me," Amber said.

"I never heard about the dirty books and the condoms."

"You were away at university."

"It was ten years ago. How can she..." He shook his head. "Listen to me, there is nothing wrong with any of the choices you made. You're perfect just the way you are."

He led her into the kitchen, where the table was set for a nice dinner. There was a vase of roses in the center. Even a tablecloth —she doubted any of her exes knew what a tablecloth was.

He took both her hands in his and looked her in the eye. "I mean it, Amber. When I met you at the grocery store, I thought we'd just have a bit of fun together. I didn't expect to fall for you, but I did. I love your unabashed sexiness, the way you created the life you wanted for yourself, the way you've put yourself out there again and again. I love your cross-stitching and your crochet peacocks and..." He grabbed an envelope off the counter. "Here."

She couldn't stop herself from opening it.

He'd signed them up for the cake class she'd wanted to take in Waterloo.

Some people saw her as the flighty youngest child, but since they'd met again as adults, he'd seemed to appreciate everything about her. It wasn't as if he only liked one part of her or wanted her to be someone other than who she was.

But though she had some rather tender feelings for Sebastian, they were all about friendship and sex. They weren't romantic.

That's a lie.

No, it wasn't. She'd been a little worried before about her teeny-tiny feelings of romance, but Sebastian had been about to say he loved her, and she'd recoiled. She definitely didn't love him. That wasn't what she was looking for right now.

Even if she was, going out with him was a terrible idea. Look at what had happened today! His parents had barged their way into his house. What if she'd been eating a donut off his cock? It was fortunate they'd only caught her wearing a revealing dress.

His parents were probably going to have a fight with her parents now.

She wasn't up for this drama. Not for a man she liked but was nowhere close to loving.

"I can't do this," she said to Sebastian, handing back the envelope. "I can't cause problems between you and your parents."

"Don't worry about them. I'll handle it."

"I'm sorry," she whispered. "I don't feel that way about you. I'm so sorry." Tears came to her eyes. He was her friend; she felt badly for not being able to give him what he wanted.

But she couldn't.

He raked a hand through his hair. "I understand. I suppose it's best that we stop seeing each other now. Just take this before you go." He handed her a box, emblazoned with the logo for Glazed, and she couldn't help the unhinged laugh that came to her lips.

"You bought donuts. For…?"

"No, not for that. Though if you really wanted…" The corner of his mouth kicked up. "I got them to make you laugh, and because you said you like this donut shop."

Oh, God.

No, this was all wrong.

She hurried to the door and laced up her impractical boots as quickly as she could.

Sebastian ate the salad by himself. He ate the mussels by himself.

He opened the bottle of wine and drank a large glass before he could even think about what he was doing.

He didn't bother lighting the candles.

He'd told Amber how he felt, and it had been a disaster.

Even if his parents hadn't come at such an awkward time, she said she didn't have those feelings for him.

It wasn't meant to be.

She'd told him she wasn't interested in a relationship, but he'd thought—from the way she kissed him, the way she looked at him—that it had all meant something.

Apparently, he'd been wrong.

He poured himself another glass of wine and sank onto the couch.

[12]

AMBER FELT LIKE CRAP.

Maybe it had something to do with the four donuts she'd eaten in the past twenty-four hours. They'd been delicious, of course: red velvet, carrot cake, crème brûlée, and London fog. She'd never told Sebastian that red velvet was her favorite, but somehow, he'd known to get one.

She hadn't had a good night's sleep, either. Two hours, tops. She'd kept wishing she was lying in bed next to Sebastian. She felt so terribly that she'd broken his heart.

She wished only the best for him.

Amber probably also felt shitty because she'd gotten a dozen texts and calls from her family in the past twenty-four hours, though aside from talking to Ah Ma last night, she hadn't answered any of them.

What had his parents told hers?

Your wayward daughter is corrupting our precious son!

Sebastian's parents had arrived in Ashton Corners from Hong Kong when Sebastian was a baby. Upon hearing that there was a new Chinese family in the next town over, Ah Ma had wanted to visit, and she'd convinced Amber's parents to go with her. Their baby sons had been only three months apart, and they'd become friends. Amber's family had been a bridge, of sorts, between Sebastian's family and their new Canadian small-town life, helping them adjust.

Their families had known each other for decades. And now...

She didn't feel up to dealing with her family yet. Instead, she was having a night out with her friends.

Amber was now tipsy on beer, in addition to being exhausted and high on sugar. She'd also had four cups of coffee earlier, in an attempt to wake herself up. It hadn't worked and probably put her body even more out of whack.

"Anyway," she said, after another gulp of beer, "when his mother basically said I was an underachieving slut, Sebastian was furious."

"Good," Gloria said. "He should have been furious."

"Once they were gone, he told me that I was perfect and he'd fallen in love with me. He had a romantic dinner all planned out." Her voice wavered. "He also signed us up for a cake class."

Roxanne and Gloria looked at each other.

"Why would he do that?" Roxanne asked.

"I told him that I want to take one. I watch baking shows all the time."

"You do?"

"Yeah." Amber paused. "I also crochet little animals as a hobby, but I felt embarrassed telling you two about those things, because you're so talented and I'm..." She gestured vaguely with her hands.

"I knew about the cross-stitching," Gloria said.

"Because I made you an intricate floral piece that said 'Fuck that shit.'"

"Yeah, and I said you should sell them."

"I don't want to turn everything I do into a business, though."

Gloria nodded. "I'm sorry, I didn't get that. But you *are* talented."

"You didn't tell us about baking, but you told Sebastian," Roxanne pointed out.

"I told him a lot of things."

Gloria and Roxanne exchanged looks again. Why did they keep doing that?

"Are you sure you're not in love with him?" Gloria asked. "I haven't seen you this upset in a long time. Like, you and Darren were together for quite a while, and I don't think you were this bothered when you found out he was cheating."

"And all Sebastian has done is treat you well," Roxanne said.

"Yeah, I fall for the losers. I'm broken. I can't fall for the guy who's actually good to me." Amber frowned at her coaster.

"And has a big dick and knows how to use it," Gloria said.

Amber snorted.

"I think you've fallen for him," Roxanne said. "You're just in denial. I'm not sure why. Maybe because of his parents."

"Yesterday was bad enough. I don't want to have to deal with that over and over again. I showed up in an I-want-to-have-sex-tonight dress."

"Think of it this way: you've already reached rock bottom. There's nowhere to go but up. How could it get any worse?"

"If they walked in on me giving him a blowjob and eating a donut off his dick."

"Huh," Gloria said. "Your imagination really is something."

"It's that old sex advice from Cosmo, right?" Roxanne said.

"Yeah, Sebastian and I were laughing about it the other day. You can see how much worse the situation could get."

"With basic precautions—such as locking the door—it seems unlikely something like that would happen. He's willing to take his parents to task for how they acted. Maybe try trusting that he can handle it and will always stick up for you."

"Seems a pity to let this one go when you like him so much," Gloria said. "I agree with Roxanne. You're in deep denial."

"I'm not." Amber knew that wouldn't convince them, though.

Gloria leaned forward. "So tell me. Exactly how big is it?"

Amber's face heated, and then she chuckled at the earnestness in her friend's face. "I'm not telling. That's my secret."

"Fine, fine. Be no fun."

"I'm fun!"

"Yeah, your boyfriend—"

"Sebastian isn't my boyfriend!"

"—is right. You're perfect just the way you are."

Perhaps it was the lack of sleep or the sheer quantity of sugar, caffeine, and booze that had passed through her veins, but Amber hiccupped and shed a few tears.

"You two are great," she said.

"We're also right," Gloria said, giving her a hug. "You'll see. Now I'm curious—do you have any pictures of your crochet animals?"

Amber hadn't planned to go to Sunday dinner at her parents' house that week. But Ah Ma had threatened to drink two piña coladas or drop dead—her threats kept changing—if Amber didn't show up, and she felt guilty. She put on the Hamlet scarf that Ah Yeh had given her and headed out the door.

There were more people at Sunday dinner than usual. Greg, Nick, and their girlfriends had made the drive from Toronto, and everyone was at the door when Amber arrived, twenty minutes late.

"You don't all need to look at me like that," Amber said after taking off her shoes. "I'm perfectly fine."

"I hear you and Sebastian aren't together anymore," Zach said.

"I ended things. It's for the best. I don't feel *that way* about him."

"Are you sure?" Mom asked.

Her family doubted her, just like her friends.

"Do you want me to fight Cecilia and Randall?" Ah Ma lifted up her leg and kicked the air. She lost her balance, and Nick and Greg managed to catch her just in time. "I have mad fighting skills!"

"Sure you do," Dad said.

"You think I am a weak old woman, but I will show you. Hi-yah!" She punched the air with her left fist, then the right.

"Okay, that's enough. You'll hurt yourself."

"Then they will have my death on their conscience. Good! They deserve it. Amber, they said you were not good enough for Sebastian. Wah, they don't know what they are talking about. You are the best girl!"

"Thanks, Ah Ma," Amber said.

"Let me get this straight," Mom said. "You had a sexual relationship with Sebastian, and he wanted it to be romantic, too, but you said no?"

Ugh, Amber wasn't in the mood to hear her mother say "sexual relationship."

"Something like that," she mumbled.

"There's nothing wrong with that. As long as you're enjoying yourself and being treated well, you do what you like." Mom paused. "You haven't had many boyfriends. Is this the sort of thing you do often?"

"I've had many boyfriends, actually," Amber said. "I just haven't told you about most of them. I thought you'd be mad about a few of them, and some didn't last long. I was hoping to avoid your interference in my life. In fact, I've had so many crappy boyfriends that I decided to take a break from dating for a while."

"And then you ran into Sebastian?"

"Yeah."

"Where?"

"At the grocery store." Amber would most certainly not say more than that.

"See? I knew it. The grocery store."

"Could we please not talk about this anymore?"

Dad put his hand on her shoulder. "We want you to know that Cecilia and Randall are wrong. You're definitely good enough for Sebastian. The question is whether he's good enough for you—and that has nothing to do with him being a doctor."

"He definitely is," Amber whispered.

"You know," Zach said, "I like the idea of you two together."

"Me, too," Mom said. "But it's your choice, of course. We won't interfere."

Amber looked around at her family. "You're serious? You won't interfere in my life anymore?"

"Ah, now you are getting carried away," Ah Ma said. "I cannot promise that."

"But I've been thinking," Mom said. "After Zach went so far as to get a fake girlfriend to avoid our matchmaking, and you clearly don't feel comfortable telling us a lot of things...maybe we got a little too involved at times. Besides, relationships aren't for everyone—your aunt Cheryl has been happily single for decades. We shouldn't force it on you. I trust you to make the right decision."

"I've made lots of bad decisions," Amber said.

"And you haven't let that get you down." Mom held out her arms, and Amber embraced her. "We're proud of you, honey, and don't listen to anyone who treats you like you're inferior."

Amber sniffed, a little uncomfortable with the compliments. "I knew Cecilia didn't like me, after the condom incident when I was seventeen."

"We talked about it back then. I told her that you were being safe and I taught you well. She didn't agree, but I had no idea she continued to hold that against you. Until yesterday."

"There was a big fight!" Ah Ma said. "They came over and there was so much yelling. Rosemary even slammed the door on them."

"I didn't mean to cause problems in your friendship," Amber said.

"Don't be sorry about that," Dad said. "They were horrible to you." He gave her a hug.

"I want a hug, too," Ah Ma crashed into the two of them and wrapped her arms around Amber from behind.

Ah Yeh had been silent, and remained so, but he hugged her next, followed by Zach.

Amber released a deep breath. She was lucky to have her family, even if they drove her nuts at times.

Just then, a loud sound pierced her ears.

"Why is the fire alarm going off?" Ah Ma asked.

"It's probably you," Dad said. "This happens almost every time you cook."

"But I haven't touched the kitchen today! I tried, but everyone told me to stay out."

"Oh, shit," Mom said. "I forgot something."

"See? It wasn't my fault!"

Ah Ma and Ah Yeh followed Mom into the kitchen, and Dad removed the battery from the smoke detector.

Zach stayed behind in the front hall with Amber.

"Sebastian is a good guy," Zach said.

"I know," Amber said miserably.

"I never thought I'd fall in love with Jo, and then...well, things changed. Just saying."

Amber was overwhelmed right now. This weekend had been a roller coaster, and she was looking forward to going back to work tomorrow and getting away from it all.

The night at Sebastian's seemed so long ago, but it had only been two days.

And she was starting to wonder...

"I don't know," Amber said. "I'm happy for you, by the way. That your ridiculous fake-relationship plan turned into something real." She thought of Nick and Lily, as well as Greg and Tasha, and a wave of yearning rushed through her.

She might be the Queen of Bad Boyfriends, but she did want to have that one day. She hadn't given up hope; she'd just put it on hold.

Was it possible Sebastian was the guy for her?

Had she really found love in the family planning section of the grocery store pharmacy?

~

Sebastian had hoped to spend most of the weekend with Amber.

Instead, he spent much of the time going over stuff for work, as well as shopping for things to make his house look more like a home. But what his place could really use was an inappropriate cross-stitch near the front entrance. His parents wouldn't approve, but...

Sebastian liked his life; however, he wondered what would have happened if his parents had never pushed him in any particular direction when it came to his career. If there had been no expectations whatsoever.

Yes, there were things he didn't tell his mom and dad—and he'd refused to move into the house next door—but overall, his life was close to what they wanted for him. Even his long-term relationships had been with women his parents generally approved of.

And then he'd started sleeping with Amber Wong.

He didn't regret anything he'd done or said to them. He would never tolerate such treatment of the woman he loved. He had zero doubts about his feelings for Amber, and for once, he'd done something without a shred of consideration for his parents' expectations.

Amber was entirely his choice. Sure, it had crossed his mind that his parents might be pleased because she was the daughter of their friends, but that hadn't really factored in. Plus, he'd dreaded their meddling.

But he'd been wrong about what his parents would say.

And Amber didn't want him.

He sighed heavily as he sat down at his kitchen table and picked up the envelope with the information for the cake class.

He'd been looking forward to doing that with her, dammit. Everything was fun as long as she was there.

He put on his winter clothes and walked to the grocery store, where he picked up a few things for the week, though he didn't need much. His parents had brought quite a bit of food on Friday.

Then he ventured to the pharmacy section. There was a small selection of greeting cards, and all the Valentine's Day cards were fifty percent off, since the day in question had passed.

He bought one.

He also bought some discounted Valentine's chocolate, remembering all the Christmas chocolate that Amber had had in her basket that day in January.

Sebastian managed a wry smile at that memory.

After returning home and putting away his groceries, he jumped in his car and headed to his parents' house. He'd promised he'd come over for dinner today, and he wasn't particularly looking forward to it.

"I won't let you speak to Amber like that ever again," Sebastian said.

"Is she your girlfriend now?" his mother asked.

They were sitting around the kitchen table in his childhood home: Sebastian, his mother, and his father.

"No," Sebastian said, "but if you see her again, you better not act like that."

"We had a fight with Rosemary and Stuart," Mom said.

"They stuck up for their daughter? Good."

Mom crossed her arms and looked at him as though trying to figure him out. Perhaps she thought this was out of character for him—he'd never been the rebellious child.

"You were okay with them setting up Diana and Zach," he said. "But for me and Amber, it's different?"

Was it because they considered Zach more respectable...and they'd never seen Zach wearing a short *I'm-here-to-have-sex* dress? Or because they had more specific expectations for Sebastian than Diana?

Not that it mattered.

Dad finally opened his mouth. "You really love her."

"Yeah. I do."

I've never quite felt this way before.

"Then if you bring her home, I will welcome her. We will try to be more open-minded. She is not who we imagined for you, but maybe she is right for you." He gave Sebastian a small smile.

Sebastian exhaled. If he'd won over his dad, then his dad would eventually convince his mother. "One other thing. Boundaries. Please don't show up unannounced and force your way in when I say no, okay? I'll try to visit you every week now that I'm close by, but at the very least, call before you get in the car."

"That is fine, Sebastian," Dad said. "We understand."

Mom didn't seem thrilled, but she nodded.

He knew his parents wanted the best for him. They'd come to this country for opportunities, to give their children a better life, but they had specific ideas of what that meant, and they were a little rigid in their thinking.

They would figure this out, though.

He felt a heaviness in his heart as he thought of Amber. He wanted her to be an important part of his life, but he'd already put his heart out there and been rejected.

Perhaps she'd come to him later, after she got his package in the mail.

Perhaps not, but it was her choice, and he'd let her make it on her own.

"I'm thankful for what you've done for me," he said to his parents, "but I have my own life now and I can decide what's best for me." He paused. "I love you."

His parents looked at each other like they didn't know what to make of his words, then turned back to him.

"Ah, I almost forgot," Dad said. "There was a big sale this weekend on paper towels. They're in the basement. I will get them for you."

"We went to London and got the bao you like," Mom said, heading to the fridge. "And those chocolate cookies—they are so hard to find."

Though they didn't say the words, this was how they told Sebastian that they loved him.

WHEN AMBER CAME HOME on Monday after work, she took down the sign that had hung above her bed for a year.

Rule #1: No Dating.

After having leftovers for dinner—her parents had sent food home with her yesterday—she sat in front of the TV, ready to crochet and watch some baking shows. She'd bought a pattern for an otter holding a heart, and she was excited to get started.

The truth was, there was a purpose to the otter. And her next crochet project, which made her giggle stupidly.

She was making them all for Sebastian. A plan had formed at the back of her mind, and she was slowly putting it into action.

As she worked on her little projects, she allowed the feelings she'd ignored for so long to bubble to the surface. She'd been so resistant to the idea of them being together, but after talking to her friends and her family, she'd been slowly changing her mind.

She didn't suddenly know in a flash that she wanted to be with him for always, but that didn't mean it was any less. She'd been impulsive in the past. Now, she was taking her time.

For some reason, she needed this time alone, and she let herself have it.

The following Wednesday, she received a small package. She got a goofy grin on her face when she saw that it was from Sebastian, and she immediately tore it open.

There was a bag of chocolate hearts with a "50% off" sticker. She was sure he'd left the sticker on deliberately.

There was also an envelope sealed with a heart. Inside, she found a card with two heart balloons and the words "Be Mine." When she opened it up, a piece of paper fluttered out.

It was the registration for the cake class. He'd added a sticky note saying he could change the name of the second person so she could take it with a friend.

In the card, he'd written, *If you change your mind, I'm here. Love, Sebastian.*

The next move was on her. She didn't expect to hear from him again otherwise—he would give her space. She appreciated that, but at the same time, she wanted to run to him and throw her arms around him.

But she would wait a little longer.

Until her plans were in order.

Until she was absolutely sure.

Screw that. She was absolutely sure now. She wanted to be with him more than anything. And unlike many of the men she'd dated in the past, he was kind and thoughtful and he made her feel good about who she was.

There was still the issue of their families, but Roxanne was right when she said the worst thing that could happen had already happened. Yes, it might be annoying at times, but it was worth it. Amber wouldn't give this up just because there were some issues. She could stand up for herself when she needed to, and Sebastian would be on her side; she knew she could count on him.

All of a sudden, she ached, absolutely ached, to have his arms around her once more.

She sent him a text.

~

Sebastian figured it was a good sign that Amber had invited him over that Friday.

Still, he didn't expect the sight that greeted him when he opened the door.

Well, he'd expected Amber, looking lovely, of course. She was wearing the same dress she'd worn on Valentine's Day. For a moment, he could look nowhere but at her.

But then he noticed the red and pink streamers. The heart-shaped balloons.

That was a surprise.

"I'm sorry about Valentine's Day." Her voice, normally strong, wavered. He squeezed her hand. "I was caught off-guard. But that doesn't mean I hadn't already been falling for you. I had—but I kept it a secret, even from myself. I can be a little dim sometimes."

He shook his head. "No, you are a bright light, and my life is so much better for having you in it."

"When you pulled a box of Magnum condoms off the shelf, I never would have imagined you saying something like that to me one day." She took a deep breath, and he couldn't stop smiling at her. "I didn't plan on it being more than sex—and the sex was amazing, even if we, uh, had trouble making it work the first time. But then we began hanging out, outside of the bedroom. I told you things that I don't usually tell other people. We spent nights together. You made me breakfast. It was…" She shut her eyes for a moment. "It was better than any relationship I'd had. It was finally the relationship I deserved—because I deserve better than what all those assholes gave me. I just wasn't looking for it with you, so I couldn't see it. But now, I'm looking, and I love you. I love the way I feel when I'm with you."

"Me, too," he said quietly.

He'd been missing something in his life. Someone he could relax around, someone he could have fun with.

But she was so much more than that to him.

He didn't have the words, though, so he pulled her into his arms and kissed her. Unlike the first time, it wasn't a kiss that came simply from lust, but one with a deeper passion, an emotional bond.

It felt so good to have her body pressed up against his again. To have her in his arms, feeling like they were both where they belonged.

When he began kissing down the side of her neck, she stepped back. "Before we get carried away, I want the chance to do Valentine's Day over again." She led him into the living room, where there were three packages wrapped in red and pink paper, and handed him one. "Open this first."

It was a pair of crochet otters, each holding a red heart.

"You made these," he said.

"Just for you."

"They're adorable."

She handed him the next package.

This one rendered him speechless. It was another crochet project, but it wasn't what he'd call *adorable*.

It was a crochet penis.

Yes, she'd made him a light brown penis. With balls, of course.

"It's very…phallic." He was unsure what else to say.

"It's meant to be to scale," she said. "Want to check?"

"Soon, I promise."

The next present was a crochet donut with pink frosting. Which, by itself, was rather cute, but he knew what she intended him to do with it.

God, he loved this woman.

He slid the donut on top of the crochet dick. It was a perfect fit.

He swallowed. "About our families…"

"We'll do our best to ensure they don't interfere too much. My mom admitted they get a bit too involved at times."

"And my parents understand that I love you and won't tolerate them talking that way. In time, they'll come to like you— I can't see how they wouldn't. But we'll figure it out together."

She nodded. "I have something else for you, too."

"You've already given me so much."

"I know, a Magnum-size crochet dick really put it over the top. Though that was a little more successful than what I'm about to show you."

She led him to the kitchen, where there was a plate of cupcakes on the counter. They had white icing and red heart candies, but they didn't look like the sort of thing that could be sold in a bakery. Rather, they looked like something that might appear on *Nailed It!*

He'd binge-watched baking shows in the past week. It had made him feel closer to her.

"As you can see," she said, "I definitely need some classes. Will you take them with me?"

"Absolutely." He smiled.

"Now, although these don't look gorgeous, they taste all right." She put a lopsided cupcake on a plate. "Red velvet with cream cheese buttercream. It was my first time making buttercream, and it's a little grainy, but..." She swiped some buttercream off the cupcake and held it to his lips.

"Mm. That's good."

She swiped up more buttercream and put it just above the low neckline of her black dress. "Want a taste?"

"Oh, do I ever. But I can't help worrying that your dress is going to get dirty."

He pushed the thin straps off her arms and unzipped the dress. She shimmied out of it.

"The bra will have to go, too." He unclasped her strapless bra and tossed it on the floor.

Now she stood before him, wearing only black lacy panties and a bite of cream cheese buttercream. She looked utterly delectable.

"Happy Valentine's Day," he murmured.

Then he licked off the buttercream and carried her to bed.

"DAMMIT, IT DOESN'T FIT!"

Amber tried, once again, to slide the chocolate dip donut with sprinkles onto her boyfriend's dick. One side of the donut split to accommodate Sebastian's girth, even though she'd selected the donut with the largest hole.

"I think that's a sign it wasn't meant to be." Sebastian stroked her hair. "I'm a little relieved, to be honest. I was worried you might accidentally bite in the wrong place."

"I would have been very careful, I assure you," Amber said, pretending to be offended by Sebastian's lack of faith in her eating-donut-off-dick abilities.

In general, he had lots of faith in her, but not here.

She tore the donut in two and handed one half to Sebastian. After they'd consumed the donut, she gave him a blowjob without any donuts or grapefruit.

That was how they spent the morning of Easter Sunday: in bed.

But at eleven o'clock, they had to get dressed in proper clothes—rather than the skimpy red lingerie Amber had been wearing for the past hour—and head to Mosquito Bay.

That was okay. Amber had had lots of time alone with Sebastian lately.

They'd officially been together for over a month, and it was, without a doubt, the best relationship she'd ever had, and she couldn't imagine it being any better than this. They went out for bubble tea together. They baked together—with limited success, but they were improving. They went grocery shopping together. They lay in bed and snuggled. They laughed a lot. Occasionally, they went out for drinks at The Tempest with her friends.

The best part was simply getting to be with him all the time, this wonderful man who loved her just the way she was.

Though Amber's family wasn't religious, they celebrated Easter with a ham lunch, which her mother prepared. There would also be noodles—Ah Yeh's noodles appeared at every family holiday—scalloped potatoes, salad, and lots of other food. Perhaps Lily and Nick would bring Nanaimo bars.

Given that all the Wong children now had significant others, this Easter lunch would be more crowded than usual. Sebastian's family would be coming this year as well.

An hour after leaving Mosquito Bay, Amber arrived at the brick house where she'd grown up. She and Sebastian walked up the flagstone path hand in hand, and before Amber could ring the doorbell, the door opened.

"Hello!" Ah Ma said. "Happy Easter!" She held up the colorful drink in her hand, garnished with a pink umbrella.

"Ah Ma, it's noon," Amber said. "Have you already started drinking?"

"These are virgin piña coladas, don't worry. Very healthy."

"Um, I'm not sure piña coladas are healthy, even without the booze."

"Who cares? I am old. I will do whatever I like!"

Just then, a six-foot-tall pink Easter Bunny walked into the front hall. He was carrying a basket of chocolate eggs and wearing a grumpy expression.

"Greg, you are supposed to smile." Ah Ma pinched his cheek, which she was barely able to reach.

"Why is my brother dressed as the Easter Bunny?" Amber asked.

"Ah Yeh ordered the costume on Amazon," Greg said with a sigh. "We took a vote, and everyone thought I should wear it. Personally, I voted for Nick."

Tasha bounded into the hall. "I think he looks cute."

Amber plucked a chocolate egg out of Greg's basket and passed it to Sebastian. She took a second one for herself.

"Hey, Amber." Zach walked into the hall, holding Jo's hand. "How was the drive?"

"Not too bad. We didn't get stuck in a snowstorm and spend the night in an unheated motel room, so I can't complain."

"It's April," Greg pointed out. "A snowstorm is unlikely."

"You never know," Ah Ma said. "I am powerful! I can control the weather. But now there is no need for matchmaking, because you have all been matched, thanks to me."

"Um," Nick said. "You guys set Lily up with Greg, not me."

"And you set Zach up with Sebastian's sister," Amber said, "rather than setting me up with Sebastian."

Ah Ma tapped her finger against her chin. "I have secrets."

"Before I forget." Amber pulled a package out of her purse and handed it to Jo. "This is for you."

Jo unwrapped the green paper.

"You made this, Amber?" Ah Ma said. "I don't understand. It looks like a banana."

"I don't think it's a banana," Jo said. "It looks more like a penis."

"Just like the shaft you drew at Chinese New Year, the last time I saw you," Amber said. "I'm looking forward to playing Pictionary against you next year, with my new teammate." She squeezed Sebastian's hand, and he squeezed back.

The doorbell rang, and Amber opened the door, revealing Sebastian's parents and sister.

"You are here!" Ah Ma said. "Just in time. Look what Amber made for Jo." She pulled Jo's gift out of her hand and held it up in the air.

Amber put her hands over her face and shook her head. Things had been going reasonably well with Sebastian's parents, but she hadn't needed them to see that.

Cecilia and Randall exchanged slightly horrified glances, but then Cecilia said, "You are very, ah, talented, Amber."

Huh. Her future mother-in-law was complimenting her crochet dick.

Yes, she expected Cecilia would be her mother-in-law one day. She couldn't imagine marrying any man but Sebastian.

"Isn't it awesome?" Ah Ma said, and her enthusiasm over the crochet dick made Amber wonder if those really were virgin piña coladas.

Ah Ma led the way into the kitchen, where Mom was absently stirring a pot on the stove as she kissed Dad.

"Okay, Mom and Dad," Nick said. "Time to break it up."

"You're all here!" Mom said. "Happy Easter, everyone! I'm especially pleased that the Easter Bunny was able to join us this year."

Everyone looked in Greg's direction and clapped.

"Can I take this costume off yet?" Greg muttered.

Amber laughed and leaned back against Sebastian, who wrapped his arms around her.

She was with her family and the man she loved for the holidays, and there was nowhere else she'd rather be. And when she got home that night, she'd give Sebastian the cross-stitch she'd made for him.

It said: *Amber Wong has the world's best boyfriend.*

SERIES EPILOGUE

Lily Tseng crossed "char siu" off her list.

It was a very long list of things to bring to Mosquito Bay and Ingleford for the Christmas holidays. Today was December 23, and they were going to visit Nick's family in Mosquito Bay for two nights. Then after Christmas lunch, they'd head to her family in Ingleford. It would be a hectic few days, but she was looking forward to them.

"What's next on your list?" Nick murmured before kissing the side of her neck. He'd managed to enter the kitchen without her noticing.

"The coconut lemon..."

How was she supposed to form words when he was kissing her like that?

They'd been together for over a year, and she'd moved into his penthouse six months ago. And his kisses were just as electrifying as they'd been the first night she'd spent with him. The night that was supposed to be a one-night stand but had turned into more. So much more.

She glanced down at the ring on her finger before turning in his arms and kissing his lips. He palmed her ass and pressed her against him as he swept his tongue into her mouth and—

"No!" She stepped away. "I have to finish my list, and then we have to get on the road. Ah Ma will call any minute now asking why we haven't left yet."

"But we're not supposed to be there until dinner, and it's only one. The drive doesn't take five hours." He gave her a devilish lopsided smile, one that he knew worked very well on her, no matter how many times he used it.

She sucked in a breath. Well, maybe she could afford to be distracted for ten minutes...

Just then, Nick's phone rang.

"Sorry," he said, pulling it out of his pocket, "this will only be a minute or two."

She suppressed a smile. It would not be just a minute or two with his family.

"Hi, Ah Ma," Nick said into his phone. "No, not yet... We still have lots of time until dinner. Don't worry, we'll be there... A blizzard? I didn't think it was supposed to snow until tomorrow... Yes, it really would be too bad if I had to spend tonight in a motel with my fiancée and only one bed, very sad, how could we ever pass the time... No, I'm not sassing you!"

Lily couldn't help laughing as she came up behind Nick and pulled him into her arms.

"No, I don't need to speak to Mom," Nick said. "Okay. Fine... Hi, Mom. Lily has already crossed char siu off her list, don't worry... Yes, I know...Yes, I know... You'll see her in just a few hours, you don't need to speak to her now..."

Lily smiled as she stepped away from Nick. He would likely have to talk to his father and possibly also his grandfather.

Next on the list: the date squares and coconut lemon squares, both of which Nick had made that morning. Well, calling them coconut lemon *squares* was a bit of a misnomer, as Nick had cut them into triangles. The coconut lemon triangles were already in a Tupperware, so she put that in one of the many bags coming to Mosquito Bay and crossed it off the list.

The date squares were still in the baking pan, but they should be cool by now. She cut those into squares—actual squares, not triangles—and placed them in another Tupperware, then into the bag.

Nick was still on the phone.

"I'll see Ah Yeh in five hours! He can tell me about his latest finds on Amazon then... Yes, I'm sure... Yes, I know... Lily won't forget. She's very organized. Okay... Okay..."

Lily moved on to the next item: Nanaimo bars. She'd made two different types yesterday. Her normal recipe, plus a slight modification in which she'd added mint extract and green food coloring to the middle layer. Christmas-y, right? She put the

Tupperware of Nanaimo bars on the kitchen island just as Nick ended his call.

"Everything okay?" she asked.

"Yeah." He raked a hand through his hair. It was adorably mussed now. "I just hope they don't call back in two minutes, like last time."

"Here. Have one of these." She picked up a mint Nanaimo bar and separated the top chocolate layer. She still maintained that eating each layer separately was wrong, but this was what Nick liked.

She lifted the chocolate layer up to his mouth. As he nibbled it, she thought of him scraping his teeth over her shoulder, as he'd done last night. Next, he licked the minty custard-flavored buttercream off the bottom layer, and God, why was she getting so aroused from watching him eat Nanaimo bars in a blasphemous manner? It was just...she knew what else he could do with that tongue...

Before eating the bottom layer, he looked up at her and laughed softly.

"What's the next item on your list?" he asked. "I hope it's 'have sex with my fiancé.'"

He ate the rest of the Nanaimo bar as his gaze swept over her body. She was wearing a red sweater and jeans, and it felt like the red sweater was much thicker than it actually was. Her skin was overheating.

"It's not on the list, sadly," she said, "but I can add it."

"Mm, yes, how about you do that."

As soon as she'd finished scribbling "sex" on the bottom of the list, Nick picked her up and carried her to the bedroom.

When she returned to her list twenty minutes later, she was in a post-sex daze. A good start to the Christmas holidays, which would end her first full calendar year with Nick Wong. She glanced at the framed photo on the wall—the two of them in formal clothes at a charity gala—and smiled.

She'd once considered herself boring, but Nick made her feel the opposite of boring. She was special, and their relationship was certainly never dull.

The two of them were carrying bags of presents to the front door when Nick's phone rang again. He sighed before answering.

"Yes, Mom. We'll be there, don't worry... No, we haven't left yet... We'll be on the road in fifteen minutes... Yes, I promise. Bye."

Lily chuckled as he slipped his phone into his pocket. She put on her boots and winter jacket, then picked up the first round of food and presents to take to the car.

"Ready?" she said.

"I just have one more thing to do."

"But I've gotten everything on my list. We don't want to keep your family waiting—"

He cut her off with a kiss on the lips.

"Now we can go." He winked at her.

"Look who's here!" Zach said. "Hey, everyone, it's Mr. Fancypants!"

Nick loved his family. He really did.

He reminded himself of this as Zach used that unfortunate nickname again.

It had started snowing, but it still wasn't too bad out. The drive had only taken twenty minutes longer than usual.

There was a stampede of people rushing to greet Nick and Lily in the front hall of his parents' home.

"Nicky!" Ah Ma said. "You are just in time."

"In time for what?" he asked warily.

"I have a new career and I'm showing off my skills."

Nick tried not to groan. After the car ride, he'd wanted a few minutes of peace before discussing wedding plans with Ah Ma.

Since "retiring" as a matchmaker, she'd become quite an eager wedding planner and had even started using the internet.

It didn't help matters that Greg and Tasha hadn't had a big wedding back in June. Rather, they'd informed everyone a week in advance that they were getting married at City Hall in Toronto, and it had been a very simple affair. Quite nice, but simple. So Nick's wedding would be the first grandchild's wedding that Ah Ma was involved in planning.

"I know what you're thinking." Dad walked in and gave Nick a hug, then Lily. "You assume it's about wedding planning, but your ah ma has decided, at the ripe old age of eighty-nine—"

"I'm eighty-eight!" Ah Ma said.

Dad waved this away. "You've been saying that for three years now. Anyway, she's decided to become a mixologist. Your ah yeh got her a cocktail shaker and other items on Amazon."

"No, I bought them myself! I know how to use the internet now."

Ah Yeh hobbled in. He was yawning and looked like he'd just woken up from a nap. "No, I had to sit beside you the whole time and help you use the mouse, which you insisted on calling a chicken."

"Wah, why shouldn't it be called a chicken? Chicken is a better animal than a mouse. They are much tastier."

"Anyway," Zach said, "Ah Ma was in the middle of making a drink for Greg. It's called the Mr. Grinch."

Nick and Lily laid their presents under the tree and put the food away, and then they entered the living room, hand in hand. Ah Ma was mixing drinks at the bar—that was new—in the corner, and Jo, Greg, and Tasha were seated on the couch.

"Hey," Nick said. "Happy holidays."

Greg grunted.

"Merry Christmas," Tasha said.

"How are you feeling?" Lily asked.

"Oh, not too bad. I'm no longer tired all the time." Tasha

smiled. She was five months pregnant, and Nick had noticed that half the presents under the tree were for the upcoming baby.

Tasha and Greg, who were now both thirty-five, had decided they wanted to start having kids right away, but Nick and Lily weren't ready for that yet. In a few years, perhaps.

Mom entered the living room, a Santa suit over her arm. "This is for you, Greg. Since you're going to be a father, I dug it out of the basement. Here, put it on."

Greg did not look enthusiastic, but then Tasha said, "Ooh, yes please," and he took the Santa suit from Mom and put it over his clothes.

"Come on, Greg!" Zach said, slapping him the back. "You're supposed to look jolly."

Greg gave him a withering stare.

"No, it is appropriate that you look like a Grinch." Ah Ma came over with a glass. "Because your Mr. Grinch drink is ready!"

Greg peered at the glass with obvious trepidation, and Nick didn't blame him. Greg then had a small sip and made a priceless expression of disgust, which had Nick and Zach howling in laughter.

"Ah Ma," Greg croaked, "what did you put in here?"

Tasha took the glass and sniffed. She covered her mouth with her hand and looked like she was going to be sick, and Greg turned to her in concern.

"Secret recipe," Ah Ma said proudly.

"Surely you can give us some hint," Nick said.

"Ah, fine. There is Blue Curaçao, pineapple juice, melon liqueur—"

"That sounds okay."

"—bitters, Goldschläger, Sambuca, lime juice...hmm, I'm forgetting something."

Well, that sounded revolting.

"Had you made this before?" Nick asked. "Did you try it yourself?"

"I am not allowed to drink all my creations." Ah Ma frowned. "Because I have a low tolerance for alcohol, you know. They forbid me."

"For good reason." Dad entered the living room with Ah Yeh, Amber and Sebastian trailing close behind.

It was crowded in the living room now, so Nick pulled Lily close and wrapped his arms around her. His mother turned on the old stereo and started playing some Christmas music, beginning with "All I Want for Christmas is You."

There was another expression of pain on Greg's face, but then Tasha pulled him close and planted a quick kiss on his lips. She seemed to have recovered from sniffing Mr. Grinch.

They hadn't all been together since Thanksgiving back in October, and it was nice to see everyone again. Nick used to hate coming to Mosquito Bay and made his trips here as short as possible, but he rather liked them now.

And it was also nice to know there would be no sneaky matchmaking.

"What's happening in here?" Amber asked.

"Ah Ma is making cocktails," Zach said.

"I will make one for you next, Amber," Ah Ma said.

"Sounds like a great idea." Zach nodded. "Yes, make one for Amber now."

"This is called the Lucky Santa."

Everyone watched as Ah Ma quickly poured a bunch of things into the cocktail shaker like a pro. She shook it with great enthusiasm, to the beat of "Jingle Bell Rock," which was now playing. For mysterious reasons, it made Greg's face turn almost as red as his Santa costume.

"Ho, ho, ho," Greg said, failing to sound jolly.

Ah Ma added a little umbrella to the glass and handed it to Amber. "Isn't it pretty?"

"Yes, it's a very pretty red," Amber said, taking the glass. Having not witnessed Greg trying the first cocktail, she didn't look sufficiently concerned as she took a sip. "That's…interesting. Here, you try, sweetie." She handed the glass to Sebastian.

Sebastian took a sip. "Interesting. Yes."

Ah Ma beamed. "It has Campari, crème de menthe, Clamato, gin, and soda water. Should I make one for you, Nick?"

"No, I'm quite alright."

Sebastian placed a container on the coffee table and removed the lid. "We brought cupcakes. Two types: red velvet and chocolate with mint frosting."

"Oh, wow," Jo said. "These look like they came from a bakery!"

Sebastian turned to Amber and smiled.

Tasha picked up one of the red velvet cupcakes. "I've been craving Coffee Crisp lately, but now I think I could eat a whole tray of cupcakes."

Ah Yeh reached for a chocolate mint cupcake before Tasha could eat them all. He had a bite. "Yes, these are very delicious, Amber. And you are getting so good at the decorations. Maybe next time you can do a Santa face. Or Shakespeare."

"Why are you complimenting her cupcakes," Ah Ma said, "but you never compliment my cocktails?"

"Because her cupcakes are much better than your cocktails."

Ah Ma came out from behind the bar and tried to swat Ah Yeh, but Ah Yeh managed to stumble to his feet just in time. She hobbled into the kitchen behind him, in hot pursuit.

Lily took the opportunity to set out the Nanaimo bars—both varieties—on the table next to the cupcakes.

"Make sure to save room for dinner," Mom said as Greg reached for a Nanaimo bar. "Prime rib and Ah Yeh's noodles, and this time, Greg and Tasha won't miss out."

"Don't worry, Greg," Nick said, "I'll still do my best to eat your share of prime rib. I know you hate it."

Greg did not deign to respond.

There was a shout from the other end of the house.

"Ma, I told you," Dad said, "no chasing people at your age. Come back and eat a cupcake."

Ah Ma and Ah Yeh finally returned to the living room.

"No cupcakes yet," Ah Ma announced. "First, you must all try my fortune cookies! I made them myself."

"Fortune cookies!" Jo said. "Wow. How do you get them into that shape?"

"Don't get too excited," Dad said. "She did try to make fortune cookies, it's true. But there were—"

"Technical difficulties," Ah Ma interrupted. "Yes. Very serious technical difficulties."

"Which resulted in our kitchen being filled with smoke. So we had to go out to Wong's Wok for dinner yesterday, and there aren't any actual fortune cookies to be eaten because they all had to be thrown in the trash."

"Then why is Ah Ma saying we have to try her fortune cookies?" Nick asked.

"There are still fortunes," Ah Ma said. "Just no cookies. You will draw them out of the hat." She picked up a top hat and walked over to Tasha. "You pick first.

Tasha stuck her hand in the hat and pulled out a small slip of paper. "'You will have a baby next year,'" she read, then patted her stomach. "Yes, that's very true. I will."

Greg was next. "'You will have a baby next year,'" he read. "Well, yes, my wife will be giving birth."

Nick and Lily looked at each other. He had a sneaking suspicion he knew what the rest of the fortunes would say.

Sure enough, his turn was next, and he read the tiny slip of paper out loud. "'You will have a baby next year.'"

"Or the year after," Ah Ma said. "This is okay, too."

"Is every fortune the same?" Dad asked.

"You will have to draw one to find out." Ah Ma held the hat out to him, then pulled it back. "Wait, no, the fortunes are not for you. Only for grandkids. Amber, you are a good girl, you can pick one now."

Amber's fortune said the same thing as everyone else's.

"Ma, really?" Dad said.

"What?" Ah Ma put her hands on her hips. "Can't I be eager for great-grandbabies?"

"You're already getting one!"

"Well, I want more, and now everyone is matched up, thanks to me."

"Um," Nick said. "Thanks to you. Right."

"Wah," Ah Ma said. "Stop being sarcastic!"

She came over to swat Nick. He managed to step out of the way in time, then he and Lily caught Ah Ma before she could lose her balance.

"They don't all need to have children," Mom said. "It's a personal choice. And remember, we acknowledged that we were interfering too much in their lives."

"You said that, not me." Ah Ma crossed her arms over her chest, the hat dangling from one hand. "Plus, this is hardly interfering!"

Dad snorted. "Since I'm not allowed a fortune, I'm taking one of these cupcakes instead."

Ah Ma glowered at her son. "Since you are being so mean, I will make you a bad cocktail to go with your cupcake."

"A bad cocktail?" Dad said. "How is this different from your normal cocktails?"

"You will see. It will be nasty."

Ah Ma's hands were a flurry of activity as she worked on the drink. Everyone watched in silence, but it was hard to keep up with what she was muddling and mixing and shaking. Eventually, she presented Dad with a glass, decorated with a blue umbrella.

He took a suspicious sniff, then tried a sip. "It's actually quite good."

"Really?" Greg said.

"You're not bluffing?" Zach asked.

Nick, too, had his suspicions.

Dad didn't say anything else, but unlike Amber and Greg, he kept drinking his cocktail. "What's that one called, Ma?"

"It's called the Mean Son."

Mom tried a sip from Dad's glass. "Yes, it's pretty good."

Nick was debating how to piss off his ah ma so he could get a drink called the Mean Grandson rather than what she'd made for Amber and Greg.

"You really like it?" Ah Ma asked. "Your taste buds must be broken. It was supposed to taste nasty!"

"I think the secret to you mixing good cocktails," Dad said, "is to make something you *think* will taste disgusting."

"Hmph. Well, now it's Nick's turn for a cocktail."

"What's the name of his drink?" Amber asked.

"Mr. Fancypants City Boy with Perfect Fiancée."

Zach howled in laughter, because of course he did.

"I agree," Nick murmured. "She is quite perfect." He squeezed Lily's hand.

"Lily, you are my favorite." Ah Ma held up a hand before anyone could protest. "Because you were my first matchmaking success story."

"You don't get to take credit for our match," Nick said. "You set her up with Greg."

"Maybe that was all part of my plan." Ah Ma tapped her cheek. "Ah mas work in mysterious ways."

Indeed, they did.

A few minutes later, Nick was handed his special cocktail.

It was truly mysterious how a drink could taste this revolting.

It was three o'clock on Christmas Day, and another holiday with the Wong family had almost come to a close. As soon as this game of Scrabble was finished, Nick and Lily would pack up and head to Ingleford.

There were four teams: Nick and each of his siblings were paired with their partners. Ah Ma, Ah Yeh, Mom, and Dad were merely watching and offering commentary.

But right now, everyone was silent as Jo began playing her word.

S-H-A...

Was Jo really going to play "shaft"?

S-H-A-C...K.

Ah Ma sighed, and perhaps Nick was hearing things, but he thought the sigh sounded disappointed.

"Double word score," Jo said proudly, "with the *k* on a double letter score. I don't think anyone can catch us now."

"I think you're right," Nick said.

He and Lily might have put on a better performance, but they'd been engaged in a serious game of footsies for the past hour.

As expected, Jo and Zach ended up winning Scrabble. They'd also won charades last night. Alas, there had been a bit of an incident during charades when Ah Ma attempted to crouch down for "Crouching Tiger, Hidden Dragon" and got stuck, but she was okay now. Dad had then decreed that Christmas charades should not become a yearly tradition, and Ah Ma had suggested Twister instead, which was immediately shot down.

As Lily was having a wedding-related conversation with Amber, Nick made a quick trip to the kitchen to get a glass of water and found his parents making out. Unfortunately, they were right in front of the cupboard where the glasses were kept, so he pulled out a festive reindeer mug instead.

"Smoochie-boo-kins," Mom murmured as he was leaving.

He figured he and Lily would be like that when they were in their sixties, and he smiled.

After quenching his thirst, Nick began packing up. He took a quick break to reply to a text from Trystan, who wanted recommendations for where to take a woman to brunch.

Nick couldn't help laughing.

Half an hour and many hugs later, he and Lily were on the road to Ingleford.

"So, your second Christmas with my family," he said. "It didn't scare you too much?"

But he knew what her answer would be.

"You know I love your family," she said. "Though it's nice to have some peace and quiet before we see mine."

"I was thinking…" Nick lifted his hand from the steering wheel and briefly touched Lily's thigh. "Perhaps a one-hour stop at a motel would be in order?" He waggled his eyebrows.

"Nick! Did you see the quantity of food I ate in the last two days? I can barely move. I'm practically waddling like a duck."

"A very sexy duck."

"Which you can enjoy when we get back to Toronto tomorrow."

"I look forward to it."

As he looked forward to all the time he got to spend with Lily. Yes, the last year with her had certainly been wonderful.

He loved spending the holidays—and all other days—with Lily Tseng.

Even if she had some very strange ideas about eating Nanaimo bars, she was his favorite person in the whole big world, and he didn't see that changing.

ABOUT THE AUTHOR

Jackie Lau decided she wanted to be a writer when she was in grade two, sometime between writing "The Heart That Got Lost" and "The Land of Shapes." She later studied engineering and worked as a geophysicist before turning to writing romance novels. Jackie lives in Toronto with her husband, and despite living in Canada her whole life, she hates winter. When she's not writing, she enjoys gelato, gourmet donuts, cooking, hiking, and reading on the balcony when it's raining.

To learn more and sign up for her newsletter,
visit jackielaubooks.com.

CPSIA information can be obtained
at www.ICGtesting.com
Printed in the USA
LVHW040942171021
700680LV00001B/20